FINALE

ALSO BY STEPHANIE GARBER

Caraval

Legendary

FINALE

A Caraval Novel

STEPHANIE GARBER

FLATIRON
BOOKS
NEW YORK

FINALE. Copyright © 2019 by Stephanie Garber. All rights reserved. Printed in the United States of America. For information, address Flatiron Books, 175 Fifth Avenue, New York, N.Y. 10010.

www.flatironbooks.com

Map by Rhys Davies

The Library of Congress Cataloging-in-Publication Data is available upon request.

ISBN 978-1-250-15766-9 (hardcover)
ISBN 978-1-250-24386-7 (signed edition)
ISBN 978-1-250-23197-0 (international, sold outside the U.S., subject to rights availability)
ISBN 978-1-250-15767-6 (ebook)

Our books may be purchased in bulk for promotional, educational, or business use. Please contact your local bookseller or the Macmillan Corporate and Premium Sales Department at 1-800-221-7945, extension 5442, or by email at MacmillanSpecialMarkets@ macmillan.com.

First U.S. Edition: May 2019
First International Edition: May 2019

10 9 8 7 6 5 4 3 2 1

For Sarah and Jenny—
I don't need tickets to Caraval because both of you
have already made so many of my dreams come true.

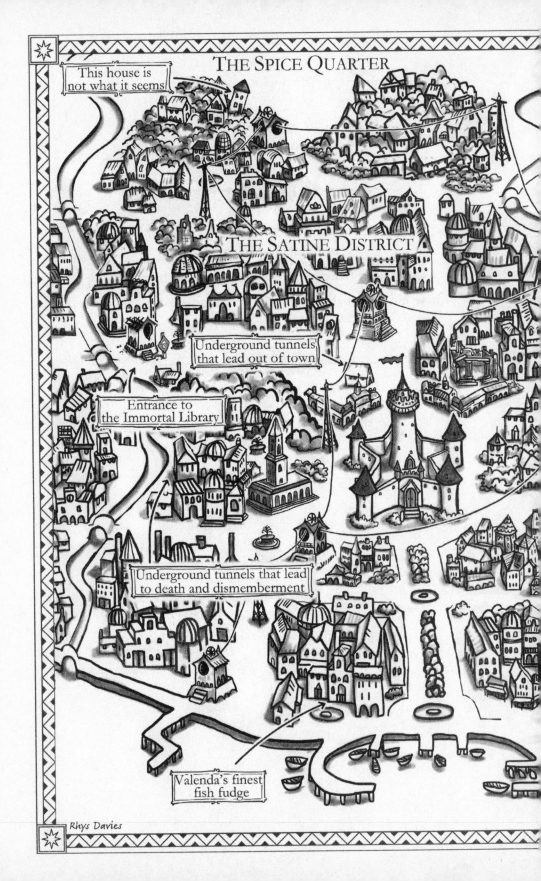

THE SPICE QUARTER

This house is
not what it seems

THE SATINE DISTRICT

Underground tunnels
that lead out of town

Entrance to
the Immortal Library

Underground tunnels that lead
to death and dismemberment

Valenda's finest
fish fudge

Rhys Davies

Beware of lice

Highly intelligent dog

THE TEMPLE DISTRICT

Actual skeletons
inside the closets

Menagerie ruins

Jacks's gambling den

UNIVERSITY CIRCLE

MAP OF ALL

Every story has four parts: the beginning, the middle, the almost-ending, and the true ending. Unfortunately, not everyone gets a true ending. Most people give up at the part of the story where things are the worst, when the situation feels hopeless, but that is where hope is needed most. Only those who persevere can find their true ending.

FINALE

BEFORE THE BEGINNING

Scarlett Dragna's bedroom was a palace built of wonder and the magic of make-believe. But to a person who'd forgotten how to imagine, it might have just looked like a disaster of dresses. Garnet-red gowns littered the ivory carpets, while cerulean frocks hung from the corners of the iron canopy bed, swinging gently as a gust of salty wind snuck in from the open windows. The sisters sitting on the bed didn't seem to notice the breeze, or the person who entered the room with it. This new figure slipped inside quiet as a thief, making no noise as she crept toward the bed where her daughters were playing.

Scarlett, her eldest, was busy straightening the petal-pink petticoat resting on her shoulders like a cape, as her younger sister, Donatella, wrapped a strand of creamy lace across her face as if it were an eye patch.

Their voices were high and light and morning-bright, in the way that only children's voices can be. Just the sound of them was magic, melting the harsh midday sunlight into bits of luminous butterscotch that danced around their heads like stardust halos.

Both of them appeared angelic until Tella announced, "I'm a pirate, not a princess."

Their mother's mouth warred between smiling and frowning. Her youngest daughter was so much like her. Tella had the same rebel heartbeat and adventurous spirit. It was a double-edged gift that had always given her mother so much hope, as well as fear that Tella might make the same mistakes she had.

"No," Scarlett said, more headstrong than usual. "Give it back, that's my crown! I can't be a queen without a crown."

Their mother's frown won as she edged closer to the bed. Scarlett was generally less combative than Tella, but both girls' mouths twisted stubbornly as their hands wrapped around opposite ends of a pearl necklace.

"Find a new crown, it's my pirate treasure!" Tella gave a fantastic yank and pearls flew across the room.

Pop!

Pop!

Pop!

The mother caught one, deftly capturing it between two delicate fingers. The tiny globe was as pink as her daughters' cheeks, now that both girls had finally looked up to see her.

Scarlett's hazel eyes were already turning glassy; she had always been more sensitive than her sister. "She broke my crown."

"A true queen's power isn't in her crown, my little love. It's here." Her mother placed a hand over her heart. Then she turned to Tella.

"Are you going to tell me that I don't need treasure to be a pirate? Or that my greatest treasure is right here?" Tella put a tiny hand over her heart, mimicking her mother.

If Scarlett had done it, their mother would have imagined the gesture to be sincere, but their mother could see the devilry in Tella's eyes. Tella had a spark that could either set the whole world ablaze, or give it much-needed light.

"I would actually say your greatest treasure is sitting across from you. There is nothing quite so precious as the love of a sister." With that, the mother picked up her daughters' hands and squeezed.

If there had been a clock in the room, it would have stopped. Occasionally, there are minutes that get extra seconds. Moments so precious the universe stretches to make additional room for them, and this was one of them. People don't get pauses like these very often. Some people never receive them at all.

These little girls didn't know this yet, because their stories hadn't begun, not really. But soon their stories would take off, and when they did, these sisters would need every stolen moment of sweetness they could find.

THE
BEGINNING

Donatella

The first time Legend appeared in Tella's dreams, he looked as if he'd just stepped out of one of the stories people told about him. As Dante, he'd always dressed in shades as black as the rose tattooed on the back of his hand. But tonight, as Legend, he wore a seduction-red double-breasted tailcoat lined in gold, accented by a matching cravat, and his signature top hat.

Shiny locks of black hair peeked out from beneath the brim of the hat, sheltering coal-dark eyes that brightened when he looked at her. His eyes glittered more than the twilit waters surrounding their intimate boat. This was not the flat, cold look he'd given Tella two nights ago, right after he'd rescued her from a deck of cards and then callously abandoned her. Tonight he was smiling like a wicked prince, escaped from the stars, ready to spirit her up into the heavens.

Uninvited butterflies took flight in Tella's stomach. He was still the most beautiful liar she'd ever seen. But Tella wasn't about to let Legend bewitch her the same way he had during Caraval. She smacked the top hat right off of his pretty head, rocking the tiny vessel beneath them.

He captured the hat with ease, fingers moving so fast she'd have thought he'd anticipated her response if he weren't sitting across from her, near enough for Tella to see a muscle tic along his smooth jawline. The two of them might have been in a dream, where the twinkling sky turned murky purple around the edges as if nightmares lurked close, but Legend was as sharp as precise pen strokes and as vibrant as a freshly cut wound.

"I thought you'd be happier to see me," he said.

She gave him her most vicious glare. Her hurt from the last time she'd seen him was still too raw to hide. "You walked away—you left me on those steps when I couldn't even move. Jacks carried me back to the palace."

Legend's lips slashed into a frown. "So you're not going to forgive me for that?"

"You haven't said that you're sorry."

If he had, she would have forgiven him. She *wanted* to forgive him. She wanted to believe Legend wasn't all that different from Dante, and that she was more than just a game piece he wanted to play with. She wanted to believe he'd left her that night because he'd been scared. But rather than looking regretful for what he'd done, he appeared irritated that she was still angry with him.

The sky grew darker as writhing purple clouds bisected the crescent moon, severing it into two pieces that floated across the sky like a fractured smile.

"I had somewhere I needed to be."

Her hopes sank at the coolness in his voice.

Around them the air turned sooty as fireworks burst above their heads, shattering into brilliant glimmers of pomegranate red, reminding her of the fiery display from two nights ago.

Tella glanced up to see the sparks dance into an outline of Elantine's palace—*Legend's* palace now. She actually admired the fact that Legend had convinced Valenda that he was the true heir to the throne of the Meridian Empire. But at the same time, the deception reminded her that Legend's life was made of games on top of games. Tella didn't even know if he desired the throne for its power, if he wanted the prestige, or if he merely wished to pull off the greatest performance the empire had ever seen. Maybe she would never know.

"You didn't have to be so cold and cruel about the way you left," she said.

Legend took a heavy breath and a sudden rush of hungry waves lapped against the boat. The vessel rocked down a narrow canal that fed them into a glowing ocean. "I told you, Tella, I'm not the hero in your story."

But instead of leaving now, he was leaning closer. The night grew warmer as he looked into her eyes the way she'd wanted him to the last time they'd parted. He smelled of magic and heartbreak, and something about the combination made her think that despite what he claimed, he wanted to be her hero.

Or maybe he just wanted her to continue to want him.

Caraval might have been over, but here Tella was, inside of a dream with Legend, floating over waters of stardust and midnight while fireworks continued to fall from the sky as if the heavens wanted to crown him.

Tella tried to turn the fireworks off—this *was* her dream, after all—but Legend seemed to be the one in control of it. The more she fought against the dream, the more enchanted it became. The air grew sweeter and the colors grew brighter as mermaids with tropical teal braids and pearly pink tails leaped out of the water and waved at Legend before diving back in.

"You are so full of yourself," she said. "I never asked you to be my hero."

She and Legend had both made sacrifices two nights ago—she'd doomed herself to captivity inside of a Deck of Destiny, in part to keep him safe, and he'd freed the Fates to rescue her. His actions were the most romantic thing anyone had ever done for her. But Tella wanted more than to be romanced. She wanted the real him.

But she wasn't even sure if a real Legend existed. And if he did, she doubted he let people close enough to see him.

He'd placed his top hat back on his head and he truly did look handsome, almost achingly so. But he also appeared far more like the idea of Legend than a genuine person, or the Dante she'd known and fallen in love with.

Tella's heart constricted. She'd never wanted to fall in love with anyone. And in that moment she hated him, for making her feel *so* many things for him.

A final firework burst into the sky, turning the entire dreamscape the most brilliant shade of blue she'd ever seen. It looked like the color of wishes come true and fantasies made real. And as the fireworks fell, they played music so sweet, sirens would have been jealous.

He was trying to dazzle her. But dazzle was a lot like romance— fantastic while it lasted, but it never lasted long enough. And Tella still wanted more. She didn't want to become another nameless girl in the many stories told about Legend, a girl who fell for everything he said, just because he leaned across a boat and looked at her with stars dancing in his eyes.

"I didn't come here to fight with you." Legend's hand lifted, as if he might reach for her, but then his long fingers dipped over the low side of the boat and idly played with the midnight waters. "I wanted to see if you received my note, and ask if you wanted the prize for winning Caraval."

She pretended to think as she recalled every word of the letter by heart. He'd given her hope he still cared by wishing her happy birthday and offering her the prize. He said he'd be waiting for her to come and collect it. But one thing he'd not said was that he was sorry for any of the ways he'd hurt her.

"I read the message," Tella said, "but I'm not interested in the prize. I'm done with games."

He laughed, low and painfully familiar.

"What's so funny?"

"That you're pretending our games are over."

Donatella

Legend looked like a freshly woken storm. His hair was mussed by the wind, his straight shoulders were dusted in snow, and the buttons of his coat were made of ice as he strolled closer, through a chilling-blue forest made of frost.

Tella wore a cloak of cobalt fur, which she wrapped tighter around her shoulders. "You look as if you're trying to trick me."

A sly grin twisted his mouth. The night before, he'd seemed like an illusion, but tonight he felt more like Dante, dressed in familiar shades of black. But while Dante was usually warm, Tella couldn't help but imagine the dream's frigid temperature reflected Legend's true mood.

"I only want to know if you wish to collect your prize for winning Caraval."

Tella might have spent half of her waking day wondering what the prize was, but she forced herself to tamp down her curiosity. When Scarlett had won Caraval, she had received a wish. Tella could have used a wish, but she had a feeling Legend had even more in store for her. So she would have said yes . . . if she hadn't sensed how very much Legend wanted that answer.

Donatella

Every night Legend visited her dreams like a villain from a storybook. Night after night after night after night. Without fail, for nearly two months, he always showed up, and he always disappeared after receiving the same answer to his question.

Tonight they were in an otherworldly version of the saloon inside the Church of Legend. Countless portraits of artists' imaginings of Legend looked down on them as a spectral piano player tapped a quiet tune, while ghost-thin patrons clad in colorful top hats danced around.

Tella sat in a clamshell-shaped chair the color of rainforest mist, while Legend lounged across from her on a tufted chaise as green as the sugar cubes he kept rolling between his deft fingers.

After that first night in the boat, he hadn't worn the top hat or the red tailcoat, confirming her suspicions that the items were part of his costume rather than his person. He'd gone back to dressing in crisp black—and he was still quick to laugh and to smile, like Dante.

But unlike Dante, who had always found excuses to put his hands on her, Legend never, ever touched Tella in dreams. If they rode a hot-air balloon, it was so large that there was no danger of her accidentally bumping into him. If they strolled through a garden of waterfalls, he stayed along the edge of the path where their arms weren't at risk of brushing. Tella didn't know if their touching would put an end to their shared dreams, or if keeping his hands to himself was just another one of the many ways he maintained control, but it frustrated her endlessly. Tella wanted to be the one in control.

She took a sip of her sparkling green cordial. It tasted too much like black licorice for her, but she liked the way Legend's eyes went to her lips whenever she drank. He might have avoided touching her, however, it never stopped him from looking.

But tonight his eyes were red around the edges, even more than they'd been the last few nights. The Days of Mourning for Empress Elantine were ending in two days, which meant the countdown to Legend's official coronation was about to begin. Twelve days from now he'd be crowned emperor. She wondered if the preparations were taking a toll. Sometimes he spoke of palace business, and how frustrating the royal council was, but tonight he was being quiet. And asking about it felt like awarding him points in the game they were playing, because this was definitely a game, and giving Legend the impression she still cared was against the rules. Just as touching was.

"You look tired," she said instead. "And your hair needs to be cut; it's half hanging over your eyes."

His mouth twitched at the corner, and his voice turned taunting. "If it looks so bad, why do you keep staring?"

"Just because I don't like you doesn't mean you're not pretty."

"If you really hated me, you wouldn't find me attractive at all."

"I never said I had good taste." She downed the last of her cordial.

His eyes returned to her lips as he continued to roll his absinthe sugar cubes around his long fingers. The tattoos on his fingers were gone, but the black rose remained on the back of his hand. Whenever she saw it, she wanted to ask why he'd left it, if he'd gotten rid of his other tattoos, like the beautiful wings on his back, and if that was why he no longer smelled of ink. She was also curious if he still wore the brand from the Temple of the Stars, signifying that he owed them a life debt. The debt he'd taken on for her.

But if she'd asked that, it would have unquestionably counted as caring.

Fortunately, admiring wasn't against their unspoken rules. If it had been, they'd both have lost this game a long time ago. Tella usually tried to be a little more discreet, but he never was. Legend was unabashed in the way he looked at her.

Although tonight he seemed distracted. He hadn't made any comments about her gown—he controlled the location, but she chose what she wore. This evening her flowing dress was a whimsical blue, with shoulder straps made of flower petals, a bodice made of ribbons, and a skirt of fluttering butterflies that Tella liked to think made her look as if she were a forest queen.

Legend didn't even notice when one of her butterflies landed on his shoulder. His eyes kept flitting to the ghostly piano player. And was it Tella's imagination, or did the tavern appear duller than her other dreams had been?

She would have sworn the chaise he lounged on had been a bright, lurid green, but it had blurred to pale sea glass. She wanted to ask if something was wrong, but again, that would have given the impression of caring.

"Aren't you going to ask me your question tonight?"

His gaze snapped back to her. "You know, someday I might stop asking and decide not to give you the prize."

"That would be lovely." She sighed, and several butterflies took flight from her skirt. "I'd finally get a good night's sleep."

His deep voice dipped lower. "You would miss me if I stopped visiting."

"Then you think too highly of yourself."

He stopped toying with his sugar cubes and looked away, once again preoccupied by the musician on the stage. His tune had ventured into the wrong key, turning his song discordant and unlovely. Around the room the ghostly dancers responded by stumbling over one another's feet. Then a raucous crash made them freeze.

The piano player folded atop his instrument, like a marionette whose strings had been severed.

Tella's heart beat wildly. Legend was always frustratingly in control of her dreams. But she didn't sense this was his doing. The magic in the air didn't smell like his. Magic always held a sweet scent, but this was far too sweet, almost rotted.

When she turned back around, Legend was no longer sitting, but standing right in front of her. "Tella," he said, his voice harsher than usual, "you need to wake yourself—"

His last words turned to smoke and then he turned to ash as the rest of the dream went up in poisonous green flames.

When Tella awoke, the taste of fire coated her tongue and a dead butterfly rested in her palm.

4

Donatella

The next night, Legend did not visit her dreams.

Donatella

The intoxicating scents of honeycomb castles, cinnamon bark pies, carmelite clusters, and peach shine floated through Tella's cracked window when she woke, filling the tiny apartment bedroom with sugar and dreams. But all she could taste was her nightmare. It coated her tongue in fire and ash, just as it had the day before.

Something was wrong with Legend. Tella hadn't wanted to believe it at first. When the last dream they shared had gone up in flames, she'd thought it could be another one of his games. But last night when she'd searched for him in her dreams, all she'd found was smoke and cinders.

Tella sat up, threw off her thin sheets, and dressed quickly. It was against the rules to do anything that gave the impression of caring, but if she just went to the palace to spy, without actually talking to him, he would never know. And if he really was in trouble, she didn't much care about breaking the rules.

"Tella, what are you getting dressed up so quickly for?"

She jumped, heart leaping into her throat at the sight of her mother stepping into her room. But it was only Scarlett. Save for the silver streak in Scarlett's dark brown hair, she looked almost exactly like their mother, Paloma. Same tallish height, same large hazel eyes, and same olive skin, just a tiny shade darker than Tella's.

Tella glanced over Scarlett's shoulder into the next room. Sure enough, their mother was still trapped in an enchanted slumber, still as a doll atop the sun-bleached quilt of their dull brass bed.

Paloma didn't move. She didn't speak. She didn't open her eyes. She was less ashen than when she'd arrived. Her skin now had a glow, but her lips remained a disturbing shade of fairy-tale red.

Every day Tella spent at least an hour watching her carefully, hoping for a flutter of her eyelashes, or a movement that involved more than just her chest rising up and down as she breathed. Of course, as soon as Paloma woke, Jacks—the Fated Prince of Hearts—had warned that the rest of the immortal Fates, whom Legend had freed from a Deck of Destiny, would wake as well.

There were thirty-two Fates. Eight Fated places, eight Fated objects, and sixteen Fated immortals. Like most of the Meridian Empire, Tella had once believed the ancient beings were just myths, but as she had learned in her dealings with Jacks, they were more like wicked gods. And sometimes she selfishly didn't care if they woke up as long as her mother woke up as well.

Paloma had been trapped in the cards with the Fates for seven years, and Tella hadn't fought so hard to free her just to watch her sleep.

"Tella, are you all right?" Scarlett asked. "And what are you all dressed up for?" she repeated.

"This was just the first gown I grabbed."

It also happened to be her newest one. She'd seen it in a shop window down the street and spent practically her entire weekly allowance. The dress was her favorite shade of periwinkle, with a heart-shaped neckline, a wide yellow sash, and a calf-length skirt made of hundreds of feathers. And maybe the feathers reminded Tella of a dream carousel Legend had created for her two months ago. But she told herself she'd bought the dress because it made her look as if she'd floated down from the clouds.

Tella gave Scarlett her most innocent smile. "I'm just going out to the Sun Festival for a bit."

Scarlett's mouth wrinkled, as if she wasn't quite sure how to respond, but she was clearly distressed. Her enchanted gown had turned a wretched shade of purple—Scarlett's least favorite color—and the dated style was even older than most of the furniture in their cramped suite. But, to her credit, Scarlett's voice was kind as she said, "Today is your day to watch Paloma."

"I'll be back before you need to leave," Tella said. "I know how important this afternoon is for you. But I need to go out."

Tella wanted to leave it at that. Scarlett didn't understand Tella's relationship with Legend, which was admittedly complicated.

Sometimes Legend felt like her enemy, sometimes he felt like her friend, sometimes he felt like someone she used to love, and every once in a while, he felt like someone she still loved. But to Scarlett, Legend was a game master, a liar, and a young man who played with people the way gamblers played with cards. Scarlett didn't know that Legend visited Tella in dreams every night, she only knew that he showed up sometimes. And she believed that the version of him Tella kept meeting was not the genuine Legend because he only visited in dreams.

Tella didn't believe Legend was still acting with her. But she knew there were things he wasn't telling her. Although Legend did ask the same question each night, that question had started to feel like just an excuse to come and see her—a distraction to hide the real reason he only appeared in her dreams. Unfortunately, Tella still wasn't sure if he visited because he truly cared for her, or because he was playing yet another game with her.

Scarlett would be upset to learn that he'd been showing up in her dreams every night. But Tella owed her sister the truth. Scarlett had been waiting weeks for this day; she needed to know why Tella was suddenly running out.

"I have to go to the palace," Tella said in a rush. "I think something has happened to Legend."

Scarlett's dress turned an even darker shade of purple. "Don't you think we'd have heard rumors if anything happened to the next emperor?"

"I don't know, I only know he didn't visit me in my dream last night."

Scarlett pursed her lips. "That doesn't mean he's in danger. He's an immortal."

"Something's wrong," Tella insisted. "He's never *not* shown up."

"But I thought he only visited—"

"I might have lied," Tella interrupted. She didn't have time for a lecture. "I'm sorry, Scar, but I knew you'd be unhappy. Please, don't try to stop me. I'm not objecting to your meeting with Nicolas today."

"Nicolas has never hurt me," Scarlett said. "Unlike Legend, he's always been kind, and I've been waiting months to finally meet him."

"I know, and I promise I'll be back to watch Mother before you leave at two o'clock."

Just then the clock chimed eleven, giving Tella exactly three hours. She had to leave now.

Tella wrapped her arms around Scarlett and pulled her into a hug. "Thank you for understanding."

"I didn't say I understood," Scarlett said, but she was hugging her sister back.

As soon as she pulled away, Tella picked up a pair of slippers that laced up to her ankles and then padded across the faded carpet into her mother's room.

She pressed a kiss to Paloma's cool forehead. Tella didn't leave her mother very often. Since they'd moved out of the palace, she'd tried to stay by her mother's side. Tella wanted to be there when her mother woke up. She wanted to be the first face her mother saw. She hadn't forgotten the way Paloma had betrayed her to the Temple of the Stars, but rather than choosing to remain angry, she was choosing to believe there was an explanation, and she'd learn it when her mother woke from her enchanted sleep. "I love you and I'll be back very soon."

Tella considered getting herself arrested.

She didn't want to get arrested, but it might have been the quickest route to the palace. Too many visitors, from all over the empire, had descended on Valenda for the Sun Festival. They overflowed the sky carriage lines and clogged the streets and sidewalks, forcing Tella to take a longer route to the palace, and to skirt the delta that led out toward the ocean.

The Sun Festival took place every year on the first day of the Hot Season. But this year was especially rowdy, since it also marked an end to the Days of Mourning and the countdown to Legend's coronation, which would take place in ten days—though only Scarlett, Tella, and Legend's performers knew him as Legend. The rest of the empire knew him as *Dante Thiago Alejandro Marrero Santos.*

Just thinking the name *Dante* still hurt a little.

Now, Dante felt more like a character from a story than Legend did. Yet the name always pricked her like a thorn, reminding her how she'd fallen in love with an illusion—and how foolish it would be to completely trust him again. But she still felt compelled to go after him, to ignore the festival and all the excitement buzzing through the streets.

Now that the Days of Mourning were over, the black flags that had haunted the city were finally gone. Dour frocks had been replaced with garments of sky-kissed blue, turmeric orange, and minty green. Color, color everywhere, accompanied by more delicious fragrances—candied citrine, tropical ice, lemon dust. But she didn't dare stop at any temporary street stalls to buy any treats or imported fizzing ciders.

Tella's steps quickened and—

She abruptly stopped next to a boarded-up carriage house. Several people rammed into her back, knocking her shoulder against a splintered wood door as she glimpsed a hand with a black rose tattoo. *Legend's tattoo.*

The sweetness in the air turned bitter.

Tella couldn't see the figure's face as he wove through the crowd, but he had Legend's broad shoulders, his dark hair, his bronze skin—and the sight of him made her stomach tumble, even as her hands clamped into fists.

He was supposed to be in danger!

She'd imagined he was sick or injured or in some mortal peril. But he looked . . . entirely fine. Maybe a little more than fine: tall and solid, and more *real* than he ever appeared in her dreams. He was definitely Legend. Yet, it still didn't feel entirely real as she watched him confidently weave through the crowd. This scene felt more like another performance.

As the heir to the throne, Legend should not have been sneaking around dressed like a commoner, in ragged brown pants and a homespun shirt. He should have been riding through the crush on a regal black horse with a gold circlet on his head and a cadre of guards.

But there were no guards protecting him. In fact, it appeared as if Legend was going out of his way to avoid any royal patrols.

What was he up to? And why had he so dramatically disappeared from her dreams if nothing was wrong?

He didn't slow his self-assured steps as he entered the crumbling ruins that edged the Satine District. They were full of decaying arches, overgrown grasses, and steps that looked as if they'd been built for giants instead of human beings, and Tella had to jog just to make sure she didn't lose sight of her quarry. Because, of course, she was following him.

She kept close to large boulders and darted over the rocky grounds, careful not to be seen by guards as Legend climbed up, up, up.

The sweetness in the air should have grown thinner the farther she ventured from the vendors, but as she ascended, the sugar on her tongue became thicker and colder. When Tella's knuckles brushed against a rusted iron gate that had fallen off its hinges, her skin turned blue with frost.

She could still see the sun blazing above the festival, but its heat didn't penetrate this place. Gooseflesh prickled up her arms as she wondered anew what Legend was playing at.

She'd almost reached the top of the ruins. A giant broken crown of white granite columns grayed by decades of rainfall and neglect rested in front of her. But Tella could almost picture the decrepit structure as it had been centuries before. She saw pearl-white columns, taller than masts on ships, holding up curved panels of stained glass streaming iridescent rainbows over a grand arena.

But what she no longer saw was Legend. He'd disappeared, just like the warmth.

Tella's breath slipped out in white streams as she listened for footsteps, or the low timbre of his voice. Perhaps he was meeting someone? But she didn't catch any sounds other than the chattering of her own teeth, as she crept past the closest column and—

The sky turned dark as the ruins around her vanished from view. Tella froze.

After a heartbeat, her eyes blinked and then they blinked some more as her vision adjusted to the new scene. Piney trees. Tufts of snow. Glints of light from animals' eyes. And air icier than frost and curses.

She was no longer in one of Valenda's many ruins—she was in a forest experiencing the middle of the Cold Season. She shivered and hugged her uncovered arms to her chest.

Light fell from a moon larger than any she'd seen. It glowed sapphire-bright against the foreign night, and dripped silver stars like a waterfall.

During the last Caraval, Legend had enchanted the stars to form new constellations. But he'd told Tella himself that he didn't have that much power outside of Caraval. And this didn't feel like any of the dreams she'd shared with him. If it had been a dream, he'd already be stalking toward her, giving her a fallen angel's smile that made Tella's toes curl inside her slippers as she pretended to be unaffected.

In her dreams it was never this cold, either. Sometimes, she felt a brush of frost through her hair, or a kiss of ice down the back of her neck, but she was never actually shivering. If she had been, she could have just imagined a heavy fur and it would have appeared around her shoulders. But all she had were her thin cap sleeves.

Her toes were already half frozen, and icy ringlets of blond hair clung to her cheeks. But she wasn't about to turn back. She wanted to know why Legend had disappeared from her dreams, why he'd scared her so badly, and why they were now in another world.

She might have thought he'd taken some sort of portal back to his private isle, instead of into another dimension, but the stars pouring out of a crack in the moon made her imagine otherwise. She'd never seen anything like it in her world.

She wouldn't have believed it at all, except this was Legend. Legend brought people back to life. Legend stole kingdoms with lies. Legend wrangled the stars. If anyone could walk through worlds, it was him.

Not only that, but he'd magically changed his clothes. When Tella caught a fresh glimpse of his dark silhouette through the snowy branches, Legend no longer looked like a commoner, but like the Legend from her earliest dreams, dressed in a finely tailored suit accented by a raven-wing-black half-cape, a sophisticated top hat, and polished boots that the snow left untouched.

Tella considered leaving the safety of the tree line to confront him when he took a few more steps—and met the most stunning woman Tella had ever seen.

6

Donatella

Tella's stomach went hollow.

The woman was made of things that Tella didn't possess. She was older, not by much—just enough to look more like a woman than a girl. She was taller than Tella too, statuesque with straight, fiery-red hair that fell all the way down to a narrow waist, which was cinched with a black leather corset. Her dress was black as well, silky and slender with slits down both sides that showed off long legs clad in sheer stockings embroidered with roses.

Tella might not have thought much about the stockings, but there were also roses tattooed on the woman's arms, black ones, matching the rose inked on the back of Legend's hand.

Tella instantly hated her.

She might have hated him, too.

Roses weren't rare flowers, but she doubted these matching tattoos were a mere coincidence.

"Welcome back, Legend." Even the woman's voice was the antithesis of Tella's, slightly raspy and laced with a seductive accent Tella couldn't place. The woman didn't smile, but when she looked at Legend she licked her lips, making them deepen to a shade of red that matched her hair.

Tella resisted the urge to pick up a snowball and toss it at the woman's face.

Was this who Legend visited in his days while he kept Tella confined to his dreams? Legend had always made it sound as if he was busy with imperial business when they were awake, but Tella should have known better than to believe him.

"It's good to see you, Esmeralda." The tone of Legend's voice chilled her to her blood. When he spoke to Tella it was deep and low, but often tinged with something teasing. This was more carnal and a little cruel, a voice that didn't know how to play. He used it as easily as the voice he taunted her with in her dreams. And for a cracked moment Tella couldn't help but wonder if this vicious Legend was the act—or if the flirtatious Legend she saw when she slept was the true performance.

"We should get out of the cold." The woman slipped her arm through Legend's.

Tella waited for him to shift away, to show a hint of discomfort, but he only pulled her closer, touching her easily when, for the last two months, he hadn't touched Tella.

She seethed and shivered as she followed the pair, creeping behind them as they reached a two-story cottage, bright with firelight that fell through the windows and then spilled out from the door as the woman opened it and they both stepped inside.

Tella felt a flare of heat before the door slammed shut, leaving her blanketed in cold once more. She should have left, but apparently she was a masochist, because rather than turning around and saving herself from more torture, she braved the moat of thorny roses surrounding the house, sacrificing the helpless feathers of her skirt as she crouched beneath the closest cottage window to eavesdrop.

If Legend was having a relationship with someone else, Tella wanted to know everything about it. Maybe this woman was the reason he'd walked away from her that night in front of the Temple of the Stars.

Rubbing her hands together to keep herself from turning to ice, Tella lifted her head enough to peek through a frosted window. The cabin looked as warm as a handwritten love letter, with a stone fireplace that took up an entire wall and a forest of candles dangling from the ceiling.

The hideaway seemed to be made for romantic rendezvous, but as Tella spied, she saw no kissing, no embracing. Esmeralda sat on the blazing fireplace hearth as if it were her throne, while Legend stood before her like a loyal subject.

Interesting.

Maybe the matching tattoos didn't mean what Tella thought they meant. But Tella was still troubled. She always imagined that Legend answered to no one except himself, and no matter who this fascinating woman was, Tella didn't like her. And she really didn't like the way Legend stood, leaning toward her, head slightly bowed, as he said, "I need your help, Esmeralda. The Fates have broken free from the Deck of Destiny that you imprisoned them in."

Blood and saints.

Tella ducked back down, sucking in cold gasps of air as her back slammed against the icy cottage wall. Suddenly she knew exactly who this young woman was. Before Legend had freed the Fates, they had been imprisoned in a Deck of Destiny by the same witch who'd given Legend his powers. The witch who Legend was speaking with now.

No wonder he was treating this woman like a queen. Esmeralda was his creator. When she had cast the spell dooming the Fates to the cards, she'd taken half their powers and then given them to Legend when he'd sought her out, centuries later. Tella didn't actually know much more about the witch. But she wasn't supposed to be so young, or so tall and attractive.

"I failed to destroy the Fates. I'm sorry. But I'm paying the price," Legend said, his voice carrying down through the cracked window above. "My magic has grown much weaker since the moment they were freed. The Fates are still asleep for now, but I think they've already taken some of their powers back. I can barely do a simple illusion."

Tella resisted the urge to stand and steal another look. *Was he telling the truth?* If the Fates had somehow managed to steal his magic, then it would explain why he'd vanished so violently from her dreams the other night, and failed to appear last night. Yet she'd seen him use a glamour in the forest to change his clothes, and he'd seemed to have no trouble with it.

Of course, that was a small illusion, and she hadn't been close enough to touch it. In one of her earlier dreams with Legend, he had explained how his powers worked. He'd told Tella: *Magic comes in two forms. Those with powers can usually either manipulate people or manipulate the world. But I can do both and create lifelike glamours that feel far more real than ordinary illusions. I can make it rain, and you wouldn't just see the rain, you'd feel it soaking your clothes and your skin. You'd feel it all the way down to your bones if I wanted you to.*

It had started raining then, inside of her dream, and when she'd woken up hours later, her thin nightdress had been speckled with drops of wet and her curls had been soaked—letting her know that the dreams weren't just her imaginings, but real rendezvous with Legend, and that his powers of illusion extended far beyond them.

Perhaps Legend was telling the truth about the Fates taking some of his magic, but he wasn't telling the entire truth. Maybe he could still create illusions, but they weren't powerful enough to trick people into believing they were real.

Tella thought back to the dead butterfly she'd found in her hand when she'd woken up the day before. Now that she really considered it, she'd seen the butterfly, but she hadn't felt it. Its delicate wings hadn't brushed her skin, and as soon as she'd set it on the nightstand, it had vanished.

"The Fates shouldn't have any of your magic," the witch bit out, "not unless *you* released them from the cards."

"I would never do that. Do you think I'm a fool? I've been trying to destroy that deck since the day you made me." Legend's tone was clipped as if he were genuinely offended, but Tella knew that *this* was all a lie. A blatant lie to the woman who'd created him. He had wanted to destroy the cards, but when he'd been given the opportunity, he hadn't. He'd freed the Fates instead, to save Tella.

"I still want to stop the Fates," Legend went on. "But to do it, I need to borrow your magic."

"You can't stop the Fates with magic," said the witch. "That's why I told you to destroy the Deck of Destiny. They're immortals, like you. If you kill a Fate, they will die, but then they'll simply return to life."

"But they have to possess a weakness." Legend's voice took on that edge once again, a voice for unraveling and stealing. He wanted Esmeralda's magic and he wanted to know the Fates' fatal weakness.

It should have given Tella relief that he was searching for a way to destroy them—she didn't want the Fates alive either—but a horrible feeling came to life inside her as she heard the decisive click of Legend's boots.

Tella pictured him moving closer to Esmeralda.

She clamped her frozen hands into fists, fighting the growing urge to peek through the window, to see if he was doing more than closing the distance in order to get the information he wanted. Was he touching the witch? Was he wrapping his arms around her cinched waist, or looking at her the way he sometimes looked at Tella?

When Esmeralda spoke once more, her voice had turned seductive again. "The Fates that were imprisoned do have one disadvantage. Their immortality is linked to the Fate who created them: the Fallen Star. If you kill the Fallen Star, the Fates he made will change from immortal to ageless, similar to your performers. They will still have their magic, and they will never grow old, but unlike your performers, they will not have Caraval to bring them back to life if they die. If you wish to destroy all the Fates, you must first slay the Fallen Star."

"How do I do that?" Legend asked.

"I think you already know. The Fallen Star shares the same weakness as you."

The pause that followed was so quiet and still that Tella swore she could hear the snowflakes falling on the roses around her. Twice in a row the witch had just likened Legend to the Fallen Star. First, when she'd mentioned the Fallen Star's Fates and Legend's performers. And now she'd just said that Legend shared the same weakness as the Fallen Star.

Did that mean Legend was a Fate?

Tella flashed back to something her nana Anna used to say when she told the story about how Legend came to be. *"Some would probably call him a villain. Others would say his magic makes him closer to a god."*

People had also called the Fates gods at one point in time—cruel, capricious, and terrible gods, which was why the witch had trapped them in the cards.

Tella shuddered at the thought that Legend might be like them. During the last Caraval, her interactions with Fates like the Undead Queen, Her Handmaidens, and the Prince of Hearts had almost left her dead. She didn't want Legend to be in the same category. But she couldn't deny the fact that Legend was immortal and magical—and that made him something more akin to a Fate than it did to a human.

Tella desperately tried to hear what the weakness was. But Legend didn't reveal it with his response.

"There has to be another way," he said.

"If there is, you'll have to find it out on your own. Or, you could remain here with me. The Fates don't know I've come to this world. If you stay, it will be like it was when I taught you how to master your powers." She purred. Actually *purred*.

Tella really did hate her.

Black thorns ripped the freezing feathers from her skirt as she lost her battle with restraint and rose from her crouch to peek through the window once again. And this time she wished she hadn't.

Legend was on his knees before the witch and she was running her fingers through his dark hair, moving them possessively down his scalp to his neck, as if he belonged to her.

"I didn't know you were so sentimental," said Legend.

"Only when it comes to you." Her fingers knotted in his cravat as she tilted his chin toward her.

"I wish I could stay, Esmeralda. But I can't. I need to go back and destroy the Fates, and I need your powers to do that." He pushed up from his knees just as the witch had been leaning into what looked like a kiss. "I only want to borrow them."

"No one ever wants to just borrow powers." The witch's voice turned biting again, but whether it was because of his request or because he'd denied the kiss, Tella couldn't tell.

Legend must have imagined she'd be vexed by his denial; he took a step closer, picked up her hand, and brushed a chaste kiss to her knuckles. "You made me who I am, Esmeralda. If you can't trust me, no one else can."

"No one else *should* trust you," she said. But her rich red lips had finally curved into a smile. The smile of a woman who was saying yes to a man she couldn't resist.

Tella knew the smile because she'd given the same one to him before.

The witch was giving Legend her powers.

Tella should have turned away, should have returned back to her world before Legend caught her there and he saw her trembling from the cold, and from all the feelings that she wished she still didn't have for him. But she remained, transfixed.

The witch uttered words in a language Tella had never heard as Legend drank blood straight from her wrist. He drank and drank and drank. Took and took and took.

Legend's cheeks flushed and his bronze skin began to glow, while the witch's harsh beauty diminished. Her fiery hair dulled to orange;

the black ink of her tattoos faded to gray. By the time Legend lifted his lips from her wrist, Esmeralda sagged against him as if her limbs had lost their bones.

"That took more out of me than I expected," she said softly. "Can you carry me up to the bedroom?"

"I'm sorry," Legend said—but he didn't sound sorry at all. His voice was cruel without the sensuousness to temper it. Then he spoke words too quietly for Tella to hear.

The witch lost even more color, her already pale skin turning parchment-white. "You're joking. . . ."

"Have you ever known me to have a sense of humor?" he asked. Then he picked up the witch and slung her over his shoulder with the ease of a young man checking an item off a list.

Tella stumbled backward on half-numb limbs, leaving a small riot of ripped-up feathers in her wake. She knew that he'd meant it every time he'd told her that he wasn't the hero, but a part of her kept hoping that he'd prove her wrong. Tella wanted to believe that Legend really cared about her and that she was his exception. Although she couldn't help but fear that all that belief really meant was that Legend was actually her exception, that her desire for him was the weakness that could destroy her if she didn't conquer it.

If Legend was willing to betray the woman who'd created him, then he was willing to betray anyone.

Tella tore through the roses, running from her hiding spot beneath the window back into the forest. She stumbled off the main path, into the trees, only glancing back once she was safely hidden behind a copse of pines.

Legend left the cottage with Esmeralda still slung over his shoulder. And in that moment, Legend no longer felt like Tella's enemy, or her friend, or the boy she used to love—Legend felt like every story she'd never wanted to believe about him.

Scarlett

Scarlett's feelings were a commotion of colors, swirling around her in garlands of excited aquamarine, nervous marigold, and frustrated gingersnap. She'd been pacing the suite since her sister had left, somehow knowing that Tella wouldn't be back in time, but also hoping that she'd prove Scarlett wrong.

She stopped pacing and looked herself over in the mirror once more, to make sure her dress wasn't a reflection of how anxious she felt. The gown's pale pink lace appeared duller than before, but everything appeared dimmer in this mirror.

The suite Scarlett and Tella rented was a threadbare tapestry of aging items. Both girls had agreed on moving out of the palace. Scarlett had wanted to be independent. Tella claimed the same thing. But Scarlett imagined her younger sister had also wanted to create distance from Legend after how he'd walked away from her at the end of Caraval.

Tella had begged to rent one of the fashionable apartments in the fanciful Satine District, but Scarlett knew that their money had to last beyond one season. As a compromise, they'd leased a suite of small rooms on the farthest edge of the Satine District, where the trim on the mirrors was more yellow than gold, the chairs were upholstered with scratchy velveteen, and everything smelled chalky, like chipped porcelain. Tella complained about it regularly, but living somewhere modest allowed them to stretch their funds. With most of the money Tella had stolen from their father, they'd secured this apartment until the end of the year. Scarlett wasn't sure what they'd do after that, but it wasn't her most pressing concern.

The clock chimed three.

She peered out her window. There were still no signs of Tella among the holiday revelers, but Scarlett's ground coach had finally arrived. There weren't many in Valenda, as people favored floating carriages to ones that rolled through the street. But, her former fiancé, Count Nicolas d'Arcy, or Nicolas as she had started calling him, resided in a country estate outside the city's quarters, far beyond any of the floating carriage houses. Knowing this, Scarlett had secured her transport a week ago. What she hadn't known was how crowded the festival would be.

People were already hollering at her coachman to move. He

wouldn't wait long. If he left, Scarlett would be stranded and she'd miss her chance to finally meet Nicolas.

Her lips pinched together as she entered the bedroom where Paloma slept. *Always sleeping. Always, always sleeping.*

Scarlett tried not to be bitter. Knowing her mother hadn't meant to abandon them forever, that she'd been trapped in a cursed Deck of Destiny for the past seven years, made Scarlett more sympathetic to her. But she still couldn't forgive her mother for leaving her and Tella with their wretched father in the first place. She could never see Paloma the same way Tella did.

In fact, Tella would probably be furious when she returned and found Paloma unattended. She was always saying how she didn't want their mother to wake up and be alone. But Scarlett doubted Paloma would wake today. And if Tella was so concerned, she should have come back in time.

Scarlett pulled open the main door to her suite, ready to call for a servant and ask her to keep an eye on their mother. But one of the maids was already there, coral-cheeked and smiling broadly.

"Afternoon, miss." The servant did a quick half-curtsy. "I came to tell you there's a gentleman waiting for you in the first-floor parlor."

Scarlett looked past the servant's shoulders. She could see the scratched wood banister, but there was no view of anything downstairs. "Did the gentleman give a name?"

"He said he wanted to surprise you. He's very handsome." The girl coyly twirled a lock of hair around her finger, as if this attractive young man was standing in front of them.

Scarlett hesitated, considering her options. Perhaps it was Nicolas, come to surprise her. But that didn't sound like him. He was so proper, he hadn't wanted to meet her while the Days of Mourning were being observed; he'd asked her to wait until today for their true courtship to begin.

There was one other person who it might be, but Scarlett didn't want to hope it was him, especially not today. She'd vowed not to think about him today. And if it *was* Julian, he was five weeks late. Scarlett might have thought he'd died, except she'd had Tella ask Legend about it, and he'd confirmed Julian was still alive. Though he didn't say where his brother was, or why he'd failed to contact Scarlett.

"Would you do me a favor?" Scarlett said to the servant. "My mother is still unwell. She doesn't need anything, but I hate to leave her alone. While I'm out, would you check on her every half hour in case she wakes?"

Scarlett handed the girl a coin. Then she quietly crept down the stairs, heart in her throat, hoping despite her better judgment that Julian had finally returned and had missed her as much as she missed him. She kept her steps quiet, but the moment she entered the parlor, she forgot how to move. Julian's eyes met hers from across the room.

Everything was suddenly warmer than it had been before. The parlor walls grew smaller and hotter, as if too much sunlight had snuck in through the windows, covering all the tattered bookshelves and chairs in the sort of hazy afternoon light that left the entire world out of focus, except for him.

He looked perfect.

Scarlett could have easily been convinced he'd just escaped from a fresh painting. The tips of his dark hair were wet, his amber eyes were shining, and his lips parted in a devastating smile.

This was the boy of Scarlett's dreams.

Of course, Julian probably starred in the dreams of half the girls on the continent as well.

All of her earlier feelings from before transformed into flames of fiery tangerine. Julian couldn't see her colors, but Scarlett didn't want to reveal her feelings with other tells. She didn't want her knees growing weak, or her cheeks turning to blush. And yet she couldn't stop her heart from racing at the sight of him, as if she were preparing to chase him should he run away. Which he had.

He must have been somewhere even warmer than here. His unusually crisp shirtsleeves were neatly rolled up, showing off lean arms. One forearm had a wide white bandage on it that contrasted with his skin, which was several shades darker than his natural golden brown, tanned from wherever Legend had sent him last. The neatly trimmed stubble lining his jaw was thicker and longer than she remembered as well, and covered part of the thin scar that ran from his eye to his jaw. He didn't wear a coat, but he had on a gray vest with shiny silver buttons that matched the lines of fancy thread on the sides of his deep blue trousers, which were tucked into brand-new leather boots. When she'd first met Julian, he'd looked like a scoundrel, but now he was pure gentleman.

"Hello, Crimson."

Her dress reacted immediately. Scarlett willed it not to shift and betray any of her feelings, but the gown had always liked Julian. The first time she'd put on the dress, back on Legend's isle, she'd been embarrassed to undress in front of Julian, and a little disappointed because the dress had looked like a dreary rag. Then she'd put it on, and when she turned and looked at Julian, the gown had transformed into a confection of lace and seductive colors, as if it had somehow known that this was the boy whose heart she needed to win.

Scarlett couldn't see her reflection now, but she could feel the gown shifting. Warm air brushed her décolletage as the dress's neckline lowered. The skirt tightened to hug the curve of her hips, and the fabric's color deepened to the ravenous pink of lips longing to be kissed.

Julian's grin turned wolfish, reminding her of the night he'd first whisked her off her home isle of Trisda. But despite the hungry look in his eyes, he made no move to close the space between them. His elbow rested against a cracked display case as a fresh ray of sunlight streamed through the window, gilding all his edges in gold and making him look even more untouchable.

Scarlett wanted to run to him and throw her arms around him, but she didn't move from the doorway. "When did you return?" she asked coolly.

"A week ago."

And you're only visiting now? Scarlett wanted to ask. But she reminded herself that she was the one who'd first put a wedge between them when she'd told him she wanted to meet her former fiancé.

Julian had said he understood, had said he wanted her to do whatever she needed. But then he'd been sent away on *another* errand from Legend.

I won't be able to write, but it will only take one week, he'd promised.

One week had turned into two, then three, then four, then five weeks without so much as a note from him to say he was still alive. She wasn't sure if it was because he'd given up on her or if he'd forgotten about her because he was so busy working for Legend.

Julian pulled at the back of his neck, looking uncomfortable, bringing Scarlett's attention back to the bandage wrapped around his arm.

"Were you wounded?" *Was that why he hadn't come by?* "What happened to your arm?"

"It's nothing," he mumbled.

But Scarlett would have sworn he blushed. She didn't even know Julian was capable of blushing. He had no shame. He moved through the world with utter confidence. But his cheeks were definitely flushed, and his eyes refused to meet hers. "I'm sorry I didn't come by sooner."

"It's all right," Scarlett said. "I'm sure you're very busy with whatever Legend has you doing." Her gaze flickered once more to the mysterious bandage around his arm and then up to his eyes, which still declined to meet hers. "It's nice of you to stop by. It's good to see you." She itched to say so much more, but she could hear the carriage horses neighing outside. Scarlett needed to leave before she mucked things up with Nicolas. "I'd love to chat, but unfortunately I was about to step out."

Julian shoved away from the display cabinet. "If you're going to enjoy the festival, I'll join you." It was the polite statement of a friend. But Scarlett's feelings for Julian had always been too strong for friendship, even when she'd first met him and hadn't liked him at all. Scarlett and Julian could never just be friends. She needed more from him, or she needed him to let her go.

"I'm not going to the festival," Scarlett said. "I'm finally going to meet Nicolas."

Julian's expression fell. It only lasted a moment. If Scarlett had torn her eyes from him for a second, she would have missed it. Almost as soon as he heard what she said, Julian walked past her to the boardinghouse front door. She expected him to leave, to let her go and close the door on them completely.

Instead he opened it with an oddly pleasant smile. "That's perfect," he said, cheerful, as if she'd just told him they were having coconut cake for dinner. "I can be your chaperone."

"I don't need a chaperone."

"Do you already have one?"

Scarlett glared. "You and I never had one."

"Exactly." With a smug grin, he swaggered past her to the idling carriage and opened that door as well. But rather than wait for her to enter, Julian slipped into the coach.

Scarlett's emotions were searing as she entered the coach and took the seat across from him. Julian might have started dressing like a gentleman, but he was still behaving like a scoundrel. She'd have understood his frustrating behavior if he'd made any effort to contact her over the past five weeks, or if he'd tried to fight for her after she'd told him that she wanted to give Nicolas another chance as well, but it seemed all Julian wanted to do was fight against her.

"You're trying to sabotage this," she accused.

"I'd say I'd never do that, but that would be a lie." Julian lounged back in his seat, spreading out the way young men always seemed to. Since the streets of Valenda weren't made for coaches, this box was particularly narrow, with barely enough room for the two of them. But Julian stretched his arms across the brocade cushions, and kicked out his legs to take up more than half the space.

Scarlett grabbed one of his knees, knocked it into the other, and pointed toward the door as the carriage began to rumble down the road. "Get out, Julian."

"No." His arms dropped from the cushion and he leaned forward. "I'm not leaving, Crimson. We've spent enough time apart." He placed his hand on top of hers and pressed it firmly to his knee.

Scarlett tried to pull away, but it was in the halfhearted way someone did something when they were actually hoping someone would stop them.

And Julian did. He slipped his brown fingers between hers and held on tighter than he ever had, as if making up for all the weeks he hadn't been able to touch her. "While I was gone, I tried to remember every word you ever said to me. I've thought about you every hour of every day I was away."

Scarlett fought the urge to smile. It was everything she had wanted to hear. But Julian had always excelled at knowing what to say. It was following through where he fell apart. "Then why didn't you write?"

"You told me you wanted space to meet your count."

"I didn't want that much space. For five weeks I heard nothing from you. I thought that you'd forgotten about me or moved on." She tried not to sound too accusing or too desperate. She felt as if she'd failed at both, and yet Julian's earnest expression didn't waver. His eyes were the prettiest shade of brown, and warmer than the light slipping through the carriage windows.

"I won't ever move on, Crimson." He took her hand and brought it to his heart.

Scarlett's heart beat wild and uneven in response, but Julian's remained steady and unwavering beneath her palm.

"I've made a lot of mistakes. I gave you space, because I thought that's what you needed. But I realized as soon as I saw you today that I was wrong. So I'm in this carriage with you now, ready to go wherever you're going, even if it means watching you with another man."

Scarlett crashed back to reality. For a moment she'd forgotten about Nicolas.

"What if I don't want you to watch me with another man?" she said.

"I'm not thrilled about the idea, either." Julian's tone turned teasing, but his fingers tensed as the carriage rattled over a bumpy road.

They were nearing the edge of the city, and drawing closer to Nicolas's estate.

"If you really want me to leave, I'll get out of this coach and walk back to the palace," Julian said. "But you should know that I'm also here because I don't trust this count."

"Do you trust me?" Scarlett said.

"With my life. But I've met your father and I have a difficult time putting faith in anyone who would make a deal with him."

"Nicolas isn't like that."

When Scarlett had first written Nicolas after learning she'd not truly met him during Caraval, he had been away from the continent mourning *her*. Her father had lied and said Scarlett and her sister had both died in an accident. He had no idea what a horrible man Marcello Dragna was.

And Nicolas was nothing like her father. He was drawings of plants, and anecdotes about his dog, Timber. He was a rule-follower like her; he believed in tradition so much he'd waited until today to meet her. Nicolas was safe. Scarlett couldn't see him breaking her heart. Julian had already broken her heart twice, and even if Julian didn't intentionally do it again, her heart would break for him eventually.

When Scarlett had first written Nicolas she'd only wanted to meet him, to cure her curiosity. Then Julian had left for so long, and Nicolas's letters had been there when Julian hadn't. Steady when Julian had been unreliable.

As a part of Caraval, Julian was ageless. He could die and stay dead if someone killed him when a game wasn't in play, but he would never grow old as long as he was one of Legend's performers. Scarlett could never ask him to give that up.

She didn't know if Legend would still hold the games now that he was to become emperor. But given how Julian had just disappeared for weeks, it was clear Legend still controlled him. Any future Scarlett and Julian might have together was destined not to last. And yet even knowing all of this, she couldn't bring herself to pull her hand away from his.

"I don't want you to walk back to the palace," she said. "But if you ruin this, I swear on the stars, I will never speak to you again. The count has to believe you're a chaperone. We can tell him that you're my cousin."

"That's not going to work unless you're fine with him believing you have an inappropriate relationship with your cousin." Julian darted closer and pressed a quick kiss to her neck.

Scarlett felt her cheeks go red. "Don't you dare do anything like that!"

He lounged back, laughing hard enough to shake the carriage. "I was only kidding, Crimson, although now I'm tempted to follow through."

8

Scarlett

Sweat beaded between Scarlett's toes as a servant led her down a hall covered in detailed wainscoting and thick crown molding.

There might have been some cracks in the molding, which gave her a hint of pause. Nicolas had never said it, but at one point, she'd imagined that he'd only wanted to marry her because of her father's wealth. But she wasn't connected to her father anymore. If Nicolas ever chose to propose, it would be because of her.

Now the palms of her hands were sweating even more than her toes. She wanted to wipe the damp on her gown, but it would be worse to have obvious streaks marring the deep pink fabric.

Scarlett took several shallow breaths, trying to calm herself as the servant opened the door to a sprawling garden covered in glass. "His Lordship will meet you in here."

Sprightly hummingbirds zipped from plant to plant, mirroring the state of Scarlett's chaotic stomach as she stepped through the doorway. Everything smelled of pollen and flowers and budding romance.

Nicolas had recently drawn her a bouquet of hybrid flowers and told her that he enjoyed experimenting in the garden. She'd thought he'd written it to sound impressive, but clearly someone played with the plants in here. There were clusters of white Valendan faisies with velvet-blue vines, silver spider lilies that shined under the light, and yellow stems of sunflowers with jade-green petals.

Not too far from the door rested a copper table set with a bouquet of bright pink peonies, a pitcher of minted lemonade, sandwiches of seeded bread, and tiny tarts covered in white plums. Enough to be thoughtful without going over the top.

Julian eyed the little feast suspiciously, as if the lemonade was poisonous and the sandwiches hid razor blades. "It's not too late to leave."

"I'm exactly where I want to be." Scarlett perched on the edge of a large copper chair. "But you're free to go whenever you wish."

"Don't tell me you really like it here." Julian's eyes lifted toward a slice of the glass ceiling covered in ladybugs. "There's something off. Even the insects want to escape."

"Ahem." Someone cleared his throat. "His Lordship, Count Nicolas d'Arcy."

Scarlett's breath caught.

Clipped boot steps, heavier than she would have expected, followed the servant's voice.

She thought she'd imagined her former fiancé as every possible sort of man. She'd pictured him short, tall, slender, wide, old, young, bald, hairy, handsome, plain, pale, dark, brooding, cheerful. She'd pictured him dressed in frilly frockcoats and dour suits as she tried to imagine the first thing he'd say upon meeting her.

She'd imagined what she'd say to him as well. But her words tangled together as he stepped forward and took her hand in his.

Nicolas was a mountain. The large hand holding Scarlett's could have just as easily crushed it as cradled it. He was almost a full foot taller than her—all muscled legs, burly arms, and brown hair so thick that even though it appeared he'd tried to tame it, a wide lock fell over his forehead, giving him a boyish appearance, which was added to by his slightly crooked spectacles.

He looked the way she would have imagined a vigilante who had a secret identity as a gentleman botanist.

Beside him trailed a great black dog the size of a small pony. *Timber.* Scarlett had heard a lot about him in Nicolas's letters. His tail wagged and his ears went back at the sight of Scarlett, obviously excited. But the dog didn't leave his master's side; he sat obediently as Nicolas brought her hand to his full mouth.

Her dress clearly liked him. Her low neckline was now rimmed with roughly cut gems that sent sparks of light all over the glassed-in garden.

"It's wonderful to finally meet you," Scarlett managed.

He smiled, wide and sincere. "I'm tempted to say you're even prettier than I imagined, but I would hate you to think me unoriginal."

"Too late," Julian coughed.

A wrinkle formed between Nicolas's thick brows as he noticed Scarlett's companion. "And you are?"

"Julian." He offered his hand.

But Nicolas refused to let go of Scarlett's. "I wasn't aware Scarlett had a brother."

"I'm not her brother." Julian kept his tone friendly, but Scarlett felt a surge of bruising purple panic as devilry sparked in Julian's eyes. "I'm not related to her at all. I'm an actor she played with during Caraval."

He emphasized the words *played with,* and Scarlett could have choked him. Julian would choose *now* to finally be honest.

Not that Nicolas appeared disturbed. The young count's broad smile remained even as he pet Timber with his free hand.

But Julian wasn't finished.

"I'm not surprised she's never mentioned me. At the start of Caraval I don't think she liked me much. But then we were given the same bedroom—"

"Julian, enough," Scarlett cut in.

Nicolas's smile finally fell. He released her fingers, as if taking them had been a mistake.

"It's not the way it sounds. Julian and I are only *friends,*" she said, deciding not to even touch the word *bedroom.* "He met my father during Caraval and he was nervous you might be like him. He wanted to come today because he's protective of me. But allowing that was evidently a mistake." She shot a narrow look in Julian's direction.

He appeared unapologetic, shrugging as he sank his hands into his pockets.

"Nicolas, please—"

"It's all right, Scarlett." The count's voice rumbled deeper than before, but the angry lines around his mouth were gone. "I won't say I'm pleased about this. But after learning the truth about your father and hearing about the *fiancé* you met during Caraval, I can understand."

Nicolas turned back to Julian, and Scarlett stared as the young men finally shook hands. "Thank you for watching out for her during the game."

"I'll always watch out for her," Julian said.

"What about when you're not needed?" Nicolas asked.

Julian threw his shoulders back and stood taller. "I'll let Scarlett make that choice."

"Julian, stop," Scarlett said.

"It's all right." Nicolas scratched his dog behind the ears. "I don't mind a bit of competition. In fact, I'd prefer to know who else is trying to win your hand."

"I wouldn't put it like that," Julian said. "Winning implies this is a game."

"It's a figure of speech," said Nicolas.

"I know." Julian smirked. "Games are what I do. But I don't think you were using it figuratively. You want to win her by proving you're the best."

"Isn't that what you want?" Nicolas asked. And Scarlett would have sworn he puffed his chest.

They were like battling peacocks. Scarlett pictured their emotions swirling in proud shades of teal and cobalt blue. Or maybe she was actually seeing their feelings?

Scarlett always saw her own emotions in colors, but she'd only seen the feelings of someone else once. It had happened during Caraval, after she'd shared blood with Julian. It was the most intimate thing she'd ever done, and afterward, she'd been able to glimpse Julian's feelings. But it hadn't lasted long, and neither did this glimpse of pride, making her wonder if it was only in her mind, since she hadn't drunk anyone's blood.

Julian and Nicolas were still staring each other down. This was not the scene Scarlett had imagined. *She* was supposed to be the one Nicolas was staring at. He was supposed to flatter and woo her, not argue with Julian.

"I don't need to prove anything," said Julian. "I'm not trying to win her hand. I'm offering her mine, and everything that comes with it, hoping she'll take it and decide she wants to keep it."

It was one of the sweeter things Julian had said, and maybe Scarlett would have accepted his hand if he actually had spared her a look during his pretty speech. But the boys were so caught up in their sparring, it seemed they'd forgotten she was there.

"I'm glad this isn't just a game to you, Julian, but maybe it should be. Perhaps we should turn this into a courtship competition," Scarlett said. The words immediately tasted like a mistake. But the bemused glances of her gentlemen felt like a victory. Instead of speaking as if Scarlett wasn't there, Julian and Nicolas were now looking at her as if she were the only one present.

"They did this in the early days of the Meridian Empire," she went on. "Young ladies from wealthy or noble families would arrange a series of tasks, so that their gentleman suitors could show off their skills. Whoever completed them first or best would then marry the young lady."

Nicolas ran a hand over his mouth, as if trying to hide his expression, but she could tell he was intrigued.

"This shouldn't be a game," Julian said.

"Afraid you'll lose?" Nicolas definitely puffed his chest this time.

Julian muttered something under his breath. His posture was tense and his jaw was clenched, making the scar that ran from his jaw to his eye turn into an aggravated white line. "Crimson, don't make this a game."

If he hadn't said that, Scarlett might have changed her mind. She'd made the challenge mostly to shock them and to stop their ridiculous fighting. But if she backed out now, it would look as if she were doing it for Julian and not for herself.

And she always felt as if she were caving in for Julian.

Julian was the sun in the middle of the wettest part of the Cold Season, gloriously warm and wonderful when he was there, but completely unreliable. For five weeks he'd vanished. Now, though he'd only been back in her life just a few hours, he'd turned it into chaos.

Sometimes, admittedly, she liked the wildness he brought into her world. But she didn't like that this time it was more about him getting his way than it was about her. He'd said in the carriage he was here because he didn't trust the count. But Nicolas was a botanist, with a dog—one look at him and it was clear he didn't have any nefarious plans for Scarlett. Julian just didn't want anyone else to have plans for Scarlett at all.

"If you don't want to play, you don't have to," Scarlett said. "But I think it will be fun. My mind is made up."

"Since when do you make up your mind so fast?" argued Julian.

"Since five weeks ago." Her smile was an exclamation point.

Julian looked as if he wanted to keep arguing. He probably would have if Nicolas wasn't there. Instead, he just swatted at an unfortunate ladybug with more force than necessary.

Nicolas's grin expanded as if he was already winning.

It made Scarlett a little nervous. But after what she'd just said to Julian she couldn't back out now, and though it might have been a little terrifying, it was also exhilarating to take control in a way she never had before. "I'll start with a simple challenge and each challenge will grow progressively harder until one of you backs out, or one of you fails to complete a task."

"What's the first challenge?" Nicolas asked.

Scarlett tried to remember what she'd read in the history books. But this was her game; she could do it however she wanted. "Each of you must bring me a gift within the next three days, but it must be something you've never given to anyone else."

"Will we get a prize if we bring the best gift?" Julian asked.

"Yes," Scarlett said. "I'll give a kiss to the winner of each individual challenge, and at the end of the game, I'll marry whoever wins."

It was the sort of thing Tella would have said. It was bold, and it made Scarlett feel bold as well.

But feelings never lasted, and the results of this game would.

Scarlett

Scarlett tried not to regret her choice in declaring her hand in marriage a game, while Julian appeared to be hiding how unhappy he was with the way their visit to Nicolas's estate had turned out. After Scarlett had laid out the rules of the game, she'd convinced both gentlemen to sit down and have some of the tea and treats Nicolas had prepared. But of course it had turned into another competition; talk of traveling turned into a battle over who traveled the most. Talk of books had turned into a contest to see who was better read. And when the talk had stopped, they'd stared each other down until Scarlett finally declared it time to leave.

Julian now leaned his dark head against the window, one booted foot slung casually over his knee as he hummed softly. Scarlett knew he didn't feel as careless as he appeared, but his melody was resonant and relaxing, making all the flourishing rows of country farms look even prettier as their coach lumbered over uneven roads.

"Do you also sing?" Scarlett asked. "I've never heard a hum so musical."

The corner of Julian's mouth hitched into a wry smile. "I have lots of practice. For years, Legend kept giving me roles as a minstrel who only spoke in song."

Scarlett laughed. "What did you do to earn that?"

Julian shrugged. "My brother has a jealous streak. I think it bothered him that I was getting so much attention during the games. He tried to turn me into a joke. But everyone likes a handsome young man with a good voice."

Scarlett rolled her eyes, but the world did turn lovelier when Julian started humming again. She looked out the window as the coach rumbled closer to an immaculately kept country house the color of Sun Festival peaches, trimmed in crisp white and surrounded by rambling faises that made her think of living lace.

Even the family out front appeared to be perfectly posed. They must have been celebrating the festival with an outdoor dinner. There was a long table atop the grass, set with flowered cloths and covered in what looked like a feast. The family of five stood around it, all drinking from earthenware goblets as if someone had just given a toast. Scarlett looked to the youngest child, a girl with long braids down her back. She held her goblet with both hands, lips smiling as if this was her first taste of wine. It was the sort of grin that hurt if a person held on to it too long.

But the smile didn't change. *Nothing changed.*

Bitter-orange pinpricks of unease crawled over Scarlett's skin as the coach trundled past and no one among the party lowered their goblets or moved at all.

Scarlett might have thought the family was a series of incredibly lifelike statues if not for the terrified plumes of phantom-purple swirling around their frozen forms. Plumes that were definitely not in Scarlett's mind. She could see their feelings so vividly, her heart stated racing with whatever fright they were experiencing.

"Something's wrong." Scarlett reached across the carriage and opened the window to yell at the driver, "Stop the coach!"

"What's the matter?" Julian asked.

"I don't know, but something isn't right." She flung open the door as soon as the carriage came to a stop.

Julian followed while she tore across the grass.

The scene looked even more unnatural up close. The only things that moved were the blades of grass around Scarlett's feet, and the ants. The ants crawled over the Sun Festival feast while the family remained frozen in their endless toast, mouths awkwardly parted and teeth stained with dark purple from whatever they'd been drinking.

"Would Legend do something like this?" Scarlett asked.

"No, he can be cruel, but he's never this cruel." Julian frowned as he checked the pulse of the youngest girl. "She's still alive."

He continued to search for heartbeats as the family remained eerily still.

"How could someone even do this?" Scarlett scanned the table, as if she might find a bottle of poison hidden among the food. But everything looked perfectly normal—flatbread, long beans, speckled cobs of corn, baskets of fresh sunberries, latticed pig pies, and—

She paused on the butter knives sticking out from the table. Dull, flat metal, the kind of utensils that cut poorly and yet someone had been strong enough to shove the tip of each one through the cloth into the table, pinning a note in place.

"Julian, come look at this." Scarlett carefully leaned over the feast, not daring to touch the knives or the note as she read aloud.

> ONE, TWO, THREE, FOUR, FIVE…
>
> IF THE SUN HASN'T SET, THEY SHOULD ALL STILL BE ALIVE.
>
> BUT ONCE THIS DAY COMES TO AN END,
>
> I'M AFRAID THIS FAMILY WILL ALL BE DEAD.
>
> IF YOU WISH TO STOP THEM FROM TURNING TO STONE,
>
> WHOEVER READS THIS MUST ATONE.
>
> RECALL YOUR LIES AND ACTS DONE OUT OF FEAR,
>
> THEN CONFESS YOUR LATEST MISDEED OUT LOUD FOR ALL TO HEAR.
>
> —POISON

"It doesn't even rhyme properly," Julian grumbled.

"I think you're missing the point," Scarlett whispered. She didn't know if the statues were capable of hearing, but if they were, she didn't want to scare them with what she was thinking. "Did you see the name at the bottom of the note? There's a Fate called the Poisoner."

It wasn't exactly the same name as Poison, so maybe this wasn't the work of a Fate. But if it was, it was a terrible sign.

Until recently, Scarlett had never thought much of the Fates—the mythical, ancient beings had always been her sister's obsessions. But after the Fates had been freed from their cursed Deck of Destiny, Scarlett had peppered Tella with questions, and studied up on them herself.

The Fates were so ancient that most people believed them to be myths that only existed as painted images on Decks of Destiny, which people used to tell fortunes. But they weren't merely painted images; they were real and had been cursed to live inside a Deck of Destiny for centuries. There wasn't a great deal of information on what exactly they could do with their powers, but the name the Poisoner seemed rather self-explanatory.

"Do you think this could mean that the Fates are waking?"

"We didn't think they'd wake up this quickly." Julian tugged at the knot of his cravat. "It could just be a prank for the Sun Festival."

"Who's capable of a prank like this?"

"The Prince of Hearts can stop hearts," Julian hazarded.

"But their hearts are still beating." Scarlett hadn't been the one to touch their pulses, but she imagined they were pounding. Hers was. She could feel her heart racing as the plumes of purple panic coming from the family began to curl like smoke from a growing fire.

"I think we should do what it asks, and confess our last lies out loud," Scarlett said. "Even if we go back to town and find an open apothecary, I have a feeling they won't be able to fix this." And Scarlett couldn't leave these people like this.

Julian shook his head as he looked over the frozen family once more. "I should have gone along with the lie and said I was your cousin."

"Why do you say that?" Scarlett asked.

"Because the last lie I told was to you." Julian tore a hand through his hair and when he looked back at her again, it hung over nervous and regretful eyes.

An awful sinking feeling turned inside of Scarlett. His lies had torn them apart before. Lying was the habit Julian couldn't seem to break, perhaps from being a part of Caraval for so long. But with all his honesty today, she'd started to hope that he had changed. But maybe she'd been wrong.

"I'm sorry, Crimson. I lied when I said I left for five weeks to give you space. I left because I was angry you wanted to meet the count, and I thought leaving would make you want me more."

It did. It made her want him—and hate him, and just then it almost made her want to laugh. It always hurt when Julian lied because it made her believe that his lies meant he didn't care. But everything he'd done today proved that he still cared. And she couldn't get mad at him for manipulating her, when she'd done the same thing to him.

"You're terrible," she said. "But I'm terrible, too. I don't really think the courtship game between you and Nicolas will be fun. The more I think about it, the more nervous I get. I only did it to test you and get back at you for leaving."

Julian's grin immediately returned. "Does that mean you're going to call it off?"

Someone coughed at the other side of the table. Choking, sputtering, wheezing, and the crashing of dropped goblets followed, as the family began to move again.

"Oh, thank you!"

"Bless you!"

"You saved us!"

Scarlett and Julian were immediately enclosed in one family-size hug as the small clan poured out their gratitude. Their bodies were shaking and warm from the sun, and the youngest girl with the braids might have hugged Julian a little longer than everyone else, forming an instant crush on him.

"I thought for certain we were going to stay like that forever," said the stout woman who Scarlett assumed was the mother.

"People passed by, but no one stopped," said one of the sons.

"Can you tell us anything about who did this to you?" asked Julian.

"Oh, yes," everyone said at once. And then all their strained faces went blank.

"Well, the person was . . ."

"I think . . ."

Several of them tried to answer the question, but none of them managed it, as if their memories had been stolen.

Scarlett debated voicing what she'd whispered to Julian, about the possibility that the Fates were waking up and Poison was actually the Poisoner, but this family had been through enough. They didn't need to be terrified by Scarlett's suspicions.

"We'd ask you to stay and dine with us," said the fatherly looking man. "But I don't think any of us will be eating after this."

"That's all right," Scarlett said. "We're just glad we could help."

She and Julian let everyone embrace them once again before they returned to the carriage. If this scene really was the work of a Fate, they needed to warn—

"Wait!" cried the youngest girl with the braids. She tore across the grass. Scarlett thought she may have come to give Julian a kiss good-bye, but she ran up to Scarlett instead. "I want to give you a gift for stopping to help us." The girl solemnly reached into the pocket of her apron and pulled out an ugly key covered in greenish-white rust and scratches, the color of buried secrets that should not have been dug up.

"That's all right," Scarlett said. "You keep it."

"No," the girl insisted. "There's more to this key than just how it looks. It's like how my family was when you drove by. I don't know what it does, but I found it this morning, on the edge of the well. One moment, nothing was there, and then it appeared. I think it's magic, and I want you to have it, because I think you're magical too."

The girl handed her the gift.

Scarlett might have teared up, this child was so precious. "Thank you." She enclosed the key in her palm.

It wasn't until after Scarlett stepped into the carriage and looked at it again that she noticed the object had transformed from an aged piece of rust to a crystalline key that glittered like stardust and bewitchment.

Donatella

Tella's limbs were shaking and her eyes were bleary by the time she neared the boardinghouse. Slipping between worlds had left her feeling like a damp sheet of paper that had been wrung out by rough hands.

Tella didn't know how much time had passed while she'd been away. From all the rumpled festival streamers and the number of sweets melted in the streets, she'd wager she'd been gone for hours. Children who'd been running around with sun-shaped pinwheels earlier were now asleep in the arms of tired parents, young ladies who'd been wearing simple gowns had changed into sleeker sheaths, and a new round of merchants had taken over the streets. Celebrations were dying and starting up again, coming back to life for the endless night of festival sunshine.

Tella was beyond late to meet Scarlett.

Her steps slowed as she entered the aging boardinghouse. She didn't want to see Scarlett's disappointment. She felt terrible that she'd let her down and failed to keep her promise. But Tella didn't regret following Legend—it was good for her to finally see him when he had no idea she was watching. She probably should have tracked him down in real life weeks ago, but she'd liked the dreams too much. He was so close to perfect in the dreams. And maybe that had been the point. In dreams, Legend was someone she wanted—someone she cared and worried about—but in real life, he was someone that no one should trust.

Tella eased the door open and slowly stepped into a room heated with trapped sunshine.

"Scar," she tried, hesitant.

"Donatella . . . is that you?" The question was barely a whisper, so soft it felt closer to a thought, and yet the voice was unmistakable, familiar—even though Tella had only heard it once in the past seven years.

She ran into her mother's room and immediately crashed to a halt at the sight of her mother sitting up in the bed.

The world stopped. The outside noises from the festival vanished. The shabby apartment faded.

Kisses on eyelids. Locked jewelry boxes. Giddy whispers. Exotic perfume bottles. Stories at night. Grins in daylight. Enchanted laughter. Lullabies. Cups of violet tea. Secretive smiles. Drawers full of letters. Unspoken good-byes. Fluttering curtains. The scent of plumerias.

A hundred misplaced memories resurfaced, and every single one appeared bloodless and insubstantial compared to the miraculous reality of Tella's mother.

Paloma looked like a slightly older version of Scarlett, although her smile lacked Scarlett's gentleness. When Paloma's lips curved they were just as they had been in the Wanted poster Tella had seen for Paradise the Lost. It was the same enchanting and enigmatic smile that Tella remembered practicing when she was a little girl.

"Why am I not surprised that you look as if you just came out of a fight?" Paloma's smile wavered but her voice was the sweetest sound that Tella had ever heard.

"It was only with a rosebush." She flung herself toward the bed and pulled her mother into a hug. She didn't smell the same way Tella remembered—the sweet scent of magic cleaved to Paloma—but Tella didn't care. She pressed her head into her shoulder as she clung tightly to her mother's softness, perhaps a little too ferocious.

Her mother returned the embrace, but only for a moment. Then she was sagging against the quilted headboard, breathing raggedly as her eyelids began to droop.

"I'm sorry." Tella pulled back right away. "I didn't mean to hurt you."

"You could never hurt me with a hug. I'm just—" Her brow wrinkled beneath stray strands of dark mahogany hair, as if she were searching for a runaway thought. "I think I just need to eat, my little love. Can you fetch me some food?"

"I'll ring for one of the maids."

"I—I—think—" Paloma's eyes fluttered all the way shut.

"Mother!"

"I'm fine." Her eyes cracked open again. "I just feel so weak and hungry."

"I'll be right back with something to eat," Tella promised.

She hated to leave her mother, but she didn't want to make her wait for a maid to plod up and down the stairs. It was fortunate she didn't wait, because as Tella raced to the kitchen, there didn't appear to be any maids at all. They must have all taken off for the Sun Festival.

The cooking galley was abandoned. No one stopped Tella as she grabbed a tray and began piling food on top of it. She pilfered the best-looking fruits from a mound of plump peaches and sun-bright apricots. Then she took a hunk of hard cheese and half a loaf of sage bread. She munched on the food as she grabbed it, her appetite returning with excitement. Her mother was finally awake, and she was going to be fine as soon as she ate.

Tella thought about brewing some tea, but she didn't want to wait for the water to boil. She searched for a bottle of wine instead. They never served alcohol here, but she was certain they had some. Tella located a bottle of burgundy in a cupboard and then she grabbed a couple of chocolate hand-pies for dessert.

She was proud of her feast as she carefully marched it up the steps.

She remembered closing the door behind her, but it seemed she'd left it cracked. Tella pushed it the rest of the way open with her elbow, losing a runaway peach in the process. It hit the ground with a dull thud as Tella stepped inside.

The room was colder than it had been when she left, and quiet. *Too quiet.* The only sound came from a fly buzzing toward the stolen feast in her hands.

"I'm back!" Tella tried not to be nervous at the lack of her mother's response. Being anxious was her sister's role. But Tella couldn't stop her sense of growing unease.

An apricot fell onto the floor as Tella quickened her pace.

And then the entire tray threatened to fall from her trembling hands.

The bed was vacant.

The room was empty.

"Paloma?" Tella called. She couldn't bring herself to say the word *Mother.* It hurt too much to cry out the way she had as a child and to hear no response. She'd vowed never to do it again. But it ached just as much to call her mother's formal name with no reply.

Her throat tighter than before, Tella tried yelling both her mother's names. "Paloma! Paradise!"

Absolutely nothing.

Tella thrust the tray onto the bed and ran into the other bed-room and then into the bathing room. Both were empty.

Her mother was gone.

Tella's legs forgot how to work. They stumbled clumsily back into the bedroom before her knees completely quit, forcing her arms to find a nearby bedpost for support.

All Tella could hear was the fly buzzing around her abandoned food, as she tried to make sense of what could have happened. Her mother was weak. Confused. Maybe she'd gone to look for Tella and gotten lost? Tella just needed to find her and—

Her thoughts cut off at the sight of something atop the dresser by the bed. A note.

Tella clumsily pushed away from the bed. Her fingers trembled as she picked the message up. The handwriting was rushed, shaking.

My loves,

I'm so sorry to leave you, but I knew that if I waited any longer, it would be too hard for me to go. Please forgive me, and do not look for me again. All I ever wanted was to protect you, but my presence will only put the two of you in more danger.

If I am awake, then the Fates are waking up as well, and all of Valenda is in peril. As long as you are in this city, you are not safe. You must get as far away from the Fates as possible. Leave Valenda immediately.

The Fates are as vicious as the stories say. They were created out of fear, and fear is part of what fuels their power, so they will try to inflict as much as possible. Fight against being afraid if you encounter them and be safe, my loves.

If I can, I will make my way back to you both.

With more love than you can imagine,

Your mother

"No!" Tella ripped the sheets from the bed and pressed them to her eyes like a handkerchief. Her tears were angry and hot. They didn't last, but they hurt. How could her mother do this? It wasn't just that she'd left, but that she'd tricked Tella to do it. She hadn't been hungry or weak. She'd wanted to get away—to leave again.

Tella crumpled the note in her fist, and instantly regretted it. If she didn't find her mother, this was all she'd have.

No. Tella couldn't think like that. She'd conquered death. She would find her mother and bring her back. She didn't care what the message said. Tella had decided long ago to never make decisions ruled by fear. Fear was a poison that people mistook as protection. Making choices to stay safe could be just as treacherous. Her father had hired horrible guards to keep himself, his money, and his estates safe. Her sister had almost married someone she'd never met to keep Tella safe. Tella didn't care how safe she was—as long as she had her mother.

A voice in the back of Tella's head warned this was a hazardous idea. Her mother had told her to leave the city to avoid the Fates. But Tella was partly responsible for the Fates being free.

And she had not sacrificed so much, and worked so hard, just to be left by her mother again.

The sun still shined too bright, merchants still filled the sidewalks, and the roads were still coated in a carnival of half-eaten holiday treats when Tella stepped outside. But beneath the aroma of heated sugar and lost pieces of celebrations, Tella picked up another scent, far sweeter than inexpensive pleasures: *magic*.

Tella recognized the aroma from the dreams she'd shared with Legend. It had also clung to her mother when Tella had held her. The magical scent was faint, but it left enough of a trail for Tella to follow through the crowds.

"'Scuse me . . ."

"Sorry, miss."

More than one inebriated person stumbled into Tella as she followed the magical scented trail through the packed streets, until she found herself near University Circle at another set of Valenda's ruins.

Tella didn't actually spend much time in this part of the city. She didn't know these ruins. They were far more intricate than the ancient arena she'd followed Legend into earlier. These passageways, arches, and arcades appeared to have been used for commerce. She really hoped they didn't lead to more portals as she started climbing the steep trail that led to them.

She probably should have changed into fresh shoes. Her thin slippers were completely ruined from the snow and then darting through the hot city; it was easier to walk once she took them off.

The granite stairs were warm from the sun, and yet Tella felt a brush of something cold running down her nape like spiders' legs.

She hazarded a glance over her shoulder.

No one was behind her. No guards stood between the trees to her sides. In fact, there didn't appear to be any guards at all.

But the slick sensation of being watched increased, along with the throbbing sensation of magic. Tella couldn't just smell the magic now, she could feel it, stronger than when she'd followed Legend. It pulsed around her as if the steps had a beating heart.

Thump.

Thump.

Thump.

Magic pounded beneath her bare feet as she continued to climb the ruins—except, suddenly, they no longer appeared so ruined.

Instead of crumbling arches, Tella saw pristine curves covered in brightly painted carvings of red chimeras reminiscent of the ones she'd spied at the Fated Ball. There were silver lambs with heads like wolves, blue horses with green-veined dragon wings, hawks with black ram horns. And—

Tella jolted back at the sight of Legend's royal guards. Seven of them. All strewn across the top of the stairs like knocked-over toy soldiers.

She stubbed her heel on a rock as she stumbled back another step. Until that moment it hadn't occurred to her that maybe the magic-scented trail she had been chasing didn't belong to her mother. If all the Fates were awake, one of them might have done this.

But these guards didn't look dead.

Maybe Tella was tricking herself, but they appeared to be sleeping.

She crept closer and cautiously pressed her finger to one guard's neck. She thought she felt a pulse, when a rushed set of footfalls broke the quiet.

Did they belong to her mother, or a Fate?

Tella's stomach tied into a knot. Before the Fates had been freed from the cards, the spell had begun to crack and ghostly versions of the Undead Queen and Her Handmaidens had temporarily slipped out of the cards and almost killed her. But Tella had survived, and she'd rather face them all over again than risk losing her mother again.

Tella chased the footfalls down narrow stairs into a poorly lit labyrinth of cells with pearly white bars. They were almost pretty, but she hated cages; the sight of each one made her bare feet sprint faster.

Her bruising pace didn't slow until the hallway opened into a brilliantly torch-lit cavern that reeked of sulfur and dank running water. It could have easily been an elaborate set for a historical play, the prettiest of torture chambers, or a training room for an ancient circus.

Red tightropes crisscrossed above Tella's head, with no net beneath. Painted circles that looked like wheels of death, all decorated with knives, spun around the edges. Beyond the wheels were pits of vibrant orange-tipped flames that burned like lakes of fire beneath narrow suspension bridges. In a corner, a granite carousel covered in decorative spikes whirled.

Cutting through the center of it all was a river of red. Tella's mother stood on the other side of it. But she looked nothing like the weak woman Tella had left lying in a bed.

Donatella

Paloma looked like a wicked version of Scarlett. Tella didn't know where her mother had found new clothes, but she now wore a floor-length black leather coat with short sleeves that showed off long garnet-red gloves. They were the same color as her corset top. On her legs, Paloma wore fitted bone-white breeches, which tucked into black leather boots that went over her knees. A dagger rested in a sheath, snug against her calf, while a thin silver rope wrapped around her opposite thigh like a pet snake.

She looked brutal and beautiful, like a criminal who'd just escaped from a Wanted poster—a myth who'd ripped herself free from a story to give it a different ending. And Tella desperately wanted to be a part of that ending.

"Please, don't leave again!" Tella cried.

Then she was running, barreling through the cavern, leaping over the stream of red and into her mother's arms. Tella hugged her with everything she had. Maybe if she held on tight enough she wouldn't have to let go this time. Tella wanted a different ending, too. She wanted one with her mother and Scarlett, smiling and laughing and making wondrous plans for the future.

"You shouldn't be here," Paloma said, her voice sharp, and yet she didn't release Tella. She stroked her ratted curls with a tenderness Tella had never been able to capture in her memories.

"I knew you'd be fierce," Paloma said. "But, Donatella, this is a fight that will destroy you if you don't walk away." She dropped her arms.

"No!" Tella grabbed her mother's wrists; she'd hold on for the rest of her life if she had to. "You belong with Scarlett and me. I don't know what you think you need to do, but please come back to us."

"I can't." Paloma tried to shake free, but Tella refused to let go. "You need to get out of here—it's not safe."

"My life hasn't been safe since you left!"

Paloma's hazel eyes turned glassy, and her voice gentled at last. "I hate that you've experienced so much pain. But I'm only going to bring you more. I'm the one who's dangerous tonight, Donatella. I'm here because I need to kill someone."

"No," Tella argued, even as she felt the blood drain from her face. "You're just saying that to make me leave."

"I wish I were. But there are things from my past that I need to make right, and I won't risk letting you and Scarlett get involved. I've made countless mistakes, but you and your sister are the only things

I've made that have brought something better into this world." Her daring smile returned, giving Tella hope that maybe her mother didn't really want to do this. Tella only had to convince her of that.

"Just come back with me to say good-bye to Scarlett," Tella pled. "She's missed you too!"

"I wish I could." Paloma reached up and cupped Tella's jaw. "I would go with you, but I have to do this, or you and your sister will never be safe."

She stroked Tella's cheek, one gentle touch, before she slipped her gloved fingers to the back of Tella's neck and pulled her closer. "I love you so much, and I'm sorry."

Something sharp poked out from the tips of Paloma's gloves and pricked Tella's nape. She felt a bite of cold and a sense of liquid being injected into her veins.

"Wh—what—" Her tongue felt suddenly heavy and useless. She wanted to ask what her mother had done. She wanted to ask why she suddenly couldn't move her arms or legs. She wanted to say so much more. But nothing came out except that one powerless *what*.

Her mother had only pulled her close so she could paralyze Tella with the tips of the gloves. This must have been what she'd done to the knocked-out guards.

"It will be all right," Paloma soothed. Her hands hooked beneath Tella's arms.

But nothing felt fine.

Tella couldn't believe her mother had left her, then drugged her, or that she was now dragging Tella's body toward the mouth of the cavern. Tella tried to fight, but her limbs wouldn't obey—she could barely even feel them.

Her mother finally stopped at one of the cracked wheels of death—the kind circus performers strapped women to and then threw knives at while the wheel spun and spun. Her mother didn't strap Tella to it, but she did tuck her behind it, hiding Tella between the circle and the granite wall.

No! Don't do this! Tella tried to object, but her tongue was so thick and heavy she couldn't even manage a squeak.

"You should fall asleep soon. Once you wake up, leave this city with your sister. I'll find you when I can." Paloma kissed Tella on the cheek, her lips lingering longer than before. But despite what she said, this did not feel like an *I'll find you later* kiss. This was an *I'm planning on never seeing you again* kiss.

Mother! Tella tried to shake the numb from her limbs. She wasn't passing out like the guards—her mother must have used up most of her poison on them. Tella could feel tingling in her toes, but she couldn't get them to move. She couldn't even crawl after her mother as she walked away. All Tella accomplished was a ragged breath, but the sound was so pathetic, it was muffled by the grate of footsteps entering the cavern. Heavy and pounding, the sort of footsteps that wanted to make an entrance.

Tella didn't know if it was her mother's drugs, but the air grew hotter as the menacing sound became louder. The intruder moved close enough for Tella to see a pair of masculine boots caked in dust. But the figure continued past, not even pausing as he spun the cracked circus wheel in front of her. It groaned alive, ticking like an off-kilter clock as it rotated.

Click.

Click.

Clack.

Tella didn't like the sound, but it allowed her to view the cavern when the fractured wedge of the wheel rotated her way. Her first peek between the broken crack only lasted long enough to see that sparks now filled the cavern, as if the air was on the verge of catching fire. The tiny flames danced around the man, making the gold on his red military coat sparkle. He stood right in front of her mother.

Paloma looked much smaller than before as she lifted her face toward him expectantly.

"I feared I'd seen you for the last time," she said.

The wheel continued to rotate, obstructing Tella's view once more. When the crack reached Tella again, the intruder was stroking her mother's hair. And her mother was gazing up at him with adoration in her eyes, as if she'd been waiting for this clandestine meeting even more than Tella had been longing to reunite with her.

This wasn't how it was supposed to be.

"Gavriel." Paloma said his name as if it were a secret that only she'd been told. "I've missed you so much. I hoped you'd come back to these ruins."

The wheel continued to spin. When the fragmented piece came around again, the man's hand was in her mother's hair.

"You're as beautiful as I remember," he said. Then his lips pressed to hers, and Tella swore all the flames in the cavern surged brighter. The sparks in the air glowed like stars. Tella could feel their heat from behind the wheel.

Tella was going to be ill. She wanted the wheel to stop, to block her from seeing anything else, but instead it began turning faster, as if it was enthralled by the kiss. Tella prayed to the saints for the embrace to end, or that she'd at least regain her ability to move, to fully block it out. But her limbs remained numb and the kiss went on, intimate and burning and so, so very wrong.

Clearly, her mother hadn't come here to murder anyone. She was here because she wanted to be with this man more than she wanted to be with her daughters. Tella might have felt a knot in her stomach if she'd had more sensation in her body.

"My memories of you did not do you justice." His lips had moved to her jaw.

"I'm glad you missed me, too," she said.

"I thought of you every day." His mouth trailed to her ear, but what should have been a whisper echoed throughout the entire chamber. "I pictured all the ways I would get my revenge against you."

Click.

Click.

Clack.

This love story had just gone very wrong. For several tense seconds Tella's heart raced. She couldn't hear anything other than the wheel until her mother's strong voice grew louder when she said, "Gavriel, I made a mistake."

"You forced me back inside that cursed Deck of Destiny once you learned I was a Fate. That's a very intentional error, Paradise."

God's blood and teeth.

This man—this *Fate*—had been trapped in the cards too. Her mother had just kissed him. What was she doing? She'd pushed away her own daughter so she could cling to one of the monstrous immortals who only saw humans as pawns and fragile sources of entertainment. Tella didn't know which Fate he was. He could have been the Assassin, the Fallen Star, the Poisoner, the Apothic, or Chaos. It didn't matter—all of them were demons.

Tella wanted to scream at her mother to leave. But Tella's tongue was still thick. Her lips were numb. All she could feel were a few rebel tingles, and even if her mouth had moved, even if she'd warned her mother, Tella doubted Paloma would have responded. Her mother already knew the man before her was a Fate, she probably knew which one he was and what terrible powers he had, and she didn't appear to care.

Another spin of the wheel showed Paloma leaning into the Fate again. "I was warned that you'd kill me to keep yourself from falling in love with me," Paloma said, her voice much more tender than the way she'd spoken to Tella earlier. "I panicked, Gavriel. I did what I thought I had to, to defend myself. We both do what it takes to survive; that's one of the things we've always had in common. But I've regretted that choice ever since. Why do you think I'm here right now?"

"That's what I've been trying to figure out," he said.

Tella had met Fates before, the Prince of Hearts and the Undead Queen. This Fate's voice was even colder, his presence more commanding and powerful, the little flames around him sparking with his every word. But Paloma didn't pull away.

"There's nothing to figure out. I'm here because I want to be with you." She rose up on her toes.

The wheel whirled, blocking out what happened next, but the stretch of silence told Tella they were kissing again.

"Do you still want revenge?" Paloma gasped finally. "Or do you want to be with me, too?"

"Maybe revenge can wait." His mouth returned to her mother's.

Tella started to close her eyes; she couldn't watch any more of this. But just as she was about to stop looking, she caught a glimpse of silver in her mother's hands as Paloma pulled out a knife and quickly dug it into the Fate's heart.

A roar echoed across the cavern.

Tella could have cheered. But she wasn't sure what her mother was doing. Fates were immortals; if they died, they just came back to life. But maybe her mother knew something Tella did not. She held her breath as the wheel came around yet again.

But the Fate wasn't lying on the ground or falling to a temporary death. He was standing, staring at Paloma as if she'd truly surprised him. Then, in a flash, too quick for Tella to see, his massive hand pulled out the dagger and thrust it into Paloma's chest and twisted.

She let out a sound that Tella knew she'd hear in her nightmares forever. It rocked the cavern walls as Tella tried to scream too. But she couldn't even manage to whisper. Her lips were still tingling with numbness. There was a similar prickling sensation in her limbs, but it wasn't enough to move them.

She tried to crawl on her belly, out from behind the wheel and somehow save her mother, but all Tella could do was watch.

The wheel of death slowed to a crawl.

Click...

Click...

Clack...

Everything had been moving too fast, and now it was all going too slow.

When the wheel finished its turn, Paloma was totally still on the ground, while the bleeding Fate looked down on her.

Get up! Get up! Get up!

Tella finally got her fingers to move. Her toes were gaining feeling too.

But her mother wasn't moving at all.

Tella dug her fingers into the ground until they started to bleed. But it wasn't enough to propel her forward.

Even the wheel had ceased spinning. The Fate fell to his knees, but her mother remained on the ground.

Tella managed to crawl forward an inch. She wasn't ready to give up yet. Her mother couldn't be dead. Her mother was too strong to die. Tella had fought too hard to lose her. The story wasn't supposed to end this way.

I will rip your arms from your chest! "You sonofa—"

A hand clamped over her lips. Cold and sweet, like apples and Fated magic.

"Quiet, my love," Jacks whispered. "There's nothing you can do for her now except keep yourself alive."

His cool fingers stayed in place until after Gavriel finally died from the wound her mother had inflicted. His massive body fell to the ground. The cavern should have filled with silence, but Tella could hear the pieces of her heart as it shattered.

Donatella

Tella wished that time would stop. For years she'd divided her life into two periods: *When Her Mother Had Been There* and *After Her Mother Had Left*. Now her mother was dead. But Tella didn't want to use this moment as a measure of time. She didn't want time to move forward at all. She wanted time to freeze, like her unmoving limbs, but even they were regaining echoes of feeling.

She couldn't walk, but she managed to crawl across the cavern's granite floor to her mother's body. But that's all it was, a body. When Paloma had been in her enchanted sleep, her face had still possessed color, her chest had moved up and down. Tella had once thought she was still as a corpse, but she wasn't—until now.

"At least he stabbed her instead of burning her to death with his powers," Jacks said. "Fire's the most painful way to die."

"That's not helping," Tella muttered.

"Well, I'm not really the comforting sort." Jacks's cool arms slipped beneath Tella's back as he picked her up from the ground.

"Put me down," Tella said. Jacks was a Fate, and the last thing she wanted was help from someone like him.

Jacks huffed a sigh. "If I leave you here, you'll die like your mother when Gavriel comes back to life. Or another Fate will just find you."

"Why do you care?"

"I don't." Jacks flashed his dimples, narrow lips parting into a sharp smile that turned him into the beautifully cunning Prince of Hearts that she'd been fascinated with as a child. "I just prefer torturing you myself."

"Too late," Tella mumbled, and she probably should have tried to fight him more.

Jacks hadn't bothered her for the last sixty-odd days, and supposedly she was his true love—the one person immune to his fatal kiss—but he was still a Fate. A murderous one. He'd been heir to the throne before Legend, and according to rumors he'd killed seventeen people to take that place. He'd even threatened to kill Tella. He was viperous and fatal. Yet Tella couldn't muster the appropriate fear. She couldn't feel anything other than numb.

Her mother's death didn't even make sense. Gavriel hadn't hurt her until after she'd wounded him. He might not have killed her if she hadn't stabbed him. Why would she risk it, when he would only come back to life?

"Who is Gavriel?" Tella choked out. "Which Fate is he?"

Jacks's cold fingers tensed against her back. "I'm only telling you this because I like him even less than I like you. Gavriel is the Fallen Star."

The same Fate who, according to Legend's witch, had created all the Fates. A venomous surge of rage briefly broke through Tella's shock. If Legend really did want to kill the Fallen Star to defeat the other Fates, he'd have to get in line.

"I'll find a way to destroy him," Tella vowed.

"Not in this condition," Jacks muttered as he carried her up a set of steps.

She didn't want to see the sky as she and Jacks finally emerged outside. It should have been black. But it was still impossibly blue, rippling with threads of indigo. Tella usually loved it when the sun stayed out so late, when it was night and the world remained light, but now it just felt wrong. The day should have ended. The sun should have fled and turned the world dark the moment her mother had died.

Tella's throat went tight. She closed her eyes, attempting to shut out the light, but that only made it worse. Every time her eyes closed, all she could see was the Fallen Star as he drove a knife into her mother.

A sob began to build inside her. She was only dimly aware of her surroundings as Jacks carried her down a brick street. She didn't know where he lived now that he was no longer heir to the Meridian

Empire and had been kicked out of Idyllwild Castle. She'd assumed he resided in the Spice Quarter, inside a crooked building with a coven of thieves, or in an underground tomb with a den of gangsters.

But it didn't smell as if he was taking her to the Spice Quarter. There were no pungent cigars. No streams of spilled liquor or urine stained the ground. Jacks had brought her to the clean pathways of University Circle, a world of leather-bound books, pressed robes, and pristine hedges, where ambitious scholars grew like weeds.

His pace turned leisurely as he approached a four-story house made of clay-red bricks and onyx columns. Tella might have asked what they were doing here, or if this was where he lived. But all she could do was let her tears fall.

It couldn't even be called crying. Crying gave the impression of participation, action. But Tella was done acting. She could barely keep breathing.

"I'd try to say something comforting, but last time you didn't appreciate it," Jacks murmured. But despite his words, he held her closer to his cool chest as he reached a pair of polished doors.

Maybe he really did plan to torture her. Or maybe he knew that even though her paralysis was almost gone, Tella wouldn't have moved if he'd left her. Maybe he knew she'd have lain on the steps leading up to his house even after the sun finally fell and the night turned cold enough to make her numb once again. Because now that she had all her feeling back, it hurt. Everywhere. Her emotions were bruised and bleeding. And for a moment she hoped that they'd bleed out.

Then maybe it wouldn't feel so impossibly painful, or so hard to breathe and think and feel anything but agony.

The door before them swung open. They stepped inside and the wretched blue sky was replaced by a ceiling covered in gold chandeliers that dangled lights over walls papered with black and red symbols from playing cards. It was a den of gambling, full of dealers who smiled like tigers and players eager as cubs.

People were laughing and clapping and rolling dice on tables with whoops and hollers, and all of it had never sounded so wrong. It was a blur of gaming chips, and fizzing drinks, discarded cravats and clacking wheels of misfortune and chance. When someone won, confetti made of diamonds and hearts and clubs and spades rained down on everyone. The room was alive in a way her mother was not.

If anyone thought it odd that Jacks was carrying a hysterical girl, no one remarked on it. Or maybe Tella just didn't notice. The drawn windows might have managed to block out the sun, but all the noise and chaos of Jacks's gaming parlor only intensified the piercing emptiness inside of her.

Jacks's arms tightened around her as he wove through the crowd. Multiple people approached him. "Can't you see my hands are full?" he drawled, or simply just ignored them.

A few steps later and they were on the stairs. The carpets went from plush to threadbare the higher they climbed. Jacks had redecorated the ground floor for his guests, but left the upper levels unchanged. Not that Tella saw much of them. Her eyes mostly stayed on the ground and Jacks's scuffed boots until he carried her through another door.

It looked like a study. There was an empty fireplace with a decorative amber rug marred by several scorch marks in front of it, a worn whiskey-brown leather couch, and a scratched desk with a lone plant underneath a glass dome. Jacks continued to cradle her as he sat slowly on the deep couch.

Tella could have pulled away. It was wrong to let him touch her—he was the same type of creature that had killed her mother in front of her. And yet she feared that Jacks's deadly arms were the only things still holding her together. She didn't want *his* comfort, but she desperately needed comfort.

Jacks's shirt had quickly dampened against Tella's cheek, but rather than push her away, he held her closer. He rubbed circles around her back, while his other cold hand wove through her curls, carefully untangling them with gentle fingers.

"Why are you helping me?" Tella finally managed. Unlike Legend, who either hid his feelings or pretended to have them when he didn't, Jacks never pretended to care. When he had an agenda, he just made threats to get what he wanted.

"You're not fun when you're this pathetic. I can't torment you if you're already miserable." His hand left her hair to press against her cheek and brush several tears away. The touch was as soft as the last kiss her mother had pressed to that very same cheek, and Tella lost what she'd been able to keep together.

No longer were tears just falling from her eyes. She was crying harder than she ever had in her life, sobbing with so much force she felt as if she might break. It was too much emotion to hold on to and too much to release.

"It was all for nothing," Tella moaned. "Everything I did to save her only worked to destroy her. I should have never tried to change the future I'd seen in the Aracle. The first time I saw her, the card only showed her in a prison. If I hadn't tried to alter that future, she'd still be alive."

"Or maybe you'd be dead too," Jacks said. "You don't know how things could have turned out differently."

"But they could have been different." Tella pictured all the other ways her mother's story could have ended. If Tella had listened to her mother as a child and never played with her cursed Deck of Destiny, maybe her mother never would have left the girls on Trisda in the first place. Or if Legend had just taken the deck, like Tella had asked, and then destroyed it before any more of the Fates escaped, her mother would be alive now.

Tella had made so many mistakes. If only she could go back and make one right. If she could just rechart her path so it led somewhere else.

That was it.

A spark of hope lit up inside her.

Tella could travel back in time and re-create the entire day. Now that all the Fates were awake, there was a way to do it. Then at least one good thing could come from their return.

Tella looked up at Jacks, seeing him for the first time since he'd carried her away. His untamed locks of golden hair made him look more like a lost boy than a murderous Fate; his unearthly eyes were the silver-blue of young girls' dreams; and his lips were so sharp she imagined he could cut with a kiss. She couldn't trust him, but to do this, she would need him.

"In Decks of Destiny, there was a Fate that could move through space and time—the Assassin. What if he could help undo this?"

"I know you're grieving," Jacks said, "but that's the worst idea I've ever heard. Traveling through time is always a mistake."

"So is trusting you. But here I am, and you haven't hurt me yet."

"*Yet* is the key word in that sentence." He ran a cool finger under her chin. "Stay long enough and I guarantee that will change."

Tella sat up straight. "Tell me where the Assassin is and I'll leave right now."

"Even if I knew where he was I wouldn't tell you, Donatella. Contacting the Assassin is not a good idea, and not just because of his nickname. Before the Fates were trapped in the deck, the Fallen Star, the Undead Queen, and the Murdered King all used the Assassin to travel through space and time, and all the different timelines made him insane. He's not always aware of when he is, and he'll disappear for long stretches. People who've convinced him to take them back in time don't always return. As I said, worst idea."

"Nothing could be worse than this! Please, Jacks." Tella grabbed his damp shirt with her fists, pulling his cruel face even closer. "Help me find him. I'm begging you. It hurts so much. Too much. Everything is painful. Each time I close my eyes I see him murdering her.

Every time it's quiet I hear the awful *click-clack* of that wheel. And I can't shut it off!"

Jacks's hand went still against her back. "What if I could take away the pain and the sadness?"

"How?" she asked.

"It's one of my abilities." He wiped another trail of tears from her cheeks.

A warning flare cut through some of Tella's grief. Myth had it that the Prince of Hearts had the ability to control emotions. But, since Jacks had not been in the Deck of Destiny when Legend had freed the other Fates, he should have still been at half power. "I thought you didn't have your full powers back."

"I don't," he bit out. "I still can't control emotions the way I used to, or give someone feelings that they don't have. But I can temporarily remove unwanted feelings. I can take away your pain for tonight." His icy fingers lingered on her cheek, a numbing promise and a warning all at once. "I won't be permanently erasing it, my love. You'll still experience it. But when your sorrow returns tomorrow, it won't be as powerful as it is now."

His other hand stroked up and down her back again until it was easier for her to breathe. Too easy. She wondered if he was using his powers to calm her. But Tella couldn't bring herself to care as much as she should have. The heartache was too overwhelming. She knew that the instant Jacks let her go, her lungs would tighten once more, her tears would return to sobs, and even if she didn't close her eyes, she'd see her mother dying over and over and over. A hundred deaths in the span of one heartbeat. Too many heartbeats and she might die, too.

"Do it," Tella said. A part of her knew how desperately wrong it was to take comfort from a Fate. But even if it was a mistake, it couldn't be as bad as this. "Take the sadness and the pain—just take everything that hurts."

Donatella

Jacks's cool hand cupped Tella's cheek. "All right, my love." He tilted her face toward his as he lowered his lips to hers.

Tella pressed her palms against his chest and shoved off of his lap. "What are you doing?"

"I'm taking the pain away."

"You didn't say you had to kiss me."

"It's the most painless way. It will still hurt, but—"

The last time they'd kissed, her heart had stopped working properly.

"No," she said. "I'm not letting you kiss me again."

Jacks ran his tongue over his teeth, thinking for a long minute. "There is another way, but"—a second hesitation—"it requires an exchange of blood."

A rigid spike of awareness shot down Tella's spine. Blood sharing was powerful. Tella had learned during her first Caraval that blood, time, and extreme emotions were three of the things that fueled magic. Tella had drunk blood before. She didn't recall it clearly, but she knew she'd been on the brink of death after her altercation with the Undead Queen and Her Handmaidens. She might have even died, but then she'd been fed blood, and it had saved her life. But blood also had the ability to take life. One drop of blood had once cost Scarlett a day of her life.

"How much blood would you need to drink?" she asked.

"I don't need to drink any, unless you wish to do it that way." He flashed her a feral smile as he pulled a jewel-tipped dagger from his boot. Half the gems were missing, but the ones that were still there sparkled, bitter-blue and ruinous-purple.

He sliced the dagger down the center of his palm. Blood, glittering with flecks of gold.

"You'll need to do the same." Jacks handed her the knife.

"What happens after I cut myself?"

"We clasp hands and say magic words." His voice was teasing, but his unearthly eyes were gleaming with grave intent as he held his bleeding palm for her to take.

He did not look human at all as gold-flecked blood continued to well in the hollow of his hand. It should have frightened Tella, but there was too much grief and too much pain, she didn't have room for emotions like fear.

She didn't even feel the dagger's cut as she pressed it to her palm. Blood welled, darker than the glittering stream running down Jacks's wrist. But he made no move to stop its flow. His eyes were on her hand, watching as two red beads fell and stained her sullied yellow sash and her periwinkle skirt. Her gown had started out the day so bright, but now it was ruined, like so many other things.

Tella handed Jacks the dagger back, but he dropped it to the ground, and took her bleeding hand in his.

His pulse was racing. His palms had never felt so hot. The blood from his wound felt eager to mingle with hers. "Now repeat after me."

The words that followed were in a language Tella didn't recognize. Each one rippled to life on her tongue, metallic and magical-sweet as if she could taste the blood flowing between their hands. It surged faster and hotter with every foreign word. Jacks had promised to take her sorrow and her pain, but something about the exchange made her feel as if she was agreeing to give him even more.

Stop, before it's too late.

But Tella couldn't stop. Whatever Jacks wanted to take, she'd let him have it—if he just took away her grief.

The last three words he spoke all at once, in a voice that thrummed with power: *"Persys atai lyrniallis."*

These words did not taste sweet at all. They latched on to her tongue like barbs. Biting and sharp and utterly unholy. The leather couch, the empty fireplace, the cluttered desk all disappeared.

Tella tried not to scream or crumble against Jacks as invisible cords of magic lashed around their clasped hands; it felt like threads of flames and burning dreams. Then the fire was spreading, searing her arms, scorching her chest, and branding her flesh as raw magic infected her veins.

"Don't let go," Jacks commanded. His other hand was now clutching her unwounded palm. But Tella could barely feel it. She was back in the cavern, on the rocky floor, watching her mother walk away from her. Then Gavriel was there, and this time there was no spinning wheel between them. Tella was seeing the Fallen Star pull the dagger from his chest, thrust it into her mother's heart, and twist until—

"Look at me," Jacks hissed through his teeth.

Tella opened her eyes.

Jacks's forehead was damp with sweat and his chest moved unevenly as his ragged breathing matched hers. He wasn't just removing her pain, he was taking it. Bloody tears streaked his cheeks and agony turned his eyes pale.

Tella clutched his hands tighter and pressed her forehead to his.

"Is this transaction too intense for you," Jacks panted, "or are you actually worried about me?"

"Don't flatter yourself."

"Don't lie to me—I feel everything you're feeling right now." His lips moved so close to her mouth she could taste his bloody tears dripping down the edges. They were bitter, full of loss and grief, but also cool and pure like ice. It wasn't quite a kiss, but it didn't hurt so much when she brushed her lips against his.

Maybe she should have let him kiss her . . . maybe it wouldn't hurt her this time.

"I promise it won't hurt this time," he rasped against her mouth.

Tella let her lips pass over his again. He was a liar and a Fate. But when she pressed her mouth to his, it felt better than anything else had that day.

Her pain shattered as he kissed her back. Everything was a tangle of tongues and tears and blood and heartbreak as Jacks continued to take her sorrow. He drank it in with every needy movement of his cold lips against hers. His hands stayed locked with Tella's, but they snaked behind her back, holding her tighter and caging her in as they both tumbled onto the floor.

This was nothing like their flawless first kiss during the Fated Ball. This kiss was urgent and wild and raw and corrupt. Full of all the terrible emotions flowing between them. A torrent of sorrow and pain. They were on the rough carpet and all over each other. Her teeth sank into his lips, biting sharp enough to draw blood.

He kissed her harder, possessively, nipping her jaw, then her neck, as his lips and teeth trailed down to her collarbone.

Before, he could feel her emotions, but now she could feel *his.* Even though he'd taken both her pain and her sorrow, that wasn't what he was feeling now. He felt desire. Desperation. Lust. Obsession. He wanted her. She was all he wanted. All he thought about. She felt it in the way the kiss began to shift from reckless and hungry to languorous and savoring, as if he'd considered this for a very long time and now he was acting out all the things he'd imagined.

A faraway place that Tella tried to ignore told her this was all a great mistake—Jacks wasn't really the one she wanted, Legend was. No matter what he did, or what he was, it would always be Legend.

Maybe she could never actually *have* him, but she wanted him. If she was going to kiss one of the villains, she wanted it to be Legend, not Jacks.

She needed to push Jacks away.

But Legend never touched her anymore. Even if Legend had been there, he might not have held her, let alone kiss her. And it felt so good to be kissed, to be cherished and touched. To feel desire instead of pain. The sorrow was almost gone, and the kiss grew more intense. Or maybe now that Tella was no longer feeling crushing despair or seeing death, she could truly feel the entire kiss, and every inch of Jacks's body as it pressed against hers.

But even in her muddled state, Tella knew she couldn't let it continue.

She ripped her bleeding hand free of Jacks's and ended the kiss.

Jacks made no attempt stop her. But he made no further effort to move away. They were both on their sides, chests pressed together, legs all tangled.

The pain and the sorrow and the hurt were gone. But so was all of her strength. She was boneless. Empty. There were splatters of blood all over her dress and her hands, and all over him. Something intimate, beyond the physical, had just passed between them.

Red tracks ran down his cheeks, ghosts of tears he'd cried for her.

She should have tried to leave. But her body was exhausted. And she liked the way it felt when Jacks wrapped his arms around her, holding her tight to his cool chest as if he wanted her to stay. After she regained her strength, she would go back to hating him. All she cared about now was that the pain was gone. "Thank you, Jacks."

He closed his eyes and took a deep breath. "I'm not sure I did you a favor, my love."

Donatella

Tella woke up haltingly. Her dreams had been feverish flashes, all fleeing too fast for her to fully remember, but she knew Legend hadn't been in them.

After two months of sharing dreams with Legend, she wasn't used to dreaming alone. She also hadn't expected to dream alone. Legend had his full powers back. Since he'd taken all the witch's powers, he probably had more power than before. But he still hadn't visited Tella's dreams.

Had he seen her following him yesterday? Was something still wrong with his powers? Or was it something else?

Tella's heart pounded, and her skin flushed hot, except for all of the places where she tangled with the Prince of Hearts's icy arms and legs.

Dirty blood and saints.

She needed to get out.

She hadn't meant to sleep there *all* night. She needed to leave and find her sister, who was probably worried to death.

Carefully, Tella slid her leg out from between Jacks's. His arms responded by pulling her closer. Air rushed from her lungs as their faces became perfectly aligned.

Even in slumber, he looked vicious in his beauty. His brows formed a cruel line; his dark eyelashes looked sharp enough to prick fingers; his cheeks were so pale they'd turned an icy shade of blue; and his lips still had flecks of blood from where she had bitten him during their kiss.

Her skin went suddenly hot. She could still taste him on her lips. Tart and bitter and deliciously sweet. Apples and grief and Fated magic. She refused to think of it as a mistake, but she couldn't let it happen again.

Giving up on graceful, Tella clumsily shook out of his grip, jumped up to her feet, and bolted for the exit.

Tella smelled breakfast porridge and bitter black tea when she knocked on the boardinghouse door. The light brown wood was warm from the freshly risen sun. It would be another hot day. The back of Tella's neck was already damp from the growing heat.

She looked down at the dirt and blood spattered across her tired periwinkle dress. She should have stolen a cloak from Jacks before leaving. If Scarlett saw the blood on her skirt, she'd ask questions Tella wasn't eager to answer. And Tella imagined that her sister already had a lot of questions.

But it was too late now. The proprietor had opened the door. She took one look at Tella and started to close it. "We don't take in charity cases."

"Wait—" Tella grabbed the edge and held tight. The woman must not have recognized Tella in her current state of dishevelment. "I have a suite here on the second floor with my sister."

"Not anymore." The owner puckered her mouth. "You and your sister have been evicted for destruction of property. Leave or I'll have you arrested."

"You can't do that." The last time Tella had been there she'd ripped a sheet from a bed, but that hardly constituted destruction of property. "My sister and I have already paid through the end of the year. So, get out of my way, or maybe I'll have you arrested."

Tella shoved on the door, hard enough to force it all the way open.

"Stop!" the owner yelled. "I will call the patrol if you go any farther."

"Go ahead!" Tella cried as she barreled up the stairs. She didn't know what was going on, but she needed to see her sister and—

Tella crashed to a halt just outside the door. Only fragments of defenseless wood now hung from its hinges. Someone had nailed a sheet to the frame, but somehow that made it even worse, like a closed casket at a funeral.

Tella yanked the fabric back with one pull.

"Scarlett?" she called. But her voice was met with only silence and chaos. The furniture was splintered and charred, the mirrors were cracked, and shards of the chandeliers covered the ground in sharp glass tears. It looked like the scene of a crime.

"Scarlett!" Tella cried again, louder than before. The painful emotions Jacks had taken away threatened to return in a new form at the thought of losing her sister. There didn't appear to be any blood, but that didn't mean Scarlett was all right. And Tella could not imagine that her sister had done all of this.

"She's right up there, officers." The proprietor's starched voice climbed up the stairs, followed by two guards in royal blue uniforms.

Tella started to panic. Her chest tightened the same way it had last night. "Scarlett?" she called one more time, though it was obvious her sister wasn't there.

By now, several guests had poked their heads out of their doors. Their expressions ranged from curious to frightened to irritated, but no one breathed a word as the guards closed in on Tella.

The female guard stepped forward first, slow and careful, as if Tella were a stray cat who might scratch or run away. "We're not going to hurt you."

"But we will if you run."

Tella's head snapped to the male guard.

And then she felt the hard press of metal as the female darted forward and quickly linked chain cuffs around Tella's wrists.

"What are you doing?" Tella shouted.

"We're placing you under arrest, by order of His Highness, Prince Dante."

Donatella

Tella rattled the dungeon bars, feeling like the Fated Lady Prisoner who'd been put in a cage for no good reason. "Your Highness!"

Magic strangled her every time she attempted calling out for Legend, but she was not in the mood to yell for someone who didn't really exist and cry out the name Dante, or even worse, "Prince Dante." But there was something pleasantly mocking about "Your Highness."

She couldn't *believe* he'd had her arrested. Was it because he knew that she'd followed him the day before? She didn't think he'd seen her, but that still didn't give him the right to imprison her.

Now she definitely didn't need to feel guilty about kissing Jacks.

Tella shook the bars again. The stone gargoyles impaled by the tops of them peered down on her with bulging eyes. She didn't know how long she'd been locked up here all alone. As she'd been dragged inside, she'd looked around at the other cells, wondering if Legend had brought his witch down here as well. But all Tella saw were the tally marks etched into the walls. There were names carved into the dry stones as well, but she didn't plan on staying long enough to make hers one of them.

"You have no right to keep me locked up!" Tella cried out.

A heavy door groaned open at the end of the torch-lit hall, followed by the confident beat of boots, which she knew too well. Legend wasn't crowned yet, but he already moved like an emperor stepping into a throne room.

Tella's eyes trailed upward from his tall black boots to the fitted black trousers hugging his muscular legs. His shirt was also black, but it was accented with a vest covered in thin wolf-gray lines that matched the cravat at his throat and the lapels of his velvet coat. The coat was the rich royal color of blackberries—a shade she'd never seen him in. But he wore the color well; it complemented his bronze skin tone, and made his hair look even blacker and his eyes look even brighter, bringing out flecks of gold that reminded her of stars at night.

No wonder they'd already started creating statues of him around the city. He might have been a liar and a villain, but he made both things look very good.

The other cells were empty, but he didn't even glance at them, and Tella had the impression that Legend wouldn't have darted his eyes around even if the cells had been full of deadly criminals. He moved like nothing in the human world could hurt him. He didn't need to look over his shoulder. According to the witch, he only had one weakness, and Tella doubted it was in this dungeon.

She couldn't believe she'd chased him into another world because she'd thought he was in danger. Even though he could have been telling the truth about losing some of his powers, she should have known that he'd do whatever it took to get them back.

"Let me out of here, you bastard!"

"I think I preferred *Your Highness*." He continued his elegant walk toward her, moving with unrushed strides down the dim hall. Someone else might have thought he didn't have any particularly strong feelings about their current situation. But Tella had spent the last two months sharing dreams with him. She was aware of his movements—aware of *him*. She noticed the tic in his jaw as he slowly raked her over, eyes traveling from her bare feet to her naked calves. His gaze tightened as he reached her skirt with all its ripped-up feathers. But instead of making a mocking comment, Tella saw lines form across his brow, as if he was trying to puzzle something out.

Was it possible he didn't know that she'd followed him to see the witch? And if that was the case, then why had he locked her up?

She glowered at him when his probing gaze traveled from her neck, to her lips, and then—finally—her eyes.

The dungeon suddenly grew very warm. His gaze was still tight and dark, but it was edged in heat that she felt all the way down to her toes.

For months Tella had pondered what it would be like when they met again outside of her dreams. She wondered if he'd touch her at last, if he'd apologize for leaving her on the steps in front of the Temple of the Stars. Once she'd even imagined him asking her to be his empress. She almost laughed at that thought now, but she was wholly serious when she said, "Just because you're going to be emperor doesn't mean you can lock me up without reason."

The corner of his mouth slowly lifted into an arrogant tilt. "Actually, it does. But I didn't mean for you to be arrested. I only told my guards to collect you and bring you to me once you were found." His voice was cool, even. Again, another person might not have picked up on the way his sentences turned razor-sharp right at the ends. He was definitely angry, and angry *with her*.

Tella couldn't believe it. Her mother was dead. The Fates were awake. Her sister had been kidnapped. *His* guards had locked her up, and yet Legend kept looking at her as if she was the one who'd done something wrong.

"What crime have I committed?"

"I told you, I didn't have you arrested. I know how you feel about cages. I was only trying to find you."

"Did you really have to use your guards?" She tried to keep her voice as even as his was, but it was difficult. She could feel Jacks's spell cracking. Her chest was tight and her head was pounding. And Legend still hadn't unlocked her cell door. "If you'd wanted to find me, why didn't you just visit me in my dreams and ask me where I was?"

A quick clench of his jaw. "I tried to."

"Then why couldn't you?" Tella said. Shortly after he'd first showed up in her dreams, he'd taught her how to control parts of them—little tricks to change what she wore and larger tricks in case she didn't want certain people entering her dreams. But even when she'd been mad at Legend, she'd always let him in. "I wasn't keeping you out."

"I know. But something else was."

Tella didn't see Legend move—he must have used his magic to hide what he was doing—but suddenly the door between them was open, and Legend was holding something in his hands—two pieces of confetti, one shaped like a spade and the other shaped like a heart.

A sharp memory returned to Tella: Jacks carrying her through his gambling den as card-suit confetti fell from the ceiling. Was this why Legend was mad at her, because she'd been with Jacks?

"Where were you last night, Donatella?"

Again, she hadn't seen him move, but he was now farther away, leaning against the bars opposite her cell, making it clear that even though they were outside of her dreams, some of the rules hadn't changed. He was still keeping his distance.

"That's none of your business," Tella snapped, "and even if it was, I don't have time to argue with you about it. I need to find my sister."

"Tella!" Scarlett's voice carried down the hall before Tella caught sight of her running forward in a storm of flushed raspberry skirts, bright enough to light up the entire dungeon.

"Where have you been?" Scarlett captured Tella in a hug so tight it cut off Tella's breath. Or maybe she couldn't breathe because of the emotions suddenly captured in her throat. Her sister wasn't dead or injured or kidnapped. She was here and safe and alive. "We've been searching the entire city for you and Paloma."

"I thought something happened to *you*," Tella choked out.

"Why would you think that?" Scarlett shot an accusing look at Legend.

He continued to lean against the prison bars, regarding Tella with narrowed eyes. "I didn't get the chance to tell her you were here."

"Oh good, you found her." Julian appeared at the end of the hall, swaggering forward as if the tension in the dungeon wasn't thick enough to choke on. He was dressed in finer clothes than Tella had ever seen him in, but they looked tired, as if he'd been wearing them since the day before. "Where was she?"

"We were just figuring that out." Scarlett turned back to her sister. "Legend told us that he thought Jacks had taken you."

The bright raspberry skirts of Scarlett's dress began to fade as she took in the disheveled state of Tella's feathered dress. She'd probably lost a couple feathers during her time with Jacks, but she doubted they'd come undone in the same way Scarlett was imagining. And after all she'd seen yesterday, Jacks didn't feel like the most dangerous immortal that Tella knew.

"Is your mother here too?" Julian asked.

Scarlett didn't say anything, but Tella could see the question in her eyes as well. Eyes so much like their mother's that just looking at them made Tella tremble all over, as if her bones wanted to break out of her skin and flee before they were forced to relive last night's horrors.

"Tella, what's wrong?" Scarlett reached for her sister's hand again.

Tella wrapped her fingers around Scarlett's, the same way she had as a child the day after their mother had vanished from Trisda. Tella had been the first of the sisters to discover Paloma was missing. She'd found the room her father had destroyed after he couldn't find Paloma anywhere. Then Scarlett had been there, taking her sister's hand and silently promising she'd never let go as long as Tella needed her to hold on.

"She's left again?" Scarlett guessed.

Tella was tempted to say yes. It would have been so much easier for her and for her sister if she just let Scarlett believe her mother had run off. But if Tella took the easy path now, it would be so much harder to take the necessary one.

Last night she'd vowed to kill the Fallen Star, and she planned to follow through. She'd find a way to destroy him, and she couldn't do it on her own.

She took a deep breath, but it became lodged in her throat until she finally managed to say, "Our mother died yesterday."

Scarlett staggered back and clutched her stomach, as if the wind had been punched out of her.

Tella wanted to take her sister's hand again, but she couldn't stop to comfort her. If Tella stopped talking, she knew she'd start crying. She had to keep going. She reached into her pocket and shared the good-bye letter her mother had written. Then Tella told them how she'd ignored her mother's warnings and followed her into one of the ruins, where Tella had watched every disturbing thing that had passed between the Fallen Star and their mother until the Fallen Star finally took Paloma's life. The only part Tella wasn't entirely honest about was the bit involving Jacks. Since they already knew she'd been with him, she told them how he'd found her and carried her out of the cavern, but she didn't add that he'd then helped her by taking away some of her grief.

When she finished, the four of them no longer appeared to be standing in the halls of Legend's dungeon. Again, she hadn't even seen Legend move, but she knew he'd created the comforting illusion they stood within now. The cold floors had turned to plush cream carpets, the stone walls had turned to white soapstone, and the barred windows had shifted to pretty stained-glass ones, covered with serene pictures of clouds in calming skies that shined pale blue light over everyone's grim faces.

Julian offered his condolences first. Somewhere during her story, he'd moved close to Scarlett and wrapped an arm around her shoulder.

Legend still remained distant. He leaned against one of the gleaming walls, but when he looked at Tella, all the earlier anger and wariness had disappeared, replaced with a look so indescribably gentle, she would never have pictured it on his face. "I wish it was in my power to bring her back. I know how much she meant to you, and I'm sorry you lost her the way that you did."

His fingers twitched, as if he were tempted to reach for her, but for once Tella was glad that he didn't attempt to touch her. Last night Jacks had held her together with touch, but Tella had the feeling that if Legend pulled her into his arms right now, she'd fall apart entirely. She could handle his glares and his barbed remarks, but his tenderness could upend her completely.

Scarlett didn't say a word, but tears streamed down her cheeks, more tears than Tella would have expected, given her rocky feelings toward their mother. Tella felt as if she should have been there to try to soothe them instead of Julian, but again she feared that it would only make her cry, too.

Then warmth encircled Tella as Scarlett broke away from Julian and folded her arms around her sister. Scarlett's chest shook, but her arms were unshakable, holding Tella impossibly tight, the same way Scarlett had that day after their mother had first disappeared.

Tella shuddered against her sister, but she didn't fall to pieces as she had feared. Their mother had once told them there was nothing like the love of a sister, and this was one of the moments where Tella could feel that truth. She could feel her sister loving her twice as much as before, trying to heal the wound her mother's death had left. It was too soon for it to heal, and Tella didn't know if the hurt would ever completely mend. But Scarlett's love reminded her that while some things never healed, other things grew stronger.

"Maybe we should leave and give them some time alone," Julian whispered to Legend.

"No," Tella said, breaking away from Scarlett. "I don't want to grieve now. I'll grieve after the Fallen Star is dead."

"We have to stop the other Fates as well," Scarlett added with a sniff. "We can't let anyone else suffer like this, or like the people we saw yesterday."

"What did you see yesterday?" Tella asked.

"A family that was petrified by the Poisoner."

"Though we weren't certain it was him, or that the Fates were really waking up, until now," added Julian.

"But you suspected it—that's why you sent guards for me?" Tella turned to Legend, but if he had actually been concerned about her safety, and not just jealous of Jacks, it didn't show. Legend's expression had shuttered, and any trace of gentleness or tenderness had vanished from his handsome face.

"Did you see any other Fates when you were with Jacks?" he asked. "Do you know who he's working with right now?"

"No," Tella said.

She might have said more. She might have told them where Jacks was and what he was doing in his gambling den; she was certain they were all curious. But Jacks wasn't the real enemy now. The Fallen Star was, and according to the witch, there was only one weakness that would allow him to be killed—and Legend shared that same weakness.

"I think we need to worry less about Jacks—who actually *helped* me last night—and more about the Fallen Star. What is the Fallen Star's weakness?"

"I don't know," Legend said.

"Yes, you do." Tella kept her eyes fixed on his. Earlier, his gaze had been full of stars, but now his eyes were soulless jet-black with midnight-blue veins, the same colors as the wings that Dante had tattooed on his back. How had she ever thought Legend was only Dante? Tella should have known from his eyes alone. Eyes didn't change color. Pupils might dilate and whites might turn yellow or red, but irises didn't change the way that his did.

"Don't lie to me, Legend. Esmeralda told you that the Fallen Star's weakness is the same as yours."

Legend's eyes flashed—gold-white. Lines briefly formed around them, as if he were smiling, but they were there and gone so fast, Tella wondered if she imagined it. Amusement was not the response she'd expected.

"What she said was useless," Legend answered, something like bitterness clouding his tone. "If we want to defeat the Fallen Star and have a chance at killing the Fates, we have to find another weakness."

"Wait—you went to see Esmeralda?" The shock on Julian's face made it clear that Tella wasn't the only one from whom Legend kept his extracurricular activities secret.

"Who's Esmeralda?" Scarlett asked, looking between them.

"I haven't heard that name in a long time," chimed a new voice, as Jovan entered the glimmering hall. She was one of Legend's most welcoming performers, but she was perhaps also the most difficult of all of them to read. She was always smiling. Always friendly, always cheerful. Since no one could possibly be that happy all the time, Tella sometimes imagined Jovan's grins were just another piece of the costume she wore during Caraval.

But Jovan wasn't smiling today. Her dark brown face looked uncharacteristically stern as she approached Legend. In one of their dreams, Legend had told Tella that most of his performers had taken on roles in the palace when the last Caraval had ended and he'd been declared the heir. Jovan appeared to be a high-ranking guard, dressed in a navy military coat with gold tassels on the shoulders that matched the gold lines striping her pants.

"Sir, may I speak with you for a moment? There's been another incident."

16

Donatella

Hairline cracks formed along the edges of Legend's illusionary windows. "Which Fate?"

"The Poisoner again. He turned an entire wedding party to stone near Idyllwild Castle. They're fine now," Jovan added quickly. "But the person who saved them isn't. The Poisoner left a note saying that the party would only become human again once someone willingly took their place. The bride's sister sacrificed herself."

Scarlett clasped her hands together, as if she wanted to send up a prayer to the saints. "Is the sister stone now?"

Jovan nodded grimly. "I'm sorry, sir. We took all the precautions you asked."

Legend rubbed a hand over his jaw. "Move the girl to the stone garden and see if any of the potions Delilah peddles during Caraval can reverse it. Did the wedding party at least get a good description of the Poisoner this time?"

"Not of him," Jovan said. "But one member of the wedding party had the impression that the Poisoner might have had someone with him."

Legend cursed under his breath.

"Do you think we should cancel tomorrow night's Midnight Maze and tell everyone to stay indoors?" Jovan asked.

"No," Legend said. "We can enact a citywide curfew for the people who aren't invited, and tell them it's because of preparation for the coronation. But if we cancel the maze, everyone will know something is wrong."

"But there *is* something wrong." Julian gave his brother a hard stare, but it still looked friendly compared to the cold gaze that Legend was capable of.

"The Fates feed off of fear," Legend said. "I don't want to turn an entire city into a feast for them. And as far as we know now, only the Fallen Star, the Poisoner, and the Prince of Hearts are awake."

"Jacks isn't a threat," Tella protested. "The Fate we need to worry about is the Fallen Star—we can't even hurt the other ones until he's dead. But Legend won't tell us how to defeat him, because he's too afraid of sharing his own weakness." Tella shot Legend her sharpest scowl.

Legend's nostrils flared, and Tella doubted it was a coincidence that the stained-glass windows filled with bleak storm clouds and lightning. "Give Tella and me a moment alone."

No one had to be asked twice. Julian and Jovan turned and walked quickly down the hall. Only Scarlett glanced at Tella, but she nodded that it was all right for her sister to leave them. This conversation with Legend was overdue.

As soon as the others were out of sight, Tella whirled on Legend, but she was caught off guard as the corridor shifted again.

The ceiling stretched four stories high as the walls transformed from white soapstone to rich mahogany wood, inlaid with bookshelves covered in pristine volumes, and cabinets full of treasures lit by delicate lights that floated like lost pixies. Her old prison cell was now a roaring fire, warming her back as extraordinarily soft furs cushioned her feet. Chairs appeared next, red-velvet with wide clamshell-shaped backs, like the ones she often favored in the dreams she shared with Legend. They rested in front of the blazing fire, inviting her to sit, while gentle violin music trailed down from the domed ceiling.

She couldn't help but compare the scene to Jacks's dark study with its worn whiskey-leather couch and its carpets dotted with burned specks from the fire. It was a place for making mistakes and bad deals. Although she hadn't mentioned spending the night with Jacks, somehow she felt as if Legend was trying to make a point with his grand illusion—that what Jacks could give her would never compare to the things that Legend was capable of.

"Are you trying to show off? Or just distract me?"

"I thought you'd be more comfortable here." Legend strode across the elegant study to lean one jacketed elbow against the mantel of the fireplace. "If you don't like it, I can change it. What was that dream you were so infatuated with? Was it the one with the zebras?" He gave her a teasing smile, looking much more like the Legend of her dreams than he had when he'd first shown up in the dungeon. His grin grew wider as Tella felt her dress change, turning sleeker as her feathers shifted into black-and-white lines of silk, mirroring the fitted gown she'd worn in the dream he'd just mentioned. She'd been excited about the zebras, which he'd created after she'd told him she wasn't sure she believed the curious animal was real. But it was the way he hadn't been able to take his eyes off of her in the dream that had given her the real thrill.

"Stop trying to distract me," Tella said. "And take the illusion off my dress. I don't want to be your next Esmeralda."

Legend's smile vanished. "You and Esmeralda—"

"Don't tell me we're not alike," Tella said. "I already got that impression from spying on you."

His eyes clouded over. "Then why are you upset?"

"You deceived her. You took all of her magic. Then you kidnapped her!"

Legend's expression didn't change, but behind him the fire blazed hotter and brighter, shifting from orange to scorching red. "If you knew her, you wouldn't feel sorry for her, Tella. She isn't innocent. I collected her so she could pay for her crimes. Esmeralda is ancient. She used to be the Fallen Star's consort, and before she trapped him and his Fates in the cards, she helped the Fallen Star create the Fates.

She's responsible for their existence, and the Temple of the Stars wants to make her face trial for that."

"What does that have to do with you?" Tella asked.

"You might remember that I made a deal with the temple." Legend removed his jacket, took out a cufflink, and folded back one of his black shirtsleeves.

It might have looked as if he were doing it because of the sweltering heat from the fire, except as he moved, Tella caught a glimpse of the brand on the underside of his wrist.

The mark was not nearly as brutal as the first time Tella had seen it seared into his skin. It was now so faint she could barely detect it, as if it were healing and disappearing. But she still remembered what it had looked like before—and what it signified. The Temple of the Stars had branded Legend in exchange for allowing Tella to enter the vault where her mother had hidden the cursed Deck of Destiny trapping the Fates.

"I vowed to the temple that I would bring them the witch who helped created the Fates. When I did, I swore it on my immortality. If I hadn't delivered Esmeralda to them, I would have died that night, and nothing would have brought me back to life this time. I know you're angry with me right now, but I'd hope you wouldn't want me dead."

Of course she didn't want him dead. Just thinking Legend was in trouble had driven Tella to chase him into another world. But saying that felt like giving too much away when he still wasn't giving anything away.

When Legend had first accepted the brand from the Temple of the Stars, in Tella's place, it had felt like such a great sacrifice on his part. But knowing the lengths Legend was willing to go to in order to get what he wanted, Tella was no longer sure if he'd made the bargain to prevent her from being owned by the temple, or if he had gone through with it to ensure she'd enter the vault and retrieve the cards for him.

She wanted to think he'd done it for her, but she still wasn't certain, and right now that wasn't what mattered. He might have given her answers about the witch, but he still hadn't given her the answers that she wanted most.

"Is *that* why you won't tell me your weakness?" she asked. "Have you actually thought I wanted you dead? You think I'd use your weakness against you?"

He looked into the fire, avoiding her gaze. "The weakness I share with the Fallen Star won't do us any good when it comes to defeating him."

"Since when do you care about good?"

"I don't—" Legend broke off. His eyes shot past her, as if he'd heard a noise outside of their illusion.

Whatever it was, Tella couldn't see where it came from until a door appeared on the wall next to the fire, and Armando stepped through it.

Tella cringed away, moving closer to the fireplace, and to Legend.

Armando was the performer who'd played the role of her sister's fiancé during the sisters' first Caraval. Tella couldn't stand the sight of his smug smile, his calculating green eyes, and the irritating way he tapped his fingers against the blade he wore at his hip. Like Jovan, he was also dressed like a member of Legend's guard, in a navy military coat with a shining line of golden buttons.

"Why is he here?" Tella asked.

"Armando has agreed to guard you when I can't be around."

"No," Tella said. "I don't want him following me, and I don't need a guard."

Legend pierced her with a look that was hotter than the flames at his back. "I didn't free you from the cards just to see you killed by the Fates."

Tella opened her mouth, but she couldn't find the proper response. Legend never talked about what he'd done to free her from the cards. The only time he'd acknowledged it at all had been that same night, when he'd told her that he hadn't been willing to sacrifice her. But then, after she'd called him her hero, he'd walked away, making her question everything.

"You're welcome to stay here in the palace." Legend pushed off the fireplace mantel and picked up his jacket from the clamshell chair. "Your old room in the golden tower is still yours if you want it, and your sister's old room is hers, too."

Tella narrowed her eyes. "What do you want in return?"

"I never wanted you to leave in the first place." Legend turned and walked through the walls of the illusion, as if he'd just said too much.

Although to Tella, it didn't feel like nearly enough.

17

Scarlett

While Tella and Legend talked about Fates and illusions, Scarlett wished she were only experiencing an illusion.

Everyone's feelings were everywhere. They came in too many colors for Scarlett to keep track of or ignore. Scarlett had never felt anything like it. It was far more intense than the brief flashes she'd seen with Nicolas and Julian. Mournful nevermore gray covered the ground like deathly fog. Anxious violet vines licked the palace hallway. And dark, fearful greens turned everything else sickly and toxic.

Scarlett couldn't breathe.

She could barely even tell Jovan and Julian she needed air before she stumbled toward the heavy door leading to the stairs. Although Scarlett and the others had left Tella and Legend alone in the dungeon so they could talk, Scarlett could still feel the crushing weight of Tella's heavy-gray grief and the spiky rage of her burning-red anger at the Fates. Scarlett hadn't been able to see Legend's emotions, but she swore they were the ones making it so hard to breathe. Or maybe it was Scarlett's own unexpected grief at the loss of her mother.

"Crimson." Julian rushed to her side.

"Don't." Scarlett shook his hand away. His concern was more than she could take. Stormy, stormy, stormy blue, swirling and fierce and—

Scarlett's vision filled with black.

"Crimson!"

Donatella

Legend hadn't just moved into the palace, he'd taken it over. Servants covered every inch of the place, buzzing around like worker bees as they either prepared for Legend's upcoming coronation or worked on the massive renovation he'd commissioned.

During Elantine's reign, her palace had been a thing made of dust and history. It had been grand in the way old stories were grand, full of curving details, threaded tapestries, and delicate artistry. But Tella imagined Legend's palace would be none of those things.

Legend possessed a fallen angel's beauty that commanded attention. He was tailored suits over inked tattoos, and lies that people wanted to believe. His palace would be breathtaking in the way that only powerful things could be.

Tella knocked against her sister's door in the sapphire wing once more. Scaffolding covered both sides of the entry, but there were no workers in sight at the moment, so Scarlett should have heard the knocks.

"Either she's not there, or she's not answering," Armando said.

"I didn't ask for your opinion." Tella knocked again, just to be obnoxious, since she was certain Legend was just being obnoxious when he'd chosen to assign Armando—whom he knew she despised—as her personal guard.

Tella wondered if Scarlett was with Julian. In the dungeon they'd looked closer than Tella had expected. In a dream a week ago, Legend had told her when Julian had returned to Valenda, but as far as Tella knew, he hadn't come to visit Scarlett until after Tella had left. Whatever reunion they'd had must have been magnificent, or maybe Scarlett hadn't been quite as over him as she'd claimed—something both sisters had in common.

Tella knocked on the door a final time, but Armando was right—Scarlett wasn't there or she wasn't answering the door. Either way, Tella couldn't stand here and do nothing, not as long as the Fates were out there.

Tella had bathed and scrubbed off the dirt from the cavern, and changed into a slender ice-blue gown with tiered skirts that she must have left in the palace. But she would never wash away what had happened in those ruins. She could still hear the *click, click, clack* of the wheel and see her mother's wounded body, unmoving on the floor.

The Fallen Star needed to be stopped—and he needed to pay for what he'd done to her mother. And if Legend wasn't going to share the Fallen Star's weakness with Tella, then she was going to find someone else who would. And she knew just the person. *Jacks.*

Cold licked the back of Tella's spine. For a moment she was back in his study, on the floor, feverish and hot except for all the places where his cool limbs tangled with hers.

It was a bad idea to go back. But if anyone knew the Fallen Star's weakness, it would be another Fate. And hadn't Jacks said something about hating the Fallen Star?

Tella glanced at Armando. He was barely two steps behind her. Losing him might be a little tricky. But she couldn't take him with her to Jacks. If Legend found out Tella was visiting Jacks again, he might actually lock her up in the tower.

She did believe that this morning's imprisonment was a mistake. But Tella also knew that she wasn't dealing with the Legend of her dreams, who she'd almost convinced herself wasn't that different from Dante. She was dealing with Legend the immortal, the soon-to-be emperor, the Legend who did whatever it took to get what he wanted. And if he wanted Tella safe—and away from the Prince of Hearts—she could picture him taking measures that went far beyond simply assigning her a guard.

Tella quickened her steps as she passed the Stone Garden. The statues had been human once, but when the Fates ruled centuries ago, they had treated humans more like objects and playthings. One of the Fates had turned all the people in the garden to stone just to have lifelike decorations. Tella didn't know if there was any life inside them, if the people who had been frozen could still look out on the world and see and hear. She swore that the statues' faces appeared more terror-stricken than they had before the Fates had been freed from the cards. She wondered if the bride's sister who had been turned to stone today was standing among them, or if they'd found a way to cure her, but somehow Tella doubted that.

Her limbs had turned shaky again as she reached the carriage house.

"His Highness would prefer it if you didn't leave the palace grounds," said Armando.

"And I'd prefer it if he didn't keep so many secrets." Tella hopped inside a floating coach that would take her to the Temple District.

With a groan, Armando threw himself into the carriage opposite her as the cozy box took off. "I hope we're at least going somewhere interesting."

"Actually, *we're* not going anywhere." With that, Tella opened the door and leaped outside. She tore the hem of her glacier-blue gown and nearly sprained her ankle from the awkward landing. If the carriage had risen any higher, she definitely would have injured herself, but it was worth the risk to get away.

Armando scrambled to the door, but the coach was too high for him to jump safely.

Tella blew him a mocking kiss. "I won't tell *His Highness* that you lost me if you don't tell." Then she picked another carriage line, one that would take her to University Circle and to the Prince of Hearts.

Scarlett

The pillows beneath Scarlett were so much fluffier than the lumpy things in her rented apartment. The sheets were far softer as well. They smelled of cool breezes and starlit nights and the only boy she'd ever loved.

Not her pillows. Not her sheets. Not her bed. *Julian's bed.* And just then it felt like the safest place in the world. Scarlett wanted to hug the feathery pillow and curl deep into the sheets until she fell back asleep.

"Crimson." Julian's voice. Gentle but direct enough to tell Scarlett that he knew she was awake.

She sat up and slowly cracked her eyes open. For a heartbeat her vision was still blurry about the edges, but there weren't feelings crowding the room. The only colors she saw were the ones that were supposed to be there. The cool dark blue of the sheets cocooning her, the sleek gray of the curtains at the corners of the bed, the warm brown of Julian's skin, and the intoxicating amber of his eyes.

His room was full of the same colors and slightly wild, like his appearance. Stubble lined his jaw, his hair looked as if he hadn't stopped running his fingers through it, and his cravat was on the floor at his feet. Scarlett didn't need to see his emotions to detect his concern. He sat beside her on the bed, but he looked ready to catch her if she took another fall.

"How long was I out?" she asked.

"Long enough to make me worry that this wasn't just an elaborate ploy to get into my bed."

Scarlett managed a smile. "What if I said it was a ploy?"

"I'd tell you that you don't need one. You're welcome in my bed anytime." He gave her a wicked grin. It would have been convincing if she hadn't just seen thin threads of worried silver ghosting around the edges of him. She wondered if he suspected that she hadn't just fainted out of grief.

Scarlett wanted to close her eyes again, to shut out the emotions coming off him, but she didn't want to shut him out.

"Thank you," Scarlett said.

"I'm here for whatever you need." Julian shifted closer to the headboard, a silent invitation. She could lean against him if she wanted, and she did.

Scarlett pressed her head to his solid shoulder and closed her eyes. But even though she managed to mute the silver worry hovering around him, she couldn't turn off everything. Earlier she'd thought the grief she'd felt only belonged to Tella, but perhaps some of it had also been Scarlett's.

"I didn't think it would hurt," Scarlett confessed. "I thought I'd lost my mother a long time ago. I was furious with her. I didn't trust her. I didn't want her back in our lives, I didn't want her . . . I didn't want her at all."

Julian held Scarlett tighter and pressed a kiss to her forehead.

She didn't know how long they sat there like that. And she didn't know if she was sad because her mother was dead, of if she was sad because she'd wanted her mother gone. She wanted to be sad her mother was dead; that's how a good daughter would have felt, and if there was one thing Scarlett tried to be, it was good. But she'd stopped trying when it came to her mother.

"Do you know where my sister is now?" Scarlett asked.

"I think she's still with Legend," Julian said.

Scarlett slowly peeled back the sheets. She wanted to get up, but given her gown's fondness for Julian, she was a little nervous as to what it might have shifted into while she was in his bed. Oddly, it was still the same deep pink garment it had been before. She wondered if the emotions that had worn her out had depleted some of the gown's magic as well.

Julian hopped off the bed, misreading her hesitation. "Do you need help?"

"I can manage," Scarlett said.

But Julian's arms were already around her. He picked her up with one quick swoop and carried her into a sitting room.

"Julian, I can walk."

"Maybe I just want an excuse to hold you." He grinned like a thief who'd just gotten away with a crime.

She let herself lean into him. It felt good to be in his arms. He was the perfect distraction from all the horrors she could have dwelled on. He set her down on a velvety couch, warm from sunbeams streaming through the floor-to-ceiling windows.

A tray of luncheon foods sat on the coffee table across from her. Julian piled up a plate with thick sandwiches and cheese for her. As she ate, she noticed that the bandage from yesterday was still around his arm, and though he'd not changed his clothes, the dressing on it looked fresh, as if he had taken the time to put a new one on while she'd been unconscious.

Scarlett gingerly touched the bottom of the cloth. "You never told me what happened here."

"It's a secret." He rocked back on his heels, just out of her reach.

Scarlett couldn't tell if he was being playful or evading. "Do you plan on wearing the bandage forever?"

He pulled at the back of his neck, definitely evading. "Why are you so interested in it?"

"Because it looks as if you're hurt and you won't tell me what happened."

"What if I gave you a secret instead?"

Before she could answer, he loped into his bedroom and returned with a cloth-bound book, so old that its ochre cover was practically paper-thin.

"I had someone take this from Legend's library while you were asleep. It's one of the oldest books he has on the Fates, and it's all about the Fated objects."

Scarlett tucked her legs beneath her to make room for him on the couch. "Are you going to read me a bedtime story from it?"

"Maybe later." He pulled a pair of glasses from his pocket, which made him look boyish and charming and sweeter than Scarlett thought was possible. "Do you still have the key that little girl gave you yesterday?"

Scarlett reached inside her dress pocket and pulled it out. "Is this what you're talking about?"

"You might want to be careful who you offer that to. I think that little girl was right about it being magical. I believe it might be one of the eight Fated objects." Julian sat beside her on the couch, his leg brushing her knees, as he started to read:

"*In Decks of Destiny, the Reverie Key predicts dreams come true. It can turn any lock and take whoever holds the key to any person that they can imagine.*

"*However, the Reverie Key's power cannot be taken. To be used, the key must be received as a gift.*

"*Like many of the other Fated objects, it chooses who it's given to, often appearing out of nowhere before it's given away to someone worthy and in need.*"

Julian's eyes met hers as he finished reading. "How's that for a secret, Crimson?"

The object shimmered brighter and warmer in Scarlett's palm. It definitely looked enchanted. Maybe it was just her muddled head, but she had the feeling that the object was hopeful she would use it, even more hopeful than the earnest little girl with the braids had been when she'd said she thought that Scarlett was magical.

Scarlett didn't feel magical at the moment. Her emotions felt fragile and dry as cracked paint. But Julian was trying so hard to cheer her up with his secret, which actually felt much more like a gift. It might not have been something tangible, but it was incredibly thoughtful. He could have said he was giving it to her as part of the competition, but he didn't. And Scarlett didn't want to tarnish this moment for him by bringing the contest or Nicolas up.

"This is perfect." She even managed to give him a smile. "But just to make sure you're right, I think we should test it out together."

Julian's face lit up, as his mouth hitched into a grin.

Scarlett thought she might have heard a knock on the door, but if Julian heard it, he ignored it. His eyes were on Scarlett as she held out a crystal key that sparkled even more than before, as if she'd said exactly what it wanted to hear.

Donatella

Tella knew she'd found the right place when she saw the door clapper shaped like a broken heart. It felt like a warning that nothing good could come from stepping inside.

Maybe she should have tried harder to get Legend to tell her his weakness before running off to Jacks so quickly. Jacks might not choose to help her again, and if he did tell her the Fallen Star's weakness, it would definitely come at a cost. But what would the cost be if she walked away? Would the Fallen Star murder more people? Would he discover that Paloma had two daughters and come after Scarlett and Tella?

Tella knocked on the door and it immediately swung open, letting her inside Jacks's gambling den.

Dice flew while young patrons clapped, all of them eager to lose fortunes that they hadn't even earned and favors Jacks would no doubt collect from them later. Everyone looked fresher than they'd been last night. The ladies' smiles weren't smudged, the gentlemen's cravats were sharp, and the drinks were unspilled. Tonight's games had only just begun.

"Aren't you a pretty thing?" A woman with red diamonds painted on her cheeks sauntered over to Tella. She was dressed to match the cards on the tables, in a knee-length skirt of black-and-white stripes, which flared over her full hips. Her fitted jacket hid shiny spade-shaped buttons, but her long sleeves were all wrong for the Hot Season, making Tella wonder if there were cards, or weapons, hidden inside them. If this woman worked for Jacks, it wouldn't have been a surprise.

Though after a second look, Tella didn't imagine this person worked for the Prince of Hearts, or that she was even a person. Copper curls that shined like coins framed a face with a light brown complexion covered in dark freckles and eyes like liquid diamonds—practically clear, and very inhuman. No, this was not a person at all. This woman was a Fate.

Tella stumbled backward, tripping on her ripped hem.

"That's not the response I usually get." The Fate's smile stretched wide, making everyone within a ten-foot radius grin in unison. Then there was a thunderous round of applause, punctuated with several loud whoops and whistles, as if more than half the room had just had a tremendous streak of luck.

This woman was definitely a Fate. Mistress Luck, if Tella's guess was right.

Her card usually represented good fortune, but Tella didn't care. She continued backing toward the door as black-and-red confetti fell from the ceiling. "Stay away from me!"

Mistress Luck's smile dimmed, and a series of gasps and disappointed groans filled the gambling den.

"You know how much most people would pay for my advice?" asked the Fate.

"That's why I'd rather pass on it. I'm sure the price is entirely too high."

The Fate shook her head and pursed her lips, but then her eerie eyes sparked with a flash of iridescent light. "Oh my, you're her, aren't you? *You're* the one who made Jacks's heart beat?" The Fate's clear eyes went toward Tella's chest as if there were a piece of eerie treasure hidden inside. "You're his weakness."

Tella froze at the word *weakness*.

Mistress Luck's smile returned and the den filled with cheers once more. "Seems I have your attention now."

Oh, she definitely had Tella's attention. This was exactly what Tella wanted. If this woman could give it to her, then Tella wouldn't even need to talk to Jacks. "What does it mean to be a Fate's weakness?"

"It means you and Jacks are both in danger. Immortals and humans are not meant to be together."

Tella choked on a laugh. "Jacks and I aren't together. I hate Jacks." But the words definitely didn't taste as true as they should have.

Mistress Luck could clearly tell from her response. "Don't humans usually avoid things they hate?"

"Sometimes Jacks is a necessary evil."

"Then make him unnecessary." Mistress Luck gripped Tella's arm as her cheery voice turned into something harsh. "Your relationship with the Prince of Hearts will end in catastrophe."

"I already told you, we don't have a relationship." Tella tried to pull free, but the Fate's grip was inhumanly strong.

"You're in denial. If you weren't drawn to him, you wouldn't be here."

Tella tried to object, but the Fate just kept talking. "You're the human girl who made Jacks's heart beat again. There are whispers you're his one true love. But that doesn't mean what you think it does. Immortals cannot love. Love is not one of our emotions."

"Then it shouldn't matter if I'm Jacks's true love," Tella said.

"You didn't let me finish." Mistress Luck squeezed Tella's arm a little harder. "When we're attracted to humans, we only feel obsession, fixation, lust, possession. But on very rare occasions, we come across humans who tempt us to love. But it always ends badly. Love is poison to us. Love and immortality cannot coexist. If an immortal feels true love for even a minute, they become human for that minute. If the feeling lasts too long, their mortality becomes permanent. And most immortals would kill the object of their affection rather than become human. It's not safe to tempt an immortal to love. And if Jacks doesn't kill you because he's tempted to love you, then I promise his obsession with you will destroy you."

A hush fell over the den at her words, as if the entire room had just been dealt a bad hand.

"If you have any intelligence, you'll turn and walk away now." The Fate finally released Tella's arm, and then she drifted back through the sea of gamblers, claps and cheers following her as she moved.

Tella tried to shake off the feel of her grip. But she couldn't shake off her words.

Love and immortality cannot coexist.

We only feel obsession, fixation, lust, possession.

If an immortal feels love for even a minute, they become human for that minute. If the feeling lasts too long, their mortality becomes permanent. And most immortals would kill the object of their affection rather than become human.

Now Tella knew what an immortal's one weakness was. Love. To kill the Fallen Star, they would need to make him fall in love. But he was definitely the sort who would murder a human before loving them.

A sharp ache panged beneath her breastbone, right around her heart. But the hurt went far deeper than that. This was not the weakness Tella would have imagined. But now she understood why Legend hadn't wanted her to know about it: Legend didn't love her, and he never *would* love her, not as long as he wanted to remain immortal.

"You look as if you're in pain again," Jacks drawled.

Tella spun around, her heart racing at the sound of his voice.

Tonight the Prince of Hearts was dressed like a debauched ringmaster, in a deep burgundy coat with a popped collar and ripped-off sleeves that revealed the black-and-white shirt beneath, which had been carelessly left unbuttoned. His white cravat hung untied around his neck, and his black pants were only half tucked into his scuffed boots.

He was the exact opposite of Legend. Legend always looked as if he could walk away from the apocalypse unscathed, while Jacks always seemed as if he'd just come from a fight—all wild, almost violently reckless in his appearance. And yet because he was a Fate, Jacks still managed to be almost painfully attractive.

"Here to see if I can make you feel better?" He sank his teeth into the corner of his mouth, drawing one sparkling bead of gold-red blood. "I'm happy to help you out again."

Tella's belly dipped and her cheeks flushed with heat. "That's not what I want."

"Are you sure about that? You definitely look as if you want something." He laughed as he flicked out his tongue to catch the blood at the corner of his mouth. Still chuckling, he sauntered off toward a nearby roulette table.

"Wait." Tella stormed after him. "I need to talk to you."

"I'd rather gamble." He grabbed the knob in the center of the already spinning black-and-red wheel and gave it another whirl, making it turn faster as the people at the table grumbled. "Place a bet and then we'll talk."

"Fine." Tella pulled out a handful of coins.

"Not that sort of bet, my love." His silver-blue eyes sparked, taunting and daring, along with something else she couldn't place fast enough. "I think we can make this a little more interesting."

"How?"

He tugged at his lower lip with two pale fingers. "If the ball lands on black, we'll talk, like you want. I'll answer the questions you came here with. But if it falls on red, you have to let me into your dreams."

"Not a chance."

"Then this conversation is over." He turned.

"Wait—" Tella reached up and clamped a hand on his shoulder.

Jacks slowly spun around, smiling as if he'd already won more than just the right to slip inside of her dreams.

"I haven't agreed yet," Tella said, "and if I do say yes to this bet, you need to promise that you won't keep anyone else out of my dreams."

"Why?" He leaned in closer, surrounding her with the crisp scent of apples. "Did someone complain?"

"I'm complaining! They're my dreams and you don't have the right to keep anyone else from them."

"I was doing it for you," Jacks said sweetly. "Dreams might seem insignificant, but they give away more secrets than people realize."

"Is that why you want inside of mine?"

His smile was all sharp edges. Suddenly all Tella could hear was the way Mistress Luck had said the word *obsession*. It didn't matter why Jacks wanted into her dreams—the fact that he wanted in them and had kept Legend out should have scared her.

Jacks had seemed safe last night because Tella had been too numb to care about all the things he'd done, but he was still viperous.

"Better decide quickly," he taunted. "The odds could be much worse and I could have asked for far more."

Whir . . .

Whir . . .

Whir . . .

The wheel continued spinning but the little white ball was losing momentum. And Tella had no doubt that when it stopped, Jacks would walk away or offer her a bet with worse odds.

"Fine," Tella said. "You have a deal."

The ball immediately stopped and slid into black.

Tella couldn't believe it. "I wo—"

The ball jumped and popped into the red slot beside it.

"No!" Tella stared at the ball, waiting for it to move again, but of course it didn't. "You cheated."

"Did you see me touch the ball?" Jacks fluttered his lashes innocently.

Tella fought the urge to smack him. "I know you made it move."

"I'm flattered you think so highly of my abilities, but I'm not Legend. I don't do magic tricks."

No. He definitely wasn't Legend. Legend was deceptive and he didn't play fair, but he wasn't a blatant cheat.

Jacks picked up Tella's hand and gave it a quick cold kiss before dropping it and striding away from the table. "See you later tonight, my love."

"We are not done here!" Tella marched after him, weaving through drunk gamblers until she caught him on the same stairs he'd carried her up last night. The carpet brought back flashes of how helpless she'd been. Her chest constricted and her feet faltered on the steps.

Jacks spun around abruptly. "Why are you so upset? What are you worried I'll see in your dreams?"

"Get over yourself." Tella took a ragged breath. "I'm here because I want to know how to kill the Fallen Star."

"If you go near the Fallen Star, he'll kill you quicker than he killed your mother."

Tella flinched.

"Good," Jacks said. "I'm glad you look scared."

"That's why I need to kill him."

"You can't," Jacks said flatly.

"What about with love?"

Jacks's eyes iced over with irritation and Tella swore the stairwell grew a little colder. "Who told you that?"

"So, it's true?" Tella said. "Love can make an immortal human long enough to kill?"

"It's true, but that's not going to happen." Jacks started up the stairs again.

"Then tell me another way," Tella called as she followed. She might have said she wouldn't leave until he answered her, but she had an inkling that wouldn't be much of a threat. Following him was probably a terrible idea as well. Mistress Luck's words came to mind once more as she trekked up the stairs:

If Jacks doesn't kill you because he's tempted to love you, then I promise his obsession with you will destroy you.

But Jacks had his back turned to her now. He didn't seem obsessed with her at all. And he still felt like her best option for figuring out how to defeat the Fallen Star. She knew he wasn't safe, but after she got what she wanted from him tonight, she wouldn't let herself see him again.

His study smelled faintly of apples and blood when she followed him inside. Tella's skin prickled once more with memories of their forbidden kiss as her eyes went to the scorched rug in front of the worn leather couch. She quickly looked away, focusing on Jacks's desk instead; on top was a map of the city, held down in one corner by a mocking Deck of Destiny.

The deck was a little faded and worn around the corners. It was nothing like her mother's magical deck, but it was another reminder of Paloma and how she'd sacrificed so much—*including her life*—to try to stop the Fates from reigning once again.

Jacks threw himself in the chair behind his desk, looking annoyed that she'd followed him inside.

"The Fallen Star killed my mother," Tella said. "I watched as he murdered her. I don't expect you to care about that, but I know you felt my pain last night. I saw you cry tears of blood."

"Everyone who owns a Deck of Destiny has seen me cry tears of blood. Don't turn this into a tragedy and think that means I care."

Jacks picked up his Deck of Destiny and began to shuffle the cards with elegant fingers. "And don't think that this means I'm on your side." His voice was so acerbic she almost didn't realize this was his way of saying he would help her.

"There's a book in the Immortal Library, the Ruscica," Jacks went on. "It can tell a person or a Fate's entire history. If Gavriel has a fatal weakness that no one is aware of, this book might reveal it. But using the Ruscica is not a good idea. You'd need Gavriel's blood to access his history, and retrieving that could get you killed. If you're determined to go after him, you'll have the best chance of finding what you need inside the Vanished Market."

Jacks cut the cards and flipped one half of the deck over. On top lay the card for the Vanished Market, which depicted a rainbow of colorful tent stalls, all selling exotic animals, wares, and foods from times past.

We might not have what you want, but we have what you need.

The Vanished Market was one of the eight Fated places. In Decks of Destiny, the Vanished Market was an auspicious, albeit tricky, card. It promised a person that they would be given what they needed. But most people agreed that what a person needed and wanted were two different things. And Tella imagined that trading inside the market was a bit like making a deal with one of Legend's performers during Caraval. She doubted she could purchase what she needed with coins.

"If there's another way to kill him, you might find your answer inside of the market," Jacks said. "There's a stall there run by two sisters who buy and sell secrets. In exchange for your secrets, they will give you one of the Fallen Star's secrets."

Tella studied Jacks, dubious. "I've only seen the Fallen Star from afar, but he doesn't strike me as the sort to sell his secrets."

"He's not, but if anyone has one of his secrets, it would be the sisters. The market exists outside of time. If you visit them, you'll learn that they have unique methods of collecting information."

"Where can I find the market?"

"Several of the ruins throughout the city were once Fated places, but to access their magic, they need to be summoned." Jacks pointed to a set of ruins to the west of the Temple District. "Look for an hourglass etched into the stones and feed it one drop of blood to summon the market. But be careful, there is always a cost to enter a Fated place that has been called forth. The market exacts a time tithe from everyone who steps inside. For every hour you spend in the market, a day will pass in our world."

"Thank you for the warning." Tella hadn't known that bit, and she was more than a little surprised Jacks had told her, since a Fate's primary source of entertainment was toying with humans. In fact, she was surprised by everything he'd told her. She'd come here half wanting to rebel against Legend and half hoping for answers. She hadn't actually expected to get any. But she had. She now knew Legend's immortal weakness, and she also knew where to search for the Fallen Star's weakness. "I imagine you want something in exchange now."

Jacks's eyes slowly lowered to her mouth.

A chill caressed her lips like a kiss. "I already told you that's not why I'm here."

"So then why haven't you left?"

His laughter followed Tella as she walked out the door.

21

Scarlett

S carlett should have been tripping over her feet with exhaustion rather than dancing into her sparkling palace suite.

After using the Reverie Key with Julian to visit a baker he knew in the north, where Scarlett tasted the best cakes of her life, he'd then brought her to see an old friend of his in the Southern Empire, where the water was the most brilliant shade of turquoise she'd ever seen and people sent messages with sea turtles. She could have stayed there longer, but Julian had wanted to take her to his distant cousin, who lived in a house with a roof made for watching the world's most spectacular sunsets. In one afternoon Julian and the Reverie Key had shifted Scarlett's tiny view of the world, making it even larger than she'd realized.

She tried to tamp down her smile. She shouldn't have been giddy as she fell back onto her bed. She should have been mourning the loss of her mother, worrying about where her sister was, or fearful of the Fates that were all waking up.

But it was difficult to be afraid of nightmares when Scarlett's thoughts were still tangled up in the dream that was Julian. She'd lied about needing to sleep because she'd felt so caught up in him she'd wanted to wake and return back to the real.

She regretted it already.

The Reverie Key was still warm in her pocket. She thought about using it to find him, and asking him to visit one more magical place. And maybe Scarlett would have done just that, if a servant hadn't knocked on the door with a delivery from Nicolas.

Scarlett didn't even need to open the card that came with it to know the gift was from him. It was a crystal watering can, small enough to fit in her palm, as if it were for pixie-size plants.

Scarlett crashed back to reality. She'd been trying not to think about the competition between Julian and Nicolas. Given everything else that had happened in the last two days, it didn't seem nearly as important as it had before. But she couldn't just ignore it.

Scarlett opened the note reluctantly. When she had received letters from Nicolas in the past, she'd always reread them until the paper went thin. But she wished this one had never arrived.

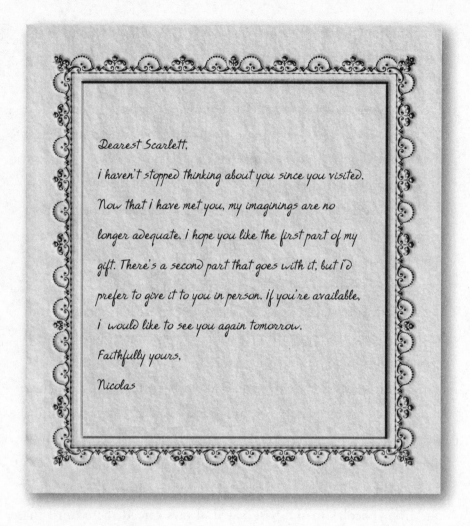

Dearest Scarlett,

i haven't stopped thinking about you since you visited.
Now that i have met you, my imaginings are no
longer adequate. i hope you like the first part of my
gift. There's a second part that goes with it, but i'd
prefer to give it to you in person. if you're available,
i would like to see you again tomorrow.

Faithfully yours,

Nicolas

If Julian had written the words, Scarlett was certain her heart would have raced, or her cheeks would have hurt from the way her smile stretched. She'd have felt something. But not even the dress managed a response.

Closing her eyes, Scarlett lay her head against her pillows.

She used to think Nicolas was her best option for marriage. And maybe he was safer than Julian. Nicolas was attractive, attentive, everything he'd made himself out to be in his previous letters. But Scarlett felt nothing for him. No, that wasn't true. She felt relieved that they weren't married.

Nicolas might have been the safer choice, but Julian was whom Scarlett wanted to choose. There was no competition between Julian and Nicolas. Julian had won Scarlett's heart a long time ago.

She went to her desk to write Nicolas one last letter.

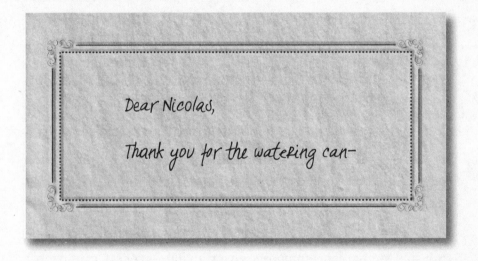

Dear Nicolas,

Thank you for the watering can—

Scarlett tried, but she couldn't write another word. After all of their lost chances, it seemed terribly callous to inform Nicolas in a letter that she'd already made her choice. She wouldn't want to be dismissed this way.

Balling up her note and tossing it in the trash, Scarlett looked at his letter once again. She couldn't give him her hand in marriage, but she could give him this final meeting. She owed that much to him.

Donatella

Valenda was a city that had been made for the night.
As Tella took a sky carriage back to the palace,
the world below her glittered with light. The churches
and sanctuaries of the Temple District glowed like
bits of moon that had lost their way, while the dimmer lights in the
Spice Quarter smoldered like ashes from a fire that refused to die.
Then there were the sleeping houses in between the districts, illuminated by guardian lampposts, giving an illusion of safety as people
slumbered in their beds.

No one knew how fragile their security was, and Tella wondered
if more Fates were waking up now. She probably should have asked
Jacks about it before she'd left him. But the Prince of Hearts had
looked as if he'd wanted to collect a higher fee for more information.

Tella's coach came to a gentle halt as it reached the palace carriage house. Mindful of her gown's ripped hem, she exited carefully.

The air tasted candied, the world glittered, and the stars looked close enough to steal and place inside of her pockets, making Tella feel as if she were inside of one of Legend's dreams, or back in Caraval. Though the sun had set, servants were still bustling about the palace grounds in preparation for tomorrow's Midnight Maze. Night dust, which made whatever it touched shimmer under the light of the nearby stars, filled buckets that servants carried around so they could brush everything from the hedges and the fountains lining the walkways to the bunnies that hopped through the gardens.

Most of the palace's staff didn't pay much attention to Tella, but she swore a few looked her way with narrowed eyes before turning to each other and whispering things about her.

She knew it was a bad idea to stop and listen—gossip rarely contained compliments. And yet Tella found herself following a pair of chattering servants to the Stone Garden. She ducked behind a female statue on the edge of the garden, with a billowing skirt that created the perfect place for Tella to hide behind as the servants brushed the other statues with more glowing night dust.

"Did you *see* her?" The first girl's voice was light and chirping, like a bird's. Tella had heard it before, her very first night in the palace, when she'd come to Valenda for the last Caraval and *Dante* had told the staff that she was engaged to Jacks. She hadn't been that angry until she'd overheard this birdy servant talking about the engagement, or rather about Jacks, and how he was a rumored murderer. They hadn't known he was actually the Prince of Hearts, and at the time, neither had Legend.

"I thought she was the former heir's fiancé," replied a second servant. Tella didn't recognize her voice. But she decided she didn't like it when she heard the breathless way she said, "I would think His Handsomeness Prince Dante wouldn't want her around."

"Oh, His Handsomeness *definitely* doesn't want her around," said the birdy girl. "I think the little trollop is just hoping to make Prince Dante her new fiancé now that her former fiancé isn't royal anymore. But everyone—except for *her*—knows that's not going to happen. The prince is probably just keeping her around because she used to belong to the former heir, and to keep her in his possession is another show of his power."

That's not true! Tella wanted to jump out from behind her statue to protest.

But maybe it was just a little true. Legend was jealous of Jacks. And according to Mistress Luck, when immortals were attracted to humans, they only felt obsession, fixation, lust, and *possession*.

"I heard," said the birdy girl, "he actually had her locked in the dungeons this morning!"

"Whatever for?" gasped the second girl.

"It wasn't because I didn't want her around," said Legend, the low sound of his voice filling the entire stone garden.

Suddenly, Tella couldn't have peeled herself away from her hiding spot if she'd tried. Moments ago, the world had been full of night dust and stars, but now he'd taken over.

The confident scrape of Legend's boots echoed across the garden and Tella pictured him moving closer, covering the frozen servants in shadows, as he said, "I want her here. If it were up to me, I'd keep her here forever. I asked her to marry me and she said no. That's why I locked her up. It was an inappropriate response, but sometimes I take things a little too far."

He paused, and she could picture him flashing a dissolute smile. "You two should keep that in mind the next time you decide to spread rumors, or you might find yourselves in a prison as well."

"We won't start any more rumors."

"We're so sorry, Your Highness."

There was a rush of sloppy slippers as if the servants were giving hasty curtsies, and then fleeing the stone garden, probably leaving a trail of glimmering night dust as they scurried off.

"You can come out now, Tella." Legend's voice took a teasing turn as he leaned an elbow on the statue that she was behind. Still dressed in the same black-and-wolf-gray suit as earlier, with a matching black half-cape slung over his shoulders, he looked both rakish and regal as he watched her rise from her crouch.

If this had been one of their dreams, when Tella and Legend were still pretending not to care, she might have rolled her eyes up at him, giving him a response that was the opposite of how she felt. But she sensed that game was now over. And yet she still couldn't be entirely vulnerable and tell him just how much what he'd said had turned her inside out. He'd lied, making himself look like an unhinged prince-ling in order to keep her reputation from being ruined.

"I think you scared those servants half to death," Tella said. "But you know they'll still repeat everything you just told them."

"I don't care what anyone says, as long as they're saying things about me." His tone was that of a shallow royal, but the look in his eyes was deep and all-consuming. His steady gaze held hers as if he had no intention of ever looking away—as if just maybe he'd been telling the truth when he'd said that he wanted to keep her here forever.

Her neck flushed with heat that spread across her collarbone.

Once again, she thought of Mistress Luck's warning—immortals only felt obsession, fixation, lust, and possession. But maybe Legend felt more. . . .

It would get around that he'd been rejected by Jacks's tarnished former fiancée. Just the rumors would make Legend look weak—a terrible way to start a reign. But he hadn't even hesitated to defend her.

It made her want to give him something in return.

"I think I know how to find out if the Fallen Star has another weakness."

Legend's eyes glittered, as if he'd just won points in the game she thought they were no longer playing. But for once she would gladly give him the points.

"We can buy one of his secrets at the Vanished Market, and I was thinking you could visit it with me."

His dark brows drew together, suddenly wary. "How'd you find the location of the market?"

"She learned it from me." Jacks's smooth voice licked a cold trail up her spine.

Tella spun around.

Jacks was standing directly in front of her, looking exactly like the Prince of Hearts she'd been obsessed with as a child. All pale glowing skin and brilliant golden hair that hung over unearthly blue eyes. His gaze was a little bloodshot, but his smile was exquisite, knife-sharp and polished, like a blade eager to be used.

"How did *you* get here?" Legend's voice was lethal, but when Tella looked back at him, his eyes were fixed on hers. They filled with something like hurt before thinning to a look that was closer to an accusation.

"The better question is, how did *he* get here?" Jacks slit his eyes toward Tella.

"I—" Tella started. But—she paused to look back up at the sky full of impossibly close stars—maybe she wasn't actually in this part of the palace? Maybe Tella hadn't stopped to listen to a pair of servants, and maybe Legend hadn't truly defended her in front of them.

Maybe Jacks was asking why Legend was there because Jacks still knew him as Dante—and Dante was not supposed to have magical abilities, like the power to enter dreams.

Tella's gaze lowered to the ripped hem of her ice-blue gown, and she willed it to mend itself, something she'd only be able to do if she was in a dream. For a moment, nothing happened.

Then, almost as soon as she'd begun to think she wasn't in a dream, the dress began to mend. The rip vanished, and a new tear inside of her heart took its place.

This wasn't real. Legend had risked nothing to defend her in front of those servants, because they were only in a dream.

Until that moment, she'd always loved her dreams with Legend— they'd felt like something special that the two of them had shared. But this felt like a deception.

Her gaze sliced from Legend's stormy eyes to Jacks's cutlass smile, feeling as if she was standing in the middle of an immortal game board. She hadn't liked how Jacks had tricked his way into her dreams, but it was almost worse that Legend had tricked her once again into believing an illusion was real.

"Both of you are terrible."

Tella willed herself to wake up, and her eyes flashed open just as her sky carriage came to a halt.

She must have fallen asleep while traveling across the city, her visions of Valenda at night seamlessly turning to dreams without her even realizing it.

She climbed out of the coach to find servants buzzing around the palace grounds and painting everything with night dust, but it didn't glitter as much, the stars no longer looked close enough to touch, and none of the servants glanced her way or whispered behind her back.

It wasn't until the following morning, when Tella was back in her borrowed palace room, that she heard the voice of a servant.

"Miss Donatella." Her name followed the loud knock that had woken her up.

Tella threw on her robe and dragged herself out of the raised canopy bed and across thick carpets. Perky sunlight warmed her skin as she opened her main doors. Two royal maids stood on the other side, the same ones who'd been in her dream last night.

They each held one end of a shiny black box, almost as long as Tella was tall.

"We have a gift from His Highness, Prince Dante," the birdy maid said as both girls set the box atop the closest couch.

"He also wanted to make sure you received this." The other maid handed Tella a crisp black envelope along with a curious smile.

But Tella wasn't about to open Legend's note in front of an audience, especially not one that she imagined would share its contents.

"You can go now," Tella said. As soon as they left, she tore off the envelope's seal. The note it contained was a simple square and covered with precise handwriting that for once made Legend easy to read.

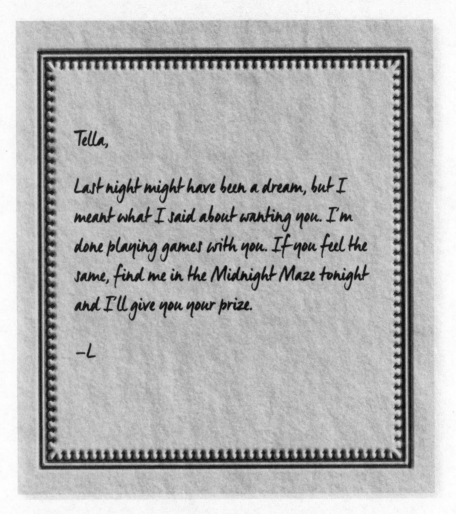

Tella,

Last night might have been a dream, but I meant what I said about wanting you. I'm done playing games with you. If you feel the same, find me in the Midnight Maze tonight and I'll give you your prize.

—L

She reread the letter, her—

"Donatella." Scarlett's voice was paired with a knock on the door, cutting off Tella's thoughts before they could go anywhere interesting.

"I'm not here right now," Tella called.

"Then you won't mind if I come in." The doorknob turned—

although Tella would have sworn it had been locked—and Scarlett stepped inside. Her lacy gown was a shockingly bright shade of red, which seemed at odds with her somber smile.

A small train of lace rosettes trailed behind her as she walked toward where Tella huddled on a couch next to the box from Legend. But Scarlett didn't really look at the box as she took the chair opposite her sister.

It was the first time they'd been alone since their mother had died, and from the way Scarlett was looking at Tella, this was clearly the main reason she was checking in. But Tella's feelings were still too raw. If she actually talked about her mother now, it would be like picking off a scab before the wound had a chance to heal.

"How are you doing?" Scarlett asked.

"I'm viciously tired," Tella moaned. "But I think I might perk up if you tell me why you looked so cozy with Julian yesterday."

Scarlett's cheeks turned bright pink and her dress shifted to the exact same color.

"I knew it!" Tella crowed. "You're in love with him again." Not that Tella really believed her sister had fallen *out* of love.

Scarlett shook her head, trying to fight her blush. She probably still felt as if they should be talking about their mother rather than boys.

But Tella needed this more than she needed to talk about broken feelings, and she believed her sister did, too. "Tell me everything."

Scarlett sighed. "I think he's stealing my heart all over again." She then told her sister about Julian's return, and how he'd insisted on coming with her to meet Nicolas, who sounded far more decent than Tella had expected. She surprised Tella again by confessing she'd challenged both gentlemen to a game. "But I think I'm going to call the game off."

"I'm tempted to tell you not to." The game was something Scarlett never would have done before Caraval, and Tella was impressed she'd suggested it. "It sounds like a brilliant idea, but you know I've never been a fan of Nicolas."

"There's nothing wrong with Nicolas. He's just—"

"Not Julian."

Scarlett's answering grin told Tella everything she needed to know. Julian might not have been perfect, but he was perfect for her sister.

"Now it's your turn." Scarlett eyed the shiny black box beside Tella.

"It's a gift from Legend. He wants me to meet him at the Midnight Maze tonight." Tella pulled out the note Legend had sent her and handed it to Scarlett. "I think this might be his way to apologize to me for tricking me in a dream without really apologizing."

"Hmm." Scarlett's brow furrowed and her dress turned a suspicious shade of mauve as she read. "I actually think he might be planning on giving you more than an apology tonight." She looked up at Tella with solemn hazel eyes. "Did you know the Midnight Maze isn't just the start of the weeklong countdown to a new ruler's coronation? It's an ancient Valendan tradition with very romantic roots. The first Midnight Maze was built by a prince for the princess he wanted to marry. The stories say that the prince told his princess there would be a prize in the center of the maze. Then he snuck there and waited for her, preparing to propose when she found him."

"So you think Legend plans to propose?" Tella said it like a joke. Legend hadn't even given her an apology for leaving her that night in front of the Temple of the Stars. There was no way he could be planning on giving her a proposal.

But Scarlett looked utterly serious. "I don't think it's entirely far-fetched. Although, in the story the proposal never happened. After the princess entered the maze, she was never seen again. It's said whenever there's a Midnight Maze, the ghost of the prince appears and searches for his lost princess."

"That sounds like more of a tragedy than a romance," Tella said.

"But it also sounds like Legend. I think he likes stories on the dark-and-tragic side." Scarlett pinned Tella with a stare that looked a little like a warning, before her eyes went back to the long black box beside Tella, as if its contents might confirm her suspicions.

"It's probably just a dress, since he knows we lost most everything when our apartment was destroyed." Tella lifted the lid. But to say what she found inside was just a dress would have been like saying Caraval was only a game, when it was so much more.

A sweet, bewitching fragrance filled the room. It made her think of every dream that she'd spent with Legend as she reached inside the box and pulled out a gown that could have made any girl fall in love.

The garment he'd sent had straps made of flower petals, a bodice made of ribbons lined in gems as small as glitter, and a full skirt formed of hundreds of silk butterflies, all in different shades of blue that together formed a magical hue she'd never seen. Some had sheer blue wings that were almost as pale as tears, others were soft sky blue, a few had hints of violet, while some had periwinkle veins. The butterflies weren't alive, but they were so delicate and ethereal, at a glance they looked real. Exactly like the gown of her dreams, the dress she'd worn four nights ago when they'd been inside a dream version of the Church of Legend. She'd thought he hadn't even noticed what she'd worn. But clearly, he had.

It was tempting to shove the dress in the box and not show up at the party at all. The Fates were still out there; she needed to go to the Vanished Market. She needed to find the Fallen Star's weakness. It was selfish to attend a party right now.

But the real truth was, she was less afraid of battling monsters than she was of giving Legend her heart once again.

Before Legend, Tella had wanted nothing to do with love. She'd believed she was destined to only experience unrequited love. Then she'd fallen in love with him, and it had been like drinking magic— indescribable, all-consuming, and fantastically addictive. Tella didn't even want to get married, but if there was one person who could tempt her, it was Legend.

"Are you going to go?" Scarlett asked.

"Of course I'm going to go," Tella said. She just didn't know what she would do if Legend actually proposed. No one knew how to make her dream or wonder or feel as much as Legend. But no one knew how to break her like Legend did, either. She still wasn't entirely over the last heartbreak, and if he did it again, she feared she'd never get over it.

23

Scarlett

Every step Scarlett took from the palace felt like a move in the wrong direction.

To avoid the chaos of Legend's Midnight Maze, which had taken over all of the outer palace grounds, Scarlett had asked Nicolas for another meeting spot. He'd responded by sending a hand-drawn map with clues. She imagined he was trying at romance, and if the map had been from Julian, it would have worked. But instead of feeling romanced, Scarlett felt as if she were making a mistake.

She should have told Tella that she was going to see Nicolas. She'd told Tella she was calling off the game. But she hadn't confessed she was telling Nicolas this in person. Deep down, Scarlett knew it was a questionable choice to leave the safety of the palace grounds.

After yesterday's incidents with the Poisoner, she'd not heard of any other Fates causing havoc for fun. But as Scarlett walked

Valenda's steep streets, she saw multiple Fates in the form of warn-ings and Wanted posters tacked up by Legend's guards.

The flickering pages were all over the city. Some cautioned people not to accept drinks from strangers. Others had the word *Wanted* above sketches that resembled Tella's description of the Fallen Star. But they didn't explicitly say that they were *actually* Fates. The party-goers on the street just strolled by them.

Scarlett wanted to shake everyone that walked past and make them read the notices. She knew the Fates fed off of fear, but every-one looked far too vulnerable.

Scarlett reached into her pocket, checking once again to make sure the Reverie Key was still there. At least she was protected—if she wanted to escape all she needed to do was shove the key in the closest lock. And yet she couldn't shrug off her unease.

Even her dress seemed uncertain.

As she followed the map to the docks at the edge of the city, Scarlett's gown turned a wary shade of brown, perfect for being overlooked. A few more steps over rickety wood and her nose tickled with the familiar scents of salt and fish and forever wet wood.

Trisda, the tiny isle where she'd spent most of her life, had always smelled like this. Rather than making her homesick, it made her want to flee, the same way Trisda had always made her want to flee. But Scarlett had decided after Caraval that she would not let fear rule her.

She counted the docks, following the map Nicolas had drawn for her until she came upon a long wharf covered with a black-and-gold carpet that led to a ship that looked like a floating palace. Its hull was carved with ornate images of mermaids and mermen holding tridents and seashells. The masts were decorated as well—giants with crowns of stars around their heads as they held out sumptuous purple sails.

It was almost offensive in its finery. This ship belonged to someone who thought extremely highly of himself. That wasn't the impression she'd had of Nicolas. He'd seemed more down-to-earth. But everyone wore their disguises.

Scarlett stopped just as she stepped onto the dock. She'd felt nervous about meeting him before, but now she felt a lick of fear that warned her to turn around. She didn't owe Nicolas anything.

Most people did not take rejection well. And it seemed especially unwise to reject Nicolas on his boat, which he could easily toss her over the side of—or sail away with her still on board.

She turned around. Scarlett wanted to be brave, but she didn't want to be foolish.

"Scarlett? Are you Scarlett Dragna?" The voice didn't sound like Nicolas.

Run. Hide. Scream. Her feelings turned bright warning red. She started to run.

But it was already too late.

A black bag went over her head.

"Let me go!" Scarlett tried to rip the bag off as she screamed. But her hands were yanked behind her and roughly tied together.

"Be careful with her," a new voice commanded. "He wants his daughter undamaged."

about how magnificent *His Handsomeness* looked tonight. Apparently, the nickname hadn't just been part of her dream. But Tella still felt a possessive urge to snap at anyone who uttered it.

Her nerves over what Legend might ask and how she would respond attacked, knotting her up as she slipped deeper into the maze. The fireflies had arrived, making everyone she passed appear a little enchanted as their laughter and flirtations tripped over her head.

Contrary to what the name implied, the Midnight Maze did not begin at midnight. It started around sundown when the horizon was a battle of colors, as if the clouds were trying to break free from the sky. They were probably attempting to reach the maze, which was full of even more colors.

Tella wouldn't have been surprised if some of it was Legend's doing. With so many enthusiastic emotions swirling around the maze, his magic should have been growing stronger. Perhaps that was another reason why he'd wanted to go through with hosting the maze—he needed it to fuel his powers before the Fates finished waking up.

"Oh, look!" a nearby partygoer exclaimed. "That door just sprung up in the middle of the hedge. Let's see if it takes us to the center of the maze."

Tella heard a rustle of dancing skirts and a muttered "Gentlemen first."

Then the giggling pack of people in front of her was gone, vanished through a door bursting with celestial blue dragonsnaps that disappeared along with them. Only a hovering parade of fireflies and

24

Donatella

Tella didn't know what pure anticipation smelled like until she reached Legend's Midnight Maze. The scent of red cloves and growing leaves permeated everything. She had expected simple leafy green hedges, but she should have known better than to attach the word *simple* to anything involving Legend. Each living wall was formed of different rare flowers. Burning orange starfire lilies. Deep purple twilight thistles. Brilliant gold creeping faisies. Champagne delights. Scorching red feverbells. All of which grew and stretched with every person that stepped inside.

During her first Caraval, Tella had learned emotions were one of the things that fueled magic, making her wonder if Legend became stronger the more people enjoyed his party, and as a result, the glamour and illusion of the party also grew.

Not that Tella had seen Legend. But she'd heard a few whispers a patch of near-silence remained. All Tella could hear was the flutter of wings, soft as dreamy lullabies and delicate as butterflies.

Her skin tickled with fluttering that she only usually felt in her stomach as she looked down to see her dress coming to life with the beat of a hundred wings. Tella laughed and butterflies burst free from a skirt that had been inanimate only moments ago.

Legend was there.

He had to be nearby. He was bringing her dress to life and making the maze shift in front of her eyes. It moved more rapidly than before, growing taller and thicker and *stronger*. Leafy crenulations formed at the top of it, giving everything an enchanted castle-like appearance.

She chased after the butterflies leaping off her dress until she found a glowing archway formed of dazzling white diamond peonies.

As soon as she was through the arch, the flowers moved behind her, sealing her away from the rest of the party and leaving her alone with Legend.

She took several heartbeats just to drink him in.

A dusting of bronze light surrounded him, making his skin glow and his eyes look a little brighter, as Legend leaned against a leafy wall on the opposite side of the enclosure. He was dressed in shades of charcoal black except for the deep red trousers he wore, tucked into tall polished boots. His coat was longer than usual, nearly to the ground, with a regal high collar lined in intricate thread the same color as the bronze light surrounding him, as if bits of the setting sun had stayed behind just to cling to him.

"You're such a show-off," she teased.

He gave her a devastating grin. "Only when I'm trying to impress a girl." His eyes took their time looking her over, sparking a little as they lingered on the delicate ribbons that made up her bodice, before finally meeting her eyes.

"You're beautiful." He pushed off the wall and stalked closer. But, for once, instead of hearing the confident stride of his boots, all she could hear were the words he'd written in his note: *I meant what I said about wanting you.*

More butterflies took off from her skirt as Legend stopped right in front of her, close enough to touch. The world no longer smelled like anticipation. It smelled like him. Like magic and heartbreak.

Please don't break my heart again, she thought. Even if he didn't ask her to marry him, he looked as if he was going to ask for something. Their secluded corner of the maze was growing brighter, full of infant stars that glittered and danced and shined, but Legend's gaze remained firmly on hers, intent and intense and as intimate as any touch.

Her breathing turned shallow.

His mouth twitched at the corner. "Have I scared you already?"

"Are you trying to scare me?"

"I thought I already told you, I'm only trying to keep you." His lips brushed a kiss to hers.

The maze, the party, the world, disappeared. His mouth was soft and then it was gone.

It happened so fast, Tella might have thought she imagined it if not for the teasing glimmer in his eyes.

"I came here to claim a prize, not to be played with." Tella held out a hand as if to collect.

Legend laughed, deep and rumbling. "I'll always want to play with you. But tonight I'm not playing. I want you, Donatella Dragna. I've never felt like this about anyone, and I've never asked anyone this, either." His voice dropped so low it made her toes curl inside her slippers and half the butterflies on her skirt take flight.

Scarlett was right. He was going to propose.

His eyes grew brighter and his smile turned tempting. "I want to keep you, Tella. I want to make you immortal."

Everything inside of Tella went still. *Immortal.* He was asking to make her immortal, not to marry him.

"I'd say you could take all the time you need to think about it. But now that the Fates are awake, I don't want to wait anymore. I don't want to risk losing you." Legend's hands wrapped around her waist. He looked as if he wanted to kiss her again, but this time it wouldn't be just a quick brush of his lips. She could feel his hands growing hotter as his fingers spread out over her rib cage.

If she leaned in, he'd kiss her until it consumed her, until she couldn't breathe without him and she gasped yes to whatever he asked.

Tella let him hold on, but she didn't lean in. She hadn't been entirely prepared for him to propose and she definitely wasn't prepared for this. "I'm not sure I know what you're asking. Are you offering to make me one of your performers?"

"No." His fingers stroked up and down her waist. "You'd be different. My performers aren't immortal, just ageless. My magic keeps them from growing old, but I can only bring them back to life during Caraval, when my power is at its peak. Outside of Caraval, there's nothing I can do for them. But as an immortal, if you died, you would always come back. No one could kill you. You'd never grow old or weak or frail. You'd be young and strong and alive forever."

The lights around them glittered like gems, spinning and whirling and promising that a forever with Legend would be full of magic as well. It'd be like living in one of his dreams. But for some reason, Tella couldn't bring herself to say yes.

Legend's mouth turned down, and his hands tightened around her waist. "I thought you'd be more excited. This way we can be together."

He still looked as if he wanted to kiss her, but rather than lean in, his fingers toyed with the ribbons of her bodice, carefully loosening them so his hands could reach through to brush her bare back.

Her eyes fluttered shut. Only the tips of his fingers touched her skin but Tella felt it everywhere. He'd told her that he wasn't playing with her tonight, but he definitely was—though she wondered if he even realized it.

People didn't really matter to Legend. People were game pieces inside of his world. He'd even turned the witch who'd created him into a sacrificed pawn so that he could go on. And yet, despite everything, Tella wanted to believe he didn't see her that way. Rather than preserve herself, she wanted to persevere. She wanted to believe he wouldn't break her heart again. She wanted to believe he wasn't manipulating her, that she was his one exception. But maybe Legend didn't know how to make exceptions. Maybe he deceived everyone.

He said he'd never had feelings like this before, and he'd never offered to make anyone immortal, but he'd not bothered to mention the one weakness she'd learned about last night.

Immortals cannot love. Love is poison to us. Love and immortality cannot coexist.

On very rare occasions we come across humans who tempt us to love. . . . If an immortal feels love for even a minute, they become human for that minute. If the feeling lasts too long, their mortality becomes permanent.

Suddenly everything became clear. Tella understood why Legend showed up in her dreams but kept his distance, refusing to touch her until tonight, right before making an offer to change her. Last night she'd thought Legend had real feelings for her—that he could love her. But it was the opposite. Legend wasn't changing—he was hoping to change *her*.

And she didn't believe it was so that she wouldn't die. Legend wanted to make her immortal so that *he* wouldn't die.

He didn't love her. He was afraid of falling in love with her, because love was his one weakness. If Legend loved her, he'd lose his immortality and become human. But he wouldn't have to worry about it if she was immortal, because immortals couldn't love each other.

Immortals felt obsession, fixation, lust, possession. And Legend was clearly experiencing those things. Tella sensed it with each press of his fingers, as he continued to toy with the ribbons of her bodice and brush hot touches against her skin.

She jolted back, eyes opening as she ripped free from his arms.

Legend blazed brighter, the bronze light around him making everything glow. He usually looked human, but for an instant he looked painfully immortal as his perfect lips pulled into a frown. "What's wrong?"

"Last night, I found out what your weakness is."

His shoulders stiffened. "What were you told?"

"That if you come across a human who makes you feel love, then you become mortal, and if the feeling lasts too long, then the change becomes permanent. Which makes me think that you don't want to change me to keep me alive, you only want to change me to keep yourself alive."

"No." His answer was unyielding and immediate. "That's not why I want to do this. I want you to be immortal so that you won't die."

"But I don't want your immortality, Legend. I want your love."

He took a step back. She didn't even think he realized he was doing it. "I can't give you that."

"Yes, you can. You just refuse to choose love over immortality."

The light in his eyes went out and the world became a little darker. "Even if that was true, could you blame me?"

"No," Tella said honestly. "But I don't want to be like you. That's why I can't let you make me immortal."

His eyes met hers again. The light was still gone but they shimmered in a way that reminded her of all the magical things he could offer. "You'll feel differently if you let me change you."

"But I don't want to feel differently. I want to feel love in its every form. I used to be so scared of it, but now I think love is another type of magic. It makes everything brighter, it makes people who have it stronger, it breaks rules that aren't supposed to exist, it's infinitely valuable. I can't imagine my life without it. And if you felt any love in your heart, you would understand."

Tella met his darkened eyes.

A flicker of pain fell over his face. But whether it was real or to convince her to go along with what he wanted, Tella couldn't tell. "You'll die, Donatella."

"I already have."

"But you won't come back this time."

"Most people don't, but that's not why you're offering me this. This makes things easier for you. You don't want to love me and lose your immortality."

His mouth parted and closed and parted again, and for a brief moment before he spoke he looked entirely lost. "It's not that I don't want to love you, Tella. I can't love you." His voice was flat and empty and utterly sincere. It didn't just sound as if he was saying this because he was an immortal, but because he truly believed that he was incapable of the feeling. If that was true, if he really thought himself heartless, then maybe he hadn't actually been tempted to love her. Maybe he just wanted to possess her. *I want to keep you.*

"You're not thinking this through." Legend reached for her hand.

A week ago, her heart would have soared because he wanted to touch her. But she forced herself to take another step back. She wasn't tempted by immortality, but she was tempted by him. She couldn't touch him again if she was going to do this. "I don't need to think about it. Sometimes you just know. And I know that I can't imagine spending an eternity with someone who will never love me."

She turned to leave.

"Tella, wait—"

She pressed forward. She didn't even let herself look back. The archway she'd walked through to meet him was gone. A flowering wall had taken its place. The velvety petals felt real against her skin. But she knew it was just an illusion. Almost as soon as she touched them, Legend parted the flowers and hedgy branches to let her through.

The leafy passageway before her was dimmer than she remembered. The fireflies had gone, and a chill had crept into their place. Bumps crawled over the back of her neck. The chill should have felt good after her heated conversation, but the wind sweeping through was fetid and wrong, a dream gone awry.

When she strained to hear, there was no more distant party laughter; any footsteps she picked up were harsh, fleeting.

Something was wrong.

"Tella—" Legend grabbed her hand, appearing by her side.

"Please, just let me go."

"This isn't about us—" He cut off. His grip on her tightened. He winced, face paling as the glow around him faded.

"What's wrong?" Tella asked.

More frantic footsteps echoed in the distance, followed by a series of muffled cries. Leaves poured off the walls of the maze, decaying as they fell to the ground.

"Get out of here," Legend said. "Go to the tower and lock yourself in your room."

"I'm not locking myself in a tower!"

"Then run away. If you ever do anything for me, do this—I think the Fates are here."

Then his lips were on hers. Severe. Quick. Hot. And gone far too soon.

Tella stumbled forward as he let her go. The maze around them was just a series of skeletal branches and rotting leaves. Tella could see right through them.

"Are the Fates doing this?"

"Tella, just go!" Legend roared.

The foul scent in the air grew stronger and sweeter, thick and charnel-sweet, like death, as two shadowy figures appeared on the other side of the hedge.

The blood in Tella's veins froze.

The pale woman wore a jeweled eye patch, and the man had a great gash slicing along his throat as if his head had been severed and put back on his neck. The Murdered King and the Undead Queen.

Her knees buckled and her throat went dry.

Tella grabbed for Legend's hand, to get him to flee with her. But a fresh hedge sprung up between them, cutting her off.

"No!" She banged her fists against the hedge's spindly, prickly, and entirely leafless branches. It was weaker than his earlier illusions, but it was enough to form a barrier between them.

"Prince Dante," the Murdered King said slowly. "I wonder if history will call you Dante the Dead or just forget you altogether after tonight."

"Tragic," cooed the Undead Queen. "Your face would have looked marvelous on a coin."

Before Tella could catch another word, the prickly hedge before her moved. It pressed against her chest, forcing her to stumble back. Faster and faster it shoved against her, herding her farther away from Legend and the Fates.

That bastard! Legend was using his magic to push her away and she was powerless to stop him—or the Fates who'd come for him.

She wanted to turn around, to battle against the wall at her back, and return to Legend. But the magical wall was relentless and she hated to admit there was nothing she could do against the Fates except hope that he was stronger. She'd survived when the Undead Queen and Her Handmaidens had tried to kill her. Legend would survive as well.

He had to.

Ahead of her the palace glowed, moon-bright against the black sky. The only spot on earth that didn't seem to be in pandemonium. The rest of the grounds were still dark; all the lights of the party were now vanquished. But Tella could hear people scrambling to leave the maze as its branches began to crack and crumble. There were still a few occasional giggles and laughs; some people must have thought this was all part of the game.

If it had been Caraval, Tella would have believed the same; she'd have imagined this was Legend's plan. But she'd felt his fear when he'd kissed her and then forced her away.

Tella's feet burned as her slippers crashed against the ground while the hedge continued to shove at her back. It scraped against the earth. She could sense the churning of dirt and hear the crush of its branches and—

The ground beneath Tella shook. She told herself to keep running. But she couldn't hear the hedge anymore. When she slowed she didn't feel it at her back. And when she turned she did not see it.

The hedge, the maze, the butterflies fluttering all over her skirt, everything that had been the party was gone. All that remained were thick spires of smoke, twisting upward.

No! No! No! Tella didn't know if she shouted the words, if she gasped them, or if she just thought them. She knew there was only one reason Legend's magic would suddenly stop.

He was dead.

"No!" This time she definitely shouted the word. Then her legs gave out and she fell to her knees.

THE

MIDDLE

Donatella

Tella could feel the black earth beneath her hands and knees, but she didn't know if it was dry or damp or prickly with grass and twigs. And she didn't know how long she'd stayed there, unable to move. All she knew was that she needed to get up. She needed to keep moving, she needed to keep running, as Legend had begged her to with his last words.

A dry sob shook her chest as she tried to rise.

Legend wasn't dead forever. This wasn't like what had happened to her mother, who Tella would never see again. He would come back to life. But for now, he was gone.

She looked back at the wreckage that minutes ago had been the maze, but he didn't emerge from the smoke.

Bedlam reigned where hours ago there had been magic and butterflies. She could hear the sound of people escaping, clumsy footsteps and heavy breathing, from those not used to running.

Tella struggled to her feet. She knew she needed to run away. Legend had asked her to flee with his last words. But what would happen to his body if she left? What if the Fates had figured out that he was Legend? What if they took his body, so that when he came back to life they could kill him over and over?

Tella ran back toward the melee.

"Leave the city!" she warned anyone she saw. "Get out of here!" She didn't know if there were more than two Fates nearby, but if they'd come to kill Elantine's heir, they weren't afraid of discovery. And they'd likely take over the palace next. Unlike the grounds outside, it was still bright and glowing, untouched by violence. *For now.* When the Fates took over the palace and then the Empire, the fountains would probably be filled with blood.

A rigid hand latched on to Tella's shoulder. "What are you doing?"

She tensed, bracing for a fight, even as she recognized the voice; low and resonant with a lilting accent that was just the tiniest bit shaky: Julian.

It was difficult to see his face in the dark. But the alarming way his fingers dug into her shoulder gave away enough. *He already knew what had happened.*

"We need to go back into the maze to get his body," she said.

"Tella." Julian squeezed her shoulder. "My brother is dead."

"But he'll come back to life . . . right?" She tried to shake off Julian's hand, or maybe she was just shaking.

"He's immortal—he'll come back."

"Why don't you sound more certain about that?"

"Because I'm trying to save your life right now. He made me swear that if anything like this happened to him, I would get you to safety."

Julian released Tella's shoulder, grabbed her arm, and pulled her in the opposite direction of the palace.

"Wait—wait—" Tella panted. "What about Scarlett?"

"She's not here." Julian tugged harder on Tella's hand, forcing her through clouds of smoke. "When she didn't show up to meet me at the maze, I went to find her . . . but she's not at the palace."

"Where is she?"

"With the count."

"But—but—" Tella sputtered. "Scarlett told me she was calling the game off."

"I wish she had," Julian grunted, his words choppy as he urged her to sprint faster. "When I went in her rooms, I found a note from the count asking to see her again today."

"Where does he live?" Tella asked.

"On the outskirts of the city—past the ruins south of the Temple District."

"Then that's where we go," she said.

There was a pause, full of nothing but heavy breathing, where Julian might have argued that he was supposed to get Tella to safety and then he would look for Scarlett on his own. But it seemed his love for her sister outweighed the promise he'd made to Legend, or

Julian knew there was no point in fighting with Tella. This was why Tella had always liked Julian. He never gave up on Scarlett.

They fled swiftly across the darkened city together, but they didn't move faster than the rumors:

"Prince Dante is dead—crushed to death by his maze."

"The former heir came back and murdered Prince Dante."

"Prince Dante was killed by someone in the maze."

"Invaders have taken over the city and beheaded Prince Dante."

Some of the claims were closer to the truth than others, but all of them had one thing in common: Legend was dead.

Her steps faltered, but she didn't stop. If anything, she ran harder. The Fates had won another round. But once Tella found her sister, and Legend came back to life, they'd all visit the Vanished Market. There they'd find a way to destroy the Fallen Star, and then they'd be able to stop the other Fates, as well.

There were holes in her slippers by the time she and Julian passed the edge of the city at dawn. It was a brilliantly bloody sunrise, as if someone had sliced opened the clouds and hazy streams of red had poured out instead of rain. On another morning it might have looked wrong, but on this particular day it felt appropriate that even the sky appeared violent.

A dusty stretch of dry, yellowing grassland rested between the city and the count's estate. The sad bark of a dog was the only sound, save for the tired trudge of Tella's and Julian's footsteps.

Tella tried to catch her breath, now that their pace had slowed.

She inhaled deeply, but the air tasted unclean, like the foulest parts of the city rather than a fresh slice of country. The stench grew stronger and the sad howling of the dog grew louder as they approached the count's estate.

Tella hugged her arms to her chest, and Julian walked closer to her side.

The count's residence looked like the beginning of a fairy tale, before the magic had arrived. The gardens were full of curious, well-tended flowers that appeared to have been planted with care. But the house itself was covered in chipping paint, the windows clean but full of cracks, and the crumbling chimneys appeared to be in severe need of repair. Even the long path they followed to the house was covered in fractures.

"I thought the count's residence was fancier," Tella said. "Scarlett described it as being much nicer."

"I don't think she saw it for what it really was the other day. I think she was too concerned about meeting the count. And it didn't smell this bad." Julian put a hand over his nose and mouth.

Tella did the same, fresh nerves clawing at her stomach. The stench was so putrid she dry-heaved as they reached the front door. It was cracked open, oozing more of the wretched odor.

The dog barked again, long and keening.

Tella halted as the door creaked all the way open and an awful incessant buzzing joined the unseen dog's anguished cries.

She didn't remember entering, but she would regret stepping

inside for the rest of her life. No servants greeted them, or warned them away. There was only the endless howling of the dog, the buzzing of the flies, and Tella's silent prayers.

Do not let my sister be dead.

Do not let my sister be dead.

Because someone was certainly dead. The morbid stench grew worse as she and Julian finally passed the entry and reached the open library.

Tella swayed on her feet as she saw the count's body. Or she thought it was the count's body. He was in the second-floor library, sitting in a great chair behind his desk, and he looked as if the skin had been burned off his body.

The dog beside him howled again and shook its sad face, trying to ward off the maggots and flies from feasting on the count's remains.

Tella tried to look away from the charred corpse; she'd seen enough death that week. She didn't need to look it in the eyes again. She'd never seen a body flayed with fire—and she wished she wasn't seeing it now. But she couldn't turn away from the macabre scene before her. It shouldn't have been possible. If the count had been burned alive, then other parts of his library should have caught fire. But it was as if someone had instructed the flames to only burn his skin.

Tella staggered back a step as something Jacks had said returned to her.

"At least he stabbed her instead of burning her to death with his powers. . . . Fire's the most painful way to die."

"I think I know who did this," Tella said. "I think the Fallen Star was here to find Scarlett."

Julian turned entirely gray. "Why would he want Crimson?"

"Because of our mother. Before he killed her, the Fallen Star said that she'd forced him back inside the cursed Deck of Destiny; he must have been free once before, and our mother imprisoned him again. It probably wasn't enough for him just to kill her—now he's coming after her daughters."

Which would also explain why their apartment had been ransacked.

Tella hoped she was wrong. She couldn't lose her sister the same way she'd lost her mother. But she couldn't imagine who else had done this, or why anyone else would do this. She'd never liked Nicolas, but the fact that he'd clearly been tortured to death made her think that he hadn't given up her sister—or at least not easily.

Scarlett might have managed to get away. All the servants seemed to have escaped so maybe they'd taken her sister with them. Or maybe she'd managed to hide and they just needed to find her.

Julian tried to pull the dog from the room as they went to hunt for Scarlett. But the animal wouldn't leave; it continued to howl and guard its dead master as Tella and Julian scoured every tainted inch of the estate for Scarlett.

"Crimson!" Julian shouted, and Tella would have sworn his eyes were glassy. He wasn't crying, but he was close. "Crimson!"

"Scarlett!" Tella called at the same time, repeating the name until her throat went raw. Her vision dulled around the edges as she combed through closets and cellars and dusty rooms full of cloth-covered furniture. By the time she and Julian completed searching, Tella's legs were shaking, she was covered in damp, and she'd found no signs that Scarlett had even been there.

Julian was a sweaty mess as well. Hair clung to his forehead and his shirt stuck to his chest as they stumbled away from the house and into the empty stables. It was the sole place on the estate that did not reek of dying.

But Tella didn't want to rest there. She didn't want to curl up in the hay and eat the food Julian had stolen from the kitchen. She didn't want to rehash any horrors, or sit in silence while her worst fears came true. She'd already lost her mother and Legend. She couldn't lose her sister.

Her chest went tight, and for a desperate moment Tella wished Jacks was there to take away the pain.

26

Scarlett

Scarlett waited for the world to rock, for the boat to sway and her stomach to roll. But only her stomach met her expectations. It bubbled with queasy unease as she sat up in a feather-soft bed and opened her eyes to find that everything was cream-and-gold columns and carpets and bedding, with delicate hints of pink.

Nothing was purple, her father's signature color. She didn't smell his wretched perfume, or see his hateful face. Yet Scarlett felt far from safe as she slid out of a bed shaped like a crescent moon and covered in gossamer-thin pink sheets.

On clumsy legs, still unsteady from whatever she'd been drugged with, Scarlett made her way between columns, all topped with disembodied heads of baby cherubs with animal eyes. Lovely and wrong. But they were not quite as disturbing as the frescoes of humans with animal parts painted on the ceiling.

Someone had a very twisted sense of decoration.

Her stomach churned as she reached the floor-to-ceiling windows and swiftly pulled back the curtains.

More endless arches and arcades of gold and white. Scarlett wasn't certain where she was, but she wasn't on a boat at the docks or on the ocean. It looked as if she'd traveled back in time to before Valenda's ruins had been ruins.

Scarlett turned and ran, her feet bounding over fluffy cream carpets, to search for a door. The Reverie Key still rested in her pocket; all she needed to find was a lock. But the only thing she found was a veil of pink curtains, barely thicker than the gauzy sheets on her bed.

Scarlett tore them apart and barreled into a sitting room full of more frescoes. But it was the gilded cage that gave her pause. It took up almost half the room. On the other side of the cage was a door. But inside the cage was a young woman in a lavender gown, sitting on a swing like a pet bird.

Scarlett could have darted past her. The captive woman's head was gently bowed and her eyes were closed, as if she'd just rocked herself to sleep. If Scarlett were quiet, she wouldn't even wake her. But she couldn't escape and leave another girl captive.

Scarlett took a cautious step closer.

There were no ill colors swirling around the captive young woman, but Scarlett felt a wave of uncertainty as she approached. There was something very familiar about all of this, but her head was still too muddled from the drugs to untangle what it could be.

The gleaming lock on the cage's golden door was larger than

Scarlett's fist. She reached toward her pocket, wondering if it would open with the Reverie Key, but her dress closed the pocket before her fingers could reach in. At the same exact moment, the captive woman's head shot up, revealing alert lavender eyes the same color as her dress.

"Aren't you precious?" Her voice was scratchy as if she'd not spoken for a long time. "Sadly, you cannot free me, little human. Only his true death will allow me to leave this cage."

"But I can never truly die," said a new voice.

Scarlett spun to her side.

For a moment she thought she was looking at an angel. The broad man before her was dressed in the purest white and surrounded by sparks that made her think the air around him was a breath away from catching fire.

Scarlett swore the gilded cage beside her looked duller now that he stood near it. His olive skin glowed and his thick brown hair had strands of gold that matched his brilliant eyes. He was clearly not human.

"Hello, Scarlett." The man before her curved his mouth slowly. It might have been a convincing smile except for his golden eyes, which twinkled and crinkled at the corners a second too late, as if he needed to remind himself that a smile was supposed to touch his entire face. "You look exactly like your mother. But she would never have paused to free Anissa if she thought she could have escaped. Paradise was ruthless."

He said the word *ruthless* the way someone else might have said the word *beautiful*. His smile even reached his eyes this time, making them glitter like stolen stars; they shined brighter than the sparks around him, which warmed the room like genuine flames. Instantly Scarlett knew exactly who the immortal before her was—the Fallen Star. The Fate who'd murdered her mother in front of Tella.

Scarlett faltered backward, shoulders slamming into the cage. She didn't know what the Fallen Star wanted with her, but she didn't want to find out. She tried to dart past him toward the door.

"That would be a mistake." His hand fell on Scarlett's shoulder, heavy and strong enough to crush her entire arm with one squeeze.

"Gavriel, be a little gentle or you'll break her," said the woman in the cage.

The Fallen Star relaxed his hand but didn't let go. "I don't wish to hurt you. I've brought you to the Menagerie for your protection."

The only thing Scarlett needed protection from was him. But saying that was probably a terrible idea. She tried to focus on what he'd just told her. When she got out of there—because she was going to get out—she wanted to be able to tell the others exactly where she'd been. "Isn't the Menagerie one of the Fated places?"

She hadn't studied the Fated places as much as the Fated immortals, but she recalled the Menagerie was some kind of zoo full of magical chimeras and humans with animal parts, which explained all the disturbing frescoes, and the woman in the cage beside her.

Scarlett wondered if captivity was what he had planned for her as well. Her swirling thoughts couldn't recall much about the Fallen

Star, other than that he'd made all the Fates, and he'd killed her mother. Maybe he also collected women like pets and Scarlett was his next acquisition.

"I think you're still scaring her," chimed the young woman in the cage.

"You don't need to fear me, *auhtara*." His grip on her shoulder relaxed a little more as he used that foreign word again. Scarlett was familiar with languages, but it was like nothing she'd ever heard.

"Why do you keep calling me that?"

His teeth flashed with another attempt at a smile that was everything it wasn't supposed to be. "It's my native tongue, for 'daughter.'"

The ornate room spun around Scarlett. She didn't know if he was trying to frighten or surprise her. She wanted to hope it was a twisted joke. But she doubted this immortal was capable of kidding. He was the monster that other monsters measured themselves against. If what he said was true, Scarlett wasn't entirely sure what that made her, but she didn't even want to know.

She didn't want to believe him.

He had to be deluded.

He had to be wrong.

This had to be a mistake. She already had one murderous, power-hungry father. She didn't deserve another one.

This couldn't be true, even if deep, deep down, a part of Scarlett reminded her how people often commented that Tella looked just like her father, but Scarlett held no resemblance to him. Her mother had also married her father after a whirlwind romance, which

Scarlett had heard servants whispering about a few years back. They said it was only a quick marriage because Paloma had been pregnant—and some of the maids had sworn it wasn't with Marcello Dragna's child.

"This would have worked better if you hadn't kidnapped her first," chided the young woman in the cage. "Poor girl is in shock."

"Quiet, Anissa, or tomorrow you'll wake up in a smaller cage." The Fallen Star turned his attention back to Scarlett. "I can see you're having a hard time believing this, but you must have had some inclination that you're not entirely human. Is there anything you can do that most humans are incapable of?"

"But I am human," Scarlett protested, even as she saw fearful shades of brilliant purple swirling all around her. It was a gift she knew wasn't normal, just like her more recent ability to see the feelings of others. "I'm not a Fate."

"No, you're not a Fate, but as my daughter, you can become one." His inhuman smile widened. She imagined he was trying to be reassuring, but there was nothing remotely comforting about a man who'd just told a captive woman he'd put her in a smaller cage and that he could make Scarlett a monster, too.

"Tell me, *auhtara,* what can you do?"

Scarlett swallowed thickly. She didn't want to answer him. But she knew this was a test, and she didn't want to find out what would happen if she failed. "I've always seen my own emotions in colors," she admitted, "but recently, I've begun to see the feelings of other people as well."

"Can you see any of my emotions?" he asked, voice still mild. Another test, and this time Scarlett didn't know what the correct answer was. She imagined most people wouldn't want her eavesdropping on their emotions. If the father who'd raised her had asked Scarlett this, then the correct answer would have certainly been no. But the Fallen Star was the Fate who'd created all the other Fates. He wouldn't want a daughter without talent.

Scarlett took a calming breath. She never intentionally attempted to see another's emotions, and the Fallen Star was a Fate, not a human. But apparently, she wasn't entirely human, either.

Scarlett stood a little straighter, shoving all her fear and worry and terror aside until she saw glimpses of colors that weren't her own. She'd expected angry reds and wicked purples. But the Fallen Star was made of magnificent golds.

He was pleased, and growing more delighted by the moment. She could see hints of eager green as he watched her use her powers to read him.

"What do you see?" he asked.

"You're happy I'm here, happier than you expected to be . . . and you're proud. I can see copper sparks of it all around you as I'm speaking."

"Excellent." He nodded once and the eager greens around him deepened into a greedier shade. "I knew you'd be talented. There was another Fate with a similar ability. He could control emotions, but the gift never worked on immortals."

"I can only see emotions, I can't control them," Scarlett corrected.

"That's because you haven't had my help." The Fallen Star reached up to pet her head.

Scarlett couldn't help it; she cringed away. If he wanted to kidnap her or put her in a cage, she wasn't strong enough to stop him. But she would never accept affection from him. Maybe it wasn't the smartest way to survive, but not everything was about survival.

The Fallen Star's hand fell away, but to her surprise, he gave her another inhuman smile. "If you'd accepted me too easily, I would have been disappointed. But you will not keep fighting me. You are my only child. When I ascend to the throne, I'll share the entire Meridian Empire with you, if you become what I want you to be."

He waved one massive hand and Scarlett's horror spiked, as sparks in the air exploded into flames that filled the space above their heads and twisted into shining shapes. She saw an image of herself sitting on a throne in a full party dress with a jeweled diadem atop her head and a line of suitors, some on their knees, others with their hands outstretched with elaborate gifts.

"I can make all of your wildest dreams come true once you come into your powers. I can make you a Fate, like me."

Scarlett bit back from saying that taking over the empire with him or becoming a Fate was not one of her dreams, as he waved his hand again and the fiery image shifted.

Scarlett was still sitting in the throne room, but she was now at the Fallen Star's feet, and instead of a diadem resting on her head, there was a cage around it.

"I'll let you choose which future you want. Think about it while

I'm gone. My lovely Lady Prisoner will keep you company, and remind you of what will happen if you try to leave the Menagerie."

He caressed the bars of the gilded cage and Scarlett realized why
this young woman was so familiar. The Lady Prisoner was another
Fate. In Decks of Destiny, her card had a double meaning: sometimes
her picture promised love, but usually it meant sacrifice.

Scarlett couldn't remember what the Lady Prisoner's powers were,
but she hoped it wasn't some form of fortune-telling when the young
woman's eyes shifted from purple to white as she said, "I look forward to watching you transform into what he wants."

Donatella

Tella hoped to find Legend when she finally succumbed to sleep. She didn't care if he was distant from her rejection or still a little dead, she just hoped he was there. Her shredded skyfall-blue skirts dragged over the floors of Idyllwild Castle, picking up bits of abandoned glitter from discarded paper stars, as she searched a ballroom that had no ball.

She knew she was dreaming, but everything felt more like an abandoned memory. Unlike the first night of the last game of Caraval, when Dante had accompanied her here, the ballroom was silent save for the *drip-drop* of a few pathetic party fountains. During the last Caraval they had flowed with deep burgundy wine, but now they barely drizzled a rusty red liquid the color of broken hearts.

Jacks sauntered out of the cage in the center of it in an elegant blur of wrinkled and half-buttoned clothing. Golden hair hung over his eyes, and it shined brighter than anything in the room. He looked untamed and more beautiful than Tella wanted to admit.

His movements were indolent yet graceful as he sliced off a wedge of a skyfall-blue apple, the same exact color as her dress.

Her cheeks felt suddenly flushed as he put the slice of fruit in his mouth and took a wide bite.

"What are you doing here?" she demanded.

"Not having as much fun as I'd hoped." He wandered closer. He smelled especially divine tonight—the scent of apples was paired with a rich spice she couldn't identify. She tried to tell herself she only liked it because when she'd been awake all she could smell was death, but the closer Jacks drew, the more she fought the urge to inhale him. Something was very wrong with this dream.

"That's not what I meant," she said in a huff. "I only gave you permission to enter my dreams for one night."

"And yet you didn't try to keep me out tonight?" His perfect lips toyed with the sharp tip of his blade. "What were you thinking before you slept?"

"Not about you."

"Really?" he taunted. "You weren't wishing I was there to make you feel better?" He continued toying with the knife, but the look in his unearthly eyes softened as his gaze trailed over her untamed curls and down to her ungloved hands, until it landed on the frayed hem of her wrecked ball gown. She almost thought he was concerned, until he said, "You look miserable."

"It's not polite to tell that to a girl," she snapped.

"I didn't come here to be polite, my love." He dropped his knife to the floor with a clatter and stalked closer. "I'm here because you wanted me."

"No, I didn't."

"So, you don't want me to take your pain away?" His eyes were the flawless blue of polished sea glass. "I can make you feel whatever you want when you wake up. All you have to do is ask."

He cupped her cheek with his cool hand and leaned in closer.

She should have pulled away. The word *obsession* returned to her mind. But when Jacks touched her, she couldn't bring herself to worry that this was a horrible idea, or hate the feel of him the way she was supposed to. His cool skin was soothing against her heated cheek, coaxing her to close her eyes, to lean into him, to take what he was offering.

"Doesn't that feel better?" His cold lips were at her ear, brushing against the sensitive skin. "Just say yes and I'll take away everything that hurts. I can make you forget it all. And I can give you things that your dead princeling couldn't."

A shiver shot down Tella's spine and her eyes flashed open. This wasn't what she wanted. Everything that hurt was everything she cared about—Legend, her mother, Scarlett, the Fates taking over the empire.

Tella shook her head and pulled away. She didn't need Jacks to make her feel better. She needed to wake up, she needed to find her sister, and then she needed to go to the Vanished Market to purchase a secret that might tell her how to destroy the Fallen Star. She didn't need to erase her pain; she needed it to propel her into action. Just because it was a negative emotion didn't mean it wasn't a valuable one. "We're not doing this."

Jacks rocked back on his heels and ran his tongue over the tips of his teeth. "You don't want to feel better?"

"No, and I don't want you!"

He laughed, tossing back his golden head and making the sound echo across the abandoned ballroom. "You say that, my love, but a part of you does, or I wouldn't even be here."

Scarlett

S carlett pretended not to be terrified. She pretended she wasn't trapped inside the Fated Menagerie. She pretended that instead of petrified shades of plum, her feelings were peaceful hues of pink that matched the gauzy crescent bed she forced herself to lie on.

She'd wanted to use the Reverie Key the moment the Fallen Star left. But the Lady Prisoner hadn't taken her lavender eyes off of Scarlett. Because of her cage, the Fate couldn't physically stop Scarlett from leaving, but Scarlett didn't want the Lady Prisoner yelling to alert a guard before she could escape. It would be safer to sneak out after the Fate fell asleep.

"Whatever you're planning, you can trust me with it." The Lady Prisoner delicately hopped off her perch and walked to the edge of her cage, watching Scarlett between golden bars. Her smile was far more convincing than the Fallen Star's, but she was a Fate, and although she was imprisoned, she'd seemed pretty loyal to the Fallen Star before he'd left.

Scarlett's *other* father, Marcello, had guards like this, younger guards who he'd told to be friendly to his daughters for the purpose of keeping an extra close eye on them.

"I'm not planning anything," Scarlett said.

"Of course you are," said the Fate.

"Are you telling me this because of your power?" Scarlett still didn't trust the imprisoned Fate, but she was curious about her. She could remember what her card represented, but she still couldn't recall her ability. "When your eyes went white earlier, were you seeing the future?"

"I used to see the future, lovely. Before I was in this cage, I was beloved for my gifts. People feared the other Fates, but they adored me, and they knew they could trust me because I cannot lie. This cage has dimmed my gifts. I now only see small glimpses of things that will come to pass. Occasionally I receive inklings of which choices are best pursued, or left unmade. But the only unfettered *gift* I still have is my inability to lie."

Scarlett watched the Fate skeptically as she began to strum the bars of her cage. The bit about being unable to lie did sound familiar, but it didn't make Scarlett trust her.

"You're still looking at me as if I'm your enemy, but I'm far more trapped than you. Do you know how horrible it is to be kept like a pet?"

No. But Scarlett had a feeling that if she didn't leave soon she'd find out. "Why did he put you in the cage?"

"It wasn't only him; it was another Fate, the Apothic—he can move metals and stones with his mind. The Apothic formed the cage and Gavriel sealed it with his fire to make it impenetrable to anyone except for him. He did the same thing to the Maiden Death, when he had the Apothic place a cage of pearls around her head. Like her, I won't be free until he's truly dead."

Her violet eyes filled with sorrow, but Scarlett could see strands of violent purple swirling around her. She wasn't loyal to the Fallen Star, but that didn't mean she would be loyal to Scarlett. All that mattered to the Lady Prisoner was getting out of her cage.

"Gavriel takes pleasure in passing out punishments. If you're smart, you'll listen to me. Once he takes the Meridian Empire's crown, it will be a dynasty of terror. The only reason he's not sitting on the throne right now is because he loves toying with humans and he wants his subjects to adore him before they come to hate him."

"He won't get away with it," Scarlett said. Legend was not her favorite, but he'd do everything in his power to keep his throne.

"Oh, sweetheart," sighed the Fate. "He's already started to get away with it. While you were sleeping like a distressed damsel, Gavriel sent a few of his loyal Fates to slay the next emperor."

"What?" Scarlett felt all the blood drain from her face. Legend couldn't be dead. Legend was immortal. Immortals weren't supposed to die. But Scarlett knew better than most that Legend could be killed—she'd seen his dead body during the first Caraval. He would come back to life, eventually. But if he was really dead now, then what had happened to Julian and Tella?

When Scarlett had left to find Nicolas, both Tella and Julian had been in the palace. Tella knew when to run. But Julian liked to fight— he was Legend's brother; he was a part of his games and now his court. And unlike Legend, Julian was mortal. If he died outside of Caraval, he wouldn't come back to life.

Scarlett's mouth went suddenly dry. She really had to get out of there and find Julian and her sister.

"I'm glad to see you're finally believing something I said. The Murdered King and the Undead Queen are currently in charge. Your history books say they were our rulers, but they answer to Gavriel. He's given them orders to make everyone as miserable as possible until the entire city is terrified. That's when Gavriel will come in like a savior and make his claim for the throne. By then people will be eager to believe whatever lies he tells. Unless you decide to stop him."

The Lady Prisoner gripped the bars of her cage as she peered across the room at Scarlett.

"You must become what he wants most. Only you have the power to defeat him." The Fate's eyes flickered from lavender to milky white. Then her shoulders slumped. She released the bars, returned to her perch, closed her eyes, and went back to sleep, as if she'd not just told Scarlett the world was ending and it was her job to save it.

But the only people Scarlett could think about saving just then were Tella and Julian. She needed to escape and make sure they were safe.

She sat on the low bed, legs bouncing up and down, no longer able to pretend she wasn't terrified. Anissa appeared to be asleep, but Scarlett waited until her breathing sounded more like a series of gentle snores.

Scarlett cautiously rose and took a step.

The Fate continued with her snores.

Scarlett took another step.

And another.

And another. And then, without meaning to, she was running toward the main doors and shoving the Reverie Key inside the lock.

Julian. Julian. Julian.

Thinking Julian's name as she turned the key was the fastest decision she'd ever made. If he was alive she needed—

Her thought was cut short as she stepped through the door and found herself standing beneath a rickety wooden loft, staring at a sea of straw and hay, with one tired and beautiful boy in the center of it all.

His jacket was gone, his shirtsleeves were rolled up, his pants were ripped, and her heart leaped into her throat the instant she saw him.

Julian's amber eyes flared at the sight of her, and probably at the sight of her dress, which had transformed into a glittering ball gown, with a full skirt covered in rubies. It was difficult to run in, but it didn't stop Scarlett from flinging forward and throwing her arms around him.

He smelled like dirt and tears and perfection. And she decided then that she was never, ever letting go of him. She wished there was a way to tether her heart to his, so that even when they were apart they would still be attached. There were things in this world to be truly afraid of, but loving Julian was not one of them. "I'm so glad you're alive! When I heard what happened to Legend, I was terrified that you'd been hurt as well."

"I'm fine. I'm fine." Julian held her tighter, as if he never wanted to let go either. "I've just been worried about you. How did you get here?"

"I used the key." Scarlett pulled away, just enough to see his eyes. "I had to find you."

Before Julian could respond, she leaned back in and kissed him with everything she had.

As soon as Scarlett's lips found his, his fingers knotted in her hair, and his tongue swept into her mouth, taking over every inch of it.

He was usually sweet when he kissed, all worshipping lips and gently exploring hands. But there was nothing sweet about this kiss. It was desperate and devouring. A kiss with teeth and claws, as if they needed to hold on to each other with more than just their hands. The back of her dress vanished, and then Julian's hands were there, branding her bare skin.

She knew there were other important things that probably needed to be discussed, but nothing felt more critical than this. If the last few days had proved anything, it was how painfully quick the world could tilt and shift. People died. People were taken. People turned out to be far different from how Scarlett imagined they'd be.

But Scarlett knew who Julian was. He was flawed and imperfect, rash and impulsive. But he was also passionate and loyal and loving—and he was who she wanted. His hand was the hand that she wanted to hold. His voice was the sound she wanted to hear, and his smile wasn't just something she wanted to see; she wanted to be the reason for it.

He'd never be perfect; he'd told her that. But she didn't want perfect—she only wanted him. Her hands went to the buttons of his shirt.

"Hold on, Crimson—" Julian gently grabbed at her wrists. "As much as I'm enjoying this, we need to pause."

He carefully removed her hands from his shirt. There was a flash of red on his arm as he moved, where his bandage had been. It was gone now, and in its place, on the underside of his arm, was a tattooed star filled in with a strong shade of red ink.

Tears instantly pricked at the corners of her eyes. "It's scarlet," she gasped.

Julian gave her a timid smile. "It's actually crimson."

"But—but—" She stammered over what to say. He'd done this when they hadn't even been speaking and he had no assurance they'd be together.

"I didn't want to wait," he said, easily reading her thoughts on her face. "I knew that if I came back and things didn't work out, I'd regret losing you, but I'd never regret having a reminder of you."

"I love you, Julian."

His smile could have saved the world. "Thank the dead saints—

I've been waiting to hear you say that." His mouth crashed against hers, consuming her once again.

"I should have told you sooner," she said, speaking the words in between kisses, unable to hold the rest back. "I should have told you the minute we left Nicolas's estate and I realized the game I'd made up was a mistake. I choose you, Julian, and I promise I will always choose you, and I will always love you. I will love you with every bone in my body, so that even after my heart stops beating, a part of me will remain to forever love you."

Julian kissed her again, sweeter this time, lips attentive and soft as he whispered words against her lips. "I've loved you since that night you showed up on the beach back on Trisda, thinking you could bribe me to run away without you. I could see how terrified you were when I showed up but you didn't back down."

"And then you kidnapped me."

His grin turned wolfish. "That was your sister. But I have been trying to steal you ever since." His hands kneaded her lower back as he pulled her close for another kiss.

But Scarlett startled at a noise from above.

Abruptly she looked up to see Tella staring down from the hay-loft. She looked as if she'd just woken up from a very unsatisfying sleep. Her hair was full of hay, her eyes were red, and her lips were turned down.

29

Scarlett

Tella looked the way Scarlett felt right after she'd been taken by the Fallen Star. Exhausted and broken and not entirely certain what to do next.

"Scar," Tella said, her voice rough from waking up. The uneven sound of her scrambling feet followed as she raced down the ladder from the loft. Before she reached the bottom rung, she jumped forward and tossed her arms around Scarlett. "I'm so glad you're all right."

"Nothing is going to happen to me." Scarlett squeezed her sister back. "I'm sorry I didn't tell you where I was going. Meeting Nicolas was a mistake."

The barn fell silent. All Scarlett could hear was the crackle of hay beneath Tella and Julian as they exchanged troubled looks.

"What happened?"

Tella released her sister as Julian pulled at the back of his neck.

"What happened?" Scarlett repeated.

"Nicolas is dead," Tella said. "We think he was murdered by the Fallen Star."

If Scarlett had been capable of feeling more emotion, her legs might have buckled, or she might have felt tears build behind her eyes for the man she'd once intended to marry. But for a heartbeat, the only colors she could see were black and white, as if her emotions were shutting off so that they didn't consume her.

She'd never imagined her game would have ended this way.

"How do you know it was the Fallen Star?" Scarlett asked.

"Because of the way he was killed," Julian answered, looking down. "He was burned."

"Poor Nicolas." Scarlett hugged her arms to her chest, wishing she could go back in time, wishing she'd forgiven Julian sooner and never rekindled things with Nicolas. The Fallen Star had undoubtedly come here looking to find her, and Nicolas had paid the price.

"How did you get away?" Tella asked. "Where have you been?"

It was tempting to make up a lie. After finally confessing her feelings to Julian, Scarlett didn't want Julian to view her differently. And Tella looked so fragile already. Scarlett imagined a feather could have knocked her over; it might break her to learn the Fate who killed their mother was Scarlett's birth father. But it was too dangerous of a secret to keep.

Scarlett started with the least shocking information, by telling Tella about the Reverie Key she'd been given, and how she could use it to escape anywhere. Tella perked up with a bit of awe and a hint of jealousy, which was better than fragility and fear. But Scarlett doubted her sister would have the same response to this next revelation. Scarlett still wasn't sure how she felt about it, but she knew she couldn't keep it to herself.

She took a deep breath. "It's a good thing I had the key, because I didn't actually get away. I was abducted by the Fallen Star. Tella, you were right about why the Fallen Star came here. But he wasn't looking for both of us, just me. He's my father."

Scarlett half expected the ground to shake or the rickety roof to collapse at her words.

Tella's face went bone-white, but her expression turned fierce and her hand felt warm and solid as she took Scarlett's and squeezed tight. "You're the same as you've always been, we just know more about you now. But it doesn't change you—not unless you let it. And this news doesn't change *us,* either. Even if we didn't share any blood at all, I would still call you my sister and I would battle anyone who tried to say it wasn't true. You are my family, Scarlett. Who your birth father is doesn't change that."

"I don't see you differently either." Julian wrapped an arm around Scarlett. But when he spoke again, his voice was tentative. "Does this make you a Fate?"

"No," Tella said immediately. "The witch who helped the Fallen Star create the Fates said that the Fates were made, not born. And Scarlett could never be a Fate—Fates can't love. If an immortal loves, it makes them human, and we both know how much Scarlett loves."

"Tella's right, I'm not a Fate," Scarlett said. But when she tried to add a smile to her words, her voice wobbled as she thought about the Fallen Star's threat to turn her into one. She wasn't with him now. But her powers had been growing on their own—what if she was already on her way to becoming a Fate?

Julian's arm tightened around her. "It's all right, Crimson, you're safe now. We won't let him find you."

"That's not what I'm worried about," Scarlett confessed. "The Fallen Star said he wanted to cultivate my powers and turn me into a Fate."

Julian stiffened beside her.

"You don't have to worry, he doesn't have you anymore," Tella said.

"What if it happens without him? I've always seen my emotions in colors. But lately I've been seeing the feelings of other people as well."

"Like our feelings?" Julian asked.

Scarlett nodded. "At first it was just glimpses. But I can feel the ability becoming more powerful—"

She cut off at the sound of a bark, near, and loud enough to draw everyone's attention to the mouth of the barn, where Nicolas's dog, Timber, barked again, more urgently this time.

Donatella

Tella loved dogs. Back on Trisda she'd even gone so far as to steal a puppy once. She'd cleverly named him Prince Tuckleberry the Dog. But after her father found her, Tella had never seen Prince Tuckleberry again. She'd spent such a short time with the animal that Tella had a limited understanding of the way dogs communicated. But clearly Nicolas's pet was trying to tell them something.

The massive black dog barked. Then he turned his great head toward the outside, as if he wanted the three of them to follow.

"Do you think he's telling us Nicolas is somehow still alive?" Scarlett asked.

"No," Tella answered. But maybe someone else was—*like Legend.*

The trio started toward the cracked barn doors and out into the late afternoon. Julian clutched Scarlett's hand as if he never planned to let her out of his sight. Tella hoped he didn't. Now that Scarlett was back, Tella needed to go to the Vanished Market and do whatever it took to purchase a secret that would show her how to destroy the Fallen Star—before he could get his horrible hands on her sister and turn her into a Fate.

Tella wanted to believe it wasn't even possible. But it should have been impossible that a Fate was actually Scarlett's father—or that Scarlett now had the ability to see other people's feelings. Not that it changed anything. Tella meant what she'd said—even if they didn't share a drop of blood, Scarlett would still be her sister.

An early-evening breeze cut through the air as Tella continued to follow Timber's lumbering steps to the back of the estate. She didn't feel the least bit rested. She felt as worn as the slippers on her feet. But her heart kicked out extra beats as Timber led them to a cobbled path so overgrown with purpling brambleberry bushes that she and Julian hadn't noticed it during their initial exploration of the grounds.

The dog halted and barked until the trio worked to part the prickly plants.

As soon as there was enough space to run through, the animal raced ahead.

The air turned acrid as Tella followed. Her nose wrinkled at the scent of blood and sweat and embarrassment. Suddenly she hoped Legend wasn't on the other side. The stench wasn't nearly as foul as Nicolas's house had been, but Tella felt a sense of building horror as an aged amphitheater came into view. She saw the steps first; their stones were almost blue in the fading light, the color of cold hands and blood veins under skin. There weren't many of them. The theater was small, the sort built for family plays or bits of light entertainment. But there was nothing entertaining about the forced masquerade taking place on the center of the stage.

The people were dressed in servants' clothes, and wearing horrible half-masks that came in sour shades of plum, cherry, blueberry, lemon, and orange. The colors made Tella think of rotted confetti that refused to fall as the servants moved about the stage, their arms and legs strung up with rope that turned them into human marionettes.

Tella cursed.

Scarlett gasped.

Julian looked as if the food he'd eaten in the barn had risen up to scald his throat.

No one appeared to be pulling the servants' strings. The cords all moved by magic, bobbing them about the stage in a forced dance full of disturbing bows and curtsies.

Tella's eyes latched on to the youngest forced participant, a boy with ringlets as pretty as a doll's and a face stained with dried tears.

"No wonder we didn't find any servants," said Julian.

"How long do you think they've been like this?" Scarlett asked.

No one knew how to answer her. If the servants had been strung up when the count had been killed, it must have been at least a full day. Most of them didn't even appear to be conscious; their heads stayed bowed as their bodies were jerked about the stage.

Tella raced toward it, hoping it wasn't too late to save them. "This looks like Jester Mad. He has the ability to animate objects. He must have tied them all up and then used his magic on the ropes to keep them moving."

"How do we undo it?" Scarlett asked. "When the Poisoner petrified that family, he left a note."

But no one found a note on the stage.

"I think we just need to cut the cords, or untie them," said Julian. Which proved easier said than done.

The poor servants' arms and limbs moved faster with each attempt to set them free. Julian was the only one with a blade; he gave it to Scarlett. But none of them had an easy time of things. They all had to jump back more than once to avoid being kicked in the stomach or punched in the face as they worked to undo the servants' bonds. Thankfully Nicolas didn't employ too large of a staff.

There were only half a dozen of them. Their hearts were still beating, but barely. None of them could stand on their own legs very long once they were freed.

"The master has infection remedies for the wounds in his greenhouse," muttered an older man as he ripped a rotted blueberry mask from his face. Tella imagined he was the butler. His eyes were the saddest of the lot, as he looked over his fellow servants all slumped across the stage.

Julian found the remedies while Tella fetched water, and Scarlett procured bandages from a small closet for the servants' raw wrists and ankles. The entire ordeal was terribly somber. Neither Scarlett, Julian, nor Tella told any of the servants what had happened to Nicolas, and none of them asked, making Tella suspect that they must have already known. Or they'd experienced enough terror and they didn't want to know.

There were lots of murmured thanks, but no one met her eyes, as if they were ashamed of what had been done to them. Only the boy with the ringlets looked at Tella directly. He even managed a crooked smile, as if she were some sort of hero, which she wasn't, not at all. She was part of the reason all of this had happened. But in that moment, she vowed that she would make up for the part she'd played in freeing the Fates. "I'll find who did this to you, and make sure he never hurts anyone again."

"He wore a mask," offered the boy. "But it wasn't like this." The child kicked at the scrap of cherry fabric that had been tied to his face. "His was shiny, like porcelain, and one side was baring teeth while the other side winked and stuck out half a tongue."

"Jester Mad," said Tella. "He's a Fate."

Several of the adults suddenly looked her way as she spoke; at least one appeared to think she shouldn't be saying any of this to the little boy. But after what they'd just experienced, none of them contradicted her.

Tella didn't go into the history of the Fates, or how they'd been freed from a Deck of Destiny, but she said enough so that once the servants and the boy recovered, they could warn others about the danger Valenda was now in.

It felt like an insignificant effort, but hopefully it would save a few other people from being turned into human toys, or from being murdered—like her mother, and Legend.

Tella's eyes scanned the dusky horizon, as if Legend finally might appear on it, shining brighter than the stars that were beginning to sneak out. She kept searching for signs of his return after all the servants were fed and bandaged and helped back to their quarters in the rear of the estate, which didn't possess any of the rot that had clung to the count's library.

Tella was ready to follow the servants inside and wash up. But Scarlett lingered outside the door on an overgrown path covered in peculiar faisies.

"Do you want to come inside with me to wash up?" Tella asked.

The air was still, but Scarlett's skirts rustled around her ankles. Tella hadn't noticed when the gown had shifted colors. Earlier, it had been a brilliant ball-gown red. Now it was mourning-black.

"I'm sorry about Nicolas," Tella said. "He didn't deserve to die like that."

"No, he didn't. I should never have tried to find him. Then he'd still be alive." Scarlett's eyes glistened with tears as she looked up at Tella. "We can't let the Fallen Star do this to anyone else."

"We won't." Tella reached out to take her sister's hand.

But Scarlett stepped back, a worried line between her brows. "I'm sorry, Tella—I thought I could stay here with you and Julian, but I need to return to the Fallen Star."

"What? No!" Tella's voice was joined by Julian as he emerged from the servants' quarters. "You can't."

Julian must have just cleaned up. His dark hair dripped water all over the overgrown path as Scarlett stepped closer to the estate and away from the servants' open windows.

"I'm sorry," Scarlett said. "But I have to do this. I think I might be the key to defeating the Fates."

"Absolutely not!" Julian bellowed while Tella yelled, "Have you lost your mind? He killed our mother and threatened to turn you into a Fate. You can't go back to him!"

"I don't want to go back," Scarlett said. "But I knew I had to as soon as I saw those servants. If they'd been left much longer, they wouldn't have survived."

"But how will your going back do anything to help other people like them?" Tella argued. She wanted the same thing as her sister. She wanted to find a way to kill the Fallen Star and protect everyone from the terror of him and his Fates. But this was *not* the way to do it. "The Vanished Market is one of the Fated places," she said. "There are sisters there who sell secrets, and I think they might have one that will tell us how to kill the Fallen Star."

"What if they don't?" Scarlett argued.

"Then we'll find another way," Julian cut in.

"I think this is the other way," Scarlett said. "The Fallen Star wants me to master my powers, and I think that might be the key to stopping him. There was another Fate there, the Lady Prisoner. She told me that to defeat the Fallen Star, I needed to become what he wanted."

"Of course she'd say that," Tella spat. "The Lady Prisoner is a Fate."

"He has her locked in a cage; she can't get out unless he dies. And even if she is trying to manipulate me, it doesn't mean she's wrong. What she told me makes sense. Tella, you said that if an immortal loves, they become human. If I conquer my powers, I could make him love. I could turn him human and then we could defeat him."

"Or you could conquer your powers and turn into a Fate," Tella said.

"And love doesn't work that way," Julian added. "Magic can do a lot of things, but I don't think you can make someone love with it. This is too dangerous."

"I'm not asking either of you to *let* me do this. It's my choice, not yours. So I'm only asking you not to stop me. Unless we find another way to destroy him, I'm the only one who can do this, and I *want* to do this. Tella, you once told me there's more to life than staying safe—"

"I was talking about having fun, not moving in with murderers!"

"Well, I don't think any one of us will be having fun if the Fallen Star takes over the empire. And we both know you'd do the same thing."

Scarlett enclosed her sister in another hug. She gave incredible hugs. She knew exactly how tight to hold, when to stay silent, and when to let go. But no matter when she let go of this hug, it would be too soon.

Tella held on tighter. She wanted to keep arguing. If she kept fighting, if she told Scarlett how terrified she was, if she went into details about Nicolas's gruesome death and reminded her of the way the Fallen Star had killed their mother, Tella knew she could convince her to stay. Tella wanted to do that so much. But she'd just vowed to do whatever it took to defeat the Fallen Star, and she meant it. She just hadn't thought it would take her sister.

She sagged against Scarlett as the sky finished darkening into a rippling black night. "Are you sure you don't want to be selfish right now and just think about saving yourself?"

"Of course I want to do that. But I need to do this—for me, for you, for Julian, and for all the servants we just helped, who don't have a chance at doing what I can. I can't do nothing when I have the ability to do something. And I have the Reverie Key; if it gets too dangerous, I'll escape."

"Keys can be stolen," Tella murmured.

"I'll be cautious." Scarlett hugged her sister tighter, until Tella finally pulled away. She hadn't wanted to. But if Scarlett was going to go back to the Fallen Star she needed to do it soon, before anyone noticed her absence. Scarlett probably wanted a proper good-bye with Julian as well.

And by proper, Tella imagined it would be the sort of good-bye that the prying eyes of a sister weren't meant to witness.

Scarlett

As Tella went into the guest quarters and tried to wash off all the dirt and sorrow and lingering traces of guilt from her person, Scarlett stood under a wedge of moonlight, preparing for another good-bye that she didn't want to have.

Julian appeared to feel the same way. His brow furrowed, his lips were pressed tightly together, and when he wrapped his arms around Scarlett, there was nothing soft or tender in his touch. "I know you said this isn't my choice, but you can't tell me that you've chosen me and then give me absolutely no say in your life."

"Is this your way of asking me again not to go?"

"No." He held her closer, tucking her head to his chest. "In the future—because there *will* be a future for us—I just hope you can talk to me about things like this rather than telling me you've already made up your mind."

"All right," Scarlett conceded. "But I hope you do the same?"

"I wouldn't ask it of you if I wasn't planning on that." Julian's fingers clutched her waist, as if he could still find a way that didn't involve letting her go.

Scarlett wished he could. She really didn't want to go back to the Fallen Star. But in that moment, she was more worried about Julian. Like Tella, he was impulsive and ruled by his emotions, which Scarlett could see were gray as storm clouds and full of worry.

"What if I try to slip you letters every few days? I don't think it will be safe to visit again." And she didn't think it would be safe to send him messages either, but she worried that if she couldn't find a way to assure him she was all right, he would come after her eventually and put himself in danger. "I can open a door with the Reverie Key to send you notes to let you know I'm all right."

"I still don't like it," Julian said.

"If you did, my feelings would probably be injured."

He pressed a kiss to her forehead, and for a moment his lips stayed there. "Be careful, Crimson."

"I'm always careful."

"I don't know . . ." He pulled away just enough for her to see his mouth twitch at the corner. "A careful girl wouldn't say she loved me."

"You're wrong. I don't think my heart could be safer than in your hands." But even as she said it, her heart felt heavy.

Julian's mouth was still forming half a smile, but his eyes were expressing something else. Scarlett always loved his eyes—they were brown and warm and full of all the emotion that drove him. Julian wasn't always honest, but his eyes were, and right then he was look-ing at her as if he was afraid the next time he saw her she wouldn't be the same.

"I'm going to come back to you," she promised.

"That's not the only thing I'm worried about." His voice was hoarse. "I've spent most of my life around magic—my brother's magic has brought me back to life more times than I can count. I've tried to walk away, but magic like that is difficult to leave. I know right now you think that if you can conquer your powers, you can control the Fallen Star, but your magic might end up controlling you instead."

His eyes left hers to glance over her enchanted dress before land-ing on the Fated key in her hand. It shimmered silver-bright in the dusky light.

She hadn't even realized she'd already taken it from her pocket. Relying on the key was becoming a habit, just like wearing her en-chanted dress. But she didn't want to depend on it, she only wanted to master it enough so that she could make the Fallen Star love her and turn him into a mortal. Then she'd be content to never use it again.

"You don't have to worry about me." Scarlett lifted her head and quickly gave Julian another kiss, wishing she could say more, but knowing it was past the time to return.

When she'd first used the key, she hadn't planned on going back, so she'd not thought about how much time was passing. She hoped the Fallen Star wouldn't pay another visit so soon. She also worried about the Lady Prisoner waking up.

After turning the Reverie Key, Scarlett kept her steps light. But once she entered her room in the Menagerie, she knew things were not as she'd left them.

The Lady Prisoner was awake, swinging silently on her perch as her lavender skirts brushed the polished floor of her gilded cage. "If you're going to sneak out, you shouldn't leave for so long. And don't look so surprised; did you really think I didn't know?" She affected a soft snore.

"Why pretend?" Scarlett asked.

"Because I knew you wouldn't leave if you thought I was awake. But you need to be wiser." Her voice turned whisper-soft and her inhuman eyes shifted from purple to white, as they had earlier that night. "Leaving here for hours at a time will get you caught with that key far sooner than you're supposed to be."

Donatella

A full day had come and gone and Legend was still dead. He needed to come back to life. Legends weren't supposed to die, and Tella wasn't done with him yet.

"How long does it usually take him to return to life?" she'd asked Julian during their initial journey to the count's estate.

"It's usually shortly after sunrise, always less than a day," Julian had answered. It had been difficult to get him to say much more. Tella sensed there was magic at play that kept him from revealing too many secrets. He did confess that Legend had a connection to all his performers—Julian would sense it when Legend was alive again—and if Legend wanted to find Julian, he'd easily be able to do so. But Legend hadn't appeared and Julian still hadn't sensed him.

Tella didn't know what time it was now, only that it felt like the darkest part of the night as she and Julian exited the count's estate to head to the Vanished Market.

Jacks had said the Vanished Market could be summoned by going to a set of ruins to the west of the Temple District. Since Nicolas lived outside the city, the trek was several miles. Julian was silent for much of it. The type of silent that made Tella think he planned to hold his breath the entire time Scarlett was away.

Tella could have done the same thing. She was all for making mistakes and doing better next time. But Tella feared that if Scarlett took one wrong step, there might not be a next time.

Tella sent a prayer up to the saints—even the ones she didn't like that much. She added a prayer for Legend's safe return as well, but she knew it wasn't up to the saints.

Legend had only one weakness that could allow him to be truly killed: love.

She'd been trying not to think about it. She didn't want to remember the way she'd practically begged him to love her just before he'd been killed.

That night she hadn't fully believed him when he'd said he wasn't capable of loving her. She'd believed he was just afraid of it because he didn't want to sacrifice his immortality and become human. And now she understood why.

She told herself to stop worrying. This was Legend, and he was ruthless when it came to magic and immortality. He would never let himself die for love. But Tella still found herself trying to remember the way he'd kissed her the night of the maze. Had he only felt lust, desire, and obsession that night? Or had his kiss been fueled by love? There'd been a moment during the maze when she'd thought the words *I want to keep you* had sounded possessive instead of romantic. But now, she found herself hoping he'd only felt the feelings she'd found so hurtful that evening.

"We're almost there," Julian said.

Tella could now see a vague outline in the distance. In the dark it was hard to tell the difference between stones and shadows, but it looked as if the ruins ahead of them contained a road, lined in fossilized trees, with crumbling archways at either end and a few frighteningly lifelike statues, which Tella desperately hoped weren't petrified humans.

At least there weren't any Fates around.

Tella halted just before they reached the edge of the ruins in a perfect patch of pale white moonlight.

"Am I foolish?" she asked.

Julian stopped and looked down at her. "Depends on what you're referring to. If you're talking about the fact that you're planning to make a blood sacrifice to visit one of the Fated places based on the words of another Fate, then no, because I'm here and I'm not a fool. But if you're talking about anything involving my brother, you might be."

"Thank you for putting that so gently," Tella said.

Julian gave her a one-shoulder shrug. "I'm just trying to be honest. When I lie it gets me in trouble with your sister."

"I don't want you to lie. I just wish you had something true to say that I wanted to hear."

He rubbed a hand across his jaw. The combination of moonlight and shadows made him look a little bit like his brother, a little sharper, a little harsher. But even in the dim, Julian's gaze was softer and kinder than Legend's ever was.

"If you want me to tell you that my brother will love you someday, I can't. I've known him my entire life. I'm one of the few people who knew him before he became Legend, and he's never loved anyone. But he has other good qualities. He doesn't give up or quit, and if you matter to him, he'll make you feel more important than anyone in the world, and . . ." He trailed off, as if he wanted to stop, but then added reluctantly, "I do think you matter to him."

But was that enough?

"Now, come on," Julian said gruffly. "If Legend were to come back right now, he might kill me for letting you stand in the road so exposed."

"Wait." Tella jumped in front of Julian before he could continue into the ruins.

"I just have one more question. He asked me to become an immortal."

"That's not a question, Tella."

"I don't know what to do." Tella thought she'd known. She'd

wanted Legend's love, but his death had made her realize she could never ask for his love again.

"That's still not a question," Julian said. "Even if it was, that's a choice I wouldn't want to make for anyone." He started to walk past her, but then he stopped and turned around. "If you do say yes, make absolutely sure it's what you want. There's no going back from becoming an immortal."

"Unless I fall in love."

Julian shook his head. "Don't count on that happening. Immortals can't fall in love with each other, and very few humans tempt them to love. No matter what my brother's done, I've never stopped loving him, but he's never loved me back." Julian's voice was perfectly even, as if it didn't really hurt, but Tella knew it had to destroy him. Legend was his brother. She couldn't imagine how devastating it would feel if her sister didn't love her.

But Tella sensed Julian didn't want her pity. He turned around almost as soon as he finished and walked toward the ruins with a quickness to his steps that made it clear he didn't want her to catch up right away.

When he did slow down, they searched the ruins together in silence. He'd said all there was to say, and even without Fates lurking nearby, they knew they needed to be discreet. They didn't use torches to seek the hourglass symbol, which Tella feared they would never find. Julian claimed to have perfect night vision, but despite what he'd said about not lying earlier, she was doubtful of this claim.

"Found it!" he said, smug and too loudly.

The hourglass was no bigger than a palm, hidden inside of a dilapidated stone arch, and gleaming as if lit by magic. It gave just enough illumination for Tella to see that spikes jutted out from the top of it, as if begging for the blood Tella needed to use in order to summon the market.

"Are you sure you still want to go in alone?" Julian asked.

"Every hour inside is a day that passes out here," she reminded him. "If for any reason Scar tries to use her key to find you, it's not safe for her inside the market. She could get caught by the Fallen Star if she takes too long to return to the Menagerie."

"What if she looks for you instead?"

"Now that's sweet of you," Tella said. "But I think we both know that she won't come looking for me with the key."

Tella had only watched from the hayloft when Scarlett had first returned, so she'd not heard all that had been said between Scarlett and Julian, but she'd seen the way Scarlett had looked at him. It was the look some people lived their whole lives waiting for, and others lived their whole lives without receiving. It was the look that Tella had kept hoping she'd see from Legend.

"I'll always be her sister, you can't steal that role from me. But I think you're her first love now, and you should be. If you kept choosing your brother over my sister, I wouldn't think you deserved her. All that I ask is that you don't muck it up. Don't just love her back, Julian, fight for her every day."

"I intend to."

With that Tella pressed her fingers into one of the spikes at the top of the hourglass and let her blood drop onto the etched stone.

Ethereal light poured from the archway. Suddenly, Tella saw an old, crooked road lined with foreign trees on the verge of losing all their brilliant red leaves. Between the trees, tents spread out like colorful bird wings, all littered with bits of nature and wear. These were not the magical tents that Tella had seen during the first Caraval. Legend's tents were perfect stretches of smooth silk, while these were covered in tattered brocades and lined in weatherworn tassels. Yet there was still something unearthly about them. Just as Tella turned her head to nod good-bye to Julian, she swore the tents all shifted, and for a moment the wears and tears disappeared and they looked even more dazzling than the tents of Caraval.

Tella boldly stepped through the arch and into the Vanished Market.

It felt like entering an illustrated history book. Women wore bell-sleeved dresses with dropped waists and low-slung belts made of heavy embroidery, while the men wore homespun shirts that laced up in the front, and loose pants tucked into wide-brimmed boots.

Between the tents, children dressed in similar clothes pretended to fight with wooden swords, or sat braiding wreaths out of flowers.

"Greetings! Greetings! Greetings! The Vanished Market is at your service. You might not walk away with what you want, but we'll give you what you need!" hollered a man dressed like a herald, as Tella ventured farther in.

Clearly they were used to visitors from other times. None of them seemed to care that the calf-length dress and worn leather boots she'd borrowed from a servant did not fit in. If anything, it seemed to excite everyone.

"Hello, sweeting, would you like something to brighten up your ashen complexion and bring your beloved back?" A woman wearing a thin gold circlet around her brow held out an amulet full of blushing pink liquid.

"What about some fresh roasted seaweeds?" another vendor called. "They heal broken hearts and noses."

"She doesn't want your rotted weeds. They don't cure anything! What the young lady really needs is this." The merchant across from him, a heavily wrinkled man with several missing teeth, thrust out an elaborate beaded headdress as broad as a parasol, with streaming veils as thin as spiderwebs. "If you are not careful, milady, soon your skin will be as lined as mine."

"Don't tell the girl that. She's beautiful!" cried a dark-skinned woman in an ivory wimple. Her shop was the most crowded of the bunch. There weren't even tables inside, just glistening piles of the peculiar. "Here, peer into my mirror, child." The woman shoved her arm in front of Tella.

"I'm not—" Tella broke off as she caught a clear gaze of the mirror. Its edges were covered in thick swirls of molten gold, just like the Aracle—a Fated object that Tella had relied upon a little too much when it had been trapped inside of a card.

Tella didn't know if it was the actual Aracle now free from the cards, but she quickly averted her eyes and took a rapid step back, before it could show any ill images of the future.

"In the correct hands, it will reveal more than your reflection," the woman cooed.

"I'm not interested! I like my reflection as it is." Tella continued to stumble away. After that she tried her best not to be distracted as merchants attempted to sell her brushes that would ensure she'd never lose her hair, drops that would turn her eyes any color she wished, and a disturbing dessert called hummingbird pie.

Every vendor was friendly and a little too eager, as if Tella were the first guest in centuries, which might have been the case, since the Vanished Market had been trapped in a cursed Deck of Destiny, too.

"I have shoes that will keep you from ever getting lost. They're yours if you trade me all of your pretty locks of hair." This enthusiastic vendor already had a heavy pair of shears in his hands.

Tella was certain he'd have chopped off all her hair without any permission if she'd not quickly darted into the next tent. It was emptier than the others, with nothing but a pair of turquoise-and-peach-striped curtains that fell from the fabric roof to the dirt floor.

A strikingly beautiful girl, about Tella's age, with flawless skin and lovely cobalt eyes the same color as her hair, sat in front of the curtains on a tall stool. She greeted Tella with an incandescent smile, but Tella swore that paintings had more depth in their eyes. Unlike the other vendors, this girl didn't offer to sell anything. She just kicked her legs back and forth like a young child.

Tella almost turned to leave, when another woman slowly shuffled forward from in between the curtains. This one was much older, with wrinkled skin and dull blue hair that looked like a washed-out version of the young girl's. They had the same cobalt eyes as well, but while the younger girl's were vacant, this crone's eyes were sharp and shrewd.

Tella felt as if she were looking at two different versions of the same person. One had lost her youth while the other had lost her mind.

"Are the two of you sisters?" Tella hazarded.

"We're twins," replied the older one.

"How?" Tella blurted. Not that it mattered. All she should have cared about was that this was the place she was looking for. But something about these *twins* filled her stomach with lead.

The younger sister continued kicking her legs pleasantly while the elder sister's lined face turned somber. "A long time ago we made a bargain that cost us far more than we'd expected. So be warned. Do not trade with us unless you are willing to pay unforeseen costs. We offer no returns or exchanges. There are no second chances. Once you purchase a secret from us, it's yours, we will remember it no more, just as you will forget whatever we have taken from you."

"Are you trying to get customers or scare them away?" Tella asked.

"I'm attempting to be fair. We don't set out to trick our patrons, but the nature of our bargains means no one ever truly knows what they are gaining or losing."

Tella didn't actually need to be told this. She knew a bargain made in a Fated place would probably cost her more than she realized. But if they possessed a secret that would reveal a weakness capable of killing the Fallen Star, she couldn't turn away. Fates were dangerous, but they kept their promises, and the Vanished Market promised people who entered would find what they needed. And Tella needed a secret. She needed it so that her sister would no longer be in danger, so that people wouldn't be strung up like marionettes, and so that no one else could be killed like her mother, Legend, or Nicolas.

"All right," Tella said. "What will it cost me to find out a secret about a Fate?"

"Depends on the Fate and the type of secret."

"I want to know how to kill the Fallen Star."

"That's not a secret, precious. Immortals have only one weakness. Love."

"But he must have another weakness—one he doesn't want anyone to know about." A way that would get her sister out of danger, because if love was the Fallen Star's only weakness, then Scarlett was the most likely person to defeat him, or die trying.

Tella couldn't let her sister die. And yet she felt as if she could hear the clock on Scarlett's life ticking as the younger, blue-haired sister continued kick-kick-kicking her feet while the older one closed her eyes in thought.

"I do have one of his secrets," she said after a time. Then she turned to her younger sibling. "Millicent, dear, open the vault."

The youthful girl pulled on a brassy tassel that Tella hadn't noticed before and the heavy curtains behind the older woman immediately parted, revealing row after row after row of shelves lined in ancient treasure chests. They came in all sizes and colors. Some appeared to be crumbling with age, others shined with wet varnish. A few looked no bigger than Tella's palm while several were large enough to fit dead bodies.

After a minute or so the older sister returned from between the shelves holding a square chest of red jasper with a heart on top of it that had fire painted around it. At a glance the orange and yellow paint appeared slightly chipped, and a little dull. But when Tella lifted her gaze up toward the older sister's face, the image flickered and for a moment she saw genuine flames lick the heart.

"If you use the secret inside correctly, it will help you defeat the Fallen Star. However"—the woman held the box closer to her chest—"before I can let you have it, I will need a secret from you."

"Do I get to choose the secret?" Tella asked.

The woman gave her a peculiar smile, one that lit her eyes without actually moving her mouth. "I'm afraid your secrets aren't valuable enough to trade, Miss Dragna. The secret we want belongs to your daughter."

"I don't have a daughter."

"You will. We have met you in our past and in your future, and we know you will have a daughter someday."

"Do you know who the father of this daughter is?" The new voice was low and deep and the sound of it made Tella's heart race twice as fast.

She spun around.

Everything in the Vanished Market blurred, colors merging together as if the world around her was moving too fast, except for the handsome boy standing in front of her, taking up the entire door-way to the tent.

Legend was there.

33

Donatella

Legend was there, and alive, so very alive that the sight of him made Tella grin until her cheeks hurt.

"You're back." She didn't even care that the words came out breathless.

She was beyond pretending that the sight of him didn't steal her breath. He looked like a wish that had just woken up. His eyes were full of stars, his bronze skin was faintly glowing, and his dark hair was a little mussed. He didn't wear a cravat at his throat, and the top buttons of his black shirt were undone, as if he'd been in a rush to leave—to get to *her*.

If her smile hadn't been stretched as far as it could go, she would have grinned even wider.

"Did you think I wasn't coming back?" His eyes met hers and the corner of his mouth hitched up into the arrogant twist she loved so much.

"I've—" Tella broke off. The words *been worried* became lodged in her throat. There was only one reason to have worried about him.

She swallowed the words as she fought to keep her smile. He was alive. He was alive and there. That was all that mattered. He was alive. She would have never gotten over it if he'd died because he loved her. And yet it hurt so very much to realize that he was only standing there now, looking like a dream come true, because he didn't love her, and she so desperately loved him.

"Ahem," said the older sister. "In case the two of you have forgotten, time moves differently here and I was in the middle of speaking."

Legend's lips formed a flat line as he turned toward the woman, eyes narrowing slightly as if he'd liked to have used an illusion to make her disappear. Maybe he was even trying, but his magic didn't work quite the same inside this Fated place.

Which was good, because Tella needed this place and this woman.

"You said that I would have a daughter," Tella said.

"Yes. The father of your child will possess magic," the woman replied. "Your daughter will be born with a very powerful gift. But this child will have one fatal weakness. In exchange for the Fallen Star's most closely guarded secret, we want you to discover your daughter's secret weakness and then return to the market and give this knowledge to us."

"Are you sure you don't want any of my secrets?" Tella asked.

She still hadn't wrapped her head around having a child, or that she'd visit this market again in the future, which made her think she'd survive all of this. But she hated to think this was the only way.

"You still haven't told us who the father is," Legend said, leaning a broad shoulder carelessly against a tent pole. But Tella swore she saw a muscle pulse in his jaw.

"We do not have permission to share that information," said the older sister, "and it's not good to know too much about the future."

Tella agreed. The Aracle card that had shown her glimpses of the future had almost gotten her killed. And yet she couldn't hold back from asking, "Can't you just tell me if *he's* the father?"

"Who else would be the father?" Legend growled.

"Don't get upset with me!" Tella snapped. "You asked the question first." *And you don't love me,* said her eyes.

His eyes flashed with gold, and then suddenly he was inside the tent and right in front of her, looking down at her with the handsome face she'd feared she would never see again. "I asked you to become immortal." One hand wrapped around her waist, warm and strong and solid, while his other hand found the back of her neck. His grin turned devilish as he pulled her closer.

Tella's breath went short. "What are you doing?"

"Asking you again." He kissed her, harsh and quick and a little bit savage. She parted her lips, but that was all she could do. The hand at her waist kept her pressed to him, while the fingers at her neck spread out, covering her throat as he angled her head back, taking complete control as he deepened the kiss. He was possessing her, owning her with every sweep of his tongue and press of his lips, wordlessly telling her once more that he wanted to keep her forever. He didn't kiss her as if he'd simply just come back to life. He kissed her as if he'd died, been buried, and clawed his way out of the grave and through the dirt just to get to her.

Tella had never experienced such a heady feeling in her life. He might not have loved her, but Julian was right that Legend knew how to make her feel wanted.

"Just say yes," he said against her lips. "Let me make you immortal."

"You're not playing fair," she murmured.

"I never said I did, and I won't this time." His thumb stroked the sensitive column of her neck. "You're too important, Tella."

But you don't love me. Although as painful as it was to know that he didn't love her now, she also knew that if he had, he wouldn't be alive right now.

"Ahem." The older sister cleared her throat. "If you wish to start making that child now, I'm afraid this isn't the place."

Tella leaped away from Legend, crashing back to a terrible reality and blushing harder than she ever had in her entire life.

"Now, I suggest we move on," the older sister continued. "If you two keep at whatever it is you're doing, weeks will have passed in your world by the time you leave ours."

Dirty saints. Tella really had forgotten about the time. She hadn't heard any bells ring, but she imagined more than an hour must have passed, maybe even longer, which meant at least a day had come and gone in her world. Another day that her sister was being held captive by the Fate who'd murdered her mother, and the people of Valenda suffered unknowable terrors, as the other Fates played with them like toys they wanted to break.

And she'd been kissing Legend.

Tella's eyes shot back to the red jasper box in the older woman's hands. That was what she'd come here for—a secret that could save them all—and she needed it, regardless of the cost.

"I'll do it," Tella said. "I'll make the trade."

"Tella, you don't have to do this." Legend turned to the older sister, tilting his head and flashing a smile that would have made most ladies swoon. "You can have one of my secrets."

The older sister pursed her lips. "We're not interested."

An offended crease formed between Legend's dark brows. "Then there has to be something else you want."

Outside, the sun was still filling the world with lemony light, but none of it reached inside the tent. The air was growing colder, filling with heavy waves of creeping silver-blue fog.

"Legend—" Tella put a hand on his arm, before the fog became too thick to see through. "It's all right, you don't have to save me. I know what I'm doing."

"But you shouldn't have to do it." He turned back to her, and though he didn't say another word, his eyes were soft, apologetic. And she knew this wasn't about him or his secrets.

Legend was thinking about the one thing that Tella hadn't wanted to think about. Or rather, the one person—*her mother*.

When her mother had possessed the Deck of Destiny that imprisoned the Fates, the Temple of the Stars had wanted Paloma to give them Scarlett, in exchange for hiding the cursed Deck of Destiny. Her mother had refused, but she'd easily offered the temple Tella. And it had felt like the worst sort of betrayal, similar to what Tella was doing now.

"You don't have to do this," Legend said.

But Tella didn't see a better choice, and she feared she couldn't risk taking the time to find one. "My sister—she's with the Fallen Star. She won't be safe until he's dead."

"I know, Julian told me before I found you here."

"Then you know that I do have to do this now." Tella turned back to the sisters before her conscience tried to convince her to change her mind. "You have a deal."

"Excellent," said the oldest. "We just need to seal your promise. If you fail to discover your daughter's secret weakness by her seventeenth birthday, or choose not to give it to us, the cost will be your life."

And before anyone could protest, the younger sister pressed a thick rod of iron to the underside of Tella's wrist.

She screamed out loud.

Legend shot forward and grabbed her free hand. "Look at me, Tella." His grip was strong and reassuring, but it wasn't nearly enough to distract her from the pain, or the sorrow. So much sorrow.

Tella was familiar with heartbreak, but this was the sort of hurt that came from breaking someone else's heart. A fragile heart. A child's heart. A daughter's heart.

Tella closed her eyes to stop the tears.

The younger sister pulled the iron from Tella's wrist. Where there had once been flawless flesh there was now a thin white scar in the shape of a lock made of thorns. It didn't hurt. The pain instantly disappeared with the brand. But although Tella didn't feel pain or sorrow anymore, she also didn't quite feel like she had before.

She thought about her mother, and the vision of when her mother had given Tella away. Tella would never know why her mother made the choices she had, but in that moment Tella believed that it wasn't because she didn't care, it was because she did care. She cared enough to do whatever needed to be done. Maybe that's why she'd chosen to give up Tella instead of Scarlett. Scarlett would willingly sacrifice herself—destroy herself—if she felt it was the right thing. Tella was more like Paloma, willing to do whatever it took, even if it was the wrong thing, if it got her what she needed. Maybe Paloma sacrificed Tella because she knew it wouldn't destroy her.

But Tella silently vowed that she would make sure her daughter wouldn't have to make these sorts of choices at all. When this was over, Tella would find a way to make it all right, no matter what it took.

Tella clutched the red jasper box with one hand and Legend's hand with the other. He hadn't let go since he'd taken hold of it in the tent. His heavy fingers remained laced with hers, keeping her tucked close to his side as they wove back through the bustling market. He hadn't tried to kiss her again, but occasionally, when she glanced at him, she saw a satisfied smile.

Tella wanted to peek inside the box, wanted to know which secret she'd promised so much for. But she didn't want to remain longer than necessary. She imagined she'd spent an hour and two, but maybe it had been longer. Maybe she and Legend had lost three or four days instead of only one or two.

When they crossed through the archway that took them back to Valenda, the sky was midnight blue, making it impossible to tell the hour or how much time had passed.

Legend had private residences all over the city. Julian was supposedly waiting for them at the Narrow House in the Spice Quarter. Of all his performers, only Aiko, Nigel, Caspar, and Jovan knew about it.

Heading there should have felt safer than lingering on the ragged streets of Valenda; it hadn't taken long for trash to collect now that the monarchy was in upheaval. Tella didn't spy any Fates, but she detected their taint taking up residence where night revelers had once been.

The jasper box in her hand grew heavier. She had the urge to open it now, but they'd already reached the Narrow House, which was indeed a slender structure. At first glance it appeared barely wider than a doorway, and just as crooked as all the other homes in this part of the city. But the closer they drew, the wider it grew.

Tella watched as decorative arched windows appeared on either side of the door. Beneath them rested flower boxes, overflowing with white foxglove, which Tella would have sworn weren't there moments ago.

The house would have looked curiously inviting if she had not glanced up to see the Maiden Death standing in the center of the second-story window, flashing a macabre smile from behind her cage of pearls.

Legend's hand gripped Tella's tighter.

In Decks of Destiny, the Maiden Death's card predicted a loss of a loved one or a family member. And it was her card that had first predicted Tella would lose her mother.

The air around her crackled and a fraction of a second later a hooded figure materialized between Tella and Legend.

Tella froze. She couldn't see this figure's face, it was concealed by his cloak, but she didn't need to. There was only one Fate with the ability to travel through space and time and materialize at will: the Assassin—who, according to Jacks, was also insane.

"The Maiden Death is here to see the two of you," he said.

Donatella

The Narrow House was another one of Legend's deceptions.

Tella had seen through the glamour outside and thought it had looked charming. But inside, it reminded Tella of the illusion Legend had created in the dungeon, when he'd turned her cell into a four-story study. The ceilings of the Narrow House stretched even higher, and the books on the surrounding shelves didn't look as flawless as they had in his illusion. Some of the volumes were aged and cracked and fragile, as if they'd experienced several previous lives before finding homes on these shelves.

Legend had one arm protectively around Tella's shoulders as they entered the vaulted room. He hadn't even wanted Tella to enter the house, but the Assassin had been insistent and so had Tella—this was her fight as well as Legend's.

The scene they'd stepped into could have been a painting called

Hostages at a Tea Party. Legend's most trusted performers were sitting stiffly in tufted red chairs that encircled a shiny ebony table, set with a pewter tea service that no one touched, except Nigel, Legend's tattoo-covered fortune-teller. Julian and Jovan were there, as well as Aiko—Legend's historiographer who captured the history of Caraval through pictures—and Caspar, who'd once pretended to be Tella's fiancé.

Behind them, the Assassin and the Maiden Death hovered like grim hosts. A few of the other Fates Tella had seen sometimes glowed, but the Assassin, who kept his face concealed by his heavy hood, appeared to collect shadows.

The Maiden Death looked exactly like her card from Decks of Destiny. Her head was covered in curving bars of pearls that wrapped around like a cage, and her dress looked more like long tatters of gossamer fabric that had been tied together. She didn't glow, either, but her frayed garment billowed around her, as if she kept a private wind on a leash.

"Do not be afraid of us," said the Maiden Death. "We are here to help defeat the Fallen Star."

"And if we wanted to hurt you, I'd have shoved daggers through each of your hearts the moment I saw you outside." The Assassin's voice was like nails pounding through glass, harsh and discordant.

"Is that really how you win people over?" muttered Julian.

"Daeshim," the Maiden Death chided in a voice far softer than her cloaked companion's, "remember what we talked about?"

"You said to be friendly. That was a joke."

No one laughed except for Jovan. "I think you need some work on your humor, mate."

"If you don't kill us all, I'll help you out," added Caspar.

"Thank you," the Assassin answered. Not that his politeness appeared to relax anyone. If anything, more tension filled the room. Watching Caspar and Jovan smile at the hooded Assassin felt like observing kittens hop toward a crocodile.

"I know you have little reason to trust us, but I come to warn of harm, not bring it." The Maiden Death's mournful eyes met Legend's and the wind that made her shredded dress billow grew stronger. "I sense your entire world is in danger if you refuse to accept our help."

"Any danger to our world is because of your kind," Legend said.

"You're not that different from us," replied the Maiden Death. "You're immortal and you have abilities like ours. But you do not know what it is like to be connected to the Fallen Star. We are his immortal abominations, and when we act out, he punishes us eternally. Your myths claim that Death imprisoned my head in pearls, but it was really Gavriel. Once upon a time, he wanted me. I refused him. So, he had my head caged in this cursed globe, to keep anyone else from touching me. I have tried to remove it; I've even died and come back to life, but the cage will remain until Gavriel dies."

"And what's your tale of woe?" Tella asked the Assassin.

"It's none of your business. You should trust me because I'm not killing any of you right now."

"That's good enough for me," Caspar said with a laugh. It seemed he thought the Assassin was telling another joke. Tella wasn't so sure.

Julian appeared leery as well. He sat opposite where the Fates stood, elbows on the table as he leaned forward with a stare that was on the verge of asking for a fight. "We all agree, everyone hates the Fallen Star. But I still find it hard to believe you'd want him dead, since killing him makes you two more vulnerable."

"Being vulnerable is not as bad as some believe," said the Maiden Death. "The Fallen Star's death would make us ageless. If we died, we wouldn't come back to life, it's true. But if we are ageless, we could still live almost as long as an immortal if we're careful. Although, not all of us want to even live that long. Some among our kind would like to have the option of finally dying. But they are not willing to openly oppose him. No one wants to spend an eternity in a cage."

"That I believe." Legend's tone was more diplomatic than his brother's, but it was clear from the heavy weight he put behind it that one wrong move from the Fates would change his approach. "Can we all have a minute alone? If you're really here to help us, I don't imagine that will be a problem."

The Maiden Death silently glided toward where Legend and Tella stood near the door. Once she left, the Assassin simply—and unnervingly—disappeared in a way that reminded everyone he could reappear, with the knives he spoke about earlier.

Tella swore the walls shuddered, as if the study had finally stopped holding its breath.

Legend loosened his grip on Tella but didn't let her go as he moved

closer to the table. This was the first time she'd ever seen him inter-
act with his performers like this. Some of his performers didn't even
know who he truly was, but these were the ones he was closest to.

There was a respectful silence as Legend and Tella reached the
table together. Everyone looked anxious to give their opinion. But
no one said a word until Legend turned to Nigel.

The tattooed fortune-teller picked up a cup of tea and took a sip
before speaking, his lips surrounded by inked barbed wire. "I couldn't
get a read on either Fate. The Assassin's eyes were concealed by his
hood and when the Maiden Death looked my way, she only met my
eyes. Her gaze never ventured to any of my tattoos."

"What's your personal impression?" Legend asked.

"Never trust a Fate," Nigel said.

"If the Assassin had wanted to hurt us, he would have," Caspar
interrupted.

"Maybe their plans involve more than murdering us in a parlor,"
said Jovan.

"Not all Fates are murderers," Aiko said.

"So you think we should trust them?" asked Legend.

"Yes," Caspar and Aiko answered at the same time Jovan firmly
said, "No. Anyone who uses a 'the' in front of their name is never
trustworthy. But since your orders were for the rest of our troupe to
head back to your island for safety, it might not be a bad idea to consider new allies."

Legend turned to Julian.

"I can't believe I'm going to say this, but—" Julian rubbed his hand up and down along the scar marking his face. "I like the Assassin's powers. He could go to Crimson if we ever needed him to."

"I don't know about that," Tella cut in. "I heard the Assassin wasn't in his right mind because he's traveled through time too much. But we may not need him, or the Maiden Death. We might already have the answer to defeating the Fallen Star."

She eased herself from under Legend's arm and held out her red jasper box as she quickly explained why it might be the answer to all of their problems.

But almost as soon as Tella undid the latch, she realized it would not be an answer to any problems. The note inside was so thin, it looked as if it might fall apart with a touch.

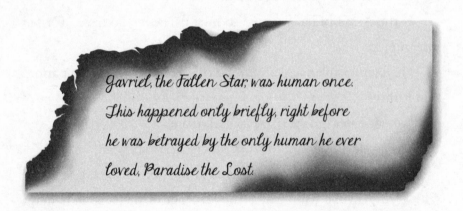

Gavriel, the Fallen Star, was human once. This happened only briefly, right before he was betrayed by the only human he ever loved, Paradise the Lost.

Tella ignored the pang she felt at the sight of her mother's name and reread the note, hoping more words would show up on the page. But they didn't.

This was not what she had wanted.

Tella wanted a list of weaknesses, a fatal flaw, or a simple plan that outlined exactly how to murder a Fate or a Fallen Star. But this secret only told her that the one person who could kill the Fallen Star was already dead.

"Never mind that idea." Tella dropped the box on the table. She would have crumpled up the useless words inside it as well, but the note had disappeared as soon as she finished rereading it. *Poof.* Gone.

She could feel her hope dwindling, but Tella refused to give up on finding the Fallen Star's weakness. And the note did reveal one thing. On the night her mother had died, Tella hadn't understood why her mother had stabbed him. But now she did. Paloma must have thought that Gavriel still loved her and that their reunion would turn him mortal so that she could kill him. Only, he'd killed her instead.

"Have you come to a decision?" The Maiden Death spoke softly from the doorway, but Tella could feel power pulsing around her as her ghostly gown fluttered, while the Assassin stood at her side collecting shadows.

Legend's handsome face appeared impassive, but Tella swore the arched doorway in which the Fates stood grew taller, making both of them look smaller. "Thank you for the offer," he said, "but we'd rather fight this battle alone."

"I don't believe you can win without us," sighed the Maiden Death. "At least take these."

There was a hiss and a pop, like a strike of the match, and then the Assassin was standing next to Tella, placing two thick discs in her palm. *Luckless coins.*

Tella flashed back to when Jacks had given her one of these. She remembered thinking the magical coin was such a special gift. But there was a reason the objects were called luckless. They could be used not just to summon Fates, but to track humans.

"In case you change your mind," rasped the Assassin.

"Hold them tight, say our names, and we will come to your aid," the Maiden Death promised.

Tella had to admit, they were kinder than any of the other Fates she'd met, and yet she still tossed their coins into a rubbish bin as soon as they disappeared.

"So what do we do now?" asked Jovan.

"I have a new idea," Tella offered.

Another girl might have remained quiet after her last scheme had failed so spectacularly. But it was for that reason that Tella felt the need to find a plan that worked. The idea was something Jacks had suggested, but she hadn't seriously considered it before. It would be riskier to her sister, because it would mean she'd need to get the Fallen Star's blood, but if it worked, it would end up saving Scarlett—and the entire empire.

"There's a book in the Immortal Library that will reveal a person's or a Fate's entire history. If we find this book and read the Fallen Star's history, it should tell us any weakness that he has."

Aiko looked up from her notebook, where she'd already begun

sketching their encounter with the Assassin and the Maiden Death. "You're talking about the Ruscica. That book could be very useful, but to access the Fallen Star's history, we would need a vial of his blood."

"I know." Tella took a deep breath, hoping this gamble would pay off. "My sister is with the Fallen Star, and once we have the book, we can send a message asking her to get the blood."

"No," Julian objected. "That would put her in too much danger."

"All of us are in danger," Aiko said.

"And Scarlett won't be alone." Legend divided looks between Nigel, Aiko, Caspar, and Jovan. "While Tella and I search for the Ruscica, Nigel, get back into the palace and find out what the Fates have planned next. Aiko, figure out which Fates are in Valenda—I don't want to be surprised by any more visits. Caspar, find a way into the palace as well and try to learn how loyal people are to the Fates in charge. Jovan, I want you on Scarlett. Sneak into the Menagerie ruins, make sure she stays safe, and when you can, slip her a note letting her know we need the Fallen Star's blood."

Tella wanted to protest—getting the Fallen Star's blood was going to be risky for Scarlett. She didn't want her sister attempting it until they had the book. But the longer they waited to ask Scarlett to get the blood, the longer she would be in the Menagerie with him.

"I still don't like this plan," said Julian. "If anyone's going to watch over Crimson, I should."

"Not a chance," Legend replied. "You'll get caught, and if something happens to you now, I can't bring you back."

Julian glared up at his brother. "You won't have to bring me back. I won't get caught."

"I'm not going to argue about this." Legend shook his head, his tone dismissive.

Julian shot up from his chair, and suddenly everyone at the table had somewhere else to look, but Tella couldn't tear her eyes away. Legend was taller and broader, but Julian's face was full of the kind of raw emotion Legend never showed. "You don't want to argue because you know I'm right."

"You're not right," Legend said. "You're in love and it makes you sloppy."

Julian flinched. So did Tella.

Not that Legend even appeared to notice her reaction.

"You're right, Legend," Tella said, drawing his attention back to her.

Legend smiled, pleased she agreed with him, until Tella went on. "Love is messy. It's not easily controlled. But that's what makes it so powerful. It's unbridled passion. It's caring about someone else's life more than you care about your own. I agree that Julian is probably in more danger of being caught, or worse, if he goes to the Menagerie ruins to watch over Scarlett, but I think it's admirable that he's willing to take that risk."

Julian stood a little taller. "Thank you, Donatella."

"But I still agree with Legend. If you're at risk, Julian, it puts my sister in more danger—if she were to find out you were there and in trouble, she'd do anything to save you. I think the best thing for her would be if you stayed away."

Julian shook his head with a scowl.

But there were no more arguments after that. It was almost eerie how no one else debated their assignments. In the end, everyone agreed to follow Legend's orders. Even Julian, who received an assignment which did not involve infiltrating the Menagerie ruins where Scarlett was being kept.

As Tella watched everyone quietly leave, she wondered if maybe Legend had manipulated them all. Did he possess another type of magic that she didn't know about? Or maybe it had something to do with how they were all bonded to him. . . .

"I know what you're thinking," Julian said. Everyone else had gone, and he was almost at the door, but he turned back and looked upon Tella. "You're wondering if we all only agreed because we're tied to Legend by magic. You're wondering if the same thing will happen to you if you accept the offer my brother made you, and become an immortal—"

"Julian," Legend warned.

"Relax, brother." A wolfish smile replaced Julian's scowl. "I was just going to tell her the truth. We all have free will, Tella. If you become immortal, you won't lose your free will. You won't feel my brother controlling you. But you'll never feel him loving you like the way I love Crimson." With that, he walked out of the room, leaving Tella and Legend alone.

The warm lights of the study dimmed as Tella heard Legend move closer. The air grew warmer and her heart beat faster, but she didn't dare look up at him. It was too easy to be hypnotized by everything about him.

Earlier, when he'd kissed her in the market, she'd felt how much he'd wanted her, she'd thought maybe it could be enough; being wanted by Legend was heady and powerful. Then she'd watched Julian. Tella had never been attracted to Julian, but for a moment she'd hated how jealous she'd been of what her sister had with him. *Enough* would never be enough for Tella. She wanted a love worth fighting for, but immortals couldn't love.

"My brother only said that because he's upset." Legend's low voice was right beside Tella and as he spoke, the world transformed. The walls turned to smoke, the abandoned table vanished, and the doorway disappeared, until it was just the two of them, standing under a velvet sky full of surreal white stars. Flickering. Glimmering. Shimmering lights. But none of them shined like Legend's coal-dark eyes when she finally looked up at him.

"There are other advantages to being immortal." His warm hand slipped around her neck before his fingers slid into her hair. "Give me a chance. Please."

Tella tilted her head back, leaning into his palm at the word *please*. The way he said it made her feel so wanted and important, once again.

His mouth twitched into half a smile, and the world went a little brighter as several stars fell from the sky, tumbling toward the earth in dazzling arcs of fire.

Tella loved it when he showed off. She loved that he was magical.

She loved so many things about him. She wanted him more than she'd ever wanted anyone—she didn't want him to let her go or to leave her alone, not even for a moment. She wanted him to chase her to the ends of the earth, to show up in her dreams every night, and to be there when she woke as well. She wanted him to love her.

But knowing what love would cost Legend, she could never ask again. Tella needed to end this, for both of them.

She knew Legend didn't love her; he had said he never would. But, just in case that ever changed, the last thing she wanted was to be the reason that he didn't come back to life when he died.

Tella gave him the sort of smile she usually paired with half-hearted apologies. "I can't do this."

Several stars disappeared from the sky.

Tella faltered, but she didn't stop. "I thought I could consider it. But I actually think I fell more in love with the idea of you than the real you."

Legend clenched his jaw. "You don't mean that, Tella."

"Yes, I do." She forced the words out, each one tasting worse than the last. But she knew that if she didn't go through with this now, she wouldn't be able to do it again.

Legend might not have been able to feel love, but from the way he kept looking at her—from the way his mouth slammed into a taut line and his eyes turned distant and guarded—it was clear he knew how to feel hurt.

Tella made herself continue, her forced smile fading. "It's sort of like how you wanted to see if you could convince the world you were

Elantine's heir. Only I . . ." She took a deep breath. "I wanted to see if I could make the Great Master Legend fall in love with me."

Legend's face became a mask of perfect calm, but what remained of the stars in their sky went out all at once, cloaking them both in sudden darkness. "If that's true, Donatella, then we both failed at getting what we wanted."

Before she could reply, he was gone.

35

Donatella

That night, Tella tried not to think about Legend. She needed to focus. She couldn't think of the hurtful things she'd said to him, or the way he'd left her in total darkness, as she penned a note to her sister that would either doom them all or save them.

Scar,

We need a vial of the Fallen Star's blood. But be very careful getting the blood, and with the Fallen Star—whatever you do, don't try to make him love you. When I went to the Vanished Market,

> I learned that the Fallen Star loved our mother once—she was the only human he ever loved, and he killed her.
>
> Be more cautious than you've ever been in your life.
>
> Love,
> T

Tella lost track of how many times she reread the note before finally giving it to Jovan, who would deliver it to Scarlett later that day, for it was already after midnight. Tella was beyond tired, but even after she climbed into bed, she fought against sleep, not wanting to face whatever waited for her—or rather, what *didn't* wait for her—in her dreams.

36

Donatella

The dreamy sky carriage came into focus slowly. It enveloped Tella like a tucked-away memory laced with hints of apples and magic. The leather cushions beneath her were buttery and trimmed in thick royal blue that matched the heavy curtains lining the oval windows. It was exactly like the first sky carriage she'd ever been in, except for its size. It was about half the size of a regular coach, leaving practically no room between her and the young man who sat opposite her, Jacks.

He grinned like a scoundrel as he tossed a shimmery white apple between his pale fingers. And for the first time Tella was glad that she'd given him permission to enter her dreams.

His apple looked as if its skin had been dipped in glitter, and yet its shine was that of a spark to a flame when compared to the Prince of Hearts. He was a little disheveled, as usual—his light brown trousers were only half tucked into his boots, his rusty-red velvet tailcoat was wrinkled, and his cream cravat was only half tied. But his skin glowed like a star, his golden hair shone brighter than any crown, and his unearthly eyes gleamed with a shade of blue that made Tella think of the most wonderful mistakes.

"What are we doing here?" she asked. She knew they were in a dream, and, like Legend, Jacks appeared to have the ability to control it.

"I thought I'd try something new. I want us to start over." He flashed his dimples in a way that Tella imagined was an attempt at an innocent smile.

She wondered briefly what might have happened if he'd given her that smile the first time they'd met, rather than threatening to toss her out of the carriage. She wouldn't have thought he was the least bit innocent or harmless, but she would have been intrigued.

"Say you could relive that day. What would you have done differently?"

"Maybe I'd have offered you a bite of my apple." He leaned forward, approaching her almost reverently, and set the glittering piece of fruit in her hands. It was colder than his skin, nearly burning in its iciness. "Go ahead and take a bite, my love. It's just an apple."

"For some reason, I don't believe you."

His grin twitched. "It may have a little magic."

"What kind?"

"Taste it and find out." Jacks's challenging stare looked like a dare, the sort that was already lost as soon as it was accepted.

If this had happened the first time they'd met, she probably would have taken a bite, half curious about the magical white fruit, half hoping to impress the even more magical boy across from her. And it probably would have put her under a spell more treacherous than his kiss had.

"I think I'll pass." She handed him the apple.

Jacks took hold of her instead. In an instant she was across the carriage and folded neatly in his lap, his cool arms wrapped around her, and his lips were close enough to kiss.

"Jacks." Tella placed a hand against his chest before he could lean any closer. "I would have been tempted by the apple, but I might have actually pushed *you* out of the carriage if you'd tried this that day."

"Then push me, Donatella. I won't stop you if that's what you want." But rather than letting her go, the arms around her tightened. Then his head tilted to the side. His lips found the sensitive place where her neck met her jaw.

"Jacks . . ." Her voice was too breathless. It sounded like an invitation instead of a warning as his mouth trailed down her neck, moving slowly and softly against her skin. His lips dropped lower, to the hollow of her throat, and her heart beat faster. When Jacks kissed her it always felt a little like he worshipped her. And with everything that had just transpired with Legend, it was so very tempting to just let him keep doing it.

"Tell me what you want, Donatella. Say it and I'll give it to you." His mouth stilled on her collarbone.

"Jacks." She pushed hard on his chest. There wasn't really enough room in the carriage for her to go anywhere, but she was able to separate his lips from her skin. Three months ago, she wouldn't have stopped him. The Tella who didn't believe in love would have played with Jacks the same way he clearly enjoyed playing with her. But Tella felt too vulnerable to play tonight.

"I'm sorry, Jacks. I don't think you can give me what I want."

The color of his eyes dulled to pale sea glass, something like hurt filling his gaze. "If I had my full powers, I could change your mind. I could make you feel more than you've ever imagined. I can even make the feeling last if you tell me who Legend is."

He stroked her cheek; his touch was affectionate—but there was nothing loving or warm about what he'd suggested.

Unlike the other Fates, Jacks hadn't been in the cards when Legend had freed them from the Deck of Destiny, so he remained weakened. But with his complete powers, Jacks could control anyone's emotions. While having him take her feelings from her for one night had been a relief, Tella wouldn't ever want to give someone that much power over her indefinitely.

"I wouldn't want that, either," she said softly.

"At least I tried." His dimples returned. "I suppose I'll just have to try harder."

He ran his fingers down her cheek once more as the dream dissolved.

Scarlett

While Tella was still asleep, Scarlett received a note sheathed inside the linen napkin accompanying her breakfast. She resisted the urge to immediately tear open the message. Instead, she took another sip of her morning cordial and slowly slid the page into her pocket.

She swore she could see puffs of demanding purple drifting up from where the message hid, as if it contained some of her sister's impatience.

The Lady Prisoner was friendly, forthcoming with what she knew about the Fallen Star's plans, and she hadn't told him about Scarlett's use of the Reverie Key. And yet Scarlett still didn't entirely trust her. She let the note sit in her pocket until later that afternoon, when the Lady Prisoner's eyes were finally closed for her nap and Scarlett could see that her colors had genuinely shifted to the tranquil teal of still waters.

The lady Fate never slept long—Scarlett imagined it had something to do with the fact that she was forced to sleep on a perch. So Scarlett read quickly, and then she penned a hasty note of her own.

Donatella,

I'll get the blood, and I'll be careful, but whatever you're doing—be quick. In three days' time, the Fallen Star plans to make his claim for the throne. He's bragged to me that his Fates will continue to torment the city. When he makes his first public appearance, he wants the people of Valenda to beg him to claim the throne and replace the Fates who killed Legend. No one will think to complain that he's crowned himself emperor until it's too late.

All my love,

S

38

Donatella

Tella had naively imagined that the Immortal Library would be as easy to find as the Vanished Market had been. It was almost as laughable as the idea that the word *easy* still remained in her vocabulary.

She gave a delicate snort.

If Legend heard it, he didn't react. His broad shoulders didn't shift, and his dark head didn't turn away from the waters of the cracked fountain he'd been staring into—the same fountain they'd kissed in front of on the night Tella realized she was falling in love with him.

If only falling out of love with him was as easy.

She'd never before wanted to stop loving Legend. But today, she kept thinking about what Jacks had tried to offer as they searched the decrepit columns that surrounded the ruins of the Cursed Wife. He didn't have his full powers, so he couldn't actually take away any of Tella's emotions for longer than a day or truly change her feelings, but she was a little tempted by the idea of feeling indifferent, rather than feeling everything.

She knew Legend remembered the night he'd carried her here and then kissed her until she'd forgotten her pain. If she closed her eyes, she could recall it all. She could remember the way he'd carried her to the mossy steps before the ruins, how they'd talked of their pasts, and then how they'd kissed. She could remember the soft, asking sensation of his lips against her mouth and her neck and the rough way his hands had dug into the rope around her waist, pulling her even closer to him as he whispered how much he wanted her.

He *had* to remember. But he refused to look at her. He practically treated her like a stranger. It was the same this morning at the other ruins they'd visited. When he spoke, it was either in short answers to one of her questions, or terse commands.

It was unfair that out of all the plans Tella had recently made, the only one that had worked involved pushing him away. She thought she could handle Legend not loving her, but she wasn't doing very well with the idea of him despising her.

She circled the fountain again, even though they'd already scoured these ruins for images that might have represented the Immortal Library and led her to the Ruscica. They'd taken turns dripping blood on anything that appeared symbolic. But either the entrance of the Immortal Library wasn't here, or it would take more than blood to open it.

Legend raked a hand through his dark hair before finally turning away from the fountain and silently starting toward the crumbling steps that led back down to the streets. They were both dressed in the sort of ordinary clothes that made people easy to overlook. Tella was wearing a short-sleeved dress the color of muddy lake water, while Legend wore simple brown pants and a homespun shirt with fraying sleeves—yet the bastard still managed to move with the arrogance of someone who knew eyes would turn his way no matter what he wore. His steps possessed the sort of confidence that some people searched their whole lives for.

"Are you coming?" he said, tone gruff, as he reached the top of the stairs.

"Depends on where you're going." The voice that traveled up from the base of the steps below them was crystallized loveliness, clear and delicate and unbreakably strong.

Tella swept closer just to hear it better. Legend tried to step in front of her, but Tella had to see who the voice belonged to.

The woman who appeared at the top of the steps was almost as pretty as the sound of her words. A gauzy peach dress billowed above the cracked ground as she moved, the same way the Maiden Death's tattered gown had, as if a magical breeze followed wherever she went. She stood taller than Legend. Her skin was pale and hard as marble, her hair nearly shorn to the scalp, and on top of her head rested a thin gold circlet, which made her look like an ancient princess.

"Aren't you a handsome one?" she said to Legend in that same hypnotic voice.

He replied with an irresistible smile. "Most people think so."

"Do *you* think so?" The entrancing woman turned back to Tella.

But as soon as she had asked her question, all Tella could see were images of Legend. She pictured him during Caraval, when he'd waited for her in front of the Temple of the Stars, with only a wide cloth wrapped around his lower half, revealing his glorious chest in all its sculpted splendor.

"You should see him without a shirt on. He's magnificent." Tella's mouth hung open as soon as the words were out. She didn't even know this woman. And she wasn't supposed to be in love with Legend anymore.

But Legend didn't smirk or grin as he normally might have. In fact, he looked murderous.

The woman laughed, the sound as captivating as her voice. It begged Tella to laugh with her. But this time Tella fought against the urge to give in as she took in the woman's appearance once more. Tella's eyes darted back up to the circlet around her head. It was covered in ancient symbols, which Tella couldn't read, but she imagined that if she could have deciphered them, the symbols would have told her that this woman wasn't an ancient princess, but the Fated Priestess, Priestess.

Her magic was in her voice. That's why Tella had answered her so honestly. Whenever Priestess, Priestess asked a question, a person had the choice between answering it truthfully or fighting the question and dying. Her voice wasn't just compelling, it was deadly.

"I can already see that playing with you two is going to be fun," said the Fate. "Would you like to stay here and play with me?"

All of the hairs on Tella's arms rose. The word *no* crashed against her skull, followed by *never,* and then the words *I'd rather kill you.* But she knew it would be a mistake to scream any of those the way she wanted to.

They needed to get away.

But the words *no* and *never* kept pounding at her skull. Pounding and pounding and—

"I'm afraid we have somewhere else we need to go," Legend answered smoothly.

Tella regained the ability to think, but it only lasted for a moment.

"That's disappointing." The Fate's mouth fell into a pout. "Where are you two going that could possibly be more interesting than spending time with me?"

Images of the Immortal Library ripped from Decks of Destiny took over Tella's thoughts. She saw magical bookshelves full of forbidden volumes, and then the Ruscica open to a page with detailed instructions of how to kill the Fallen Star.

"We're going to ruins around Valenda in search of the Immortal Library," Legend said. His voice was still completely level. Tella didn't know if he wasn't even trying to fight the questions, or if the magic affected him more than her, making it impossible to hold off from answering.

Sometime between now and the last question, the Priestess had moved closer to him. Her long white fingers were on his arm, trailing up to his neck. "That place isn't meant for humans. What would I need to do to make you stay here with me instead?"

The question wasn't directed at Tella this time—it didn't press against her skull. And yet she sensed the Fate had placed more magic behind it. Tella could feel the question filling the ruins with a sickly sweet stench as the Fate's hands climbed into Legend's hair, the same way Esmeralda's had, and Tella feared the Fate wasn't just using her powers to compel Legend to answer a question. She wanted to possess him.

"Nothing will change his mind!" Tella shouted, drawing the wretched Fate's attention her way.

The Priestess's lips thinned. "You don't have a strong sense of self-preservation, do you?"

"I'm stronger than most people think," Tella said.

She thought she saw a fraction of Legend's missing smile return.

And before the Fate could ask another question, the earth began to shake. The ruins rattled. The steps split, the cursed fountain cracked in half, wine spilling all over the ground, as the remains of the ruined mansion collapsed in a thunderous cloud of dust and debris.

The dust was so thick Tella couldn't see Legend or the Priestess, but she thought she heard the Fate's footsteps running away as Tella searched for a safe place to hide until the earthquake ceased.

All she could see was dust. But she didn't choke on it, and though the world around her was collapsing, she realized that nothing had actually touched her.

"Legend?" she called tentatively, although she was fairly certain the Priestess was now gone. "Tell me you're doing this."

The dust vanished, the shaking stopped, and the ruins returned to as they had been. The only cracks that remained were the ones that had been there before. An illusion.

Legend appeared next. But unlike the ruins, he looked much different than before. Damp hair clung to his brow, and his bronze skin looked gray as he stumbled toward Tella.

Legend never stumbled.

Her arms went around him instinctively, and either he was truly weakened or they'd reached a temporary truce, because he didn't push her away. He leaned heavily against her, making it impossible for her to move. He had drained himself using too much magic.

Legend was private about many things, including anything involving his powers. But she knew his magic was at its peak during Caraval because it was fueled by all the emotions of everyone in attendance. He'd probably been stronger at the palace for similar reasons.

"You didn't have to go to all that trouble to scare her," Tella said.

Legend's fingers found her hair and combed through her curls, an idle gesture that he probably didn't even realize he was doing. "I didn't want her asking questions you might refuse to answer."

"I'm not that stubborn," Tella huffed.

"Yes, you are," he murmured, "but I like that about you." Legend's hand left her curls and wrapped around the vulnerable back of her neck—definitely an intentional gesture. He stroked her skin with fingers that made her think he wasn't as weak as he seemed and then he tilted her head back until she was looking up at him.

His color was already returning to his handsome face, making him look a little untouchable, even as he continued to touch her.

Her teeth sunk into her lower lip. For a weak moment she hoped this wasn't a temporary truce, and that he'd finally seen through her speech from last night.

He released her neck and pulled away. "We should go."

"But I've just gotten here."

The Prince of Hearts appeared at the top of the steps. He leaned against a crumbling rail, an elegant mess of wrinkled clothing, lazy movements, and golden hair, which hung over eyes that appeared as if he'd been watching them for a while.

Ice coated Tella's skin. But it was different from the chill she felt whenever Jacks looked at her, because his eyes had moved next to her, latching on to Legend, who Jacks, along with the rest of the empire, had only known as Dante—a young man who was supposed to be dead, a young man who'd just used a frightening amount of power, a young man who didn't curse at Jacks, or try to protect Tella as he had with the Priestess.

She swiftly turned to see Legend. His broad shoulders were stiff, his expression was fixed. He stood still as a statue beside her, the same way he had the night of the Fated Ball when Jacks had used his powers to briefly stop everyone's hearts from beating.

"Jacks! Stop this!" Tella demanded.

But the Prince of Hearts didn't even acknowledge her. His blue eyes had taken on a ravenous look, and in that moment Tella could see what he was thinking. Unlike the other Fates, Jacks was at only half power; he wanted the rest of his powers back, and Legend was the one with the ability to restore him.

"Stay away from him!" Tella begged. Legend was already weakened from using so much magic; she didn't want to think what a power exchange with Jacks would do to him right now.

But the Prince of Hearts continued to ignore her; his rabid gaze stayed on Legend's frozen form. "You know, I wondered if you were Legend during Caraval, and then again when I saw you in her dream. But then you died."

"He's not Legend," Tella lied.

Jacks finally tilted his head her way, but none of the mischief that had been in his eyes last night was there. He looked more like the cruel boy she'd first met in the carriage who'd threatened to push her out just to see if she survived. "If he's not Legend, then who created the illusion I just saw, and how is he alive? The reports I heard said the new heir had been killed."

"Those were rumors," Tella said. "I started them to keep the Fates away."

Jacks laughed but his eyes remained cold. "For once I hope you're lying, my love. And if you're not, then I'm so sorry."

Tella clutched her breastbone and doubled over, suddenly dizzy and nauseous and unable to breathe. The ruins, Jacks, Legend, everything turned into a blur, and stars burst before her eyes as pain blinded her.

"What the hell—" Legend cursed, finally free of Jacks's control.

"Don't make another move toward her," Jacks warned, "unless you wish her to die."

"Jacks—" Tella gasped as she dropped to her knees, no longer able to stand. "Why . . ."

"What have you done?" Legend roared.

"I'm giving her a heart attack," Jacks said calmly. "It will kill her very soon, unless you give me my full powers back right now. *Tick. Tock.* She doesn't have long left."

"Jacks . . ." Tella panted. She couldn't believe he was really doing this. "Don't . . . do . . ."

"I'll do it," Legend said. "Stop hurting her, and I'll restore your powers with some of mine. But only if you swear right now, in blood, to never use any of your abilities on Tella or on me again."

The prince's mouth tightened and his eyes might have flashed back to Tella.

"Fine. You have a deal. I won't, unless one of you asks me to." Jacks took a dagger from his boot and sliced his hand, creating a spill of blood to seal the promise.

Tella started gasping, panting for air. "You're a demon!" She might have cursed Jacks more thoroughly, but all she wanted to do was breathe. She'd *trusted* him. She'd thought that he actually cared about her, and he'd tried to kill her.

Legend's arms went around her, holding her up as she continued to fight for oxygen. "You scared me," he murmured.

"What will this cost you?" she asked against his chest.

Instead of answering, Legend carefully walked her to the edge of the fountain, seeming to have mostly recovered from his earlier use of magic, as he helped her sit on the rim. "Stay. I'll be right back."

He turned back to the Prince of Hearts. "We're not doing this here." Legend stalked into the ruins of the decrepit mansion without waiting for Jacks to follow.

As soon as Jacks and Legend were out of sight, Tella shoved up from the fountain with shaky arms and shuffled in the direction they'd gone. Jacks was only supposed to take a fraction of Legend's power. But she didn't trust him, and she'd seen the power exchange between Legend and the witch—she had watched as Legend drained Esmeralda of *all* her magic. She couldn't let that happen to Legend.

Jacks might have left her too weak to do much, and even at her best, she wouldn't be able to tear two powerful immortals apart. But it wouldn't prevent her from trying if necessary.

She crept closer to the ruined mansion that Jacks and Legend had entered. The entire structure was skeletal, a corpse made of bricks and stones instead of bones. Tella pressed her hands against the dirty walls to keep herself from collapsing as she peered through a jagged hole.

She knew from her own experience with Jacks that blood exchanges could be intensely emotional. Jacks's mouth was latched on to Legend's wrist. Blood stained the corners of his lips, while his face twisted into something sadistic and hungry as he drank.

Unlike Jacks, Legend appeared to feel nothing. He looked like a study in apathy—until suddenly Legend ripped his wrist away from

Jacks's mouth with enough force to knock the Fate several steps back. "Tella isn't yours." The words were razor-sharp.

Jacks responded with a bloody smile. "She will be."

Tella gripped the wall to stay standing as she again remembered the way he'd flashed his dimples and said, *I suppose I'll just have to try harder.*

Was this his way of trying?

She continued to watch as Jacks wiped the blood from his mouth with the back of his hand. "She forgave me before. She'll forgive me again. And now that this transaction has taken your ability to visit her dreams, it shouldn't be difficult to win her."

Tella shoved away from the wall, ready to march inside and tell Jacks just how difficult and unforgiving she could be. But her legs had other ideas. They crumpled beneath her and brought her crashing to the hard ground. "Bastard!"

"I hope you're not talking about me."

She looked up.

Legend towered above her. But his coloring was off again—he looked pale instead of glowing bronze—and his dark hair had fallen out of place. "I asked you to stay by the fountain."

No. He'd *told* her to stay. But she didn't want to fight with him about it, not after what she'd just seen him do. "I'm sorry about the dreams."

"I don't care about the dreams." His voice turned rough in a flash. "I care that you almost died."

"I don't think he really would have killed me."

"Yes, he would have, Tella. He's a Fate; you're a human and the object of his obsession. There's only one way your story with him ends—unless you let me make you an immortal."

She didn't even see him move, but suddenly Legend was on his knees in front of her. His eyes met hers in a way that was both fierce and tender all at once, while his warm hands cupped her cheeks.

"What—what are you doing?" she stammered.

"I gave up too easily." His thumb stroked her jaw. "You asked me to let you go, but I can't."

"I already told you. It was just the idea—"

"You lied." Another quick move and his hands left her face so that one of his arms could slide under her legs while another went behind her back.

"Legend—" Tella protested. "I don't need you to carry me."

He continued picking her up, and cradled her to his chest, so close she could feel his steady heartbeat. "He tried to kill you. I need to carry you."

All the air left her lungs as he marched across the ruins and started down the steps. "I'm still not letting you make me an immortal."

"We'll see." His voice had softened, and she might have called it sweet, but there was nothing sweet about the way he smiled. It was a smile that promised she'd enjoy this new game, even as she lost it.

39

Donatella

Tella had never been so cold inside one of her dreams. Her breath came out in thick white puffs that lingered like fog, as she wandered through a house of cards, which was actually more nightmare than dream. All of the cards were either queens with her smiling likeness, or kings with Jacks's cruel face, winking at her whenever she dared look at them.

"I know you're here somewhere!" Tella called. She didn't know how he'd gotten into her dream. She'd taken precautions to keep him out after he'd tried to kill her. But clearly those measures had failed.

Jacks sauntered out from between a pair of red queens with her face that both had the audacity to blow him kisses.

She stormed forward and slapped him across the cheek, hard enough to leave a red mark against his pale skin. "I will never forgive you for what you did today."

Every king and queen on the cards scowled or covered their

mouths in shock. Some looked as if they might even march out of their cards and attack, but Jacks waved them off with a lazy hand as something that was probably supposed to be sadness flickered in his silver-blue eyes.

"You were never in danger, Donatella." His voice was far more serious than usual. "I knew he wouldn't let me kill you."

"That doesn't justify what you did!" She tried not to shout, tried not to show how much he'd hurt her, how much she cared. She'd never meant to trust him, but he'd been there when her mother had died, he'd cared for her when Legend hadn't. She knew he was a Fate, she knew he had little to no conscience, but she'd started to believe he was trying to fight against his nature for her. "What would you have done if he refused to give you his power? Would you have let me die?"

"I knew he wouldn't refuse."

"That's not an answer." Tella clamped her hands into fists. She wanted to slap him again—she wanted to tackle him to the ground and take the entire house of cards down with him and hurt him the way that he'd hurt her. But Legend was right, Jacks was an immortal and she was clearly his obsession. There was no good ending to their story. He wasn't even capable of the same emotions as she was. If he felt any guilt, or if he had any real feelings for her, he'd have never tried to kill her.

"Why do you care?" Jacks said. "You just said you'd never forgive me."

"You're still ignoring the question."

Jacks rubbed the cheek where she'd slapped him as he leaned back against one of his paper kings. "Would you even believe me if I said no, that I wouldn't let you die—that I would never let you die?"

"No," Tella said. "I won't ever believe you again. And I want you to stay out of my dreams." She knew he'd made a blood vow not to use his powers on her, but if he wanted to she knew he'd find a way around the vow, like he did with everything else. "How did you even get *in here* tonight?"

The paper king that Jacks leaned against gave Tella a crooked smile. "You and I have a connection. I've never needed permission to enter your dreams."

Tella's blood ran cold. "No, we do not have a connection. And after this, I never want to see you again."

The paper king's smile faded, but Jacks looked undisturbed. "You say that now, but you'll come back to me."

40

Donatella

Time was rushing faster than blood could pour out of a sliced artery. In two days, the Fallen Star would make his claim for the throne—unless they managed to stop him.

Yesterday, the Fates had continued to torment the city by torching every church in the Temple District that did not worship one of the Fates. The air was still tinged brown from smoke. The flames had been put out by a band of brave citizens before the fire could spread to other parts of Valenda, but the damage had marked a fresh tipping point. It was exactly as Scarlett had predicted would happen in her last note. People were ready for a deliverer. When the Fallen Star appeared, all of Valenda would think he was their savior.

Tella prayed to all the saints that she would find a way to kill him inside the Immortal Library, before they ran out of time. Unfortunately, it seemed the Fated library still did not wish to be found. Or perhaps it had never been in Valenda to begin with.

Tella spied an untouched statue of the Prince of Hearts as they searched the scorched Temple districts for symbols of the library. The statue bore little resemblance to Jacks. Its face looked much kinder. Its cheeks were round instead of hollow. Its smile looked impish rather than evil, and its lips didn't appear quite so sharp.

Legend pressed a warm hand to the small of her back. He hadn't stopped touching her since the day before. It would have been smarter to separate, at least by a few feet, as they searched for symbols to lead them into the library. But it seemed Legend had adopted a new strategy when it came to winning Tella. "Ready to move on, sweetheart?"

Tella narrowed her eyes.

Legend gave her an amazed smile. "What about 'dear heart,' or 'angel'?"

"I think we can both agree I'm far from an angel. And you're not going to convince me to become an immortal with a term of endearment." She pulled away, but he quickly grabbed the sash around her waist and wound it around his fist to draw her close. It was cloudburst-blue, the same color as her striped dress. Yesterday's drab clothes hadn't kept them unnoticed, so Tella opted for prettier attire today.

"You're right, I think 'little devil' is more fitting." He kept reeling her to him, dark eyes full of laughter. He didn't seem worried that the world around them was literally crumbling—he looked at her as if she was all that mattered.

"Please tell me I'm interrupting something," Jacks drawled as he stepped out from behind the Bleeding Throne fountain directly across from them. The basin was dry—its crimson waters probably used to put out fires—leaving behind bits of cracked red that would have normally matched Jacks's haphazard attire. But for once, the Prince of Hearts looked immaculate. His golden hair was neatly tied back, his clothes were pressed, his boots were polished, and his tailored white suit was the color people usually associated with angels.

Legend instantly moved in front of Tella like a shield.

Jacks's pale lips fell into a frown. "I'm not here to make any threats—I keep my vows. I just have a gift for Donatella."

"I don't want any gifts from you," she spat.

Jacks tugged at his cravat, dissolving his impeccable appearance with one frustrated pull. "I know you hate me again, but hopefully this will prove that I'm not really your enemy." He held out a bound scroll of paper. "This is why you haven't been able to find the Immortal Library."

Tella pointedly ignored the scroll. "We're done making deals with you."

"There's no deal involved. Consider this gift my apology." Jacks's eyes slowly met hers. Today, they were a brilliant blue with threads of bloodshot red, as if he were so torn up he hadn't slept. But Tella knew that was a lie since he'd appeared in her dreams. "Even if you don't want to accept it, it's what you need if you want to find the Immortal Library. You can only locate the library if you've been there before, or if you use the Map of All."

The scroll began to glow in Jacks's hands—just like the Fates often did.

Tella tried not to look at it. The Map of All was a Fated object, similar to the Reverie Key, but instead of finding people, it located places. It was said that if a person touched the map, it would lead that person to the place they wanted to find most—even if that location was in another realm. It could reveal hidden portals, and doors to other worlds. It was priceless and mythic, and made other treasures feel as thin as slips of paper.

It was difficult to resist the urge to grab it right out of Jacks's hands. "We don't need your map."

"But we'll take it," Legend said. With one lightning-quick move, the rolled map was in his hand.

Tella expected a protest from Jacks, but he merely placed his pale hands in his pockets. "I hope you can now find what you're looking for." He gave Tella a final look, meeting her gaze with sad, hooded eyes and so much sincerity he could have been a picture of a saint on a confessional wall.

But while she could believe he was upset that she hated him again, she doubted he truly regretted what he'd done. Tella had no doubts that Jacks wanted her, but wanting someone wasn't the same as loving them, and yesterday he'd proved that he wanted his powers even more than he wanted her.

Jacks walked away without another word.

Legend unbound the map. His face was aloof, but the quickness with which he unrolled the scroll betrayed a hint of his eagerness at possessing the Fated object, despite its unsavory source.

The paper was a bland shade of oatmeal, but Tella watched as it shifted in Legend's fingers. It started out blank, but as he held on to it, a spot of dark blue ink appeared. It grew into the smoldering remains of the Temple District, sketched piles of ash forming alongside statues of Fates. Tella saw the Prince of Hearts statue and the Bleeding Throne fountain. Then she appeared. First her untamed ringlets took shape, followed by her heart-shaped face, and her striped gown with its sweetheart neckline and tiny cap sleeves.

She waited for a rendering of Legend to materialize next, but all that showed up was a tiny star at her feet.

She was where Legend wanted to be.

"Don't look so surprised." He flashed a crooked smile, eyes filling with the same teasing look he'd given her earlier when he'd called her *sweetheart*. But she noticed that he didn't even brush her finger as he handed her the magical map.

Was it possible that Legend was actually falling in love with her?

Not that she wanted him to. Not anymore. No matter how much just the thought of the possibility of his love made her heart start to race. She didn't want him to become human and thus susceptible to death for her. And he'd made it clear, over and over, that he didn't want to, either.

Tella looked down at the map as it began to shift again. She didn't want to trust the map—it felt too much like trusting Jacks—and she imagined Legend had to feel the same way. But she was grateful he'd taken the Fated object.

The uncontrollable feeling that time was moving too fast and they were moving too slow was back. Whenever Tella thought about Scarlett, Tella's heart clenched with fear. She reminded herself that her older sister was cautious, and the letter she'd sent yesterday promised she would bring them the Fallen Star's blood tonight. But Tella couldn't help but fear that something was about to go wrong, and even if Scarlett managed to get the blood, it wouldn't do them any good if they didn't find the Ruscica. Tella and Legend didn't have the luxury of wasting time—and the map was too incredible to ignore.

As Tella and Legend followed the Map of All, it didn't just outline a route for them, it revealed a strange sense of humor as it affixed odd labels to several of the places, plants, and animals that Tella and Legend passed—and some that they didn't pass.

HIGHLY INTELLIGENT DOG
BEWARE OF LICE
ACTUAL SKELETONS INSIDE THE CLOSETS
VALENDA'S FINEST FISH FUDGE
UNDERGROUND TUNNELS THAT LEAD OUT OF
   TOWN
UNDERGROUND TUNNELS THAT LEAD TO DEATH
   AND DISMEMBERMENT

Tella had almost stopped thinking about where they were actually heading, when the path on the map finally ended just south of the Satine District. The words *Entrance to the Immortal Library* appeared. But all Tella could see was an out-of-use sky carriage house with a set of rotted boards nailed crosswise in front of the main door.

The words *Danger* and *Do Not Enter* were painted crudely over the boards, with symbols of skulls and kissing spiders painted beneath them.

Tella had never encountered the deadly arachnids, but she'd heard the stories. Kissing spiders attacked at night, while people were sleeping, laying eggs inside of a person's mouth and then sealing their victim's lips shut with their webs. There was no way to destroy the webs. They remained in place until the spiders hatched, and by then the victims were always dead.

"This is all a glamour," Legend said.

Tella looked down at the map. The words *He's right* hovered over the image of the infested carriage house, and yet she still felt reticent to enter. "If it's a glamour, why are you ripping the boards off the door?"

"There's a mental magic attached, like the illusions I use. We have to treat this as if it's real to get through."

Tella clamped her mouth shut as they stepped inside. She told herself that none of it was real. The rotting scent snaking up her nose was in her mind. Whatever squished beneath her slippers was not fungus; the yellow spiders crawling over her arms were not really there.

"This is the oldest magic I've ever felt . . ." Legend trailed off, and for a moment she thought she saw something like admiration in his eyes as the walls around them begin to crumble and a waterfall of spiders poured down from the ceiling.

Tella fought the urge to scream lest one, or more, landed in her mouth.

Legend captured her hand and propelled her forward through an avalanche of spiders. She felt their tiny legs crawling everywhere as the murderous spiders multiplied, covering every inch of her skin.

Tella didn't know if death by illusion was possible. Then she remembered what Jacks had said about needing to summon Fated places with blood. The wound on her palm from when she'd exchanged blood with Jacks was nearly healed, but Tella imagined she could reopen it with her nails.

She pulled her hand free from Legend's and scratched her healing wound, drawing a fresh surge of blood.

Drop it there, instructed the map, pointing to an eruption of spiders in the corner of the room. There were too many for Tella to make out a symbol, but she obeyed the map and instantly the spiders, the fetid ground, and the decaying walls all vanished.

One blink and the world was falling apart, and then she and Legend were in a courtyard made of sandstone walls covered in star jasmine that smelled as sweet as it looked. Tella took a timid breath. She wasn't sure if this was another illusion or the Fated library, but it was extremely preferable to that cascade of killer spiders.

Above them half the sky was intense with sunlight, while the other half shimmered with stars. At one end of it was a decorative sandstone arch with two massive statues on either side, formed of sparkling peach sand. The statues' lower halves were feline, while their torsos were human, one male, one female. Their heads would have appeared human as well if not for the curving horns poking out from the tops of them.

The male statue opened his mouth. "Welcome, fellow immortal and young mortal."

"We hope you find what you seek," added the female. "But be warned, there is a small tithe to step inside and read our books." Both statues' mouths slammed shut with an audible snap.

Tella's jaw crashed to a close as well. She fought to part her lips, to open her mouth to speak, but she couldn't.

She turned to Legend. He shook his head, his mouth as closed as hers.

Their silence must have been the cost of entering the library.

41

Donatella

The silence inside the Immortal Library was absolute and alive. Tella could feel it swallowing up her footsteps, and sucking up the sound of flipping book pages, and flickering wicks inside hurricane glasses, but the worst was the feel of the silence keeping her lips pressed painfully shut.

Legend reached out and took her hand once more. His eyes silently promised they were in this together, and then he pressed the world's softest kiss to her knuckles. She felt it from her fingertips all the way down to her toes, reminding her there were good uses for closed lips, as they ventured under an archway made of books and farther inside the Fated place.

Everything smelled of dust trapped in light, cracked leather, and wayward dreams. Breathing in and out through her nose, Tella looked down at the Map of All. It had transformed once they'd entered the library. It now revealed an entire kingdom made of books that could have either been a book lover's nightmare or their wish come true. There was a *Broken Spine Castle*, an *Unread River*, a *Ravine of Ripped Pages*, a *Poetry Valley*, a set of *Novel Mountains*, and then finally the *Ruscica and Books for Advanced Imaginations*.

The most direct route to this room was through an area referred to as the Zoo. Tella wondered if it would have books in cages, but the Zoo didn't even have bookshelves. The volumes all roamed freely in this room as they clung together to take the shapes of different animals. Tella spied bookish rhinos, papier-mâché elephants, and very tall giraffes that milled about in an oddly peaceful silence. The elephant sniffed at Tella with its leathery-gray trunk of books, while a paper bunny made of loose pages noiselessly hopped after Legend. The bunny continued to follow as they left the Zoo and reached the Reading Chamber, where books formed couches and chairs and one massive throne.

A warning flashed on the map: *Do not sit on the throne.*

Tella was instantly curious, but not enough to test the map, especially when they were so close to what they wanted. According to the map, all they had to do was climb the staircase made of books, which rested behind the throne, and they would find the Ruscica room.

The steps were too narrow for them to walk side by side.

Tella reluctantly released Legend's hand as she started to climb. The bookish stairs were the type of steep that made it feel treacher-

ous to turn around. They were unsteady, shifting beneath her slippers. But Legend touched her back or her shoulder every few steps,
letting her know that he was still there. He was with her, and he
wasn't leaving even though she couldn't see or hear him.

It made her wonder at all the other things he'd said to her in the
past without words. By the time they reached the top of the steps and
the room with the Ruscica, Tella was grateful the library swallowed
up sound. It didn't enhance her other senses, but it made her more
aware of them, and more aware of Legend as he came up beside her
and silently brushed his fingers against hers. The movement was
quick and subtle, and she might not have noticed it if she'd been
standing there waiting for him to speak, rather than paying attention to his silence.

The map didn't give any indication of where in the room the
Ruscica rested, forcing her and Legend to split up as they searched.
Many of the volumes had spines covered in numbers, symbols, or
languages she didn't read. There were also a few spines with titles
that she would have liked to read, had she not felt pressed for
time.

Mermaids and Mermen and How to Become One
Ten Essential Rules of Time Travel
Shape-shifting for Beginners
Cakes, Cakes, and More Cakes
Turning Your Shadow into a Pet
Love, Death, and Immortality

She might have picked up the book on cakes or immortality, had the latter not been sitting right next to a thick flesh-colored volume with one word crudely stitched into the spine: *Ruscica*.

The book slid out from the shelf in a cloud of red-tinged dust that made the tips of Tella's fingers tingle as she took it.

She found Legend on the opposite side of the silent room. When she showed him her prize, he smiled. Neither of them knew if it would have the information they needed, but Tella finally felt victorious as Legend took her hand again.

After the Maiden Death and the Assassin had visited his home in the Spice Quarter, Legend had decided they needed to move every night. But a part of Tella thought he was just showing off his many homes. His four-story coastal cottage looked as if it had been built around the same time as Count Nicolas's estate, but whereas Nicolas's estate had appeared as if it was in need of magic, Legend's house was the opposite. Full of glittering windows and expansive balconies that looked over the foaming ocean, the house sat on Valenda's rocky coast the way that Tella imagined Legend would have sat on his throne, demanding attention by simply being there.

They'd started about a mile away, and Legend's fingers stayed entwined with hers for the entire walk. She should have broken free; earlier his touch had grounded her, as he pulled her through the spiders and steadied her in the library. But now, he wasn't helping, he was making a claim. Tella reminded herself that nothing good could come from this as she looked down on their clasped hands. But she didn't let go. He had long fingers, strong palms, neatly trimmed nails—and no traces of ink.

She lifted their hands, peering closer. "Your black rose is gone?"

"Did you really think I'd keep it?" He dragged her hand up to his mouth and brushed a kiss to her knuckles. "You don't have to be jealous of the tattoo anymore."

"I wasn't jealous."

"Then maybe I should have left it on longer." The rose reappeared on the back of his hand.

"You're wretched." Tella lifted her free hand to playfully smack him with her book.

He caught her wrist before she could, and then he took her other hand and trapped them both behind her. They'd finally reached the porch of his cottage, and in one quick move he spun her around and pressed her back to the door. "I think you like me because I'm terrible."

"No." Tella wiggled against him, but he didn't budge. "I've decided I like nice boys, like Caspar."

"Lucky for me he doesn't like girls that way. And I can also be nice. But I think you like it when I'm not."

He freed her wrist and wrapped his hands around her hips. Tella's heart raced as his fingers spread out, claiming her as he drew her closer.

Maybe one more kiss wouldn't hurt.

Waves crashed against the nearby coast, filling the air with salt and damp, while Legend continued leaning—

The door behind her opened wide.

Tella stumbled backward, and she might have fallen if not for Legend's arms tightening around her.

"Sorry about that." Julian ran a hand through his hair, looking mildly embarrassed, though she sensed he actually wasn't. There was something hard in his eyes that wasn't normally there. And was it Tella's imagination, or was he refusing to look at her?

He'd promised Legend he'd stay away from the Menagerie, where Scarlett was being kept, but knowing Julian, he was finding ways to meet with Jovan, who was supposed to be watching her sister.

"Is Scarlett all right?" Tella asked.

Julian finally looked at her, and he even managed to smile. But Tella couldn't shake the feeling something was wrong. "I just need to talk to my brother."

Legend's arms slowly left her waist. "I'll find you when we're done," he whispered.

Tella stepped inside the house and shut the door behind her. But she couldn't bring herself to go up the curving wooden staircase to her bedroom just yet. If Julian was lying and Scarlett wasn't all right—if she'd been hurt trying to get Gavriel's blood, or if she wasn't able to get it at all—Tella didn't want to be protected from the information.

She stood close to the door, hands pressed against the warm wood, but there was only silence, save for the ocean waves. Wondering if the brothers were giving her a chance to walk out of earshot, she took a few noisy steps from the door and quickly tiptoed back in time to hear Julian say, "What are you doing with Tella?"

She jolted at the sound of her name, her alarm taking a new direction as she moved closer and peered through the door's spy-hole.

Legend's response was too low for her to hear, but she could see his expression. His dark brows slashed down and the look in his eyes shuttered.

"I know you don't love her," Julian said.

Tella staggered back a step. She already knew Legend didn't love her, but the way Julian said the words made it sound so much worse. It didn't matter that his voice was soft. The words were like a period at the end of a sentence, small but absolute in their power.

"If you care about her at all, then you should let her go rather than try to change her."

Silence.

Tella dared to look through the spy-hole once more. The sun was almost set. Night was taking over the sky as Legend looked down on his brother with something like an accusation. "That's her choice to make, not yours. Although you didn't object when I told you that a blood oath could make you ageless."

"And I hate myself for it sometimes." Julian's voice turned harsh. "I hate not just watching you lose yourself piece by piece, but benefitting from it. Then I saw you with Tella. I thought, maybe after you saved her from the deck, you would change."

Tella held her breath, but nothing about Legend changed.

He looked like the Legend who'd left her on those steps in front of the Temple of the Stars—closed off and cold and utterly unreachable. "If I'd changed, I'd be dead."

"You don't know that," Julian argued. "Maybe you would have just done things differently. You're careless with your life. You take chances because you know you can't die. That's fine if that's how *you* want to live, but don't be careless with her life." He looked up at his brother, brown hair sheltering eyes that appeared to be waging a battle between abandon and hope. "Do you remember what the game was like when it first began?"

"I try not to."

"You should, it was fun."

"It was barely a traveling carnival," Legend mumbled.

Julian smiled, as if hope had just won. "It was. But it still inspired people to dream and believe in magic. It made *me* believe in magic."

Legend eyed his brother as if he'd lost his mind. "You know magic is real."

"Just because something is real doesn't mean you believe in it. The Fates are real, but I don't put my faith in them. I used to put my faith in you, and I want to do it again. I know you can be better than this."

Legend laughed, but it sounded so far from humorous that it made Tella sad, not just for Legend but for all of them. "When did you become such an idealist?"

"When I met a girl who loved her sister so much she was able to wish her back to life. You might possess magic, but love like that is real power."

"And yet all the love in the world wouldn't have brought Tella back without my magic."

"She never would have died without your magic, either." Julian's smile disappeared. "Tella would have found another way. She didn't and doesn't need you to save her. She needs to save *you*."

42

Scarlett

Scarlett stared in the mirror that rested above her marble-pink vanity and tried not to cry at what she saw. Tella wouldn't have cried. Tella would have willed her pain into power and used it to find a way to fix everything—no matter the cost.

Scarlett could do that, too. She could do it for her sister, for Julian, for everyone in the empire, and for herself. Even if it felt impossible at the moment.

At least her sister and Julian couldn't see her right now.

Scarlett continued to stare at her new reflection in the mirror, as her thoughts took her back to the night before, after she'd delivered her last note to Tella and Julian, when everything had gone so awry.

Once a day, since Scarlett had first arrived in the Menagerie, the Lady Prisoner's purple eyes turned milky-white, letting Scarlett know she was glimpsing a fragment of the future as she told Scarlett, *The only way to defeat the Fallen Star is to become what he wants most.* But all the Fallen Star wanted from Scarlett was for her to conquer her powers, and control the emotions of others. And her original plan had been to do just that—to cultivate her powers to change his feelings and make him love her, so that he would become mortal.

But over the last couple of days the Fallen Star had made it clear that if Scarlett mastered her abilities, it would be the catalyst that would turn her into an immortal Fate.

He'd told her this to encourage her to conquer her powers. But Scarlett knew that once she was an immortal, she would no longer be able to love. Love was such a fundamental part of what drove her, she didn't even know who she'd be without love. What if it made her like her father, who only wanted power?

So, despite Anissa's warning, Scarlett had planned to get the blood that Tella and Julian needed for their Fated book.

"Are you certain you want to go through with this?" asked the Lady Prisoner. "I can't lie, so if I make a threat, I have to be willing to follow through. And if he catches you, your magical key won't get you out of one of his cages."

"I know," Scarlett said. "But if this works, neither of us will have to worry about being caged at all." Which was one of the reasons she'd chosen to trust the Fate. Scarlett didn't believe Anissa's concern for her was genuine, but she did believe that Anissa wanted out of her cage. "I think this will work, but if you're having second thoughts—"

"Gavriel and I have had skirmishes like this for decades." The Lady Prisoner

hopped off her perch to move closer to Scarlett. "I can handle whatever he throws my way."

"So can I," Scarlett said, feigning confidence she didn't feel as she dropped the wineglass from her hand, shattering it against the marble floor. Sharp shards of glass landed around her feet while garnet wine spread out, staining the hem of Scarlett's pink dress as the Lady Prisoner reached through her bars and picked up the largest glass fragment.

A moment later Scarlett cried out, loud enough to alert the guard outside her door. He clattered in an instant later. One look at Scarlett, forced against Anissa's cage, as Anissa reached through the bars to press a shard of glass against Scarlett's neck, and a moldy green cloud of fear formed around the guard as he reached for his sword.

"I wouldn't do that, unless you want me to kill her." The Lady Prisoner tilted her spike of broken glass to the most defenseless part of Scarlett's throat.

"Now," she went on conversationally. "Fetch Gavriel. Tell him what you've seen and that if he doesn't come here right now, I'll slit his daughter's throat."

The guard immediately did as he was told. Like Scarlett, he knew the Lady Prisoner couldn't lie.

"I hope this works," the Fate whispered once he left. "I really wouldn't enjoy killing you."

"I don't particularly want to die," Scarlett said, hoping she hadn't overestimated her value to the Fallen Star. Scarlett knew that he didn't care for her, and he certainly didn't love her. But based on the amount of time he spent each day working with her to conquer her powers, she knew that he very much cared about her abilities and what she could do for him. And yet her palms began to sweat as he stepped inside.

Scarlett didn't know, and didn't want to know, what the Fallen Star had been doing, but there was blood spatter on his bone-white shirt and fury in his eyes. The room grew hotter as it filled with the violent red sparks surrounding him.

"Use your fire on me and I'll kill her," the Lady Prisoner called from behind her bars. "If you want her, come get her yourself."

Scarlett didn't have to pretend to tremble at the words. Because of the Lady Prisoner's inability to lie, if the Fallen Star did use his flames, then she would be compelled to follow through with her threats. But both Scarlett and the Lady Prisoner had agreed on the risk. If the Fallen Star used his fire, then he would defeat Anissa before she was able to stab him with the broken glass and collect the blood that Scarlett needed.

Gavriel's sparks disappeared and he crossed the room faster than Scarlett could blink.

She stumbled to the side as the Lady Prisoner shoved her out of the way and sliced the Fallen Star's throat with her glass.

The cut was bloody and perfect.

Too perfect. But Scarlett wouldn't realize that until later.

She ran to the Fallen Star as he dropped to his knees and pressed her handkerchief against his bleeding throat to collect his spilling blood as he closed his eyes and died.

It was the ugliest thing Scarlett had ever done. Was this what it was to be a Fate? It lasted less than a minute, but it felt like an eternity before his golden eyes closed and his body went limp. Scarlett couldn't stop her legs or her hands from shaking. She knew they hadn't killed him forever, though he deserved it. He'd killed her mother and countless others. Still, it felt wrong.

And Scarlett was already imagining what the Fallen Star would do in his fury when he did come back to life. She needed to move quickly.

She dripped blood across the marble floors as she ran to the bathing room with the bloodied cloth to squeeze the Fallen Star's blood into a vial. Why, why hadn't she thought to hide the vial somewhere on her person to have right at his throat?

Drip. Drip.

It was taking too long to fill the vial.

Drip. Drip. Drip.

"What are you doing with that, auhtara?"

Scarlett's eyes shot up to the bathing room mirror, her trembling limbs turning to liquid. The Fallen Star stood behind her like a bronze statue that had been sliced open. His skin was pale as the dead and his neck was still bloody, but he was very much alive. Had he been pretending? Or did he just recover that fast?

He knocked the vial to the ground, shattering the glass, and wrapped a hand around her throat, choking off her air. "Disappointed I'm not dead?"

"Please," Scarlett rasped. "I—I only took the blood because I thought if I drank it then maybe it would help me finally conquer my magic."

"Then you should have just asked. I would have given it to you, auhtara. But now I have to give you something else instead." His fingers squeezed her throat again and her world went dark.

When Scarlett woke later on, her head felt too heavy to move, and there was something tight around her neck, grating against her skin.

"The cage will probably take a while to get used to." The Fallen Star's voice held a hint of diversion.

Scarlett's eyes flashed open to a world of red. There were vertical rows of ruby-red beads fitted around her head—he'd imprisoned her in a cage. A sob shook her chest. She tried to rip it off; her fingers tore at the gems, tried to bend their bars and

rip them off, but they were ineffectual, and soon she was weeping too hard to do
anything else.

The Fallen Star reached in between the ruby bars to stroke Scarlett's damp
cheek. *"Don't betray me again. My punishment won't be so kind next time."*

The memory faded as Scarlett looked in her vanity mirror. The ruby
cage encasing her head looked like the bloody cousin to the cage worn
by the Maiden Death. But rather than looking powerful like that
Fate always did in Decks of Destiny, Scarlett thought that she looked
entirely powerless. She hadn't been able to sleep wearing it, so there
were deep circles beneath her eyes, and since her hair had been down
when he'd put it on, strands of her dark hair stuck to her throat, held
in place by the unmoving collar of the cage.

Anissa had tried to tell her it was pretty, and that it matched
her scarlet earrings. They'd once been a treasured gift from
her mother. *Your father gave these to me,* she said, *because scarlet was my*
favorite color. They used to make Scarlett think that Marcello
Dragna, the father who'd raised her, had once been a better man.
But, Scarlett realized, her mother must have been referring to the
Fallen Star.

Scarlett tried not to think about her mother. But for once, she
wished she could go back in time to talk to her and ask her what
to do.

Scarlett hadn't contacted Julian and her sister. She'd been too
ashamed and embarrassed to slip them a note letting them know that
she'd failed in getting the blood, and she didn't want them to see her

like this, even for a second. Scarlett knew that she had to be even more careful now. She couldn't risk using the Reverie Key unless it was an emergency.

She couldn't make another mistake and she couldn't run away. If Scarlett wanted to save herself and everyone else before the Fallen Star took the throne the day after tomorrow, she had only one choice left: to conquer her power and use it to make him love her.

She took a deep breath and left her bedchamber to meet him.

Tonight, he was dressed in brown leather pants, a loose white shirt, and a pale gold cape that matched the victorious gleam in his eyes. He'd been in an excellent mood ever since he'd placed the cage around Scarlett's head; he liked being able to demonstrate just how much power he had over her. But tonight he appeared almost boyish in his excitement.

When Scarlett took a seat beside him on the marble bench near Anissa's cage, he grinned and stroked the curving ruby bars surrounding Scarlett's face. "My Fates have finished tracking down the members of the royal council. Now all their severed heads are sitting on pikes at the docks. There are no more barriers to stop me from claiming the throne tomorrow night."

"Tomorrow." Scarlett tried to keep the panic from her voice. "I thought you were waiting another day?"

"I've never been good at being patient." He jumped up from his seat. "But don't worry, to help prepare you for tomorrow's coronation, I've brought a gift that I'm hoping will aid you in finally conquering your abilities."

The Fallen Star called for his personal guard to open the door, and a young woman who looked as if someone had taken a magic cloth to wipe away half of her coloring stumbled into the room. Her hair was a faded shade of red, and her skin was pallid white, with dull black tattoos peeking out from beneath her long black gloves. Yet the colors of her feelings were anything but dim. Vitriolic shades of rotted plum swirled around her in spiteful, enraged circles.

The Fallen Star strode toward his captive the way a hunter might approach trapped prey. "I rescued her from the Temple District when it was on fire yesterday. Unfortunately, she's not very grateful; I've already had to punish her. She might be difficult for you to work with, unless you find a way to control her." He ran a finger down the young woman's cheek.

The woman snapped her teeth over his fingers, biting the tips.

The Fallen Star ripped his hand from her mouth before she could draw blood. "Behave." His voice remained gentle, but his words were followed by a burst of flames that singed the ends of her hair.

"If you succeed in controlling her emotions, then I will take that cage off your head. But if you don't, I'm afraid the results will be unpleasant." His gaze traced the lines of rubies imprisoning Scarlett's head. "I've been wondering if perhaps you haven't conquered your powers because you've lacked the proper motivation. Hopefully you have it now. I'll come back in the morning to view your progress, and for your sake, *auhtara,* I really hope there is progress."

Donatella

Tella couldn't sleep. She tossed and turned until she'd ripped all the cool silk sheets off her bed. But as soon as she did, they rearranged themselves, tucking her back in. She didn't know what kind of glamour it was, but she knew it was somehow Legend's doing.

He was so frustrating and confusing and impossible not to think about.

He hadn't come to see her after his conversation with Julian. And now that Jacks had taken away his ability to meet Tella in her dreams, she knew she wouldn't see him there, either. But even if he had, she didn't know what was left to say.

She needs to save you.

But Legend didn't want to be saved the way Julian wanted him to be. And Tella didn't know if she *could* really save him, or if she might just become the reason he died and didn't come back to life.

She sat up, abandoning the idea of sleep, and pulled back the delicate blue curtains that surrounded her canopy bed. Everything in the room had a dreamlike quality, from the sparkling chandeliers to the fur-thick rugs and extraordinarily fluffy cushions on her chairs. She imagined that like the sheets that tucked themselves back in, it was all mostly an illusion, but she enjoyed it just the same.

Padding over the soft floors, she wandered to the Ruscica sitting on her desk. It glowed faintly, full of Fated power. But unless Scarlett appeared with the Fallen Star's blood, none of that power would be unlocked, and they'd have no way of defeating the Fallen Star. Her mother's death would go unavenged, Valenda would burn, and Scarlett—

Tella stopped her runaway thoughts before they went too far.

Scarlett might not have appeared with the blood yet, but the night had only just begun. It was too soon to worry. She was probably going to come later, with or without the blood. Scarlett possessed a magical key, and if something had gone wrong, she'd have used it to escape.

Tella ran her fingers over the ancient cover of the Ruscica. She'd never even opened it, and yet she was putting a lot of faith in it. She wished she didn't need blood to read it. But when she opened the book, her wish didn't come true. The pages were blank and untouched.

Tella eyed the writing set on her desk. The nib of the glass-tipped pen was sharp enough to draw blood. Jacks had said she needed the Fallen Star's blood to read his story. But Jacks was rarely entirely honest.

Curious, Tella pricked her finger with the pen nib and let the blood drip into an ink bowl, filling it with red, until there was enough to write inside the magic book.

Tell me a story.

She watched as her blood soaked into the paper and slowly re-formed into a new set of curving words: Welcome to the life of Donatella Dragna.

Not what she'd hoped for. Tella already knew this story, and yet she was curious to read what the book said about her.

A table of contents formed beneath the greeting. She'd have expected it to mark her life in years, but the table favored significant events. They appeared to be listed in order of their occurrence. Some were obvious, like *The birth of Donatella Dragna, Donatella and Scarlett's mother vanishes,* and *Donatella's first kiss.* But she was surprised by some of the other captions:

> *Donatella spends a week pretending she's a mermaid*
> *Donatella steals a goat and names him Cuddles*
> *Donatella steals all her sister's underclothes*
> *Donatella writes her first letter to Legend*
> *Donatella marries the Prince of Hearts*

Tella's blood ran cold. She looked back over the table of contents, to see if there was anything else that wasn't true. But none of the other claims were false.

Maybe the book had a sense of humor like the Map of All? Or maybe Jacks had given her a fake map that led to a fake library where she'd gotten this fake book.

She hadn't married Jacks. Tella wasn't married. She wasn't even sure she ever wanted to *get* married.

According to the table of contents, the event happened right after her mother had died. Tella violently flipped through the book until she found the dreaded chapter in question. She read each word carefully, but there were sections that stood out more than others.

If her heart had not been so heavy with grief and pain, Donatella would have known better than to trust the Prince of Hearts.

If she'd not been burning with despair, she would have realized the danger in repeating magical words as her blood mingled with his.

If she'd not just watched her mother die, she would have known that the Prince of Hearts was not taking her grief away because he cared. The Prince of Hearts did not know how to care. He only knew how to take what he wanted, and he wanted Donatella Dragna.

But poor Donatella was too grief-stricken to see it. When he told her to speak, she repeated his words, creating an immortal bond that would forever tie their souls together in eternal matrimony.

No way in all the hells. Tella didn't want to believe it. But a part of her felt it. If she was being really honest, she'd felt it since the night it had happened, when she'd decided to lie there with him, to sleep beside him instead of leave. She'd felt it again, when she'd gone back the next day to ask for help. And again, when she'd felt so betrayed and so hurt by him after he had nearly killed her, when all she should have been was angry.

If it had been a human wedding, she'd have just slammed the book shut and pretended it had never happened. But this wasn't something she could ignore or pretend away.

This was an immortal bond that would tie her soul to Jacks's forever.

44

Donatella

Tella didn't care that it was the middle of the night, that she'd forgotten her cloak, or that the streets of Valenda were far more dangerous than they'd ever been now that the Fates had taken over. She marched to Jacks's as if she were deadlier than anything she might encounter.

Once at the door, she pounded her fist and then stormed inside the moment it opened. A riot of clacking and clicking and clapping assaulted her immediately.

It seemed that rather than hiding from the Fates, half the city had just come here. Tella wondered if Jacks had altered their feelings to get them there, or if all of them were as foolish as she was.

Heavily perfumed bodies brushed against her as she moved through the crush. The last time she'd been at Jacks's it had been mostly men, but tonight the gentlemen were outnumbered by the ladies. All of them were coiffed and clean. None of them were covered in sweat like Tella.

A horrid spike of jealousy shot through her at the thought that she might find Jacks with his arms around another girl. But was she really jealous or did she have that sudden feeling just because they were immortally married?

Married!

Tella still couldn't believe it. She'd flirted with trusting him again after he'd given her the map. But she never should have trusted him enough to let him trick her like this in the first place.

"Aren't you full of fire tonight?" The lively crowd parted as Mistress Luck strode closer to Tella, all green-velvet-clad curves and cryptic eyes. "Seems you really can't stay away from him."

"Where is he?" Tella spat.

The Fate pointed toward a wall covered in black-and-white hearts. "There's a door hidden there; it will take you to the gaming room where Jacks likes to play. But—"

Tella strode off without hearing the woman's warning. It wouldn't have mattered what she'd said.

Tella tore through the door and down a set of stairs, which landed her inside a room that looked as if it had been attacked by a deck of playing cards. Everything was black and white with violent hints of red. The white walls were striped with crooked lines of glittering red spades, while the floor looked as if someone had plucked handfuls of clubs, diamonds, and hearts and tossed them everywhere. In the center of the room, the heavy round table was equally wild, piled high with chips, cards, bits of jewelry, a few fancy shirts, and half-empty bottles of liquor. The chairs encircling it were full of gamblers, all in various states of undress, explaining the clothes mixed with the chips.

The only one who remained mostly dressed was Jacks. He'd lost his jacket from earlier, discarded his gold cravat, and his shirt was open, missing all of its diamond-sharp buttons.

"Everyone out!" Tella shouted.

A dozen heads turned her way, intoxicated faces all wearing various shades of surprise. Save for Jacks. His silver-blue eyes met hers expectantly and then he grinned like the devil he was. He'd known this moment was coming. "Hello, wife."

Still looking at her, Jacks gave a lazy wave of his hand toward the table. "Ladies and gentlemen, I'd introduce you to my bride, but I think I'd rather kick you out so we can chat in private."

Tella expected a few murmurs of protest, but Jacks must have been using his newly restored powers to control everyone's emotions. There were no objections from the group, and within a minute, his court of half-naked gamblers was on the stairs.

"That was quite an appearance." Jacks leaned into his winged chair and kicked one scuffed brown boot onto the table. "Have you come to consummate the—"

Tella launched herself at him before he could finish. His chair fell back, bringing both of them with it.

"You foul, heartless, wretched, cheating, manipulating, apple-sucking demon!" The curses were inelegant, not nearly as dirty as they should have been, and her blows were ineffective. He'd easily caged her wrists in his cool hands, so she didn't even hit him, but it felt good to fight him. It felt good to wrestle against his grip.

"You tricked me into marrying you!"

"You begged me to help you."

"I wanted you to take my emotions away, not make me your wife."

"But I've been a good husband. I told you how to find the Vanished Market, I gave you that Fated map."

"You also threatened to kill me! And you nearly did!" Tella panted as she finally ripped her wrists free from his icy hands. She would have tried to hit him again, but she needed to stop touching him.

She pulled herself from him, then she shoved up from the ground until she towered over him. He wasn't even breathing heavily. He just looked up at her as if he were a misbehaving angel with gold hair hanging across his pale forehead.

"I want you to undo it," she demanded. "I want the marriage revoked, and then I never want to see you again."

"Why would I agree to that?" he droned. "There's nothing really in this solution for me."

"You want to be married to someone that hates you?"

"Maybe I like the intensity of it." He grinned at her as he pushed up from the floor, leaving the chair lying between them.

Tella could barely breathe she was so furious. She would have walked out if she could have. But this marriage wasn't something she could ignore or pretend away. Even now she could feel it in the way she hated him. Fiery and all-consuming, so much stronger now that he was standing in front of her like her own personal villain.

"If you don't undo this, I swear I will kill you." She stepped over the chair, until they were so close she had to crane her neck to look up at his sharp face. "If I remain your wife, I promise that I will make you fall in love with me. I will become everything you've ever wanted, and the moment you are mortal, I'll stab the closest sharp object through your chest and end your heartbeat once and for all."

"Don't be so dramatic." Jacks sighed. "If you want out of the marriage, there's a simpler way to do it."

He reached in his boot and pulled out a dagger.

Tella scrambled back, nearly tripping on the fallen chair.

"Don't worry, my love, it's for you to use on me." He flipped the dagger in his hand and held the hilt toward her. "Immortal matrimony cannot be undone with signatures and pieces of paper. To sever our connection, you have to wound me."

"And doing that will undo the marriage?"

"'Undoing' implies it never happened." Jacks's voice switched from sharp to dull in a flash. "What's done cannot be undone, but it can be severed. All you have to do is use the knife and say the words: *Tersyd atai es detarum.*" He stepped over the chair until the space between them was gone once again.

Tella cautiously accepted the blade. It was the same jeweled dagger they'd used the night he'd taken her emotions, when he'd also married her. She slowly tipped it toward Jacks's throat.

He didn't flinch. He didn't even appear to breathe, though his lips remained parted as he looked her directly in the eyes, his gaze the saddest shade of blue she'd ever seen. She didn't believe it was real. And yet, the look on his face was so convincing, it made her wonder just enough to hesitate.

"Should I make this easier for you?" He spread his shirt apart, baring his chest of smooth, sculpted skin, like marble with a heartbeat. She could hear the rapid pulse of it as it moved in tandem with hers, pounding harder with every breath she took. When they first met, his heart hadn't beat at all. Then it started again—because of her.

She gripped the dagger tighter, but didn't make another move.

"Why are you hesitating, my love?"

"Why are you making this so easy?"

"You think this is easy for me?" Jacks leaned forward until his skin pressed against the blade. For once he didn't smell like apples. He smelled like liquor and heartache, and when he spoke, his words were almost too soft to hear. "You think it's in my nature to be kind?"

"There's nothing kind about what you did to me."

"You're right," he whispered. "What I did was purely selfish. So stab me before I decide to be selfish again. The longer we're bound together, the more difficult it will be for you to fight it. You might hate me, but you'll find yourself wanting and needing to be near me. So if you really wish to end this, do it now. Cut me and sever everything that ties us together."

Sweat slicked the jeweled hilt in Tella's hands. She wanted to do this. She wanted to slash him and be done. But something about the words *sever everything that ties us* gave her pause.

Maybe he'd known all along that as soon as she found out they were married she'd come here demanding that he end it. Maybe that's why he was giving in so easily, because that's what he actually wanted—to sever everything that tied them together. She was supposed to be his true love. She was the one who made his heart beat again—which meant she was also his greatest weakness.

"If I do this, if I sever our connection, will I still be your true love?"

"Why would you care?" Jacks's lips thinned as if he couldn't wait to be rid of her, but the look in his eyes said he wanted to devour her. "I imagine after today you won't be kissing me again."

"Just answer the question, Jacks."

In a flash, he wrapped his cool hand around her shaking one and dragged the dagger lower, creating a line of pink skin as he moved it to the center of his chest. "I don't know if you're my true love, Donatella. All I know is that I want you to be."

His hands left the dagger and slid around her waist. For a moment she couldn't move. His fingers were colder than they had ever been, creating chills that went deep beneath her skin.

"I know what I did was wrong. But if you're looking for a sad story where I justify what I've done, you're not going to find it. I'm the villain, even in my own story. But you were supposed to play a different role." Misery filled his eyes. "You were supposed to be my true love. You were supposed to want me, not him. You were supposed to be as obsessed with me as I am with you." He gripped her even tighter, the dagger threatening to pierce his skin, as he leaned his cool forehead against hers.

"If you're holding back from ending this because you think I'll kill you or hurt you once our connection is severed, that thought could not be further from the truth. When I told Legend I'd kill you if he didn't give me the power I needed, I didn't mean it—I wouldn't have done it. A part of me even hoped he'd say no, so that you would walk away from him and choose me. I'm selfish, and I want you, but I would never harm you."

"You already have," Tella said. And then she slashed his chest with the dagger.

45

Donatella

It was only supposed to hurt him, but Tella doubled over in agony as the knife pierced Jacks's skin and she said the words to free herself. Her ribs and heart were suddenly on fire. She couldn't breathe. It felt as if someone had ripped into her chest and taken something vital.

Her vision blurred, and when it finally returned, the entire card room was out of focus, except for Jacks. For the rest of her life, whenever she thought about heartbreak, she would see the way he looked at her. His arms had fallen away from her. His face was twisted in pain. Bloodred tears leaked from his eyes. But he wasn't clutching his open wound, or doing anything to stop the blood traveling down his chest and puddling on the floor.

Tella knew she'd made the right choice, but it didn't feel at all as she'd expected.

"Why are you still here?" He fell back onto a chair, still letting the blood from his chest drip everywhere. It wasn't a fatal wound, but it was deeper than she'd intended. Tella didn't like the idea of killing him, even if it was temporary.

"You should do something about that." She stepped toward him, ready to stop the flow herself.

"Don't." Jacks shoved out a shaky hand, the look in his eyes now cold as frost and curses. "You should leave. You got what you wanted."

But Tella was no longer sure what she'd just gotten.

She should have felt triumphant. She'd never wanted to be connected to Jacks. And yet her legs shook with every step she took away from Jacks and his house.

For a split second, it was tempting to go back and undo what she'd just done. She had, without realizing it, felt just a little bit less alone when they'd been connected. But he wasn't the person she wanted to be connected to.

A tremor racked her body and something like a cramp tore at her stomach. There was an emptiness inside that she'd never felt before.

With every house Tella passed she pictured the people sleeping inside. She imagined husbands and wives huddled close. She saw sisters sharing rooms, and boys with dogs at the foot of their beds.

But Tella didn't have a dog.

Tella had a sister, but her sister now had someone else.

And Legend would never be Tella's husband. In truth, Tella wasn't even sure that she *wanted* a husband—she just wanted him. She wanted everything about him. She'd always wanted everything about him.

Even before she'd known him, she'd fallen in love with the boy who'd had the passion to make his one wish come true and the audacity to call himself Legend.

Then she'd fallen in love with him again when she'd met him. She'd loved him as Dante, but she loved him even more as Legend. Dante had helped her forget, but Legend had taught her how to dream again, and she loved all the dazzling dreams they shared and the exquisite lies he told with his illusions. But she loved the imperfect truth of him just as much. She loved how protective he was, and how playful he could be. She loved the boy who'd called her an angel and a devil in the same conversation.

She loved the way he teased her, and she didn't want him to ever stop. She wanted to hear the rest of his stories—and to become a part of those stories. But more than any of those things, she wanted to forever be by his side, whether he was with her as she was fighting a nightmare or chasing a dream, or if it was the other way around, and she was helping him achieve a new dream. *Even if that meant sacrificing one of her dreams.*

Maybe *that* was love. All this time, she'd wanted him to love her, and she'd hurt knowing that he hadn't, but maybe she hadn't really been loving him. She'd chosen him, she'd fought for him, she'd felt for him, but she hadn't been willing to sacrifice what she wanted for him.

Tella started running toward the coast, racing back toward Legend's house, her heart beating faster when she was finally near enough to hear the crashing ocean waves. It was past the middle of the night, on its way to dawn but not there yet. It was that peculiar period of time that wasn't quite night or morning, but something in between.

If Scarlett had been there, she would have urged Tella to think on it longer. But what if Tella didn't have time to waste? That week alone she'd seen her mother murdered, Legend die, her sister kidnapped, and the empire overrun by Fates. She couldn't even imagine what the coming days would bring if the Fallen Star ascended to the throne. But she'd rather go through them knowing that no matter what, she had a present and a future—a forever—with Legend.

Tella slipped inside the house and quickly darted into a bathing room to wash the blood from her hands. She thought about putting on a new dress as well. The mirror showed a girl with wild curls and a hastily thrown on sapphire-blue gown, but Tella was too impatient to change.

She raced up staircase after staircase. By the time she reached the fourth floor, she was breathless. The hallway leading to Legend's room was dim with night, but she could see delicate strands of light sneaking out of the cracks beneath his door.

She knocked softly. Then a little louder.

Somewhere in the distance, waves were still crashing, but there was no sound coming from inside Legend's room.

She tried the doorknob, not actually expecting that someone as private or secretive as Legend would keep his door unlocked. But the glass knob turned easily.

Tella felt a thrill race across her shoulders. She'd never been in any of his private rooms. Not during Caraval, not at the palace, not since he'd brought her to any of his houses. She was almost positive he'd cast an illusion over her own bedroom to suit her tastes. But as she entered his rooms, the only glamour she saw was the light.

There wasn't a single lit candle in sight, yet globes of soft yellow and white lights danced around, making everything glow.

From where she stood, Tella could see his illuminated bedroom and his sitting room. His suite was well appointed, but simpler than she would have expected. Before knowing him, she might have imagined Legend's sitting room lined with sumptuous red velvet curtains and full of low cushions for seductive rendezvous. But there wasn't a speck of velvet in sight. There weren't any low cushions or curtains, either. Impeccable floor-to-ceiling windows provided a spellbinding view of the ocean while letting waxy moonlight slide over the ebony floors, the neat desk, the full bookshelves, and the wide charcoal couches.

Everything looked so perfect, Tella imagined she might smudge it if she stepped fully into the room. She tiptoed past into what was clearly Legend's bedroom.

His bed took up nearly half the space, and with its heavy iron frame and black silk sheets, it was exactly what she would have expected. Legend lay in the middle of it; his shirt was gone and he was on his stomach, sheets low enough to reveal the exquisite wings tattooed on his beautiful back.

Tella couldn't have held back her smile. She knew many of his other tattoos had disappeared, but she'd so badly wanted this one to be real.

The wings were as mesmerizing as she remembered. Soulless jet-black with midnight-blue veins the color of lost wishes and fallen stardust. And they were one of her favorite things about him. She itched to reach down and trace them, to run her fingers down his spine and wake him up. But while she'd shared countless dreams with Legend, she'd never seen him sleep, and she was curious.

Her eyes left the wings and trailed to his face. It looked as if he'd fallen asleep while reading. One bronzed hand held a book near his slumbering head, while hair black as raven feathers fell across his forehead. It was a very human pose, and yet his skin faintly glowed with inhuman light. He looked perfect and tempting, and in that moment Tella felt like a girl from a fairy tale who'd stumbled upon a sleeping god that would give her a prize if she woke him with a kiss.

And she was tempted to do just that, to sweep his hair back and press her lips to his brow, when something behind him caught her attention. She'd been so drawn to seeing Legend asleep on his own bed that she hadn't even noticed the enormous mural painted on the wall behind it.

Tella took a couple steps away to take it all in. Haunting and bright and sad all at once, the artwork almost covered the entire wall.

From the distance, it looked like an overwhelming picture of a night sky on fire. But as she drew closer again, Tella could see that this wasn't a depiction of sky or fire, but a series of smaller images; a kaleidoscope of stars and night and hourglasses, hot-air balloons and top hats, skulls and roses, death and canals, waterfalls of tears and blood and ruins and riches. It was beauty and horror and pain and longing.

Legend's soul was painted on this wall.

She didn't imagine he'd want it seen by anyone, and yet she couldn't tear her eyes away. She swore the mural moved as she drew even closer and looked until it was no longer a picture at all—it was a story.

Tella saw images from Caravals past as well as some that appeared to be from Legend's life outside of the game.

During the last Caraval, he'd told her that his tattoos were there to help him remember what was real. After the game was over and some of his tattoos had disappeared, she'd imagined that was a lie. But now she wondered if there had been something honest behind what he'd told her, because he'd clearly painted his past on his walls.

Her eyes traveled to the lower right of the wall, where the mural abruptly stopped. She imagined the images right before that naked patch would either be from the last Caraval or the past two months of Legend's life.

Her pulse sped up as she found the final image. It was of her and Legend during Caraval. They were in front of the Temple of the Stars and he was holding her close. It must have been the moment right after he'd freed her from the cards. He was clutching her as if he had no intention of ever releasing her, even though he had.

If these pictures were memories, he clearly saw things differently than she did.

Tella knew she was pretty, and that when she smiled, she could convince people she was more than pretty; she was beautiful. But in this picture, she could have been a goddess the way he painted her on those tragic steps, while he looked more like a grim shadow.

Was this how he saw himself?

"What do you think of it?" Legend's voice was low and rough with sleep.

Tella whirled back toward the bed to discover him sitting on the edge of it, bare feet on the ground, black pants covering his legs, and nothing on his flawless chest. His bronze skin glowed a little brighter, and his pants were so low she could see the definition of—

"Donatella." His voice was a low growl. Her eyes shot up to his face. Stubble coated his jaw, dark hair hung over his forehead, and though his eyes were hooded, his gaze was far from tired. He could have set the room on fire from the intensity of his stare. "You need to stop looking at me that way."

"How exactly am I looking at you?" she challenged.

His mouth slowly curved, as if he was about to challenge her right back. "I'm half naked, I'm in my bed, and you're staring at me as if you want to join me here."

"Maybe I do."

His eyes flashed with white gold and suddenly he was on his feet, towering over her. "Tella, I'm not in the mood for games right now."

She took a tremulous breath. She hadn't changed her mind, but for a moment she feared that he'd changed his. "I'm not playing a game."

She stepped closer to the bed and took another ragged breath. She'd never felt more vulnerable in her life, but if she put her guard back up he would never take his down. "I want you to make me an immortal."

Legend's brows drew together, wary. Not the response she'd hoped for. "Why did you change your mind? Is this because I didn't come to your room tonight?"

"No." She would have told him to get over himself, but she was about to throw herself at him even harder and crack her heart open even wider. "Most of my life, I've romanticized death. I used to love the idea of something being so tremendous that it was worth dying for. But I was wrong. I think the most magnificent things are worth *living* for." She took another step, until she was standing right in front of him. She reached up and placed a hand on his bare chest, right at his heart.

He sucked in a deep breath, but he didn't move away, he didn't reject her, as her hand traveled upward toward his neck. She spread her fingers out, feeling his Adam's apple bob up and down as he swallowed.

"Tella—" The word was a plea, and she couldn't tell if it meant he wanted her to stop or keep going. But she sensed that he still didn't believe her.

Her heart raced as her fingers slowly traveled to his jaw. Usually his skin was smooth, but tonight it was coarse, rough against her palm as she cupped his face and tilted it so he could only look at her.

"I think you're spectacular, Legend, and I want to spend an

eternity with you." She leaned up and slowly brought her mouth toward his.

Legend was still, but he let his lips brush against hers once. "You really mean this?"

"More than I've ever meant anything."

His eyes closed. Then his arms were around her. He picked her up in a rush, laid her on the massive bed, and took her lips with his again. The mattress beneath them was soft, but everything about Legend was solid. When his tongue slid between her parted mouth, he tasted like the ocean air that slipped in through a cracked bedroom window, salty and tempting and untamable.

Her hands explored the smooth expanse of his back, while his mouth left hers to find her neck. He pressed a more delicate kiss to the base of it, making her shiver everywhere, before his lips continued down. His tongue darted out, softly licking her skin, tasting her as he trailed kisses over the column of her throat, pressing kiss after kiss after kiss.

It was gentlest way he'd ever kissed her, and yet there was something even more intense about it. As if, despite what she'd said, he didn't believe her, as if he still didn't think they had a future, but he was determined to hold on as long as he could.

"I don't deserve you." His hands lowered to her calves, bunching the fabric of her dress up toward her thighs.

"Yes, you do," she whispered. She could barely remember how to breathe. His movements were confident and intentional. He knew where to touch and what to do.

But when he dared a glance at her eyes, he looked terrified. "Tella, I don't want you to do this because you feel pressured."

"I'm not sure which part of *this* you're talking about. But I came to you. I don't feel anything except how much I want to be with you. I gave you my heart when you kissed me at the fountain, and I've never taken it back. I love you, Legend."

His body froze above hers.

Damn the saints! She cursed herself as well for letting the words slip out.

Before she could respond, he was off the bed and halfway across the room. "We have to stop," he said jaggedly. "We can't do this, and I can't change you."

"Why not? Because of what I said? I wanted you to know how much I want this."

"It's not only that." His chest moved up and down with a deep breath. "You deserve better, Tella."

No. He couldn't let her go again. He couldn't walk away again, but she could see he was already preparing to. The white lights in the room were growing dim, getting ready to disappear, just like the stars had the last time he'd ended a conversation by leaving. "Don't you dare do this. I know what I want, and I want you."

"You might not if you let me change you." His low voice was barely a whisper. He closed his eyes, and when he opened them, he looked more like the shadow painted on his wall than the Legend she loved. "You should go. I'm not selfless or altruistic. I always find a way to get the things that I want. Right now, I'm only able to do this because no one has ever looked at me the way you did when you said those words now and—you deserve to have someone who will look at you that way. You deserve someone who can love you, someone really worth living for, rather than an immortal who only wants to possess you."

46

Scarlett

The moon had dissolved and the stars had fled to watch over another part of the world, leaving Valenda's night sky a flat, inky black. The only spots of bright came from a few glowing windows lit by burning lamps and candles like the ones blazing inside of Scarlett's Menagerie suite, where she panted in front of the Lady Prisoner's gilded cage.

Scarlett's brow was drenched in sweat that she couldn't fully wipe away because of the ruby bars trapping her head. The gemstone globe had grown even heavier over the last few hours as she tried and failed, again and again and again, to alter the angry emotions of the young woman Gavriel had brought to her.

Scarlett needed to do this. If she could control the feelings of this woman, then she could control the feelings of the Fallen Star and stop him before he took the throne in less than one day.

But despite her best efforts, Scarlett couldn't do anything beyond reading the young woman's feelings. Scarlett could see her rage and anger cascading down her straight back like a fiery cape. Scarlett imagined getting burned by it if she dared step too close. The woman sat on the marble bench that rested next to the Lady Prisoner's cage, and hadn't moved from there since the moment the Fallen Star left.

Scarlett had felt relief at first. She'd expected the young woman to attack her, after the way she'd bitten Gavriel's fingers. Instead she'd chosen to sit as perfect as a model for a portrait until she moved to take her long black gloves off with her teeth.

Her arms were covered in scrolling tattoos of faded black roses and vines that ended in two damaged hands, covered in fresh stitches. The woman's fingers had been removed, and from the sight of the stitching, it looked as if it had just been done.

Scarlett reared back. This must have been how he'd disciplined the woman for misbehaving earlier. Was this how the Fallen Star planned to punish Scarlett this time if she failed?

Scarlett tried speaking to the young woman, but she never uttered a word. After a couple of hours, the woman rested her cheek against her stubby palm, feigning boredom. It might have been believable if not for the fiery emotions she still wore like a destructive mantle.

Scarlett tried to calm her by channeling soothing thoughts. When that didn't work she tried to project images and emotions that might make the young woman feel drowsy, excited, sad, or happy.

Nothing.

Nothing.

Nothing.

"I can't do this," Scarlett finally said. She had tried to push every emotion on this woman, but instead of making her feel, it only drained Scarlett. She could barely hold her caged head up, and she couldn't even think about what would happen when the Fallen Star returned; she didn't want to find out how he would punish her for this failure.

It was time to leave. Scarlett was feeling the sort of bone-deep exhaustion that told her dawn was getting closer. The Fallen Star could come back any moment and discover she had not succeeded. Scarlett needed to use the Reverie Key and get out of there. She'd thought too highly of herself to imagine that if she stayed here long enough she could defeat him, rather than the other way around. She hated the idea of Tella and Julian seeing her caged, but she needed to return to them so they could come up with another plan.

"If you leave now, you will never win against him," said the Lady Prisoner, stopping Scarlett as she approached the main doors. Until that moment Anissa had been particularly silent, content to swing on her perch and watch Scarlett's repeated failures with the young woman. But now the Fate was on her feet, gripping the golden bars of her cage as her eyes turned an eerie white. "Don't quit. This isn't supposed to be your true ending, but it will be the start of it if you leave now."

"I would stay if I knew what to do, but—" Scarlett cut off as the doorknob turned. *Blast it!*

She'd hesitated too long. He'd come back.

Except when the door opened, it wasn't the Fallen Star. Morning light poured through the doorway as a servant boy wheeled in a cart laden with food, which he promptly set on the dining room table.

Scarlett hadn't realized how hungry she was or how stale the air had become until suddenly it was filled with the scents of breakfast cakes, strawberry puffs, honeycomb spirals, brown-sugared sausage, seasoned eggs, and piping-hot tea.

The young woman finally moved from her chair. She rose, walked over to the tray on the dining room table, clumsily picked up the pot of tea with her palms, and dumped it over all the food before Scarlett could stop her.

Her cloak of anger briefly flickered with burnished threads that looked something like victory. But like most feelings of success, it didn't last long. After a moment the threads shifted to red-black feelings of hatred and rage and bitterness.

A new plan formed as Scarlett watched the young woman's writhing, uncontrolled emotions. She was miserable, but not without reason. The Fallen Star had cut off her fingers and then given her to his daughter as a training tool. Scarlett would have been furious, too.

The thought gave her a wild flicker of hope. Maybe there was a way for her to shift the woman's emotions, after all.

"I'm disappointed," Scarlett said. "I would have thought you'd be cleverer at defying my father. I might not be able to control your feelings, but I can see them. He's the one who chopped off all of your fingers?"

The woman sat still as a placid doll, but Scarlett could see the vivid colors of her emotions crackling like a fire after a fresh log had been tossed into it.

"The Fallen Star is the one you hate and you think acting like a spoiled child with me will hurt him, but you're wrong. If you really want to injure him, help me." Scarlett picked up a soggy strawberry puff and took a bold bite, as if she wasn't about to make a risky proposition. This woman might have hated the Fallen Star, but that didn't guarantee she would help Scarlett. Her loathing was so horrible and heated and powerful, Scarlett was unsure if the woman was capable of feeling anything else.

But Scarlett had to try. Anissa was right; if Scarlett left now, it would be the start of the wrong ending. Scarlett could use the Reverie Key to escape, but she and her sister and Julian would only be safe for so long, and the entire Meridian Empire might never be safe again.

"I have no love for the Fallen Star either," Scarlett confessed. "I may be his daughter, but he murdered my mother and put this cage around my head. If you want to hurt him, help me deceive him—find a more effective use for your hate. I can see it burning you up, but you can use it to burn him instead. Or you can stick to dumping over pots of tea."

Scarlett finished off her sodden strawberry puff as she attempted to read the woman's response. But her anger and hate were so powerful, if she felt anything else, Scarlett couldn't see it.

She glanced back at the Lady Prisoner, once again sitting pretty on her gilded swing. "This should be very interesting."

And then the doorknob turned.

This time, the Fallen Star strode in. A heavy gold cape with elegant red embroidery and dense white fur hung from his shoulders. It was too much for the Hot Season, but she doubted he cared. It looked powerful, which was of ultimate importance to him.

The pleased smile he'd worn during his last visit was gone; that victory had already turned into history, and now he was hungry for something more.

"I've brought you another gift." He snapped his fingers. A streak of sparks shot out, and a pair of servants carrying a box nearly as large as Scarlett stepped inside.

"I think you'll like this present. But let's see your progress first, or this might not be the gift that I give you." His golden eyes cut to Scarlett's tea-soaked breakfast.

"I think you'll be pleased." Scarlett forced herself to grin. "You might be able to tell from my morning meal that frustration was one of the emotions I effectively projected. I also—"

"I don't need a summary. I want a demonstration, and I'd prefer to see an emotion that deviates from her natural state of anger and displeasure. I want her to feel adoration, for me."

The Fallen Star sat on the marble bench. "Make her worship me. I want her to feel as if I'm her god."

Scarlett's stomach turned queasy. Even if the woman were inclined to go along with Scarlett's plan, she couldn't picture her doing this. Feigning confidence, Scarlett looked at the woman through the ruby bars of her cage, but doubted she would help.

Scarlett was going to have to try again.

Please. Please. Please work, she silently chanted. Her heart pounded and her fingers clenched as she pictured the woman getting up from her bench and falling to her knees in reverence.

Across from her, nothing changed; the woman's emotions were a firestorm of bold and searing colors. The intensity was so extreme it took Scarlett a moment to realize the young woman's eyes had softened. Then her lips began to move. Until this point her pale mouth had been a thin line, but now it parted as if a silent gasp had escaped at the sight of the Fallen Star.

It was the most extraordinary thing to watch.

The woman fell to her knees, tears glistening in her eyes as if the Fallen Star really were someone she worshipped.

It was beyond what Scarlett had pictured. Scarlett might have believed she'd done it, if not for the hateful colors that continued to cascade from the woman's shoulders and down her tattooed arms. Thankfully, the Fallen Star couldn't see them. If he had, his eyes wouldn't have glittered as he watched the woman kneel before him.

"It's remarkable. I never thought she'd look at me like this again. Lift your head," he instructed.

The woman obeyed.

The Fallen Star reached out and stroked her neck, making the woman quiver with what he must have interpreted as pleasure.

His lips formed a flawless sneer. "It's really too bad your magic is gone and you're absolutely useless now. Even touching you disgusts me." He pulled his hand away. "You should get out of my sight before I decide to remove more than your fingers."

The woman broke into tears.

The Fallen Star laughed, vicious and bright. Scarlett wasn't certain what she was watching, but she imagined his reaction wasn't purely from what he perceived as Scarlett's actions. Somehow he had a history with this woman, and Scarlett sensed it went far beyond cut-off fingers.

"Now that's gorgeous. She responds as if she really does worship me and I've broken her. This is very good, *auhtara*. You didn't just make her feel, you've given her real feelings. But"—a wrinkle marred his perfect brow—"I don't sense that you've tapped in to your full magic yet. Let's see what happens when you take them away. I want every hint of love and adoration gone. I want her to feel nothing. Turn her into an emotionless husk." His voice dripped with cruelty.

Scarlett fought against betraying her disgust, once again focusing her full attention on the woman, as if Scarlett were the one in control of her.

But nothing happened.

If anything, the young woman sobbed harder. She wailed thick, sloppy tears, as if her emotions had gone out of control.

Scarlett didn't know what the woman was doing. Her true emotions hadn't ever changed. Her tears weren't real, but they were effectively infuriating the Fallen Star.

The air in the room grew thick with heat; the walls began to sweat.

He glared at Scarlett. "Make her cease."

"I can't," Scarlett admitted. "I—"

"Stop this or I'll put a stop to it," he threatened.

The woman fell face-first onto the floor, hysterical as a child. It echoed off every surface.

The Lady Prisoner covered her ears.

Scarlett furiously tried to project calming thoughts and images. She didn't have to read the Fallen Star's emotions to know how destructive he was feeling. He rose from the chair. Flames licked his boots.

"Just give me a minute," Scarlett pleaded. "I can fix this. I'm learning."

"That won't be necessary." The Fallen Star pulled the woman up from the ground by her neck. And then he snapped it.

THE ALMOST-ENDING

47

Donatella

Tella's dreams tasted of ink, blood, and unrequited love. She was inside Legend's mural. The night smelled of paint, and the spying stars looked like smudges of white gold rather than sparkling orbs. When she looked down, the paint from the moonstone steps stuck to her toes, turning them a glowing white.

She was in the mural's last scene, standing on the steps outside the Temple of the Stars. But unlike in the painting, Legend was not with her.

There was only Tella and the steps and the godlike statues, which glared down on her as the Maiden Death glided near.

"Go away!" Tella didn't need another prediction of a lost loved one right now.

"Does that ever work?" asked the Maiden.

"Not usually, but it always feels good to say."

"You need more in your life that feels good."

"Thus telling you, the bringer of all doom, to go away."

The Maiden Death sighed. "You refuse to understand me. I try to prevent the doom, not herald it. But, after tonight I will not come to you again unbidden. For if you do not summon the Assassin and me when you wake, then it will be too late to save your sister or the empire."

The Maiden Death lunged forward, grabbing Tella's hands and—

Tella shot up in bed, drenched in sweat from her head all the way down to the backs of her knees. Her hands were dry, but as soon as she opened them they turned damp.

Two luckless coins rested in her palm, one for the Assassin and the other for the Maiden Death.

Tella jumped out of bed and threw on a robe. She didn't want to believe the Maiden Death, and she really didn't want to call for her help. But even if the Maiden Death had not come to her in a dream, Tella would have known something was wrong—she should have been woken up much sooner.

The night before, she'd crawled into bed with the windows open, hoping the sound of the ocean waves would drown out the echoes of Legend's rejection.

You deserve someone who can love you . . . rather than an immortal who only wants to possess you.

She didn't know if he'd just said it to push her away—if he'd taken his brother's advice to let her go—or if that was how he truly felt. But halfway through the night, she'd realized it didn't matter. Legend was right. Tella did deserve more than someone who just wanted to possess her. The problem was, she wanted that *more* from Legend.

She could lie to herself and say she didn't want Legend to lose his immortality for her. But she knew that if he ever offered her his love, she'd take it and hold on to it forever.

Tormented by all these thoughts, she hadn't expected to find sleep. And, if she had fallen asleep, Julian was supposed to wake Tella up as soon as Scarlett dropped off the Fallen Star's blood. But either Julian hadn't woken her, or Scarlett had never appeared last night.

Tella pounded on Julian's door and swung it open at nearly the same time.

"Jul—" Tella faltered at the sight of his empty bed.

She left and marched down the stairs, but Julian wasn't on the lower levels. He wasn't anywhere at all.

All she found was a note pinned to the back of the front door.

I can't wait here anymore. Crimson didn't check in last night— or bring blood. I'm worried something has happened to her. I'm going to find her and bring her back.

—J

48

Scarlett

The Fallen Star dropped the woman's broken body, letting it fall to the floor with an ugly thud.

"I'm sorry you had to see that." He stepped over the body to reach Scarlett, and only then did his mouth fall into an impeccable frown. "It seems you're still not quite there, but I'm glad you're finally making progress." His fingers ignited. He brought one to the ruby bars imprisoning her head. At once the entire cage sparked and vanished, freeing Scarlett's head and neck.

Her shoulders sagged, finally rid of the weight of the cage. Her head had never felt so light. But she couldn't bring herself to thank him. After the initial relief passed, all she could do was stare at the dead woman on the floor. "Was that really necessary?"

"Don't feel bad about her death. Long ago she betrayed me. I was always going to kill her. I almost killed her when I found her imprisoned by the Temple of the Stars, but I thought she might be useful first."

He reached out to smooth a damp lock of Scarlett's hair from her cheek, his touch surprisingly light.

Scarlett still wanted to pull away; she wanted to use the Reverie Key and finally flee. She'd failed at getting the blood; she'd failed at conquering her power. But, as the Fallen Star continued to push away the hair stuck to her face with something like affection, Scarlett flashed back to the first time they'd met and how he'd mentioned the striking resemblance she'd had to her mother—the woman he'd made a child with, the woman he'd killed, and, according to a note that Tella had sent, also the one woman the Fallen Star had loved.

Maybe Scarlett had been going about this entirely wrong. Maybe she didn't need to conquer her powers to make him love her. Maybe Scarlett could bring back the feelings of love Gavriel had had for her mother and make him human long enough to kill him.

She took a shuddering breath at the thought. She didn't want to use real love as a weapon, or to murder or kill. But love was the only weapon Scarlett had. And this wasn't just about her. This was about the woman lying dead on the floor, and all the people across Valenda and the entire Meridian Empire who would suffer if she did not stop Gavriel.

"How did you meet my mother?" Scarlett asked softly.

His hand stilled against her hair.

The question instantly felt like a mistake, but Scarlett pressed on. "My other father—"

The hand on her hair dropped away entirely and the peaceful peach colors that had briefly surrounded him darkened to an orange on the verge of catching fire.

But at least she was still getting him to feel. Apathy was the opposite of love, so even though she was clearly taking his emotions in the wrong direction, at least she was taking them somewhere. She just needed to do a better job guiding his feelings so that he felt what she wanted him to.

"I meant to say, the man who raised me," Scarlett corrected. "Although, he wanted nothing to do with me until I became old enough to marry off. I hate him."

The Fallen Star's eyes sparked with a little more interest. Hate was an emotion he understood. But Scarlett would have to be careful, or he would latch on to it instead of love.

"I don't want to hate you, too. But you keep frightening me," she said. "And I don't believe that makes me weak, I think it makes me smart. I'm grateful you took the cage off, but if you want me to keep working to unlock my powers, you need to give me a reason to trust you. Clearly, my mother had a relationship with you. Or, she slept with you at least once."

His nostrils flared. Scarlett was dancing on a knife's edge. "Our relationship was more than that."

"Then tell me about it," Scarlett said.

"I think I'd like to hear this story, too," chimed Anissa.

Flames licked the bars of her cage as Gavriel shot her a glare.

"You're being scary again," Scarlett said.

"I am scary. But I do not wish to scare you."

The corpse on the floor gave Scarlett a different impression, but she didn't want to argue with him. Not when he was motioning for her to follow him out of the room and into the halls.

He rarely let her leave her rooms.

Everything was monstrously large and tinted with magic, making Scarlett even more aware of her fragile humanity, as they passed ancient pillars that were as thick as small cottages and frescoes covered in chimeras and human-animal hybrids. As one of the Fated places, the Menagerie's appearance had been restored once the Fates who'd been trapped in the cards had woken up. But Fated places required blood and tithe sacrifices to become fully alive, so thankfully the creatures in the paintings weren't real. Even so, Scarlett swore their eyes watched and their ears listened when the Fallen Star finally spoke.

"Paradise was the boldest thief I ever met. There was nothing she was afraid to steal. She loved the thrill and the danger and the risks. I think that's why she was attracted to me."

"Why were you attracted to her?" Scarlett asked.

"It started when she threatened to kill me."

Scarlett wanted to think he was joking, but he appeared entirely serious. "Before we met, Paradise was hired by the Church of the Fallen Star." His rich voice swelled with pride and Scarlett filled with dread.

She had heard of the Temple of the Stars, but she'd not known there was a church dedicated solely to the Fallen Star. Although she shouldn't have been surprised. The Temple District had everything, including a Church of Legend, which no longer sounded strange in comparison to the way Gavriel described his house of worship.

"The Church of the Fallen Star wanted her to steal a Deck of Destiny from Empress Elantine. Others had tried before, but all of them had been caught and killed for their failure—my church didn't want anyone to know they wanted this particular Deck of Destiny, because it was the deck imprisoning me and all the other Fates. Eventually they recruited Paradise. By then word had spread of the job's deadly reputation. But Paradise wasn't afraid to accept it. And unlike everyone who went before her, she succeeded in stealing the cards."

His mouth curved into a smile so small Scarlett doubted he was even aware of it. He really had admired her mother.

"Paradise didn't trust my church not to betray her. So, she only brought them one card—the card that happened to imprison me. She said the rest of the deck was hidden somewhere safe and that she'd share its location after her payment was delivered. She'd planned on fleeing the city. But things didn't go as she planned.

"The Church of the Fallen Star first formed in order to track down this Deck of Destiny and set me and the other Fates free. Before paying Paradise, they had to make sure the cards were authentic, so a member of their congregation sacrificed himself to release me."

Just the word *sacrifice* made Scarlett want to cringe, but the Fallen Star's smile twitched wider, the way someone else might at a fond memory. If he was actually trying not to frighten her with this story, he was doing a wretched job.

"As soon as I was released, I went after Paradise to find the Deck of Destiny and free all of my Fates. But she no longer had the deck. While my church had been releasing me, Paradise and her lover had used the deck to read their futures, and they'd seen the magic in the cards. Paradise still didn't know exactly what the cards were, but she was clever enough to recognize that they were worth far more than my church was offering. She had planned to ask for a larger sum. Only when she woke the next morning, her lover had taken the cards and vanished. I found her tied to a bed. She had no idea who or what I was when I arrived. She threatened to kill me if I didn't untie her, and I was instantly intrigued."

His voice turned wistful as if he were reaching the romantic part of the story, and yet the fiery colors around him where growing rabid, licking at the steps, clawing at his cape, and making Scarlett nervous that her plan was not going to work the way she wanted.

"We started as reluctant allies. The world had changed so much since I'd been trapped that I was in need of help to locate the Deck of Destiny, and she needed someone to protect her from my church. Neither of us wanted the other to know how intrigued we were with each other. I didn't admit to myself what I truly felt for her until the day she told me she was pregnant with you."

This was the part where Scarlett would have expected him to look her way. And he did. But it would have been better if he had not. There was something almost savage in his golden eyes—they held all the violence of hate mixed with the passion of love, as if all of this had happened yesterday rather than eighteen years ago.

"I was going to make Paradise an immortal after she gave birth. But before I could tell her who I was, she found out on her own and chose to turn on me. She had located the complete Deck of Destiny and instead of sharing it with me, she put me back inside one of the cards. I wanted to spend eternity with her, and she betrayed me."

The Fallen Star stopped abruptly, pausing on a landing that overlooked a glistening white canyon. He'd never taken Scarlett here before, but she recognized the cracked wheels of death scattered around the edge, and the river of red cutting through it. This was the place Tella had described when she'd told Scarlett how he'd murdered their mother.

Scarlett took a step back.

He immediately grabbed her arm. "I'm not going to harm you—I need you, and this is why." He squeezed until it hurt. "Paradise took the strongest feelings I'd ever had and used them against me. If I'd loved her she could have killed me. Love is the one weakness I've never been able to defeat. Humans try to make it sound as if it's a gift. But once they find love, it never lasts, it only destroys, and for us it brings eternal death. But I believe that once *you* conquer your powers, you can permanently take away this fault that would allow me to return human love."

49

Donatella

"Next time I see my brother I'm going to put him on a leash." Legend's voice was low, but Tella swore it rattled the artwork that lined the hall.

After finding Julian's note, Tella had gone to wake Legend. It appeared he hadn't slept much after she'd left him the night before. He stood in his open doorway in a wrinkled black shirt he must have just thrown on. His dark hair was in tangles, crescent shadows lived beneath his eyes, and his movements weren't quite so precise as usual.

"I knew that girl would get him killed," Legend muttered.

"She's not just some girl! She's my sister, and she's been risking her life to fix the mistake that we both made."

Legend scrubbed a hand over his face. "I'm sorry, Tella." He looked at her again, and the shadows beneath his eyes disappeared. But Tella knew that they were still there, hidden under one of his illusions. He cared about his brother. Julian might not have felt it, but Tella had seen it, and she could hear it in his voice when Legend said, "I'm going to go find them."

"*We're* going to find them," Tella corrected. This was her sister. She'd let Scarlett go back to the Fallen Star, and she'd asked her to steal the blood for the Ruscica—which had clearly been a fool's errand. "Before you tell me it's too dangerous, just know that I'll be going after my sister and Julian no matter what you say. If you don't want to bring me with you, I know someone who will." She held out the luckless coins she'd found upon waking up.

Legend glared at the discs and they vanished.

"Bring them back!" Tella said. "I know they're still there, even though I can't feel them."

"What are you going to do with those things?" Legend grunted.

"I'll contact the Assassin and ask him to help me rescue my sister. He could take her in and out of those ruins in a blink."

"You're the one who said the Assassin is mad."

"The Fallen Star is far worse, and I'm not going to stay here while my sister's in trouble. I don't love this idea, but I think the Maiden Death and the Assassin might be our best option to get your brother and my sister away from the Fallen Star."

Legend worked his jaw, and Tella braced herself for another argument.

"If we do this, you go in with the Assassin, find your sister, and get out of there right away."

"Are you actually agreeing with me?"

The coins reappeared in her hand, but Legend looked as if he already regretted his decision. The muscles in his neck were taut. "I still don't like any of this. But Aiko and Nigel haven't seen either the Maiden Death or the Assassin in the palace, Jovan hasn't seen them in the ruins, and Caspar hasn't heard any chatter about them working for the Fallen Star. I don't want to trust them. But while I can get us into the ruins where your sister is being kept with glamour and illusion, if Julian and Scarlett are both there, it will be a challenge to get all four of us out undetected. Just promise me, Tella, if we do this, you won't take any unnecessary risks."

Legend met her gaze, the dark crescents beneath his eyes back. It only lasted for a second, but for that moment, he looked more human.

50

Scarlett

Upon reaching the door that led back to her room, the Fallen Star gave Scarlett a luminous smile, as if they'd just had their first father and daughter heart-to-heart. She must have been a better actress than she'd thought. If he'd known that Scarlett would never become the reason he became invincible—that she would never master her powers and make him immune to love—he would have put her in another cage.

Scarlett was ready to reach for her Reverie Key as soon as the Fallen Star returned her to her suite and left. But once they stepped inside of her rooms, he welcomed more Fates to join them. Her Handmaidens, lesser Fates, recognizable from the red thread sealing their white lips shut.

"Oh, goody!" Anissa cooed from inside her cage in the center of the sitting room, though she looked far from happy about this arrival.

"What are they doing here?" Scarlett asked.

The Fallen Star waved a hand toward the box he'd brought in earlier. "They've come to help prepare you to meet the empire."

"They'll also make sure their mistress knows everything about you," Anissa murmured as soon as the Fallen Star left. "The Undead Queen spies through Her Handmaidens. Queenie and Gavriel had an affair long ago. We Fates might not love, but we are very passionate and jealous. She wasn't happy to hear he'd made a child with a mortal, and I'm guessing she's been curious about you."

Scarlett didn't know if this was the Lady Prisoner's way of warning Scarlett not to escape right now. But it didn't matter. Her Handmaidens were already upon Scarlett. They removed her gown with unnatural speed, tossing it onto the carpet, along with the precious Reverie Key still inside its pocket.

Throughout the entire process, Scarlett fantasized about darting for her dress and the key. But if she left now the Fallen Star would immediately know that she was gone and he'd be quicker at tracking her.

Scarlett's best choice was to endure until Her Handmaidens left. She swallowed her embarrassment as their prodding hands insisted on washing her and helping her with her underclothes. They rolled her hair into curls with hot tongs, and then piled it atop her head, before lining her eyes in kohl, painting her lips with ruby lacquer, and brushing golden dust all over her skin until she glowed like one of the Fates. Although when she peered in the mirror she looked startlingly similar to her mother.

Scarlett shivered as Her Handmaidens left to open the box that Gavriel had brought earlier.

If it had come from almost anyone else, the dress inside would have been a wondrous present. The bodice was gold, with thin off-the-shoulder straps of tiny yellow diamond stars that glittered in the light and cast iridescent flecks of rainbows around the room. The skirt was full and red as heartbreak, except for when she moved. A twist or tilt of her hips and a burst of gold fell from her waist down to the hem, where the gold glittered and shone and winked like tiny comets.

Scarlett had never in her life hated something so exquisite. She didn't fight as Her Handmaidens helped her into it, hoping now that their job was done they would finally leave. But as soon as Scarlett was dressed, a new escort appeared.

His face was too handsome to be human. He had dark brown skin, eyes framed by thick, long lashes, and lips with a natural curve that made him look as if he always smiled. His vicious green cloak was the color of poison ivy leaves during the Hot Season. It crashed around his ankles as he gave Scarlett a bow so perfect not even a drop spilled from the full goblet in his hand.

Definitely another Fate.

Sweet threads of magic mingled with the excited pops of gold swirling around him.

The Lady Prisoner stopped swinging. She watched this new young Fate with a warring combination of boiling red fascination and yellow loathing as he held out his free hand and took Scarlett's.

"It's so lovely to meet you, Your Highness." The rings on his fingers sparkled as he brought her knuckles to his lips and gave them a gentlemanly kiss. "We'll be spending a lot of time together. I'm Poison."

Scarlett immediately retracted her hand, flashing back to the immobile family she'd found during the Sun Festival.

"Seems she's already heard your name and doesn't like it much," the Lady Prisoner said from her cage.

"I'll change her mind." Poison grinned, flashing perfectly straight teeth. "I'm going to become her greatest friend."

"Doubtful," Scarlett gritted out.

Poison clutched his heart, jewels glittering on his fingers. "I thought you were supposed to be kinder than your father. Whatever I've done to offend you, please forgive me. Otherwise it's going to be a very tedious evening." He held an arm out for Scarlett. "I'm here to escort you to the coronation."

"Be careful," the Lady Prisoner warned.

"Calm down," Poison said. "You really think I'd hurt Gavriel's daughter?"

"It wasn't merely her that I was warning." Anissa's voice softened by a fraction and her eyes took on that unnerving shade of white. "Torture and death are on their way."

Scarlett shivered.

Poison held her a little closer. "Don't fret, little star. I think all she's saying is that it will be a dramatic party."

Without further ceremony, Poison swept Scarlett from the room and out into the lavish halls before descending into a series of under-ground passages that led them from the Menagerie into the royal palace's Golden Tower.

The Fate kept up a steady stream of chatter as they climbed and climbed to the top of the tower. Scarlett felt hot beneath her heavy dress and shimmering makeup. But Poison only grew more and more animated with each flight of stairs, as if the Lady Prisoner's warning truly had excited him.

He didn't stop until they were just outside the room where they were to meet her father. "I meant what I said about being friends. You might not like me, little star, but if you need me, I'll be here."

His charming smile slipped into something more toxic as the doors before them opened, letting them into the room where the Fallen Star waited.

Tapestries of violent wars clung to the walls while ripe yellow av-arice clung to the Fallen Star. He stood in the center of a cadre of guards, muscled young women and men who must have been Valen-da's finest, but next to Gavriel they looked like children playing dress-up. The air around him was electric with sparks; his eyes were full of flames; the cape he wore flowed from his shoulders like liquid gold.

His eyes flared when she walked in. There was a flicker of pale pink surprise, the color of fragile hearts, and for a moment so fleet-ing it might have been Scarlett's nerves playing tricks, she imagined he was seeing her mother.

He took her arm from Poison and walked her to the balcony.

From the careful way he handled her, no one would have guessed he'd killed someone in front of her a few hours ago.

Claps and screams of joy erupted as they stepped outside. The glass courtyard below was overflowing with people. Children sat atop their parents' shoulders, while others crowded inside fountains and climbed up trees, all of them with no idea what they were truly cheering for.

Her eyes latched on to a little boy wearing a paper crown and staring at the Fallen Star as if he just wanted to be noticed by him. Other children and adults peered at Scarlett the same way, admiring her merely because she was in a stunning gown and standing on a balcony beside the man with all the power.

Scarlett wanted to vomit. She wasn't their princess or their savior; she was their failure. She didn't even listen to what the Fallen Star was saying until she heard the words *Paradise the Lost*.

Scarlett's focus sharpened.

"History knows Paradise as a thief and a criminal, but I knew her as my wife." Gavriel closed his eyes and wrinkled his brow in a show of manufactured sorrow. "She's the reason I returned to Valenda. I wish I could say that I came to save all of you from the villains who killed your last would-be emperor, but I was on my way here before then. I traveled here from halfway around the world as soon as I heard a rogue by the name of Dante Thiago Alejandro Marrero Santos was to be crowned emperor. I knew I had to stop him. He was not Elantine's lost child. My wife, Paradise the Lost, was."

Mouths all over the courtyard opened in sighs and *ahhhhs*. Everyone was eager to believe him although he had no real evidence.

The audience cheers died to a respectful hush as Gavriel promised to rule the way his dead wife would have wanted. His voice even cracked and Scarlett thought she saw several ladies swoon. No one seemed alarmed that if he'd been married to Paradise he should have looked significantly older.

"And now," the Fallen Star said, "I would like to introduce someone very special. Together Paradise and I had one child, your new princess, Scarlett." He placed the ruby diadem atop her head. "She is my sole heir, but do not worry, I plan to rule for a very long time."

The courtyard erupted in applause. Perhaps a few intuitive individuals took his last words as a threat rather than a promise of prosperity, but Scarlett did not see their faces as the Fallen Star waved a hand and Poison stepped forward, carrying a gold crown so heavy most mortals would have bowed under its weight. It felt symbolic, for soon every human in the empire would be crushed beneath the fists of the Fate who wore it.

Scarlett tried to part ways from him as they left the balcony, but the Fallen Star linked his arm with hers. "I want you by my side tonight."

Together they traveled down all of the steps of the Golden Tower to the throne room and into a nightmare masquerading as a party.

Scarlett

It was the sort of celebration that would make it into history books and eventually turn into romanticized fairy tales that made even the horrible parts seem attractive. A hundred years from now people who heard of the Fallen Star's coronation celebration might wish they'd attended, although many of the humans actually there were looking as if they wished they'd not been part of the lucky crowd allowed inside.

Scarlett didn't know how the guards had decided who to let in from the courtyard, but she wondered if they'd been told they'd be rewarded if they survived the night, for despite all the abuse, no one appeared to be fighting back.

Near the stairs she'd just come down, Her Handmaidens were sewing up the lips of guests with thick red thread. Then there was the Unwed Bride in her veil of tears, kissing all the married men until their wives began to cry. The Prince of Hearts was there looking debauched, but Scarlett didn't watch him long enough to see what he was doing. Or maybe he was the one controlling emotions so that all the humans behaved.

Priestess, Priestess smelled of suffering as she wove around guests in a gown made of layers of veil-thin material that billowed as she moved. Scarlett had never spoken to her, but Anissa had told her that the Priestess's gift was her voice. The Fate could make a person betray their mother or their lover or their most terrible secrets.

Scarlett tried to steer herself father away from the Priestess—not that there were many safe places. The throne, where Gavriel would have traditionally sat, was now gushing blood, like the Bleeding Throne in Decks of Destiny, though Scarlett didn't know if it was the actual Bleeding Throne or just a replica. Across from it was a cheery polished wood stage that reeked of mortification and torment. It was just like the scene behind Nicolas's estate. Scarlett watched while Jester Mad moved people around it as if they were marionettes. Their arms and legs were tied up with strings, which Jester Mad magically controlled to make their movements jerky and doll-like.

Scarlett wanted to cut them all free, but they didn't appear to be in as much danger as the ring of people around Poison, all nervously holding goblets of bubbling purple liquid. She wasn't sure what sort of game he was playing. But she remembered Anissa's warnings about torture and death as she noticed a few of the room's newest decorations: lifelike stone statues and melting ice sculptures of people who all held goblets in their hands.

Scarlett dug her heels in and looked up at her father. "I think your Fates are taking things too far. I thought you wanted your people to adore you."

"They're only having fun."

"I'm not." She tore her arm free from Gavriel. "I want you to stop this."

Scarlett knew that there might be consequences, but fighting this would be worth it. "This doesn't make me want to finish conquering my powers and become one of your Fates."

Gavriel's face wrinkled with irritation. "Poison, turn them back into humans; my daughter is not fond of this game."

A few minutes later most of the statues and sculptures were human once more. But the evening's horrors were not over.

Just as Poison was returning his last statue back to life, Scarlett spied a handsome face among the guards near the doors. Golden-brown skin, playful mouth, and warm brown eyes locked on to hers. *Julian.*

Scarlett should have looked away. She should have done something to cause a distraction so that Julian could flee this wretched party. His disguise kept the Fates away from him for now, but that hardly made him safe.

"That young guard," the Fallen Star said, following her gaze. "Do you know him? Should I bring him over here? Perhaps we can use him to test your new powers."

"No," Scarlett said. But again, she should have done things differently. She should have said anything other than that one word. As soon as it was past her lips, the Fallen Star turned toward the closest Fate—Priestess, Priestess of the hypnotic voice.

"Bring that guard with the scar on his face over here," the Fallen Star instructed.

"Don't, please," Scarlett said. But *please* appeared to be about as effective as the word *no*. It only made the Fallen Star grin something vicious as the Priestess slipped her arm around Julian and coaxed him forward.

"I don't think I should test my powers here," Scarlett said. "What if I fail like before? I don't want to embarrass you."

"I don't think that's going to happen this time." Gavriel gave her an unsettling smile as the Priestess appeared, holding on to Julian's arm.

A lock of brown hair fell across his forehead. He looked far more boyish than the scoundrel she'd first met on Trisda and far too mortal as the Priestess dug her fingers into his arm.

Her skin shone like marble, and her flowing gown made Scarlett think of virginal sacrifices—though she had a feeling that Julian was to be the sacrifice in this scenario.

But Julian didn't cower; he stood straight and tall, surrounded by brave bursts of goldenrod and reckless whirls of brass. "Thanks for bringing me over here," he said. "I was hoping to ask the new princess to dance."

Amusement lit the Fallen Star's eyes. "First I need you to answer a question." Giddy sparks filled the air as he turned to the Priestess. "Ask him how he knows my daughter."

The Fate repeated the question and when she spoke, her voice was all Scarlett could hear. It was the sound of shining lights, full moons, wishes on the verge of being granted.

Julian answered without hesitation, "She's the love of my life."

Scarlett's heart broke and burst all at once.

The sparks around the Fallen Star grew into wild flames. "Perhaps this is why you've failed to conquer your powers. Do you love him as well?"

The Priestess repeated the Fallen Star's question to Scarlett. Suddenly, all she could think about was Julian. They were back in Caraval, tangled on a bed as he fed her a drop of his blood to save her life. She loved him then and she loved him now. But she couldn't confess it to Gavriel.

"Don't battle the question, *auhtara*, or it will kill you."

Tears streamed down Scarlett's cheeks. "Yes, I love him desperately."

"How disappointing." Gavriel motioned to the Priestess, who began to drag Julian away.

"Stop!" Scarlett tried to follow them.

The Fallen Star wrapped one bright red hand on the verge of catching fire around her arm and wrenched her toward the bleeding throne.

Excruciating pain tore across her shoulders. Scarlett cried out, drawing looks from all over the ballroom.

"I'm not planning on hurting him, and I'd rather not hurt you again, but I will if you don't behave." The Fallen Star's hand lost its heat, but his grip on Scarlett's blistering arm remained. He guided her back to the bloody throne as the Priestess brought Julian to Jester Mad's revolting stage.

"I don't want him hearing us and putting on a performance like the one you incited with my *gift*."

"What are you talking about?" Scarlett said.

"I think we're past pretending." The Fallen Star dropped his lips to Scarlett's ear. "Nothing you've done this last week has been a secret. Did you really think Anissa wouldn't tell me everything you were up to?"

Yes, Scarlett had.

"I'll have to punish you again for that later, unless you prove yourself right now." Gavriel sat upon his bloody throne, and forced Scarlett to perch on the arm of it like a decoration. He'd called her a princess earlier, but she was just a pawn. Blood stained the back of her beautiful gown as she wondered how else Anissa had betrayed her. But now wasn't the time to worry.

The entire party watched as Julian was brought to the stage across the room. Scarlett willed him to run, but he must have been afraid for her, because he didn't fight as Jester Mad and the Priestess tied strings around his arms and legs.

"Now," Gavriel whispered. "I want you to use your powers on him to take away his love for you and replace it with hatred. Once I see true loathing for you in his eyes, I will let him leave here alive."

"I can't do that." Scarlett's voice shook with every word. And it wasn't just because every part of her being was repelled by the idea of making Julian despise her. "I can't control emotions."

"Then he will die," Gavriel said reasonably. "And if I feel you attempt to shift my feelings in any way, I will set this entire room on fire and kill every human inside."

Scarlett took a fragile breath as her eyes darted around all the helpless people in the room. Half were watching her now. The rest were turned toward Julian, tied up like a puppet on the stage. And still the colors around him were fierce and bright and full of the deep, unending crimson love. She'd never felt so much love in her life. It was pure and unselfish, without fear or regret. All he wanted in that moment was for *her* to be safe.

And she had to take all those feelings away for him to live.

Scarlett could have cried. She looked at him and mouthed the words *I love you,* knowing she might never say and truly mean those words again. If she succeeded in conquering her powers, she wouldn't just be taking away Julian's ability to love her. She'd finally become one of her father's Fates and lose her own capacity to love.

So, before she tried to erase Julian's love, she let herself feel it one final time. She let her love out to touch his, the way two separate instruments might play together to create a more beautiful song, and suddenly Scarlett knew how to change what Julian was feeling—how to shift his song so that it no longer matched hers.

Before, she'd always tried to project a feeling or an image onto another person. But what she needed to do was to push against his feelings. She needed to reach with her magic and twist them until their colors began to shift and shift and shift and—

"No!" Julian thrashed against the strings holding him to the stage. He might not have heard the Fallen Star's instructions, but he knew the Fate's ultimate goal for Scarlett. Julian knew this assault against his emotions was because of her magic—magic he'd warned her against. "Don't do this, Crimson!"

The Fallen Star clapped and sparks shot out from the tips of his fingers.

On the stage, tears tracked down Julian's cheeks. He was fighting her, battling her powers with everything he had. But even his fighting was helping her magic win. She could see his love shifting to anger.

Scarlett started to shake.

The Fallen Star grabbed hold of her again to keep her from falling off the arm of the throne. She didn't know if it was from battling Julian, or if it was because she'd finally accessed her full powers, but her body no longer felt under her control.

She could feel the magic she was using, filling her and surrounding her the way her love for Julian had moments ago. It was heady and powerful. Without even trying, she could see more than just Julian's emotions. Scarlett saw colors across the room. The eager green of several Fates danced around a rainbow of terrified and morbidly curious human colors, and she knew that if she wanted to, she could twist them all with a thought. It was wondrous in all the wrong ways. Every inch of her skin prickled. When she briefly glanced down, her skin was glowing and shining with gold dust—and Fated magic.

"Finally." The Fallen Star tightened his grip on her arm. "You're almost there, *auhtara*."

Julian screamed again. "Don't do this, Scarlett!"

The name sounded wrong. He never called her Scarlett. But the name didn't hurt as much as it should have.

"You're close," the Fallen Star said. "Let go of your feelings for him and take hold of the rest of your power!"

Scarlett pushed harder and Julian's face turned into a snarl. She could see the edges of his emotions turning brown, the way something does after it's been burned.

Julian bucked against his bindings. "You lied, Scarlett! You said you would always choose me." His feverish eyes met hers, but for once there was no warmth in them.

She wasn't saving him. She was destroying him.

Her magic faltered.

She couldn't do it.

Anissa had said over and over that Scarlett needed to become what the Fallen Star wanted most to defeat him, but the Fate had betrayed her. And Scarlett knew that even if this was the only way to best her father, it was too much of a betrayal to everything she believed in. If she let Gavriel push her into doing this, how much further would he be able to push her once her love was gone and she was a Fate? Would Gavriel threaten to kill Julian again if she refused to take away Gavriel's ability to love? And would she be able to resist him—would she even want to?

Scarlett leaned into her magic once more and untwisted Julian's emotions, freeing them until they were no longer tangled and knotted and hateful.

He stopped thrashing and his head sagged, but he still managed to look at her with the most beautiful brown eyes she'd ever seen. They were glassy and red—he was still in pain, but he was also still in love with her.

The Fallen Star squeezed Scarlett's arm, making blisters break out over the skin that he'd already burned, but it wasn't enough to change her mind. He could scorch her, torture her, put her in a cage again, but he could never make her hurt Julian.

"What are you doing?" he demanded.

Scarlett smiled for the crowd, as if this were part of the show he'd forced her to put on, but she kept her voice low, knowing that defying him publicly could earn Julian a very swift death. "I'm making a new deal. If you want my powers, I will give them to you, but not like this. He goes free right now, or you get nothing from me."

Blood from the throne gushed faster, coating the Fallen Star's arms in red. "I could kill him for your disobedience."

"But then you would never get my powers." Scarlett continued to smile as more heads turned their way, probably curious as to why the show had suddenly stopped. "Do this now or I will never do anything for you again."

"Very well. I will give you what you want." The Fallen Star motioned for Jester Mad and the Priestess to undo Julian's binds.

"See how generous I can be?" asked Gavriel. "Your precious love will soon be free, but when I see you again, I expect you to make good on your promise. You will accept your power, you will become a true immortal, and you will take away the weakness that makes me able to love. Fail at this and I will torture everyone you care about until you are begging me to save them from their misery and finally kill them."

52

Scarlett

Scarlett had no idea how long it would be until the Fallen Star came for her that night, but she had no intention of being there when he did. As soon as she was allowed to leave his horrendous party she raced back through the tunnels until she reached her rooms in the Menagerie.

The Lady Prisoner leaped from her gilded perch in a flurry of violet fabric the moment Scarlett stepped inside. "What—"

"Do not talk to me, you duplicitous disappointment of a woman."

Anissa's face fell into a pretty frown. "I tried to warn you; I told you that I cannot lie."

"I said not to talk to me!" Scarlett ripped off her bloody gown once she reached her bedroom and hurried to put on her own enchanted dress. It warmed against her skin, as if it had missed her. Then it grew thicker and stronger as the fabric shifted from soft satin to supple raging red leather, which hugged her chest and flared out at her waist.

"Scarlett, listen to me," the Lady Prisoner said. "Whatever you're planning—"

"Stop talking!" Scarlett took out her Reverie Key and headed toward the door. "If you're not a traitor, then save your words to distract or misdirect Gavriel when he comes for me."

"But the torture—"

Scarlett ignored whatever Anissa said next. She shoved the Reverie Key in the doorknob, thinking only of Julian, hoping he'd already gotten far away from the palace—as she turned the magical object and opened the door.

At first she thought the key hadn't worked. She was in a dungeon hallway, far more foul than the one Legend's guards had used to lock up Tella. The air smelled of damp water and things left to die. Behind the iron bars, Scarlett saw a variety of torture devices, racks and chains and ropes, and then Julian, dangling from a ceiling.

Her legs buckled. She'd seen him wounded, she'd seen him dead, and yet neither of those things made this sight easier.

Julian's hands were chained over his head and linked to a hook in the ceiling that left him hanging over a bloodstained drain. His shirt was ripped off, his chest was red and sweating, and his beautiful face was half covered in a metal mask that Scarlett could only partially see because his head was bowed, as if he couldn't lift it anymore.

Her father must have had his Fates grab him as soon as he'd escaped the party, or he'd foolishly come back for her.

"Crimson—" His voice was raw and muffled.

"It's going to be all right." She tried to sound confident but her words cracked as her heart tore in half. "I'm—I'm going to get you free."

"No," Julian groaned, "you . . . you . . . need to get out of here."

"Not without you." Scarlett rose up on her toes to get him down from the hook on the ceiling, but it was too high to reach. She needed a ladder or a stool.

Frantic, she ran back into the hall. A few other prisoners called after her, but she ignored them as she searched for and found a short stool that must have belonged to an absent guard. She dragged it back and wasted no time in stepping on top of it.

Julian's emotions were weak, gray shadows. He swayed as she looked for the lock that held the cuffs on his wrists chained together. Only there was no lock, it was an infinity chain. She'd have to lift him to free his hands from the hook in the ceiling, but his wrists would remain shackled.

His eyes flickered open and shut. "I love you," he moaned. "If I die . . . it was . . ." The colors around him flickered and disappeared completely.

"No!" Scarlett said. "You're not going to die! We will get through this together or we won't get through it. Do not give up on me, Julian. I'm saving you, I'm saving you, I'm saving you, I'm saving you."

Scarlett repeated the mantra as she used all her strength to lift his limp body from the ceiling hook. His skin was clammy from sweat and cold. He slumped against her, nearly knocking them both to the floor with his weight.

"Julian." She said his name like a demand as she wrapped an arm around his feverish back and helped him to stand. "We need to get to the cell door, and then I can use the Reverie Key to get us out of here."

"I'm afraid your key won't help you this time." Every single bar inside the prison caught fire, filling the dungeon with violent tongues of red and orange, as the Fallen Star appeared on the other side of Julian's cell. Poison, an ever-present goblet of toxins in his hand, stood at his side, with an enthusiastic grin twisted further by the firelight.

Scarlett tried to run with Julian to the door, not caring that it was burning up, but the Fallen Star reached it first. He opened it wide and out of her reach as he stalked into the cell.

He'd taken off his crown, but his regal clothes were still soaked in blood. Red droplets sprayed the stones on the ground as he approached.

Scarlett's dress immediately shifted. With a flurry of metallic crashes, it changed from raging red leather into a savage gown of steel-plated armor.

Gavriel laughed, star-bright and vicious. "Her Majesty's Gown—that dress never did like me."

"Isn't that what Queen Azane changed into when she died?" Poison asked. "I thought she was more the lover sort than the fighter."

"Maybe she just doesn't like either of you," Scarlett spit out.

"She definitely never liked me. It's a shame, too. Azane could have been glorious." The Fallen Star's fingers lit with flames. "I don't want to hurt you."

"Then don't." Scarlett tightened her arm around Julian, her eyes searching for another exit, but there were only three impenetrable walls and burning bars before them. "Let us go."

"I'm trying to help you, *auhtara*." He took another step and before Scarlett could evade him, he pressed his burning hands onto her steel-plated shoulders.

Scarlett screamed and let go of Julian. Her dress's armor grew thicker but it wasn't enough to stop the pain, and she wasn't strong enough to break free. When he'd burned her earlier it was nothing compared to this.

"Stop fighting me, I'm saving you, *auhtara*." Golden eyes met hers. "If you leave with that boy under your arm you'll share the same fate as Queen Azane, who turned into that gown, and Reverie, who became the key in your hand. They were Fates who fell in love with humans and let themselves become mortal and die. But magic cannot die. So, when their human bodies perished, their magic was transferred into objects. Is that what you want?"

"If it means I'll never become like you, then yes," Scarlett panted; the air was almost too hot to breathe. She kept trying to break free, but his grip was too tight. All she could do was reach back and press the Reverie Key into Julian's palm. "Go—"

"You can't ask me to leave you!" Julian gritted his teeth, took her hand, and pulled with more strength than a boy who'd just been tortured should have had. It still shouldn't have been enough to free her—the Fallen Star gripped her tighter, searing her metal dress and branding her skin until she cried out again—but in that same painful moment, Scarlett's gown shifted.

During one ragged breath, the magical dress left Scarlett in only a thin chemise as it changed into two metal gloves that latched on to the Fallen Star's hands.

All around them, the flames on the bars turned to smoke.

Gavriel cursed.

Scarlett coughed, but she was free of his grip. Her dress had smothered his flames. She saw him battling against it, melting the armored gloves on his hands, destroying her dress, which had sacrificed itself so that Scarlett and Julian could escape.

"Stop them!" Gavriel yelled at Poison.

Poison stepped in front of the lock, holding out his lethal goblet, about to toss its contents and turn them to stone, or worse. "It seems we won't be great friends after all."

Scarlett and Julian ground to a screeching halt.

The raging Fallen Star was behind them, still batting the gloves. Poison was in front of them, ready to turn them to stone. They were trapped. Scarlett clutched Julian tighter—when suddenly all of the prison bars began to crumble and re-form around Poison. The thick metal poles herded him away from the door as they formed a new cage, trapping him.

Fetid air, full of smoke, turned magical and sweet.

"Legend's here," Julian wheezed. "He's doing this."

"Use the key now!" Legend roared.

Scarlett couldn't see him, but she didn't hesitate to obey. She darted forward with Julian toward the door.

But Poison was still too close. He was caged, but that didn't stop him from throwing out the contents of his goblet.

Julian shoved Scarlett behind him, blocking her from the toxin and letting it cover his chest and arms.

"No!" Scarlett screamed, grabbed Julian, and thrust the Reverie Key in the lock, as she thought of her sister and safety.

She found only one of them.

53

Scarlett

Scarlett fell through the doorway in a screaming blur of agonizing color. Blistering orange, searing yellow, and violent garnet. Her shoulders were burning. She'd felt the pain before, but now it was all she could feel.

"Get her damp towels and cold water." A pair of strong hands picked her up and carried her to a cloud-like bed.

"No," Scarlett choked. "Take care of Julian first."

"I'm fine, Crimson." Then he was next to her, holding a cold cloth to her shoulder, easing a bit of the burn as her head fell against downy pillows and the world went in and out of focus.

She didn't know how long she lost consciousness for, but when it returned, she was in a cloud of pink and gold, back in her bedroom at the Menagerie, surrounded by marble columns, disturbing frescoes, and familiar faces. But Julian's was the only face she truly saw.

The horrible mask was still covering half of his face. But the chains around his wrists were gone. He was standing up without any help. His chest was smooth and brown instead of red and sweating, and he was taking even breaths as he unfolded a damp cloth to cover her neck and her chest.

"Is this real?" she asked.

"You tell me." He pressed an affectionate kiss to her forehead with the side of his mouth.

"But . . . how are you unharmed?" Scarlett sputtered.

"You told me that we were getting through this together, or we weren't getting through. And"—Julian's brow wrinkled in something like confusion—"whatever was in Poison's goblet healed me."

"I wish some would have been poured on Scarlett," Tella said.

Scarlett turned to see her sister. She was perched on the other side of the bed, her delicate hands pressing another cold cloth to Scarlett's other shoulder. At first glance, she looked stunning in a gown covered with dark blue ribbons and pale blue lace. But when Scarlett looked closer, she saw her sister's eyes were puffy and her cheeks were splotchy, as if she'd been fighting back tears all day.

"Tella? How did you get here?"

"I had a little help." She nodded toward the columns flanking the window, and the room's other guests. Fates.

Scarlett jolted back.

Tella had gone insane. She'd brought the Maiden Death, along with another cloaked Fate who looked extraordinarily out of place, as gauzy curtains fluttered behind him. He wore a rough woolen cape over slouched shoulders and a hood that kept his entire face concealed. Scarlett had to run through the list of Fates until she remembered the Assassin, the mad Fate who could travel through space and time.

"It's all right," Tella said, though Scarlett swore her sister's voice was higher than usual, as if she was still convincing herself of this. "They want the same thing we do."

Scarlett didn't want to trust any of them. But, she knew her sister hated the Fates as much as she did. Tella wouldn't have trusted these two without a good reason, and Poison had probably saved Julian's life with whatever he'd thrown on him.

"Is Poison working with you two?" Scarlett asked.

"We have no alliance with Poison," answered the Maiden Death as the Assassin shook his head.

"Poison works for himself," called the Lady Prisoner.

Scarlett shot up in bed. She'd forgotten all about the other treacherous Fate on the opposite side of the open doorway. "We need to get out of here!" Scarlett yelled. "She's a spy."

"Of course I'm a spy," the Lady Prisoner said. "That's why he put me in here. But I'm also on your side." She hopped off her perch in a dramatic whirl of lavender skirts and clutched the bars in front of her. "I want out of this cage. Why do you think I sliced his throat that day?"

"Maybe you were bored." Scarlett knew the Lady Prisoner couldn't lie, but she really didn't want to listen to her.

She wanted to hate all the Fates. She didn't want to look in the

Maiden Death's sad eyes and remember how awful it had felt to be inside of a similar cage.

Scarlett didn't know why the Assassin would be aiding their cause—he was more powerful than anyone and yet the sooty-charcoal emotions swirling around him conjured feelings of brokenness and misery.

"Tella, why did you bring them here?" Scarlett asked.

"They sort of brought me. The Maiden Death is the one who told me you were in danger, and the Assassin is how we got inside. He brought me here to search for you, while Legend went to look for Julian. Did you two see him?"

"He helped us get away," said Julian. "He was using his illusions to fight the Fallen Star and keep him busy while we left."

Tella's face went paper-white. "You shouldn't have left him down there."

"He can handle himself," Julian said.

"What if he's been captured instead and they figure out who he is? They'll drain all of his magic. We need to get him." She turned to the Assassin. "You—"

"If you go down there to save one person, you'll never defeat Gavriel," Anissa interrupted. "You'll just keep repeating the same mistakes—sacrificing one of you to save another one of you."

"But we can't just leave him!" Tella's face went from pale to red, as if she was afraid Legend would lose more than just his powers. She looked ready to battle the Fallen Star herself.

Scarlett's ribs tightened. Her gaze darted to the empty space on the floor in front of the Lady Prisoner's cage, where a body had rested earlier that day. Murder was how the Fallen Star solved problems. "We're not going to leave him."

"The only way to win this battle is to become what the Fallen Star wants most of all." Anissa's violet gaze met Scarlett's.

"I can't do that," Scarlett said. "I tried. If I come into my full powers I'll become someone else—"

It hit Scarlett then. Maybe that *was* what she needed to do. Her father wanted her to change, but he also wanted *someone else*. Scarlett saw it whenever he looked at her with a brief bit of tenderness. He still wanted Paradise, the only women he'd ever loved. He'd killed her, but he regretted it, because like all immortals, he was obsessive and possessive. He missed her. Scarlett's mother was what he wanted most of all.

In the background Scarlett heard her sister objecting to something, but all the words turned into white noise as Scarlett finally saw how she could defeat him. The idea was extreme and possibly preposterous, but if love was Gavriel's only weakness, then she needed to become the one person he loved. "Assassin? Can you take other people with you when you travel through time?"

"What do you need to travel through time for?" Julian asked as Tella simultaneously said, "We're wasting time."

Scarlett barely heard the Assassin's soft "Yes. But if you go back in time and make even the smallest change, you may not be able to return to this timeline, and those you love here will never see you again."

"What if I just went back in time to steal a dress and observe someone in order to imitate them?"

"You may not change anything," said the Assassin. "But time travel rarely goes as planned—you may end up doing more than just stealing a dress and observing."

"Who is it you want to observe?" Tella asked.

But from the shake in her voice, Scarlett could tell her sister already had an inkling of what Scarlett had just figured out.

"I want to go back in time and see our mother." Scarlett's words should have sounded impossible. But she was standing in a room full of impossible people—three Fates, one boy who didn't age, and a sister who had died and come back to life.

Scarlett's idea was possible. It was just extremely dangerous. If she failed, the Fallen Star could kill her the way he'd killed her mother, he could put her in another cage, or he could keep the promise he'd made earlier and torture everyone she loved. But if it worked, she could save them all, along with the entire empire.

"I know how all of this sounds, but I really believe our mother is the key to killing the Fallen Star. Remember the secret you shared in your letter? The secret that told us he loved her? I've seen it in the way he looks at me sometimes. He sees her in me, and it changes him. If I can go back to steal some of her clothing and observe her, then I might be able to convince the Fallen Star that I am her. If I do this, I think he'll become human enough to kill."

Tella shook her head. Scarlett had never thought that blond curls could look angry, but Tella's appeared furious as they bounced around her face. "She's already dead, Scarlett. The Fallen Star killed her."

"That's why I need the Assassin's help. He can bring me to the Fallen Star and say that he's taken Paradise from the past."

Tella scowled, hands fisting the cloth she'd been holding as if she could turn it into a weapon. "Even if you convince him you're Paradise, what if he just kills you?"

"He won't." At least, Scarlett hoped he wouldn't. "Not if I convince him that I'm Paradise when she was first pregnant with me."

"Crimson, there has to be another way."

"He's right," Tella pleaded, "I don't think you're hearing yourself—this is a dreadful idea."

"No, it's not," rumbled the Assassin. "I've seen it work before."

Every head in the room turned his way. He hadn't moved from his position by the pillar, where he stood collecting shadows, or maybe he was creating them. Scarlett had been living with a Fate, but the Assassin's power was far more potent than the Lady Prisoner's. When he spoke, the room shuddered at the sound of his gravelly voice.

Yet, Tella still had the audacity to glare at him. "If you've seen all this, why didn't you just tell us this is what we needed to do?"

"In my experience, humans don't like it when I say I visited their futures and know they will die very painful deaths unless they do what I say. It only works if I let them figure it out."

"Though sometimes people need guidance," the Maiden Death added.

"They're right," came Anissa's voice from the other room.

Tella's frustrated scowl deepened. "Scar, this isn't our only option. I have the Ruscica from the Immortal Library. If we can get some of the Fallen Star's blood, then—"

"I tried to get his blood," Scarlett said. "That plan didn't work out."

"She ended up in a cage like hers." The Lady Prisoner nodded to the Maiden Death.

Everyone went quiet.

Tella looked as if she'd briefly forgotten how to argue. Julian looked as if he wanted to lift Scarlett off the bed and hold her in his arms forever—but that would have to wait.

"This is our best chance," said Scarlett.

"You're overlooking only one thing." The Maiden Death inclined her head toward Julian and then Tella. "If this plan works and Gavriel feels a moment of love, one of you will have to kill him. If Scarlett tries to kill Gavriel, he might stop loving her and then he won't be human."

"Why can't you or the Assassin do it?" Tella asked.

"The Fallen Star wanted to ensure that none of us ever killed him, so the human witch who helped him create us worked a spell. If one of his Fates tries to kill him, they will die instead."

"Then I'll do it." Tella's fiendish smile could have rivaled one of the Fates'. "I'll gladly kill that monster. If he's still in the throne room, I can sneak in and do it."

"That's not going to work," Jacks drawled as he strode into the bedroom. "You'll never get near him. But I can get you close enough to kill him."

54

Donatella

"What are you doing here?" Tella demanded.

"It's lovely to see you too, darling." Jacks looked only at Tella as he tossed a black apple back and forth between his long fingers as though he didn't have a care in the world. His lazy gaze grazed over her elegantly layered dress; she hadn't gone to the coronation but she'd wanted to be prepared in case she needed to blend in. The gown was all deep-water-blue ribbons mixed with sky-blue lace that made her look like a package that could easily be undone with the right tug.

He, on the other hand, hadn't changed from the awful night before. There were bloodstains on his shirt. He looked as if he'd just buttoned it up over his wound after she'd left—as though she'd not stabbed him in the chest last night and ended an immortal bond. She'd thought he was letting her go too easily, but clearly he hadn't really let go.

"How did you find us?" Tella asked.

"The Fallen Star has been holding your sister here for a week. This isn't exactly a brilliant hiding spot, and I'll always be able to find you, Donatella." He took a bite from his apple before dropping it to the floor. It thumped against the marble and rolled out of the room and through the open doorway until it disappeared under the Lady Prisoner's gilded cage. "We might not be *connected* any longer, but what was between us will never be fully undone."

"That's why I want you to leave!" Tella tried not to yell; Jacks always seemed to enjoy it when he was the one upsetting her. But the thin control she'd had over her emotions fled the moment he appeared. "I'll never trust you again."

"You will if you want to save Legend." Jacks leaned against the closest column and crossed his legs at the ankles. "Gavriel is having Legend brought to the throne room as we speak. He likes magical pets. Gavriel plans to have the Apothic put him in a cage and then seal it like Anissa's, so that Legend won't be able to use his full powers or escape—unless Gavriel is dead."

Tella shook her head. She didn't want to believe him, but she feared something had happened the moment Julian explained how Legend had helped them escape. Legend had insisted Tella stay with the Assassin as she searched for Scarlett while Legend went to look for Julian. He was supposed to find him and leave. He wasn't supposed to be a distraction or a martyr.

Julian released a curse, saying several of the things Tella was thinking.

Jacks laughed as he took in the crude mask covering half of Julian's face. "Seems as if you've also had a visit from the Apothic and Gavriel."

Julian gave him a foul look. "I can live with it."

"That's the point," Jacks hummed. "This cage will keep Legend as his pet and his prisoner. Even when Legend dies and returns to life, he'll come back in the cage, and only Gavriel's final death will free him."

There was a scratching noise, like a match being struck, as the Assassin disappeared and reappeared within the same heartbeat. He'd been by the window and now he was standing closer to Scarlett, holding a bundle of bright clothes in his hands. "He's telling the truth. The Apothic is almost done building a cage around Legend right now."

"Then get him out of there before it's done," Tella said.

The Assassin didn't move, except for the shadows that clung to him, which seemed to grow even darker. "If I do what you ask, Gavriel will know it was me and it will ruin our chances at killing him."

"See?" Jacks clapped. "I told you that you need me."

"No, we don't," Tella said.

"Yes, you do." Jacks gave her an indulgent smile, as if he knew this argument was already won. "I heard your plan. You'll never sneak in there successfully. No one else here can help you. The Assassin will be with your sister. Gavriel knows his Maiden Death hates him. The only way you'll get close enough to kill him is if you enter the throne room with *me*. Gavriel already expects it. He sent me to look for you so he could use you as leverage against your sister. He'll let me bring you in."

Tella shook her head furiously. There had to be another way. Jacks would betray her again. He always helped her and there was always an unexpected cost. *But he did always help her.*

"What's in this for you?" Tella asked. "Why betray the Fallen Star for us?"

Jacks gave her a knife-sharp smile. "It's not for all of you. Just you. And I won't be helping for free. Gavriel will expect your emotions to be under my power when I deliver you, and it can't be an act. He'll see through it. If you want to get close enough to kill him, you'll have to let me control your emotions so you adore me."

Tella snorted. "I'm supposed to believe that once this is done you'll just let me go back to hating you?"

"No, once this is over, your emotions will belong to me forever." Jacks's voice was unabashedly unapologetic. "That's the price of my help. You get to save your Legend *and* kill your monster, and I get you."

"You're delusional!" Tella said. "I'm not living the rest of my life under your spell."

"Then Legend will live the rest of his immortal life in a cage. Do you want to save Legend and the empire, or yourself?" Jacks flashed his dimples, giving Tella a playful smile.

"You're mad," said Julian.

"Don't do this," said Scarlett.

But both of their objections sounded reedy and dull compared to the ringing in Tella's ears. Because Jacks wasn't mad; despite her words, she knew he wasn't delusional. He was determined and willing to do whatever it took to get what he wanted, and unfortunately, he wanted her.

"If you do this," Tella said slowly, "I will hate you forever."

"No, my love. If I do this, you'll finally stop hating me." Jacks's smile vanished and for a moment he looked like pure desolation, a shell of a person with hollowed cheeks, fractured eyes, and bloodstains on his chest. He was an immortal who couldn't die but who could never fully live, because the things he wanted to consume were devouring him instead. Tella imagined wanting someone without loving them was like an endless hunger—even if you managed to hold the person you wanted in your grasp it would never be enough, and letting them go would be even worse.

She should have known that things between them couldn't be severed with the slice of a blade. Or perhaps that cut had led to this. Maybe Jacks had let her end their marriage because their bond had made him care for her in a genuine way, which went beyond his immortal feelings of obsession, fixation, lust, and possession. But now that their connection was severed, all that remained were his selfish impulses.

Mistress Luck had warned her that if Jacks didn't love her, his obsession with her would destroy her. If Tella said yes, that was exactly what would happen. If Jacks controlled her emotions, she would only feel things that gave him pleasure or worked to slake his unquench-able thirst for her.

Tella desperately wanted to believe there was another way, but she couldn't think of one. And as she looked around the room all she could see was the damage Gavriel had inflicted. Julian in his metal half-mask. The Maiden Death in her cage of pearls. The Lady Pris-oner kept like a human pet. Then she pictured Legend, trapped in a cage far less lovely than the Lady Prisoner's, wearing a mask like Julian's while the Fallen Star showed him off to his friends, forever.

Tella took a shuddering breath. Legend was supposed to spend forever with her, not trapped inside of a cage, and even though that was never going to occur, she still couldn't let this happen. She couldn't let Legend be trapped for eternity, and she couldn't be the reason that they failed to kill the Fallen Star. She might have first wanted to destroy him because of her mother, but it was about far more than that now.

She hated it, but Jacks was right—without his help she'd never get close enough to kill the Fallen Star.

"Tella," Scarlett said, "you don't have to do this."

"Yes . . . I think I do."

"My brother wouldn't want this," Julian said. "We'll figure out another way."

"We've been trying, and it hasn't worked. The Fallen Star is the emperor, you're in a mask, and Legend is in a cage. He definitely wouldn't want me to do this," Tella said. In fact, he'd probably be furious at her for it. "But I know he would do this for me if the situation were reversed." He'd saved her from the cards, he'd saved her from Jacks, and now it was finally Tella's turn to save him. She turned back to Jacks. "What do you need from me?"

"Wait—" Scarlett protested.

"Don't try to stop them," the Assassin said. "You wouldn't like that outcome."

There was another tiny scratch and then the hooded Assassin was taking Scarlett's hand. An instant later they were both gone.

Jacks shuddered. "I forgot how creepy that always was."

"You're not one to judge what's creepy," Tella said.

"You'll change your mind about that soon. Now, if you wouldn't mind giving us some privacy." His eyes cut to Julian and the Maiden Death.

Julian looked as if he wanted to argue. But the Maiden Death helped him from the room, leaving Jacks and Tella mostly alone.

Jacks had moved closer, to lean against the marble column opposite Tella.

She shoved off the bed but didn't take another step, knowing this might be her last moment to consciously make the choice to stay away from him. Tella was so ruled by her feelings, she didn't know how real her future choices would be once Jacks manipulated her emotions. "Do we need to cut our hands again?"

He looked intrigued by the idea, but then he shook his head. "I was only at half power when I changed your emotions before. I needed a strong physical connection to make the exchange work.

I don't now that Legend's given me my full powers back. But because of the vow I made him, I do need your permission."

"You have it. But—but—but—" There was something else she was going to say, only suddenly Tella couldn't remember exactly what they'd been talking about. Her head felt light, and a little dizzy, as if she'd just drunk half a bottle of wine.

Cool arms wrapped around her as she started to sway. Jacks's arms. His fingers were cold, perhaps a little too cold, and yet the gooseflesh they sent across her skin had never felt so wonderful.

A small voice told her that it shouldn't have felt that way, that she was forgetting something she needed to remember, but then Jacks was whispering in her ear, "It's all right, I've got you."

He spun her around to face him. His mouth quirked into half a smile, as if he were a little nervous to give her an entire grin. Not that he had any reason to be anxious. His grin was feral and dazzling, and suddenly Tella had the overwhelming desire to become the reason for all of his grins.

Why was she always pushing him away?

She knew Jacks had lied to her and manipulated her. But so had Legend. Legend had rejected her over and over. Just thinking of it made her feel dejected, as if he were pushing her away all over again. He didn't want her. He'd told her to find someone else—someone who looked at her the way Jacks was looking at her now.

His eyes glittered silver and blue. She usually thought of them as unearthly, but then they appeared deceptively sweet, as if he wanted nothing except for her to be happy.

"How are you feeling now, my love?"

Love. She liked it when he called her that. She knew he couldn't actually feel love, but it would be all right because Tella could feel enough for the both of them. She might have started out as his obsession, but now Jacks was hers.

She gave him one of her prettiest smiles. "I feel like I want to spend the rest of my life with you."

Jacks's dimples returned and they were glorious. "I think we can make that happen."

55

Scarlett

Scarlett wondered if the Assassin always kept his face shadowed by his woolen cloak and hood. It was unnerving not to see the person who'd whisked her back in time. But it was too late for Scarlett to worry about that, or any of the decisions that had led her into this ice-covered alley from years long since passed, with a Fate who possessed a reputation for madness.

"Put this on." He shoved a dress into her hands, then gave her a heavy raspberry-red coat lined in thick gold fur. It went down to her knees, giving a bold glimpse of the dress's striking black-and-white diamond pattern.

"Shouldn't I be trying to blend in?" Scarlett asked.

"You will." The Assassin inclined his hood toward one end of the alley, which appeared to lead to the Satine District. It was just as fancy as in the present day and full of people to match. Everyone who passed the alley wore vibrant coats lined in dyed furs. Some even carried fur parasols that looked as if they'd been made from leopard pelts.

"It's going to start snowing," the Assassin grunted. "As soon as it does, your mother will walk by on that sidewalk. Follow her and steal her clothes, but whatever you do, do not change the past. Today she's learned that she's pregnant with you. You cannot mistakenly prevent yourself from being conceived, but if you alter the past, other parts of your world might be undone."

"Like my sister's birth?"

"Yes. Be careful, princess. Follow your mother and observe her until you're able to steal the dress you need to deceive Gavriel. Then leave as quickly as you can. I'll be waiting for you beneath the broken lamppost."

There was a tiny scratching sound and then the Assassin was gone.

Scarlett hurried to put on the clothes he'd given her. Her scorched shoulders burned whenever fabric touched them, but the cold air and the rush of time travel had dulled much of the pain.

The first snowflake fell a moment later and Scarlett started toward the mouth of the alley, where icy bricks turned into neat lanes covered in crisp flakes of white that glinted like the start of something new, something that she hoped would be quick and simple.

When she'd first proposed the idea, she'd imagined going back in time to spy on her mother and steal a dress from her would be like when she was very young and she would sneak into her mother's closet to try on her fancy lace slips—a little risky, but not in a way that could cause real damage. Scarlett wasn't going to change the past. She was just going to observe her mother, take one of her gowns, and maybe a bit of her perfume along with it. But that was it.

The hard part was supposed to be convincing her father she was the Paradise of the past once Scarlett returned. Seeing her mother walk down the snow-covered street was not supposed shake Scarlett's world, or make her forget how to breathe. If anything, seeing her mother as Paradise the criminal was supposed to ease some of the guilt that Scarlett had been carrying around.

But as Scarlett followed her mother down the street, for the first time Scarlett saw her not as she'd been in Scarlett's memories or imaginings. Scarlett saw Paradise as the woman who Tella had always believed her to be.

Paradise glided over the street in a skirt that was such a pure shade of white it made the freshly fallen snow look gray. She smiled at everyone she passed, tipping her head and making her red feathered hat bob. These people must not have known she was a criminal, or they all liked her so much that the ones who did know kept her secret. She looked the way Love might have looked if Love looked in a mirror, infectiously happy and radiantly beautiful.

She skipped inside a fanciful dress shop with a pretty purple awning, and Scarlett didn't even think before following her. There was a display of imported hats in the corner and Scarlett darted right to them, hoping to hide from anyone's notice. Not that she needed to worry. The eyes of the women in the shop went directly to Paradise.

There were only three of them, but Paradise commanded their attention like a queen ruling over her subjects.

The lady setting up a display of ribbons dropped a spool. A plump woman who'd been about to step into the back snapped around. And the young girl who'd been spinning in front of a mirror froze.

"Hello, Minerva," Paradise called to the plump one who'd been about to leave. "Is my order ready?"

"I have no idea what you're talking about, darling."

"Yes, you do. Gavriel ordered a dress for me. It's supposed to be a surprise, but I found out about it, so I plan to surprise him instead." Paradise clutched her chest dramatically, reminding Scarlett a bit of Tella. "I'm going to wear it tonight and ask Gavriel to marry me."

"You're asking a man to marry you?" cried the girl who'd been spinning. "That's forward."

"I'd rather be forward than backward." Paradise spoke far faster than Scarlett, as if she wanted to cram as much as possible into every moment of life, an observation that Scarlett tucked away for her performance. "In my line of work, life is often very short, so I don't want to waste any of it waiting for a question that I could easily ask myself. I'm also rather certain he's going to say yes." She winked.

Even from Scarlett's position behind the hats she could see the head of the young twirling girl exploding with thoughts. Her brief conversation with Paradise had just splintered the way she viewed the world, opening up a door that the girl hadn't even known existed.

"But," Paradise added, "if he's afraid of marriage, or of me, I'll know it's time to move on."

"To Marcello Dragna?" said the lady with the ribbons. "He's very handsome and rich."

"Then you should marry him." Paradise laughed. "He'd probably be much happier with you than he'd be with me. Marcello only *thinks* he could handle me. I believe he wants to tame me, like a caged tiger at a circus, so he can show off to his friends."

"That sounds sort of like what you're trying to do with Gavriel," mused Minerva.

"No, I like Gavriel outside of his cage, and I don't have any friends to show off to, except for you, Minerva."

Minerva muttered something too low for Scarlett to hear before slipping back into the door she'd been about to go through as Paradise had entered. A moment later she reappeared with a creation in her hands that was far too extravagant to be called a gown. It was a riot of cream and black and rose and pink with splashes of flowers and lace and stray gold leaf. Long sleeves attached to a decorative bodice that was fitted through the hips, until the skirt flared out in ruffled tiers that ended in a train of gold and rose flowers with lacy black leaves.

It didn't look like Scarlett's idea of love, but she could see how it could have been her mother's, and Gavriel's.

Paradise gasped. "It's sublime."

"Each of these layers can be easily removed with a quick tug, if you need to run."

"Or if I want to have some fun with Gavriel," chimed Paradise.

The twirling girl turned red as berries, the lady with the ribbons broke out in a laugh, but Minerva didn't crack a smile. She looked as wary as Scarlett was feeling.

Scarlett knew her mother went on to marry Marcello Dragna, not Gavriel. But the entire exchange still left Scarlett with a deep, heavy feeling of dread as the conversation between the women ended. The ill feeling remained with Scarlett as she followed Paradise from the dress shop back into another icy alley.

Scarlett had no love for Marcello, but as much as Scarlett hated him, if Paradise never married him, then Tella would never be born. Scarlett quickened her steps as her mother disappeared around the corner.

Scarlett knew she wasn't supposed to interfere. The Assassin had warned her not to change—

Her back slammed against a brick wall of a dead-end street, as Paradise placed a knife to Scarlett's throat.

She fought to take a ragged breath. Seeing Paradise like this was like peering in a threatening mirror. This was the mother Scarlett had originally expected to meet. But she couldn't feel triumphant about it; if this encounter went the wrong way it could destroy the entire future Scarlett knew, or end Scarlett's life.

"What's a pretty little girl like you doing following—" Paradise cut off abruptly. She must have seen the resemblance as well, though her response was to hold the blade closer to Scarlett's throat.

"Who are you? Why are you trying to look like me?" She spoke even faster than she had in the shop. "Tell me in the next ten seconds or I'll slit your throat and walk away before your body hits the snow. One. Two. Three."

"I'm not here to hurt you," Scarlett said.

"Not the right answer." Paradise flashed a vicious grin. "Four. Five."

"I'm here because your family is in danger."

"Don't have a family," she sang. "Seven. Eight."

"Yes, you do, in the future."

Paradise didn't even bother to respond to this claim. "Nine."

"You have a daughter," Scarlett said. "You're pregnant with her right now!"

Paradise stopped counting.

"How did you know that? I've only told one person that, and he wouldn't say a word." Her eyes narrowed on Scarlett and then went wide. "Where did you get those earrings?" She dropped the box she'd been holding and touched her own ears, where a matching pair of jeweled baubles rested.

"They were from you," Scarlett said. "You told me my father gave them to you because scarlet was your favorite color. It's also what you named me."

Paradise stumbled back, but continued to hold out the knife. Gray mist swirled around her; she was confused but no longer feeling hostile, though on the outside she kept her expression severe.

"You also change your name to Paloma," Scarlett said. "You leave this identity and turn into something close to a legend."

This made a hint of her grin return, but it didn't meet her eyes the way Scarlett's grins always did. "All right, say I do believe you, why are you here?"

To save the world. To stop a monster. To see you. "I'm only here to steal a dress."

Paradise laughed, softening a little more. "Then you're a terrible thief. I must not have raised you very well."

Scarlett was tempted to tell her the truth, to tell Paradise that she'd been a dreadful mother, that she'd left when her daughters had needed her most and she hadn't come back. But Paradise wasn't that woman yet, and Scarlett wondered if maybe she'd never actually been that woman.

Somewhere along the way Scarlett had come to believe her mother didn't love her, or really love anyone. If she'd loved her daughters she wouldn't have left them or hurt them—people didn't hurt the ones they loved. But until Scarlett had appeared, her mother had been bursting with love. She'd been full of so much love she was going to ask a man to marry her. But she didn't. In Scarlett's world she went on to betray him instead, and Scarlett wondered if Paradise did all of this because Paradise loved her.

Even now Scarlett could see the love taking over Paradise's emotions as her eyes continued to dart from her earrings to Scarlett's face. In this timeline they'd only just met, but Paradise was already choosing to love Scarlett.

Scarlett could scarcely comprehend it. Whenever she loved, she loved fiercely, but it never came this easily, and she wouldn't have expected it to come so effortlessly to Paradise.

Clearly, Scarlett had never really known her mother. But there were a few things she did know about her.

"You were the best mother you could be," Scarlett said. "You sacrificed everything for my sister and me."

"You have a sister?" Paradise's entire face lit up, making her look even more magnetic, and Scarlett wished Tella could have seen how happy their mother was to hear she was having a second daughter. "I can't wait to tell your father about this."

"No! You can't tell him. Whatever you do, don't tell him." Again, Scarlett almost left it at that. The Assassin had warned her not to interfere with the past, but maybe Scarlett had been part of the past all along. Maybe she wasn't just here to steal a dress, or to see a mother she'd never understood. Maybe Scarlett was here to help make sure her mother made some of those choices Scarlett had never understood. Because she understood them now.

If Paradise married Gavriel and raised Scarlett with him, the future would change—Tella would never be born, and there was a good chance that all the Fates would be freed from the cards very soon.

"Gavriel is not what you think he is," Scarlett said.

Paradise took a harsh step back, some of the sharp edges returning to her expression.

But Scarlett didn't stop; either she was wrong and she'd already changed the future irreparably, or she was right and she needed to press forward, to stop her mother from making an irreversible mistake.

"I don't know how much I'm supposed to tell you, or if I'm supposed to be saying any of this. But you don't marry Gavriel. He's not the father of your second child. Gavriel is a Fate. He's the Fallen Star and he was trapped inside the Deck of Destiny that you stole from Empress Elantine. He wants to find the deck again so he can free all the Fates and take over the empire. You stop him from doing this—you trap him in a card again. But then you still have to hide, because his church—the Church of the Fallen Star—comes after you for running with the cards. So you marry Marcello Dragna and go away with him."

Paradise laughed, but it held none of the amusement of her earlier laugh. "No, I would never marry Marcello."

"But you do," Scarlett said. And it struck her that out of all the impossible things she'd just shared, this was the one Paradise remarked on. It made Scarlett wonder if deep down her mother was already aware of Gavriel's true goals and identity.

Scarlett tried to read her mother's colors. There were competing emotions warring each other, but Scarlett could see that Paradise was in love and uncertain, and despite her calm exterior, she was terrified of what Scarlett had just said.

"I'm sorry," Scarlett said.

"Why are you apologizing?"

"Because I know you love him."

"Criminals don't love."

"If that were true, I don't think I would be here. But I am. I'm here because you did whatever it took to take care of me—the daughter you're pregnant with right now. That's part of what makes you so re-markable. You leave Valenda, but people still tell stories about you. Even Empress Elantine talked about you before she died. She told my sister that when you loved, you did it as fiercely as you lived. You were willing to do whatever it took to protect the ones you love, even if it hurt you or them in the process."

And Scarlett realized then—she was the exact same. Everything she'd just said would cause Paradise and Tella and herself a world of pain. But if Paradise took a different course, then the future would change; everything Scarlett cared about might be lost and the Fallen Star might never be defeated.

Paradise was shaking her head, as if she could clear her muddled emotions. "And I thought you were just here to steal a dress."

"Like you said, I'm not a very good thief."

"I might have been wrong." Paradise reached down, picked up her box from the dress shop, and held it out to Scarlett. "Take it, you earned it with your story."

"Does this mean you believe me?"

"I don't know, but I don't think I'll be getting engaged tonight," Paradise said, careless and flippant. She sounded a lot like Tella when Tella was pretending not to feel.

"I'm sorry," Scarlett said.

"You don't need to keep apologizing. But there is one thing you could do for me." Paradise gave Scarlett a trembling smile. "Put the dress on. I didn't get to try it on today, and I want to know if it would have looked as fabulous as I'm imagining. I'll watch the other alley to make sure no one unwanted pops in."

Paradise darted around the corner.

Scarlett wanted to protest; she didn't feel like stripping in a frozen alley once again. But after all she'd told Paradise, this was the least Scarlett could do for her. It was the last thing her mother would ever ask of her. And it turned out to be the last thing her mother would ever say to her, as well.

When Scarlett finished dressing and turned the corner, Paradise was gone.

Scarlett picked up the bottom of her new dress and ran to the end of the alley, hoping to catch her mother. She looked up and down the street at all the people in their bright coats walking through the falling snow. If Paradise was among them, Scarlett didn't see her. All she found was a broken lamppost and a dropped knife.

Her mother had left again. Scarlett couldn't be surprised, and she didn't let herself feel hurt, not this time. Paradise might have been her mother, but she was also just a pregnant girl who'd been told she'd have to make a terrible choice. Scarlett couldn't blame her for running, and maybe Scarlett shouldn't have blamed her so much before. Scarlett loved Tella and Julian despite their imperfections; it was time to start loving her mother the same way.

And when the Assassin appeared an instant later, Scarlett imagined that this was how it was meant to be all along, and that her mother really had done the best she could. She might have run away from Scarlett just now, but Scarlett believed that when she went back to the future, she'd find things unchanged.

"Did you do what you needed to do?" he asked.

"Almost." Scarlett picked up the knife her mother had dropped. It was a white dagger with a star-shaped stone in the hilt. Scarlett wondered if it had been a gift from Gavriel as she used the knife to cut off her silver streak of hair. Months ago, that little streak had felt like such a great cost to Scarlett, but it was nothing compared to what her mother had sacrificed. "I'm ready now."

As soon as he said it, the Assassin took her hand and then they both were standing in the candlelit court of the Fallen Star.

56

Scarlett

Tella had always been more dramatic than Scarlett. As a young girl, she'd played at being a mermaid, a pirate, and an assassin while Scarlett had just tried to make sure Tella was safe. Scarlett was not an actress. But it was time for her to put on the performance of her life. She needed to become Paradise the Lost, or she might not survive the night.

Scarlett schooled her features into the edged expression her mother had worn when she'd pulled the knife on Scarlett. Then she struggled against the Assassin's grip as he roughly dragged her past Jester Mad's forsaken stage, tables of half-eaten food, and goblets left abandoned on the floor. The party was over, but perhaps Poison had turned all the maids to stone, because the mess remained.

The Fallen Star leaned back in his bloody throne, playing with the flames at the tips of his fingers while drops of red trickled over his shoulders, as if he'd already grown bored with his kingdom.

The humans were gone, but a few Fates remained.

Scarlett saw Jacks, lingering near the foot of the throne and chatting with Poison as if they were old friends. But she forced herself to not pay close attention to Jacks or her sister. Scarlett was pretending to be Paradise, and young Paradise wouldn't have known who Tella was or been concerned about the adoring way she gazed at Jacks. At a glance her emotions appeared to be a blissful shade of pink, but every few seconds they flickered with rotted hints of brownish-yellow, as if they were infected; she'd sacrificed too much. Tella didn't even appear to notice Scarlett's entrance, or Legend—who was trapped in an iron cage to the left of the throne.

Legend's grim cage was so much smaller and harsher than Anissa's, with a mockery of a swing that was covered in spikes. He looked miserable and weak and he couldn't tear his eyes from Tella's dreamy face. He appeared to be shouting to her, but there must have been an enchantment on his prison, like the one on Anissa's cage that dimmed her powers, because Scarlett didn't see any illusions, and his voice did not break through.

"You might want to fight even more," the Assassin whispered.

They were almost at the throne.

Scarlett ripped herself free from the Assassin's grip. "Let me go!" She brandished the white dagger that Paloma had dropped.

The Fallen Star finally saw her. His gaze went from the hooded Assassin to Scarlett, golden eyes widening as they caught on her dress—the dress he'd bought for Paradise—with its splashes of cream and black and rose and pink and flowers and lace and stray gold leaf. The flames at his fingertips died. The blood from the throne stopped flowing and for a moment the chamber was entirely silent.

"What have you done," he breathed. His eyes left Scarlett's to narrow on the Assassin. But Scarlett couldn't tell for certain if he was upset because he believed that she was actually Paradise, or he thought that she was Scarlett.

"I took her from the past for you." The Assassin shoved Scarlett forward with the flat of his hand.

Paradise wouldn't have stumbled, so neither did Scarlett. She took a firm step, then she cringed and made a look of disgust. Paradise shopped in the Satine District and liked pretty things. She might have been a criminal, but she would have been revolted by the bleeding throne Gavriel sat upon.

"Why are you sitting on that thing? And who are these people?" She spoke with the same rapid tone her mother had used, and wrinkled her nose as she made a show of looking around, but she didn't allow herself to appear too bewildered. Paradise hid her true emotions. "What's going on here, Gavriel?"

The Fallen Star held her gaze, his golden eyes flickering like match-flames on the verge of starting a wildfire. As if he was seeing a ghost. The lie was working; he believed she was Paradise. But he didn't appear to be in love with her.

He addressed the Assassin through gritted teeth as turbulent emotions writhed around him. "Please explain to me why you've brought *her* here." The knuckles gripping the throne turned white as he said the word *her*. "Last I heard, you wanted nothing to do with me."

"I changed my mind, but I doubted you'd be satisfied," the Assassin answered roughly. "So I brought her as a gift."

"I am no one's gift!"

The Assassin ignored her, grabbing her arm again and shoving her closer to the throne.

"Let her go!" Gavriel thundered.

The Assassin dropped her arm. "She's pregnant with your daughter. I know you've had difficulties with the child. I thought you could fix it, if you raised her yourself."

"What—" Scarlett sputtered. "How does he know this? I haven't told anyone I'm pregnant except for you." Scarlett held the Fallen Star's eyes again, trying to remember the way her mother had looked when she'd talked about him in the dress shop. But mimicking a look of love wasn't going to be enough to make him love her. And just then she was less worried about him loving her, and more concerned he might do something rash, like kill everyone in the throne room. The fire still hadn't gone out of his eyes.

"All of you, get out!" he ordered, and every Fate obeyed. Poison glided to the nearest door. The Assassin bowed and turned. Her Handmaidens, who Scarlett hadn't even realized were still there, evaporated like smoke. Jacks, who was closest to the throne, began leading Tella by the elbow, but Tella stopped as they neared Scarlett. Her face snapped toward her sister and her hazel eyes regained their focus, as if she'd been suddenly yanked out of a dream.

"Wait—" Tella tugged at Jacks's arm. "That's my mother. She's alive—"

"Get her out of here!" the Fallen Star bellowed. His throne burst into flames, filling the room with heat.

Jacks tugged Tella away with a hand around her waist, but she continued to fight him. "No—Mother!"

"Gavriel, what's going on?" Scarlett said, trying to rip his attention away from her sister, who appeared to be going off script. "What is that girl talking about?"

"Don't listen to her." The Fallen Star marched down from the burning throne, leaving a trail of blood behind him, but it looked almost peaceful compared to the emotions attacking him. Usually his angry feelings flared out like sparks that wanted to set anything nearby on fire, but these emotions seemed to be burning him, digging into his shoulders and arms like barbs at the end of a whip.

He wasn't angry with her or the Assassin, or even Tella; he was furious with himself. His emotions had erupted when she'd appeared, but they had flared when Tella said the word *alive*. He truly regretted killing Paradise.

But it still wasn't enough to make him love her now.

When he had loved Paradise in the past, Paradise had also loved him. And Scarlett didn't love him at all. Maybe that's what she really needed.

She thought she could do it. She'd brought her sister back to life with love. Scarlett was loving. She knew the colors of love and the shapes they took. She knew what it felt like to fight for love and to lose it and to give it with no design of getting anything back in return. And maybe that's why it wasn't working now. She didn't want to give him her love.

She'd seen him do too many horrible things. And even though he was mostly angry with himself right now, the emotion was so strong, it made her think he might do something hideous very soon, either to her or her sister, who was still dangerously close.

Scarlett had to find a way to change his feelings. She tried to find a spark of love for him again. She hadn't wanted to love her mother, either, but Paradise was more deserving. Or maybe no one deserved love. Maybe love was always a gift, but it was so much harder to give it to the Fallen Star because he'd spent his entire existence battling against it. He saw it as a disease rather than a cure.

"It's going to be all right. I'm going to take care of you, and I'm going to make sure that our child is absolutely extraordinary." He gave her a smile that was all teeth and inhuman hunger, without a shred of love.

Her plan wasn't working the way it was supposed to.

Donatella

Tella should have tried harder to stop her sister from going through with this plan.

The Fallen Star looked almost bored when Tella had stepped into the throne room with Jacks, but now he looked as if the wrong word might cause him to set the entire throne room ablaze. His eyes flickered like flames. But it was the way he stared at Scarlett, with a terrifying brand of protectiveness, that told Tella he might lock her sister up in this tower as easily as he might set her on fire if she said the wrong word.

Panic shook Tella's limbs. Jacks's arms tightened around her, pulling her closer to him. But not even his reassuring touch could completely calm her. If she didn't do something soon, Tella feared that she was going to watch history repeat itself with the Fallen Star and her sister.

"Tella," Jacks whispered, "there's no saving her. Your sister's plan isn't going to work. We need to get out of here before he takes his rage out on you."

An intense bolt of fear washed over Tella—Jacks was right. She would be much safer if she went with him. He would never let anything happen to her. Jacks would protect Tella until the end of time.

But Tella could not leave her sister to fight the Fallen Star on her own. Scarlett would never win. Even if the Fallen Star kept her alive, it didn't look as if he would ever love her. If Tella couldn't kill the Fallen Star, she at least needed to help her sister get out of there.

"Trust me, Jacks, I have an idea." It was a terrible idea, but many of her most successful ideas were.

"Mother!" Tella cried. "He's not going to take care of you." She broke away from Jacks and leaped between Scarlett and the Fallen Star.

The Fate's eyes turned red and flames erupted once more.

Scarlett

The moment Tella lunged between Scarlett and Gavriel, his hands burst into flames, creating an arc of sparks and black smoke as he reached for Tella's delicate shoulder.

Scarlett didn't even think—she just shoved her sister out of the way and flung herself in the Fallen Star's path.

Sparks flew.

Tella screamed.

Scarlett might have screamed too. The Fallen Star collided with her, his hands scorching the same shoulders he'd burned earlier that night. All Scarlett could feel was pain. Then his arms were holding her up instead of burning.

"Paradise." The flames on his fingers went out, and for the first time since she'd known him, he looked frightened. His brows were pulled tight together over eyes shot through with red. "I didn't mean to hurt you."

"Did you also not mean to kill her?" Tella accused.

Gavriel released Scarlett and his hands flared into fire once more, incandescent balls of fire forming in his palms.

"Stop this!" Scarlett screamed. "Paradise wouldn't have wanted you to hurt her daughter, *or* your daughter."

The Fallen Star's eyes cut back to her. The flames of his fingers went as black as betrayal.

He'd caught her slip—he knew that she was not his Paradise—but Scarlett wasn't sure it was a slip. Her performance had failed to elicit any feelings of love, so maybe it was time to stop performing.

She took a step toward him, looking in his injured eyes instead of at the hands that had burned her multiple times. She couldn't think about self-perseveration—it was too closely related to fear, and she remembered what her mother had written about fear giving Fates power.

Scarlett refused to be afraid. Fear was poison to love. And love was poison to fear. She still couldn't bring herself to love him. But she could bring herself to be vulnerable, and maybe that would get through to him.

"I know you're afraid of love, I know it's hurt you in the past and you see it as a weapon. You think love is a disease, but you've become the disease. Your fear of love is destroying you and everyone you touch. And it doesn't make you powerful, it makes the world around you tragic." Scarlett waved a hand around his catastrophic throne room, with its ugly stage, its awful cage, and a throne still burning with angry fire. "You told me you didn't love Paradise, but I know you did."

He didn't flinch. But he didn't lash out, either.

"You loved my mother and I know that she loved you. The Assassin did go back in time. He took me to see Paradise and she was bursting with her love for you. She wouldn't want any of this for you, and she wouldn't want you to do the things that you've done."

His eyes finally lowered to the gaping hole in Scarlett's sleeve and the ruined skin beneath it, blistering and burning from where he'd touched her.

Scarlett took a tremulous breath and forced herself to take a step closer. "I forgive you."

For the longest heartbeat of Scarlett's life, his expression remained indecipherable, but the flames lighting up his hands turned from black to gray, the color of regret. They crackled as they licked his fingertips, the only sound in the throne room, until finally, softer than anything Scarlett had ever heard: "I did love her. I loved her so much it scared me, and then I never let myself love again." A golden tear fell down his face. "I wish I could take back what I did to her." Another tear fell, followed by another and another.

Scarlett didn't know if they were all for her mother. His eyes were wells of endless pain, as if her father was finally feeling the weight of all the unspeakable things he'd done.

The flames lighting his fingers died.

When he cried another tear it was clear instead of gold; it was human and it was beautiful and it was the last thing he did before Tella stabbed him in the heart.

"No!" Scarlett fell with Gavriel to the floor. Tella's knife had reached his heart and he was dying quickly. It was what Scarlett wanted, but she wished she'd never had to want it.

His mouth twitched with something too forlorn to be called a smile. "We both know I don't deserve your sorrow. . . ."

With the last of his strength, Gavriel picked up the white dagger she'd dropped. His fingers could barely produce sparks, but somehow he managed to quickly melt the blade of the dagger until it formed a crude flame. The flame-shaped blade glowed with a color she'd never seen before. If she had to describe it she would have said it looked like magic, reminding her of what Gavriel had said in the dungeon, about Fates transferring their power into objects.

He placed the knife back in Scarlett's hand. "When I pass . . . this will free the ones I trapped. . . . Use it the way I would not have. . . ."

Then the Fallen Star died.

And Scarlett cried. She cried for the horrors he had been, and she cried for the wonders that he could have been instead.

Donatella

Tella felt as if the whole world should have stopped or cheered for her. She'd just slayed the Fallen Star. She'd killed the monster who'd murdered her mother.

She'd also come close to dying. She could still smell the smoke and the char from the flames that would have scorched her. Her hands shook and her heart raced. But then Jacks was there, sliding a cool, comforting arm around her and pulling her close. "It's all right, my love."

But it isn't all right, said a tiny voice inside her head. The same annoying voice urged her to pull away from Jacks—there was a truth about him that she'd chosen to forget. But Tella didn't want to remember it. She liked the seductive lie that was Jacks. She liked his cruel games and his teasing smiles and the way he bit her whenever they kissed. The throne room might have looked like a page ripped from a horror story, but Jacks was her Prince of Hearts and he'd turn it all into a fairy-tale ending. She leaned into his touch and the world became hazy.

"I did it," Tella said, her voiced tinted with disbelief.

"Of course you did, my love. But we need to get out of here now." Jacks held her tighter as he tugged her away from Scarlett. Tella had seen her fall to the floor with the Fallen Star, but she hadn't gotten up. She remained slumped against his lifeless body.

"Wait, my sister—"

"Look at me, Donatella." Jacks twisted her around until she was facing him. "Do you still want to spend the rest of your life with me?" He asked the question as if it were the only thing that mattered in the world. Never in her life had Tella felt a question with so much power. Though Jacks looked almost powerless as he asked it. He was a mess of gold hair, sea-salt blue eyes, and bitten lips, beautiful in a way only broken things could be, and Tella wanted him exactly how he was. She wanted him fractured and chaotic and completely untamable. The feeling was as consuming as what she felt from him whenever he kissed her—as if it would never be enough, even if she gave him everything.

"You are the only thing I want right now."

A ghost of Jacks's smile returned, and yet it looked so much more real than every other smile he'd given her. He looked happy. Despite the death and the wreckage and the smoke in the air, he glowed in a way she'd never seen him glow before. "You're all I want as well. But we need to leave right now or someone might try to stop us from being together." He released her shoulder to capture her hand.

He roughly pulled her through the disastrous throne room as if their lives depended on leaving. Jacks stormed past Jester Mad's abandoned stage, spilled puddles of wine, and a mirror that looked as if it had a person trapped inside. He barely stopped to open the massive doors that led to the sparkling glass courtyard.

Night had taken over and winking stars reigned from above, reflecting on the glassy ground as—

"Tella!" Legend's voice cut through the night, loud enough to startle the sky and tie her stomach into a knot.

Tella closed her eyes, as if she could undo the effect Legend had on her. She didn't want him anymore. She couldn't even look at him when he'd been in the cage; one glance at him and feelings she didn't even know she possessed had erupted. She hated Legend. She hated everything about him. But somehow the low sound of his voice still tangled her up.

"Don't stop." Jacks jerked her hand so she was flush against him once more. She willed her feet to run with him. To go wherever Jacks went. He was the boy she wanted to follow to the ends of the earth. But her body was betraying her to Legend, again. Her legs wouldn't move, and her toes had dug into her slippers, as if begging for purchase against the ground.

Jacks yanked harder on her hand, his icy grip tightening around her fingers. But Tella couldn't even look away as Legend approached.

He looked like the ending of a doomed love story. His dark clothes were ripped, there were fresh burns on his chest, and eyes that had once been full of stars were desolate, black with desperate gray cracks, and painful red lines snaking through the whites.

Her throat went tight. It shouldn't have hurt her. She hated him—she hated him for all those months he'd played with her heart. Even now he still held a piece of it. *He'd always hold a piece of it,* said a tiny voice inside of her. But Tella ignored the voice. She wanted to take her heart back and give it fully to Jacks.

"Why can't you leave us alone?" she cried. "Haven't you tormented me enough?"

Legend's eyes met hers, wide and pleading.

But Tella was done giving in to him.

"Undo whatever you've done to her!" Legend roared at Jacks.

"He hasn't done anything," Tella said. "You're the one who keeps hurting me!"

"I think that's her way of asking you to leave." Jacks smirked and gave Tella's hand a gentle squeeze. He no longer held her as tight—he knew that she belonged to him.

"Tella, listen to me," Legend begged. "You can fight what he's done to you."

"The only one I want to fight is you!" She pulled free from Jacks, prepared to finally shove Legend away forever. But as soon as she let go of him, Jacks vanished and the world shifted. Magic filled the air, thick and sweet. The glass courtyard beneath Tella's feet turned into smooth moonstone steps as the golden tower behind Legend disappeared and a new illusion took its place. A temple made of glowing white, topped in a domed roof covered in outstretched wings—the Temple of the Stars. Above it, radiant red fireworks mingled with more stars than Tella had ever seen, re-creating the moment that Legend had walked away from her, right after saving her.

Tella's heart stopped beating altogether. She could still picture the flat way Legend had looked at her that night, and the coldness in his voice as he'd told her that he wasn't the hero in her story. But now his eyes were brilliant as stars once again, full of bits of gold that glittered in the night. He was gazing at her the way he had in the painting on his wall, as if he never wanted to leave her, as if he adored her, as if he wanted to be her hero after all.

"Undo this illusion!" Tella said, unable to stand the sight of it—or him. He wasn't a hero. And she'd never wanted a hero. She was the hero of her own story, and it was time to save herself from him. "Bring back the courtyard and Jacks."

Legend's brows slashed down, the feeling in his eyes intensifying. Once upon a time, the brilliant look in them could have convinced her that he had the ability to give her the world. But now Jacks was her world, and there wasn't room for Legend. If she was being honest, there had never been enough room for him; he was too all-consuming.

"I know you think you want him, but he's controlling your feelings," Legend said, his voice growing lower and deeper with every word. "You have to fight against it."

"You're just jealous! You don't want me, but you don't want

anyone else to have me." She tried to shove against his chest, to push him away at last. "Please, stop torturing me. Just let me go."

The edge of Legend's mouth slowly lifted. "You're the one holding on to me, Tella."

"No—I—" She looked down to see her fingers gripping his frayed shirt.

Two warm hands wrapped gently around her shoulders as Legend held her in place.

Her heart beat faster. She really needed to pull away. But she couldn't move. Her body was remembering a time when he wouldn't get this close to her, when he wouldn't put his hands on her. All she'd wanted was his touch, and now he was holding her as if he planned on keeping her for a very long time.

His smile grew. "I'm not jealous of Jacks. I know your feelings for him aren't real. And you're wrong if you think I don't want you. I've wanted you for so long, and I'll never stop wanting you." His grip grew firmer as he pulled her even closer, until she was pressed against his chest.

Her breaths came out short, in tiny, angry gasps. But no matter how hard she tried to push him away, she still couldn't manage to do it. When she thought of Jacks, her heartbeat calmed, but then it craved the way that Legend made it pound. Because he didn't just own part of her heart—it belonged to him fully.

No! Tella tried to shake the thought out of her head, she tried to remember Jacks and the way he made her feel, but all she could feel right now was Legend as one of his wonderfully warm hands traced down her spine. "Do you still want to know why I walked away that night on these steps?"

No, she said, but somehow the word "Yes" came out instead.

His palms heated, and the hand on her shoulder slid to her neck and into her hair, tilting her face up, forcing her to look into his eyes. They were still glassy and dark with flecks of gold that looked like shattered stars, and she told herself she hated them.

Jacks's eyes were beautiful; Jacks's eyes were the ones she adored. But Legend's eyes had captured hers, and she couldn't stop staring into them. She told herself his eyes were just another illusion, the same as all the feelings that were threatening to take her over. She shut her eyes, but it didn't help. It only made her more aware of Legend's deep voice as he said, "I'm sorry I left you that night. I shouldn't have left, I shouldn't have hurt you. And I shouldn't have gotten scared and run away when I realized that I was falling in love with you."

Tella's eyes flashed open, and words spilled out before she could stop them. "You told me you weren't capable of love."

"I didn't think I was."

Legend moved his hand from her hair to cup her cheek, holding her face as if he'd never touched anything so precious. "I can't say that I understand love, or that I'm very good at it, because I've never loved anyone before. But I love everything about you, Donatella Dragna. Everything." His hand dropped lower to stroke her jaw. "I love the secrets you haven't told me, and the lies you've tried to get away with. I love your stubbornness and your persistence. I love the way you always pretend not to care when I visit you in dreams. I love that you never stop fighting for what you want or the people you love, even when they don't deserve it. I love you, I don't intend to stop loving you, and I hope that somewhere deep inside, you still love me, too." His mouth slowly lowered to hers, moving incrementally closer, warning her that if she didn't want to kiss him, she needed to pull away.

But she no longer wanted to pull away, and she wasn't even sure she could have. Love really was another type of magic. She was trembling all over. Shaking off the rest of the spell that Legend had broken when he'd told her he loved her. *He loved her!* Her limbs trembled harder with something like wonder at the thought.

She couldn't bring herself to speak, so she tried to tell him that she loved him with a kiss when his warm lips finally pressed against hers. They were so perfect and soft and sweet and gentle. Even though she was supposed to be letting Legend know that she loved him, she felt as if he was the one repeating the words with every languorous press of his lips, as if they weren't in any rush, as if they had all the time in the—

Abruptly Tella shoved him away. It was the last thing she wanted to do. She loved him, she knew she did. She wanted his lips on hers until she forgot how to breathe. She wanted to hold on to him forever, but he wouldn't *have* a forever if she didn't let him go right now.

His jaw tensed and the pained look returned to his face. "What's wrong?"

"You need to leave." Tella didn't recognize her own voice, as if she were battling herself with every word. She wanted to be selfish, she wanted to keep him. She loved him—which was why she forced herself to push him away. "You need to leave me before you stay like this."

"It's too late."

"No, it's not." Tella shoved him again.

He didn't even stumble backward on the moonstone steps.

She turned to run. If he wasn't going to leave, she would. But before she moved an inch, his hand clasped around her wrist and he pulled her back, binding her to him with his arms. "Tella."

"Let me go." She could already see him changing. She could see it in his smile, in the way it filled with love as it lit up his entire face. She tried to pry his arms away, but it was less than half-hearted. She'd always thought he was beautiful, but when he looked at her the way he was looking at her right now, he was absolutely everything. "If you don't let me go, I'm not going to be able to fight you anymore."

"Good, because I don't want to fight you. I just want to love you." He lifted her a little and pressed another kiss to her lips. "This is my choice, and I choose you, Donatella. I don't need immortality. You're my forever."

THE TRUE

ENDING

Welcome, welcome . . .

You have been invited to the official coronation of
Scarlett Marie Dragna,

to take place on the 1st day of the Harvest Season.

The festivities will begin at twilight
and hopefully never come to an end.

Scarlett

Anyone else might have thought it was the perfect dress. But there wouldn't be another perfect dress for Scarlett. She would never replace her Fated gown. But the piece of artwork she wore today was lovely— entirely fitted save for in the back, where a train flowed behind her, whiter than untouched snow and decorated with silk red roses. It matched the cape Poison had sent as her coronation gift, which was covered entirely in flower petals. It was glorious and extravagant and though Scarlett would have looked like a true empress in it, she couldn't wear it.

Poison had returned everyone he'd turned to stone to their human forms and agreed to a truce with Scarlett. But after one night with the Fallen Star as emperor, Valenda was still wary of all things Fated, and as the daughter of a Fate, the city was cautious of her as well; it didn't matter that she'd never stepped into her full powers.

"You look spectacular." Tella grinned wider than a cat that had just caught a bird as she stood behind her sister in the gilded mirror that matched everything in the imperial suite—even the drapes had gold leaves sewn between the gauzy panels. And it was all Scarlett's. Part of her was constantly tempted to use the Reverie Key and disappear from such an enormous responsibility. But she didn't think the key had come into her possession for that reason.

"The whole empire is going to fall so madly in love with you that Julian might get jealous," Tella said.

Scarlett laughed under her breath. "Julian's already jealous—he actually thinks Poison has a crush on me."

"Poison does have a crush on you. Why do you think he agreed to a truce with you so quickly?"

"Maybe because my sister is nicknamed the Fate Slayer."

Tella's cheeks pinked with pride. "You think I could get a Wanted poster with a picture of me on it and that title beneath it?"

"You're not a criminal," Scarlett said. "You're a hero."

"Yes, but I've always wanted my own Wanted poster." Tella laughed, but her face turned wistful in a way that let Scarlett know she was thinking about their mother again.

"Do you believe our mother really was Empress Elantine's daughter?" Scarlett asked.

"I don't know that we'll ever know for sure. But I like to think she was. When Empress Elantine talked about Paradise, she'd sounded fond and regretful." Tella rambled toward the wall of windows, and pulled back a pair of curtains to look out at the crowd already forming in the glass courtyard for that evening's ceremony. "We could always ask the Assassin to take us back in time to see her again and find out for certain."

"Maybe," Scarlett said. But she doubted it. After the Fallen Star's death, the Assassin had disappeared along with most of the other Fates. Poison was the only one who'd stayed behind, and Scarlett really hoped he didn't have a crush on her. Fates' affections tended to turn into deadly obsessions, as it had with Jacks and Tella. Thankfully, no one had seen Jacks since Legend's love broke the spell he'd placed on Tella.

Scarlett didn't know if Jacks had fled with some of the other Fates to the northern kingdoms, where it was rumored that other Fates had been living quietly. Now that the Fallen Star was dead, the Fates he'd created were no longer immortals, but were ageless. They could live supernaturally long lives, but they could also die if they gave people reason to come after them.

Scarlett would have spies look into it once she was officially crowned empress. She still wanted to track down some of the crueler Fates, like Jester Mad, the Murdered King, and the Undead Queen and bring them to justice. For her sister's sake, she wanted to make sure Jacks wasn't coming back, either.

"Excuse me, Your Highness." The crisp voice of a maid followed a soft knock on the door. "Mister Julian is here to see you."

"Let him in." Scarlett crossed the room with a speed that was probably improper for an empress. But she couldn't help herself, just as she couldn't stop herself from grinning as Julian stepped inside.

Her mother's dagger, now infused with the Fallen Star's magic, had removed the Fated iron mask from his face with one touch. Scarlett couldn't even tell that Julian had ever worn it. He looked both dapper and rakish in the suit he'd had made for tonight's coronation. Scarlett especially liked his gray vest and the thin red stripes that matched the flowers in her gown.

Tella closed the drapes with a dramatic swish. "I think it's time for me to go."

"You don't have to leave," Scarlett said.

"It's all right. I'm sure the two of you would rather smolder at each other in private, and I need to go and write a letter to Legend."

Julian gave Tella a crooked smile. "I think my brother's in the palace right now."

"I know. But I'd much rather write him a letter." Tella skipped to the door with an impish look on her face, which probably should have concerned Scarlett. But she was too distracted by Julian to worry about anything else.

As soon as Tella left, Julian stalked deeper into the room. His eyes slowly raked over the fitted lines of Scarlett's white gown, leisurely moving from her hips all the way up to the golden circlet she'd wear until she was officially crowned. "I wasn't sure you'd have time to see me today."

"I am very important."

"I know," he said solemnly.

"Julian, I'm only joking." She swiped his arm playfully. He took the opportunity as an excuse to steal her hand.

ENCORE

"You look bewitching," he said, pulling her closer. "But I think your dress is missing something."

He lifted the coat folded over his arm to reveal a present resting in his hand. The box was small and thin, and tied with a simple red bow that made her think he'd wrapped it himself.

"I told you I didn't need any gifts today." But she was grinning wider as she opened it.

Inside was a pair of crudely stitched gloves that went only to the wrist. For a moment, she wondered if this was his way of proposing. Gloves used to be a symbolic gift that gentlemen gave ladies they wanted to propose to. But the custom was out of style, and these didn't seem to be ordinary gloves. When Scarlett touched them, they began to shift. They moved the way her Fated dress used to, transforming from simple white gloves with crude stitching to long, elegant sheaths of deep ruby lace.

"Where did you get these?" Scarlett breathed.

"I went back to the dungeon and there were a few scraps of fabric from your dress that I sewed together."

"You sewed these yourself?"

A sheepish grin. "I didn't trust anyone else to touch them."

Scarlett hugged the sheaths to her chest. If she didn't already love him, she would have fallen in love with him then. Julian tried to act like a scoundrel, but he was the sweetest person she'd ever known. "You know, that dress always fancied you more than anyone else."

"Of course it did." He smirked. "It was always reflecting your feelings."

In the past she might have protested, but Scarlett didn't even want to deny it. "Thank you, this is the most perfect gift."

"I'm glad you like it." His smile returned but it looked a little bashful again as he tugged on the back of his neck with one hand. "Gloves were once a symbolic gift."

"Yes," she blurted.

His brows danced up. "I haven't even asked."

"Whatever you ask, the answer is yes." She threw her arms around his neck.

His hands tightened around her waist in response. "What if I asked for half your kingdom?"

"Then I'd say you could have all of it. Everything that's mine is yours, Julian."

"What about these?" He touched her lips.

"Especially those." To prove it, Scarlett pressed her mouth to his. "Now you're mine as well."

He pulled back just enough to give her a wicked grin. "I've always been yours, Crimson."

Legend

Legend did not believe in endings.

For most of his immortal life, he believed his world would come crashing down if he fell in love and became human. Instead, his world had become more precious, particularly the pieces involving her.

He stifled a laugh as he read her letter again. Tella wouldn't like it if she knew he was laughing, but she was one of the rare things he found funny.

It was one of the many reasons he loved her.

Year 1, Scarlett Dynasty

Dear Caraval Master Legend,

I no longer believe you are a liar, a blackguard, or
a villain, but I'm wondering if you'd like to become
those things again, because I would very much like
your help.

My sister is about to become an empress, which
will make me a princess. I know you might not see
this as a problem, but I assure you it is. I was not
meant to wander around a palace or be followed
around by guards. But I don't want to make my
sister look poorly by misbehaving; I promised her
that I would not cause any scandals. So I need you
to, please, cause a scandal for me, Legend. Kidnap
me and take me on a new adventure.

I know it's not really kidnapping if I ask you
to steal me away, but I think it would be fun
to pretend. I also think it might make a very
interesting game, and I know how you like to play.

Yours forever,
Donatella Dragna

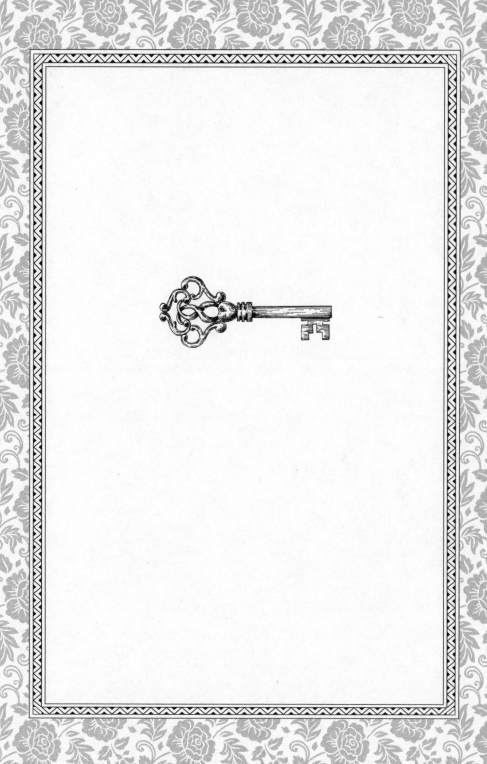

GLOSSARY OF
FATES AND TERMS

DECK OF DESTINY: A method of fortune-telling. Decks of Destiny contain thirty-two cards, comprised of a court of sixteen immortals, eight places, and eight objects.

THE FATES: According to the myths, the Fates pictured inside Decks of Destiny were once magical, corporeal beings. They supposedly ruled a quarter of the world centuries ago until they mysteriously vanished.

THE GREATER FATES
The Murdered King
The Undead Queen
The Prince of Hearts
The Maiden Death
The Fallen Star

Mistress Luck

The Assassin

The Poisoner

THE LESSER FATES

Jester Mad

The Lady Prisoner

Priestess, Priestess

Her Handmaidens

The Unwed Bride

Chaos

The Pregnant Maid

The Apothic

THE FATED OBJECTS

The Shattered Crown

Her Majesty's Gown

The Blank Card

The Bleeding Throne

The Aracle

Map of All

The Unbitten Fruit

Reverie Key

FATED PLACES

Tower Lost

Phantasy Orchard

The Menagerie

The Immortal Library

Castle Midnight

The Imaginarium

The Vanished Market

Fire Undying

LUCKLESS COINS: Coins with the magic ability to track a person's whereabouts. When the Fates still reigned on Earth, if one became fixated on a human, they would slip a luckless coin into their purse or pocket so they could follow them wherever they went. The coins were considered to be bad omens.

ALCARA: The ancient city from where the Fates ruled, now known as the Meridian Empire's capital city of Valenda.

RUSCICA: A book found in the Immortal Library that will reveal a person's or a Fate's entire history, if that person's or Fate's blood is fed to the book.

ACKNOWLEDGMENTS

In the Caraval series I talk a lot about dreams coming true. I think part of that might be because writing this series was truly one of my dreams come true. It still feels like a miracle to me that I get to write books, and I thank God every day for that miracle.

I have loved writing this series and being able to share it with others. But I never could have written it on my own. There is a fundamental group of people that I need to thank. These acknowledgments might be simpler than the ones I've written in the past—as I type these now, I feel as if I've already put all my words inside of this book—but my gratitude for everyone mentioned below comes from the deepest place of my heart.

Thank you so much, Sarah Dotts Barley, Jenny Bent, Mom, Dad, Allison, Matt Garber, Matt Moores, Ida Olson, Stacey Lee, Kristin Dwyer, Adrienne Young, Kerri Maniscalco, Katie Nelson, Julie Dao, Liz Briggs, Amanda Roelofs, Patricia Cave, Bob Miller, Amy Einhorn, Rebecca Soler, Liz Catalano, Nancy Trypuc, Donna

Noetzel, Cristina Gilbert, Katherine Turro, Jordan Forney, Vincent Stanley, and Emily Walters—and everyone else at Flatiron Books, Macmillan Audio, Macmillan Library, and Macmillan Sales—Molly Ker Hawn, Kate Howard, Lily Cooper, Melissa Cox, Thorne Ryan, and everyone at Hodder and Stoughton, Erin Fitzsimmons, Anissa de Gomery, Kristen Williams, Lauren (FictionTea), FairyLoot, and OwlCrate.

If you're reading these acknowledgments, I want to thank you too—for picking up this book, for stepping into this world, and for sticking with me throughout this entire series. I am so thankful for every reader, every blogger, every bookstagrammer, every bookseller, every librarian, and every teacher who has read this book or supported it in any way. It has been one of my greatest joys to share these characters and their stories with you.